Untitled

Pete Hartley

For Richard.

ACKNOWLEDGMENTS

My interminable thanks go to Emma Ritson who provided the original untitled oil painting for the cover of this book and to Alice Burns who posed for the picture so perfectly; to the Science staff at Lark Hill for biological advice; to the much loved unnamed proof reader and a much valued associate for scrutinising the text and suggesting vital improvements; and to you for at least reading this far.

PH

ONE

"There is one condition. I cannot tell you my name."

He inhaled the aroma of spent tobacco. "That may make things rather difficult for me." He wrote *27ᵗʰ September 1956, 10.10 a.m.* at the top right-hand side of the blank page of foolscap paper.

"If it were easy, I wouldn't need your help."

His nib was poised over the faintly lined sheet. "If I am to open a file, I must know the name of my client."

"Put whatever name you wish to call me."

He glanced at her hands. The left ring finger was banded. He wrote *Mrs A.* "I will need an address."

She opened the clutch bag on her knee and handed him a business card. *Post Office Box 21, Tower Road, Twickenham, London.*

"You live in London?"

"I have done."

He looked to his right and her left and through the arched window behind her. His top floor office was level with the Town Hall clock face. It indicated thirteen minutes past ten. "Why did you specify ten past ten?"

"He told me to."

"Who did?"

"The person I want you to find."

"And what is his name?"

"I have no idea."

Mr Coward wrote *Mr B* on the paper. "He specified ten minutes past?"

"This day. This time. This place. You."

The sleeve of Mr Coward's suit collected specs of cigar ash from the desk as he shuffled to suppress his irritation. "You know this man?"

"Intimately."

Mr Coward raised his bushy white eyebrows. "But you don't know his name?"

"I don't know his name."

"And you want me to find him."

"I suspect that you may be able to help."

"I'm a stockbroker."

"And a very good one. I have no doubt."

She had blue-green eyes with just a hint of hazel sparkling through, though everything inside the confines of the offices of C.E. Coward took on a brown or beige hue. Even the diminutive Mr French, who rustled the tanned pink pages of the Financial Times over in the far corner had a cigarillo shade to his skin. "That's speculation," he said.

"What is?"

"Your flattery."

"Well if anyone should spot speculation, it's a successful stockbroker."

"Or a foolhardy one."

"This is not speculation, Mr Coward. This is desperation."

He wrote *30?* on his sheet. "Do you have a family?"

"If you mean, do I have children?"

"That is what I mean."

There was an almost imperceptible hesitation. "No."

He imposed a deliberate delay. "Husband?"

"No."

He let her see him focus on her ring finger.

"I am engaged. To the man I want you to find."

He inhaled audibly. "You are engaged to man whose name you do not know?"

"He asked me to marry him and I agreed."

"When's the big day?"

"A decade ago."

"What happened?"

She straightened her coat. "We agreed to marry when the

2

war was over. I believe the war is over."

"You haven't seen him in ten years?"

"Thirteen."

Coward crossed out *Mrs A* and wrote *Miss A* in its place. "Would you like a cigarette?"

"Thank you."

The maple cigarette case was adjacent to the mahogany cigar box. Coward stood to allow her to select one of the contents. He lit it with his silver petrol lighter. He realigned the boxes on his desk as she inhaled. "Did your fiancé fight in the war?"

"I'm not sure."

"You are not sure."

"He was a pacifist. But I think he was in the armed services."

"Think?"

"We didn't talk about it."

"You must have seen his uniform?"

She drank smoke and exhaled it like a screen star. "I saw a uniform, but I don't know that it was his."

"Was he wearing it?"

"It was in a suitcase."

Coward focussed on the Town Hall clock again. Twenty-three minutes past ten. She could see that he struggled to decide what to do. He was finding her to be fascinating and perturbing in equal measures. Was this a compelling puzzle or puerile waste of time? He had stocks to sell and shares to buy. The telephone line to London could be so unreliable, she imagined. She pondered on how much time he would give her.

"When was it that your fiancé told you to come and see me?"

"Two days ago."

"How?"

She opened her bag again. "This postcard arrived."

He took the card. On the front was a sepia picture of Alsace on the French border with Germany. On the reverse was the address *Post Office Box 21, Tower Road, Twickenham, London, Angleterre*, and the message *C.E. Coward, Stockbroker, 27 September 10.10 am.*

"How did you know where to find me?"

"That is your telephone number."

"Where?"

"Written very small along the vertical edge. You may need a spyglass."

Coward peered closely. He opened the drawer of his desk and without looking, located a magnifying glass. "Well, the town is correct but the number is not."

"It is reversed. That's how I know this came from him. It was one of our codes."

"One of them?"

"One of them."

He looked at her face, her hands, her ring finger, thought, then said, "Miss . . . Miss A, I have no idea where your fiancé might be."

"I believe you can locate him. What would be your fee?"

"I'm afraid I cannot enter a business transaction with you."

"Why not?"

"There are insufficient formalities in place."

Her voice elevated by half an octave and accelerated in its rate of delivery. "Mr Coward, my privacy and my anonymity in this matter is everything. I can tell you nothing about certain aspects of myself and my past, but I can pay you, and I am prepared to leave a substantial deposit." She extracted a buff envelope from her bag.

He held up the palm of his writing hand, the pen pointing skywards. "If you cannot provide me with information, how can I help you?"

"I did not say I would not provide information. I simply said I would not tell you anything about some aspects of myself. I cannot. I will tell you about us. About my fiancé and I. Everything. Everything that I can."

He slightly adjusted the alignment of his cigar box. "Then do that. Write it all down, and send it to me. If, when I have read it, I feel I may be of service, then I would accept your initial deposit, and begin proceedings to attempt to locate your . . . lover. If that is not too strong a word for him."

"It is too weak a word, Mr Coward. Far too weak."

Three days later, on the last day of September 1956, she posted an envelope to be delivered by registered mail. It contained two fifty-pound bank notes and a manuscript.

4

TWO

I shall not tell you which station it was. It was crowded.
Everyone was in uniform, or so it seemed. Everyone but us. It
was Easter Monday 1943. Hundreds of people, mostly Army,
heading back after leave. I was wearing civvies and so was he. I
suppose that is why we stood out. That is why we were drawn
to each other. There was a space at his table in the station café.
Normally I would have avoided sitting there, but we had already
made eye contact of that rare strain: instantly deep, and longer
than one normally would. I asked if it was anyone's seat. He
said it was mine. I sat down.

The coffee was weak, and there was no sugar. He offered
me a cigarette, and I accepted. He made sure his hand touched
mine as he lit it.

I cannot remember the first thing he said to me or I to
him. It was small talk. Then he asked me where I was going, and
I said I had a few days' leave, and was heading to catch a
connecting train at. . . I shan't say where. He said we would be
on the same train. Then he said, "First-class I presume?"

I said, "No, third, sorry." I don't know why I apologised.
It just came out like that. Then I said, "How about you? Are
you first-class?"

He said, "No. Second."

I smiled and sniggered and said, "There is no second-
class."

"I always travel second-class," he said. He didn't elaborate on that. There was no need. From that moment onwards we had a bond.

He had a first-class ticket, of course, and insisted that I joined him. He said he would pull rank on any ticket inspector. I asked him what rank he was but he ignored my question. It turned out that our train was not the one the most of the troops were waiting for, and it was relatively quiet. We found a vacant compartment and he put my bag on the luggage rack. We sat in the two window seats, facing each other. I felt it was time for introductions.

"I'm . . ."

"Don't," he said, cutting in firmly but calmly. "Don't tell me your name."

"Alright," I said.

"And I will not tell you mine. Not for a very long time. Perhaps not ever."

This all sounds very odd, but along with this – rebuttal – there was a total acceptance. It's difficult to explain, but was entirely palpable. It was in his voice and in his stare, which was at once both penetrating and affirming. Some people might call it love, but I don't call it love. It wasn't love, not at that time. I can't give it a name.

"I don't want to know what other people have called you," he said. "We designate names at the worst possible time. Long before the individual is formed into a proper person. Sometimes they are deformed from the outset, simply because they have been given the wrong name."

I thought about my own name. I wondered what his was. "And is that true of you?"

"I'd like to get to know you," he said. "But I want to know who you are, not who you have been or what you have become."

"Are they different things?"

"Quite different."

"You're not going to tell me your name are you?"

"No, I am not. But I would like to introduce myself." He held out his hand and I clasped it. "How do you do," he said. "I'm the man sitting opposite you, in the second-class compartment."

"I suppose my third and your first averages out at a second," I said.

"And that description suits the décor much more adroitly."

For the next half of an hour we discussed the classification of the stations we pulled into, and of the people on the platforms. All the time my connection station was nearing, and I didn't want it to, and just at the worst time we were joined by an elderly, and somewhat pompous, lady. Our witticisms felt immature and we fell silent. Then my stop came.

"Well, goodbye," I said and held out my hand.

"Not at all," he said. He took a silver card case from his jacket. "Contact me. Tell me the next time we can meet. But no names, or there will be no meeting. Ever."

Our fellow passenger stared.

I looked at the card. There was a telephone number on it, that's all.

"Remember to dial in reverse order."

"For whom should I ask?"

"For the man in the second-class compartment."

I dialled the number three times. Those first three attempts went unanswered. My fourth was a week later. I recognised his voice with a single word.

"Hello?"

"It's your second-class companion."

"Good afternoon."

"I can meet with you. This Saturday." It was Wednesday.

He paused. Then said, "Do not be precise; just the county. Tell me where you are stationed."

"Buckinghamshire."

"How about Aylesbury?"

"Aylesbury would be fine."

"What time could you get there?"

"It will depend on the trains. I'm sure I could be there in good time for lunch. I'm afraid I would have to be back before midnight."

"I will wait for you at the station. Do not wear a uniform. I'll be there from ten-thirty."

"I could telephone again when I know the train times."

"No. Don't do that. I may not be here. I will be at Aylesbury station on Saturday. God willing, you will be there too."

"I'll be there, even if God doesn't will it." I don't know why I said that. All I know is that I meant it.

I cannot tell you where my posting was. I'm not being truculent - I simply can't. At that time my hours were midnight until eight in the morning. There were thousands of girls based there, far too many to be accommodated within the confines of the camp. I was billeted half an hour away by military bus.

When that Saturday came, I skipped the bus and walked to the railway station, where I changed out of my uniform and into the civvies I'd packed in a rather cumbersome carpet bag which I fastened tight so that he could not see the contents.

The train was late, and slow. I arrived at Aylesbury just after eleven in a blind fret that he wouldn't have turned up, or wouldn't have waited, but he was there, as promised, wearing the same suit and coat he had when we first met. It was a quality fabric, and a fitting style for a first-class traveller.

We shook hands and without hesitation he proffered his arm for me to take. "I have a table booked," he said.

The soup was vegetable, and watery, but a significant improvement on that which we were served at the base.

"So what's all this about no names?" I said.

"I have already painted you," he said.

"Painted me?"

"But the picture is not finished."

"You are an artist?"

"You are a picture."

"As yet untitled."

"And that is what you will remain."

"Why?"

"Because, as I explained, your name is almost certainly the wrong one. I wish to know you, completely know you . . ." His spoon was poised mid-way between bowl and mouth. ". . . without naming you."

"And why cannot I know your name?"

"I am not my name and my name is not me. I don't want you to misunderstand me, and I wish to entirely and perfectly understand you."

"Why?"

"Because you are a first-class person with a third-class ticket." He carried on eating.

"I am thrifty. Out of necessity."

"You are telling me too much."

"If we are not to talk about ourselves then what shall we

talk about?"

"You will talk about me, and I will talk about you."

I finished my soup. "You are quite the strangest stranger I have ever met."

"And you are quite the most beautiful person I have ever met."

"I am plain."

"You are not allowed to talk about yourself."

"You, on the other hand have a classical cut."

"I blame that on my father – the god Zeus."

He finished his soup and the waitress cleared the bowls. In terms of his features he could have been telling the truth. There was more than a hint of the Mediterranean about him, but less Latin and more Greek.

"Does talking about our parents not count as talking about ourselves?"

"I suspect my mother was lying when she made that claim."

I saw the first chink in his armour. "Completely?"

He paused. "Not entirely."

I felt both thrilled and compassionate. I'd tricked him into revealing something of his past. His comment and his countenance suggested possible illegitimacy. I wanted to pursue the inquiry but his face forbade it, so I complied with his code that all questions must be about the present and the future, not the past. "Will I see this painting of me?"

"If I live to finish it."

"How long will it take?"

"I may need you to sit. In order to establish the detail."

"It's not a nude is it?"

"Would it bother you if it is?"

"Not at all."

"The next time you have leave."

"Alright."

The main course was served. He had fish; trout in fact. I had the beef Wellington. It was tender and tasty but I couldn't finish it. I'd lost my appetite, but only for the food.

After dinner we just walked the streets looking at the shops until he escorted me back to the station and saw me onto my return train. I had no idea when or how we might meet again.

THREE

I timed my return from the station near my base in order to
merge with the influx into the camp for the dreaded 'graveyard'
shift. I was back on duty again at midnight, having had no sleep
for twenty-four hours. Our work was tedious and boring, but it
required intense concentration, because we had to be
scrupulously accurate. I don't know how I managed to
concentrate that night, but somehow, I did, though not
persistently.

By this point there was no question that I had fallen in love
with my enigmatic stranger.

Until then, I had not really confided in anyone, but my best
friend Vera had surmised something was preoccupying me. It
was so tedious you see. So very tedious, and so very hush, hush.
We did not talk about our work to anyone, not even each other.
So gossip was the only joy. Gossip was glorious.

When I got back to our billet the day after the Aylesbury
adventure and slept solidly for twelve hours Vera knew
something exciting was afoot. She was very trustworthy. I told
her what had happened and swore her to secrecy. She thought I
was making it up, but I convinced her it was true and she was
thrilled by it all.

"It sounds a bit, well - let's be honest – a bit bleedin'
risky."

"I think that's why I'm enjoying it so much. So many

people are getting their share of danger. The only threat to us here is a splinter from a broken pencil."

Whenever there was levity, Vera's south London background bounced through her voice. "Is he – you know – all there upstairs?"

"We are surrounded by the choicest lunatics, Vera, compared to them he is the epitome of normality."

"But is he bleedin' barmy?"

"He's mysterious, there's no doubt about that." I was bubbling too, and it all felt rather fun in a youthful way, but I made it clear I didn't want anyone to overhear us, or see our joy and be curious. I think that's why Vera suddenly said, "Shall we go on the roof?"

"Alright."

I shan't tell you where we were billeted, but it was, and is, a very grand place, an historic place. Hundreds were stationed there. Thousands. Some worked at that place but, as I have explained, loads of us were bussed out to other bases – mine in particular. Vera had something of an architectural mind and hence she had discovered a route onto the roof of the house. Someone had stashed some deckchairs up there. Sometimes, in fine weather, we crept up and sat there in the sun. No one ever found us.

It was one of those glorious April days that you sometimes get when it is uncharacteristically warm for the time of year. The sky was cloudless, we were completely sheltered, and the sun even rebounded off the lead flashing beneath us.

Every now and then an aeroplane traversed the blue as we lay back in our chairs.

"He wants to paint me nude," I told Vera.

"He wants to see you nude, more like," she jibed.

"I said I didn't mind."

"And do you?"

"No I don't."

"You've found a right one there, haven't you?"

"To be honest, I don't really like clothes very much," I said. I stood up and slipped off my skirt and blouse.

Vera laughed.

"The hell with it," I said, and took my underwear off too and stood stark naked. I must stress that this was the roof of a very grand property and edged with a decorative façade, we were surrounded by chimneystacks, completely alone and couldn't be seen from the ground. I sat back in my seat, shut my eyes and soaked up the sun.

There was a giggle and a rustle and Vera had done the same. In truth, it was not the first time we had done this. There had been a couple of days at the end of September 1942 when we had first discovered the pair of deckchairs stowed up there by goodness knows who, and under the influence of giddiness and Pimm's we had removed some of our clothes and infused our pale bodies with Phoebus' probing rays. I had remained there longer than Vera, and when she had left me alone I decided I wanted to be entirely nude. There was some aspect of me that rejoiced in the rebellion against decency and I needed to push the protest to its limit.

This time we were not drunk, and it didn't feel like we were rebelling, but rather revelling in our youth and natural femininity. There we were, a pair of romantic nymphs. All we needed was a painter. I knew one, but had no idea how I might meet him again.

We giggled some more. It all felt triumphantly liberating, as if we had shaken off not just our uniforms but all the conformity the war was imposing upon us.

We looked at each other. Vera was shorter than I, and more buxom.

"Do you think he'll include that?" she said, looking at my torso.

"What?"

"Whatever that is?"

"This," I said, stretching the scar on my abdomen, "is my brush with death."

"Really?"

"Emergency appendectomy, last summer. About a month before you arrived."

"God. Was it painful?"

"Agony. And quite frightening. I thought my number was up. I couldn't get over the thought that it would be a terribly trivial way to die during a war. Anyway, they whipped it out and stitched me up. Think it will put him off?"

"Painting you, or making love to you?"

"Do you think he intends both those things?"

Vera spread her skirt on her seat to make it more

comfortable to sit on. "He's a man isn't he? If he's half as attractive as you make him sound, I think I'd skip the first option if I was you."

"I'm actually really thrilled by the idea I might be preserved in paint."

"Did you arrange to meet up again?"

"No. When we parted he simply asked if I'd still got his number, and I said of course."

"Then you must dial it – mustn't you?"

"I will."

I returned to our rooftop haven for the next two days while the spring heatwave persisted. Vera had a bit of leave, so I went alone and on both days I stripped naked and sunbathed. It was a gentle and persistent warmth. I took a towel and lay flat out and snoozed, sometimes on my belly and sometimes on my back. The sky remained almost completely clear with just the occasional cloud, and the frequent criss-crossing of aeroplanes buzzing their reminders of our overshadowed lives.

My first-class stranger remained firmly in my mind. I thought about him all day, every day and all night too, since all my nights were spent awake. I let a week pass, and then called his number. There was no reply. I tried again at two-day intervals and there was nothing. I left it again, three or four days I think, and then there was a reply. It was a woman's voice.

"Hello?"

The fact that it was a woman threw me completely and I said nothing.

"Hello? Hello, can I help you?"

"Erm, is the gentleman there, if you please?"

"Which gentleman?"

"The gentleman from the second class compartment."

"I beg your pardon?"

"Or rather the first-class compartment."

Despite her polite tone she sounded rather affronted. "I'm terribly sorry, I'm afraid you must have dialled the wrong number."

"I do apologise; I don't know his name."

"There is no gentleman here. Not at the moment."

"Oh. Thank you."

That was it. There may have been a few more pleasantries, but none that I can recall. I was in a kind of shock. I didn't know what to do, but decided there was nothing I could do. That was that.

I told Vera on our way to the canteen.

"Woman's voice? What age do you think she was?"

"Impossible to tell. Two phrases won't leave my head. *No gentleman here*, and, *not at the moment*."

"Odder and bleedin' odder."

"Should I try again?"

"Do you want to?"

"Of course."

"Then do. But leave it a day or so. And call at a different time."

So I did. The next time I called it was a Saturday afternoon. This time it was a man's voice, but not his."

"Hello?"

"Oh, hello. Is that the first-class gentleman?"

"Matter of opinion I'm afraid."

"The artist."

"Ah, no, he's not here."

"Please don't tell me his name."

"I wasn't about to. And you should not mention yours."

"No I shan't."

"Good," he said. "Don't want to spoil anything. You are untitled, I gather."

Then I asked a rather peculiar question. I don't know why I did so. It must have been prompted by some deep insecurity I suppose. I said, "Is there more than one of me?"

He said, "Well, yes. And no."

"I see," I said, not seeing at all.

"Impossible for me to explain, I'm afraid."

"I'm sure. Could you get a message to the artist for me? To the first-class artist?"

"I can do better than that. I can tell you when he will be here."

"Please do."

"Could you call again this time next Saturday?"

"Yes, yes I can."

"Good, I'd do that if I were you."

"I will, thank you, tell him I will. I will call him on this number, next Saturday."

"I'll let him know."

"Thank you," I said, with perhaps a touch too much emphasis.

"I can tell you my name, if you like," said the man.

"Yes, I would like that."

"My name is Edwin."

"Edwin."

"Yes."

"I'm the girl from the second-class compartment."

"Are you?" said Edwin.

"Yes."

"Well you make a first class picture."

FOUR

It was the longest week under the sun. Or so it seemed. As Saturday drew close I got more and more nervous. I was determined to wait until one-thirty. That was the time that I had spoken to Edwin, and I somehow felt it would increase my chance of speaking to . . . the artist.

There was no reply.

I went to call again at two, but there was one hell of a queue at the telephone, and some silly girl was pouring her invented heart out to a G.I. on the other end. She clearly wanted us all to know that he was American.

My turn came and again there was no answer.

I left it until three, and this time it was his voice.

"Yes, hello?" He sounded out of breath.

"It's me," I said. "The second-class girl."

"Hello you."

"Hello," I said.

"It's good to hear your voice."

"And yours."

I could also hear either a wireless or a gramophone. *Smoke Gets in Your Eyes* was playing. "How's the portrait coming along?"

"Which one?"

"The one of me."

"Would you like to see it?"

"Yes, I would. Very much."

"When's your next leave? We'd need two or three days."

My pulse raced. "Not for weeks I'm afraid. The middle of June."

"There may be another by then."

"Gosh, don't you paint anything else?"

"Fauna."

"Fauna?"

"Yes."

"Does that include me?"

"I wouldn't paint you if it didn't."

"I bite, you know."

"I hope so," he said. "What date in June?"

"The tenth. For one week."

"The tenth it is then."

"Is that alright for you?"

"I'll make it so."

"Can you do that?"

"I will."

"How shall we meet?"

"Aylesbury again. I'll meet you at the station at the same time."

"Lovely."

"Could you stay all week?"

I must admit, my head spun a bit when he said that. I thought about hesitating but discovered that I hadn't. "Yes, that would be lovely."

"Bring your things then. For a week. From the tenth, at eleven."

You can imagine how hard the next seven weeks were. No harder, I suppose that all those poor folk with boys in the forces, especially the Navy, but this was peculiar, I didn't even know his name. I still don't. Yet I'd agreed to spend a week with him. With whom? Where? Vera said it was madness and she was right. Yet I was desperate to do it. It *was* madness, a kind of insanity. It all made no sense at all, but it was as if I had no option, some strange force held me, and made me want to be held by him - this nameless shadow that had brought such intense light into my life.

May of that year was a bit of a turning point in the war. We began to get snippets of better news. We took Tunis ending the

German grip on Africa, we burst the dams on the Rhur, and the allies attacked Sicily. There was still a long way to go, but people were daring to hope above and beyond what was regarded as simply obligatory optimism. Of course there was still the constant flow of depressing news. Everyone knew someone who knew someone who had lost someone. I now knew someone else that I didn't want to lose. I had no idea how much danger he was in, what kind it might be, or – should misfortune strike - how on earth I would ever discover what might have happened to him.

We were told our work was central to the war effort, though you would not know that from the detail of our day-to-day drudge. Every time I thought I might be passing on a piece of paper of some significance, I wondered if in some way it might be making my anonymous artist more safe, or even putting him in greater danger. I had deduced that he was not in the Navy, but felt sure he was enlisted in some way, unless of course, he was a boffin of some kind. I was well familiar with those. He would have fitted in very well with the team I knew; eccentrics every one.

Spring raced through the hedgerows but dragged through my veins. Every hour was a day. I rejoiced when it was June, and crossed off the days to the tenth.

I packed my case, promised to post a card to Vera, and caught a train. Third-class.

FIVE

Kendal's Lodge was a small, furnished rural property, that had previously been assigned to a gamekeeper or some such person, I imagine. Perhaps the war had put paid to that? I formed the impression that housing an estate employee was no longer its primary purpose. A key had been left hanging under the roof of a small woodshed at the back. There were many personal items about the place. The first thing I saw when we walked through the door was an envelope with a name and address.

Edwin Heap, Kendal's Lodge, West Barsham, Norfolk.

The lodge smelled slightly damp, but apart from that was very cosy. It was tastefully furnished, clean and homely. I felt like an invader.

"Don't worry," said my first-class artist. "There's nothing of mine here, apart from a few brushes and the odd stick of charcoal." He put the car keys in his trouser pocket. "Well, here we are."

There was the first real pause during which I thought he might attempt to kiss me. But he didn't.

"It's charming," I said.

"A touch clammy," he said. "The closeness of all the overhanging trees I think, but that usually vanishes if we get a fire going, or if the weather lifts a bit."

It had been a damp drive. Intermittent showers had plagued our journey. It had been dry at Aylesbury, but raining at

19

King's Lynn, and at the small station where the car had been left. The keys had been entrusted to the Station Master, who was known to my artist. He addressed him as Mr Painter, which, I have no doubt, is not his name. The windscreen wipers on the Ford were neither consistent in their operation nor efficient in their effect, but somehow we saw through the showers and after an hour or more we arrived at a pair of grand gates. Impressive as they were, I do not think they marked the principal entrance to the estate. There was a key on the car ignition ring that opened the padlock. Once we had driven through, my artist had to stop the car and lock the gates behind us. For some reason, I liked the thought of that. He wasn't locking us in, but locking everything else out.

Another five minutes brought us to the lodge.

There was a tiny vestibule, then a living room and kitchen from which stairs led to two bedrooms. The lodge did not have a bathroom. The water closet was outside, along a short path away from the back door. There was a fireplace in the living room and a stove in the kitchen. Next to each was a small stack of logs. More were to be found under a slightly ramshackle shelter near the privy.

He carried my case upstairs.

"I've got Heapy's bed," he said, not opening that door, and this will be your room.

My recollection is of a room filled with light, though that cannot really have been the case as the whole lodge was closely shrouded by woodland and the day remained depressingly overcast. Two things caught my eye, one was a double bed, and the other was an easel erected with its back towards us and sporting a large canvas attached to a board that was perhaps three feet wide and four tall. This alone should have cast the room in dimness for it stood close to the tiny window. Instead I had this feeling of a Turneresque halo of abstract brightness emitting from it. A paint-splattered cloth protected the floorboards beneath.

I hesitated, but he made no indication that I should, so I went around to the front of the easel and looked at the painting.

It was a picture of a woman sitting in a railway compartment. She was nude. It was a very good likeness; right down to my appendectomy scar.

SIX

We became lovers after a lovely day during that week in June 1943. The dam of no return was breached. He was caring, considerate and careful. Thank goodness.

To begin with, neither of us mentioned the scar on the painting. I said that he'd got a good likeness of my face and that my hair was flatteringly depicted.

He put the picture away in his room and, despite it being summer, lit a fire in the living room. He made sardines on toast for supper, served on blue willow-patterned plates. The rain lifted and we took a short, muddy, walk in the woods. There was a stack of pale ale next to the privy and we opened a couple of those when we got back and talked our way into the darkness.

Our identities, occupations and pasts were off the menu. We talked about the curiosities in the cottage, and of how we both held autumn, not summer, as our favourite season.

I asked him about Edwin, and he spoke of him with mild derision but sincere affection. He went so far as to admit that they had been school friends. He didn't say where, but some of his comments suggested they had boarded. I asked who actually lived in the Lodge. He said no one normally, but that Edwin's family used it at certain times of year and sometimes at the weekends.

"And so do you," I said. "Or the painting wouldn't be here."

"And so do I."

"You hinted there were others. Other paintings."

"Did I?."

"Do they have titles?"

"Of course not."

In one corner of the room was a gramophone and a stack of shellac records, and next to it a black Bakelite receiver.

I suddenly made what should have been a blatantly obvious connection. "The telephone," I said, staring across at it. "That's the number I rang."

"It is."

"A woman answered."

"You'd have to ask Edwin. Probably his mother."

"Probably?"

"You'd have to ask Edwin."

We talked more, I think it was about the freshness of wood fires compared to those of coal. It grew very dark very quickly. We had a few candles and a storm lantern, but the best thing to do was to head for bed. I stood to say goodnight. He took me in his arms and we kissed. It lasted quite a while, and became quite passionate, but that was all that passed between us on that first night.

I took a lantern to the privy, then washed as best as I could in the kitchen and went to bed. I couldn't sleep at first. It was a strange bed, not very comfortable, though bigger than I was used to, and the forest and the lodge had their choirs of night noises. I remember running my finger up and down the length of my appendectomy scar, and pondering the precision with which he had reproduced it. It was but a thin line cross-hatched with stitch marks, on the picture, but the position, length and inclination, were precisely correct.

I didn't sleep well and when daylight came I just lingered, not knowing when to get up. Eventually I heard him go downstairs and start doing things in the kitchen, so I got up and got dressed. He'd lit the stove and cooked the most delicious breakfast. There was a cool larder off one corner of the kitchen and it was miraculously stocked compared to what we were used to on the base, or what you could get in the high street. It was all from the estate, he explained, and hence not subject to rationing. I could see why he and Edwin spent time there whenever they could.

After breakfast was done and washed up we gathered a few things and drove to the coast. The day was better than the previous, but not overly warm with a cool breeze blowing off the North Sea. We cuddled against that.

It wasn't easy avoiding personal history details. He was better than I, which made me wonder if this was a game he'd played before with someone else, perhaps with more than one person.

We drove along the coast a little, sometimes stopping at fairly remote places, and sometimes in the small resorts. We had haddock and chips and strong tea, and then drove back to the lodge. The stove had gone out of course, but neither of us was hungry so we didn't bother eating, except for some rather scrumptious oatmeal biscuits that we found in the larder.

It wasn't cold, but he lit another fire in the living room, and we sat there with light ale, biscuits and cigarettes, cuddling on the sofa. It was heaven.

"So when's the sitting?" I asked.

"Sitting?"

"For the painting. Isn't that why you asked me here?"

"Tomorrow, if you like. If the light's right."

"And if it isn't?"

"Then it's back to the coast and you'll have to unveil on the beach."

"In between the tank traps and landmines?"

"You'd trigger a premature invasion. Lure Gerry in, and wipe out a whole battalion."

I sniggered, and said, "How did you know about my appendectomy?"

"Is that what it is?"

"It's on the painting. It's very accurate."

"If you say so."

"How did you know?"

"I saw it."

I pulled back from the embrace. "When?"

"In the restaurant in Aylesbury."

"How?"

"You'd missed a button on your blouse. Sometimes when you leaned forwards it bowed apart and I could see the beginning of it. I guessed and hoped it was your appendix."

"Why hoped?"

23

"I like the idea, that you'd survived an emergency. Makes you even more precious."

"It's rather unsightly."

"You'd be too perfect without it."

"That's an opinion not an observation"

"It's both."

I finished my cigarette and tossed the butt into the fire. "Have you done this before?"

"Done what?"

"Brought anonymous women here."

"You are not anonymous, you are untitled. It's not the same thing."

"Have you?"

"Personal history is off the agenda." He threw his cigarette into the fire and kissed me. Then he said, "Tomorrow I'll show you where they are buried."

"Who?"

"Your predecessors."

We kissed again. Then we went upstairs, and shared the same bed.

The next morning the weather had turned warmer. We had a cold breakfast, and then I sat naked on chair in the bedroom while he adjusted his portrait. It didn't take long - less than an hour. The scar in the picture looked just the same to me.

It was a wonderful week that will always soar in my memory. The weather remained changeable but we found a spectacular closeness. I suppose many others experienced something similar. The war made moments into fleeting eternities. Whenever we went off the estate we saw others comparable to ourselves, maximising the rationed intimacy and desperately devouring the temporary. What they didn't have, was our shared anonymity.

I did not discover his name.

One morning when he was up before me and downstairs cooking breakfast, I spotted a suitcase beneath the bed. I lifted the lid just a little. Inside, I saw the sleeve of the uniform of a Royal Air Force officer with two thick rings just above the cuff. A Flight Lieutenant. I don't know if the case was his. He didn't bring it when we arrived or take it when we left. I did not draw it to his attention. I didn't want to know. The fact that we did not discuss our pasts meant all we had to consider was the present and the future. The first was idyllic, the other too uncertain to contemplate.

The penultimate day was the most perfect. We remained on the estate but walked for what must have been miles before settling by a river. We saw a kingfisher. Halcyon.

He asked me if I would marry him. He made it clear he was not proposing. He simply wanted to know if I could contemplate a proposal knowing only that which I knew about him. I said I could and I would. We left it at that.

One thing bothered me. Each night when I climbed into his bed, I removed the shift I had been wearing beneath my blouse on our first date and through which I knew he could not have seen my scar.

The week was over all too quickly. The best week of my life. The final night was the finest of them all. We drove off the estate and to a restaurant on the coast. I had lemon sole. A gentleman by the name of Mr Rudd played melodies on a baby grand. We heard, but did not listen to, the conversations of others. Of course, throughout the week we had been reminded of the war. Whenever there was droning in the sky, or military vehicles on the roads, or uniformed swarms in the streets, the war was back among us, but when we stayed on the estate or, as on that Friday night, when we sat tucked away in the corner of the restaurant, then there was no war, or rather it was in another world, and there was just us, just our tiny world, and it was such a special world; a nameless place.

We drove back through the phoney night of June when late evening is still light, so when we returned to the lodge beneath black-leaved trees the darkness was doubled and redoubled. We fumbled our way to bed, and to love beneath the sheets, the thatch, the advancing cloud, and the zenith of night that never knew sun.

The morning drive to the station was in silence. It was as if all that needed to be said had been spoken. Anything that might have been voiced was too charged with sentiment to be admitted. My eyes were wet. His jaw set forward. It was not determination he showed me, but resignation petrified into a bulwark. It was not a destination he was driving towards but another state, another existence. It was a place outside of love. A place of duty, of pain, and the promise of no return.

He did not accompany me onto the train. He was to catch a later one, so we parted on the platform. That carriage has remained with me. I despised the floor-embedded bristle mat for daring to claim some of our shared soil from the soles of my shoes. Half the springs in my seat had failed inclining me back towards the door. The window was scratched in a great arc.

Advertisements offered solace. Fry's chocolate, and Cadbury's chocolate, and Camp coffee, and Venus soap, that saves rubbing.

We made no arrangements to re-establish contact.

Back at our base Vera stared at me over something masquerading as cold ham and chips.

"Well?"

"It was – idyllic."

"And his name?"

I shrugged.

"You went the whole week and you still don't know his bleedin' name?"

I shook my head.

"What did you call him?"

"You."

"All the time?"

"When there's just two of you there isn't a great need for names."

"What about in public, then? You know - to get his attention."

"I managed."

Somewhere, further along the canteen, some girl squealed and a cup smashed.

Vera said, "What about the portrait? Did you see the portrait?"

"I sat for him while he improved it."

"What – naked?"

I nodded. "It was very detailed, even before I sat. Very."

"Good likeness then?"

I undid my battledress jacket and then unfastened one button half way down my blouse, and leaned forwards to create a bulge and a gap.

"What are you doing?"

"Can you see my scar?"

"What?"

"Can you see my scar?"

"You've got a bleedin' vest on."

"Even if I hadn't – could you see my scar?"

"What?"

"Could you?"

"No, I don't think so."

"Not any of it?"

"I don't know. Tiny bit perhaps. Why?"

I told her about the precision of the painting.

"That's a bit wonky," she said.

"Yes," I said.

We were thrown back into the dull nameless routine of our work. If anything it was more mundane than ever but, we were told, more important than ever. I was on the night shift again and that meant that each day had eight hours of darkness and six of frequently interrupted sleep. I tried my best to be conscientious but having been through the wonderful week in the woods, I found it all the more tortuous, and there was the added uncertainty that I would ever meet with him again.

I left things for three weeks then telephoned the lodge. There was no reply. I tried again three days later, and then at the following weekend. Nothing. I tried on and off for another month. Nothing.

Had he not given me his name so that I could not trace him? Had he used me? As a model and a lover. Or had he been posted, or worse?

Of course our arrangement also meant that he had no way of contacting me. He didn't know who I was or where I was based. There was no point my anticipating, or hoping for, letters. I was without a name and without an address. It had been a most strange, and you might think, somewhat perilous adventure. I was in a turmoil of emotion; very much in love but also with a deep sense of rejection, which might actually have been misfortune. It was the war – anything might have happened to him. Should I have been in mourning? I was.

The journey between the camp where I was billeted and the base where I worked became unbearable. This was partly because Vera and I were placed on different shifts, so instead of having a friend with whom I could confide, I could only resort to general chit-chat or slump into long periods of dreary silence. The bus journey passed the railway station, and hence was a daily reminder of the escape I had made for our first date, and the staccato tempo and weary sway of the drive stirred up a sick sadness especially after a long night shift. I felt abandoned.

Then one September morning, when I arrived back at my bed, there was an envelope on my pillow. It was addressed to *The Second-class Stranger*.

SEVEN

The note simply stated the station where it had all begun, and three different dates and times when he planned to pass through. I faked an illness to skip my shift and made sure I was there for the first.

Our table was taken but we sat at another across the café. He was changed. Only slightly, but I noticed. There was an edginess to his demeanour that had not been there before. He smoked more. His eyes did not meet mine as much, but when they did, the sincerity was still there, the desire just as deep.

"Hello you," he said.

"Hello you," I returned.

"How are you?"

"Hell of a migraine and vomiting relentlessly."

"Really?"

"It's what I told the medic."

"And he believed you?"

"So it seems. I'll have to keep my head down."

"Let me get you some tea."

"Thank you."

While he was at the counter it felt like every other traveller was a potential squealer. It was as if they all knew I should be on duty. Of course they didn't. At least I hoped not. When he came back with my drink I said, "I phoned the lodge. Several times."

He said, "I haven't been back since we were there."

"My portrait?"

"It's finished."

"Does it have a title?"

"Of course not."

He lit my cigarette, then another one for himself."

"Can I see it?"

"Edwin sold it."

"Edwin did?"

"Settled a few debts I owed him."

I was confused. I had supposed he had wanted to paint me for personal reasons. It turned out I was simply a model. On reflection, I suppose he had never suggested anything else. Even so, part of me felt affronted, part flattered, and part, well, to be honest, exploited. Overall, though, there was a sense of being special. Not everyone is transformed into a cultural artefact.

We exchanged chit-chat. Then I raised the question of our meeting again. He asked for a list of my leave dates. I scribbled down what I knew. He put it in his pocket and said he would consult his own diary. Then he would get in touch again. Then I asked how he had known where to find me. And how he had got the letter onto my bunk.

"Edwin followed you."

"When?"

"When we last parted. I asked him to. I couldn't let you go completely."

"So you know who I am. You know my name, rank and number and even the location of my bunk."

"No. I know none of those things. Edwin does. He won't tell me. On pain of death."

"So Edwin got your note to me."

"He's a useful sort."

"Will you ask him to do something for me?"

"What?"

"Will you ask him to let me know if anything happens to you."

"He's very considerate. I'm sure he will do that."

"Thank you."

"But you must understand, like many of us, his whereabouts are not his to determine."

"Of course not."

He gripped my hand. "What will be will be, I'll do my best to get a note to you."

I returned the grip and said, "I'm not sure I want us to continue on that basis." He looked crestfallen. A train pulled in and lots of people got up. Crockery clattered. "It was heaven," I said, "while we were together, but when I couldn't get in touch, it was nothing short of sheer hell. And let's be serious, we can't spend the rest of our lives not knowing who the other is; or was."

His focus pulled tightly on something beyond the window of the café. When he turned back to me his expression had changed. It was filled with fragile hope, and a kind of hunger for joy. "We cannot be legally married without declaring who our parents said we were. But that's not who we are, nor is it the person to whom we will be making our pledges. We will know each other fully and authentically. But now is not the time for that. War makes frauds of us all. When there is peace I will ask the true you to be wedded to the true me."

"The true me has already said she would."

"First the war must end."

"Are you fighting it?"

"That would be a betrayal."

"A betrayal?"

"Of what I truly am."

"And what's that?"

"A peacemaker."

"Oh."

"That's what all artist are."

"Peacemakers?"

"Constantly at war."

I was desperate that we should somehow stay in contact, so I gave him the address of a Post Office box that my step-father rented for his business. I told him to clearly address any letter to me using whatever code name he wished, and that I would write home and forewarn my step-father, so that he would not open it. After the war, when my step-father died, I took over the box and have rented it until this day.

Over the station café counter was a large clock. Paint had peeled from the five numeral. I did not let myself read the time. I knew his train would be soon. I wanted him to miss it. He put a ring on the table.

"I will buy you a better one. Until then please wear this. I believe it once belonged to my grandmother."

I held out my left hand. He slipped the ring onto my third finger. It was slightly loose, but it is still there.

He boarded the 6.45 train. We kissed through the window of the door. First class. The train pulled out forever. That was the last time I saw him. A quarter to seven on the evening of Wednesday 22nd September 1943.

EIGHT

Inside the office, a well-combed cranium skimmed the far side of the file-stacked desks until Mr French, four foot six inches tall but looking at least fifty years of age, emerged into view in his splendidly tailored chocolate brown suit.

"I really am most grateful," she said.

"I haven't done anything, have I?" said Mr Coward.

"You have agreed to help me."

The diminutive Mr French placed the Willow Pattern tray with two cups of coffee and a sand coloured side plate with four Nice biscuits on the mahogany desk. Mr Coward passed her a cup and saucer.

"Thank you."

"You present a very interesting puzzle."

"Interesting is not an adjective I would select."

"No, perhaps not." Coward placed the other cup and saucer on his blotter pad. "Did you hear from this Edwin fellow?"

"No."

"Did he know of the reversed numeral procedure that you used?"

"I have no idea."

"But your friend Vera did."

She hesitated. "Yes, yes, she did. I told her."

"Either of those people could have sent the postcard from

Alsace."

She hesitated even more. "Vera was killed in 1944 on a trip to London. By an unexploded bomb."

"She's living in Köpenick. East Berlin."

"What?"

"Eight hundred kilometres from Alsace."

"She died in London in . . ."

"Do you know what 'Hut Six' means. I do not."

"Hut six?" She felt unsteady, and nauseous, and knew she must have turned distinctly pale.

"Don't let your coffee go cold."

She sipped from the cup.

"I don't know what it means." He drank too. "But my wife does. She won't tell me. Official secrets she says. Evidently you know. I'm not expecting you to tell me. I expect you've signed it too: Official Secrets." He indicated the Nice biscuits. "Please."

She declined. "What exactly do you know about Vera?"

"Only what my wife told me."

"How does your wife know?"

"I have no idea. But I trust her absolutely."

"Of course."

"She made enquiries."

"Very kind of her." She sipped more coffee. She was feeling steadier.

"I need to ask you something rather intimate."

"I may not answer."

"That is your prerogative."

"Go ahead."

"Your appendectomy scar."

"What about it?"

"What length is it?"

"Quite long."

"You've made comparisons?"

"A . . . military . . . nurse was of that opinion. She said she'd seen shorter."

"Where approximately is it?"

She put her cup down, stretched back and with the index finger of each hand indicated the position on the outside of her skirt. "Here to here."

"Mmm. Beneath the waist of your skirt. Always? Is it at

all possible he could have glimpsed the top edge of the scar in the way he described – through a bulge in the fastening of your blouse?"

"I was wearing a shift."

"If you hadn't been."

"I was."

"If you hadn't been."

"It's just possible I suppose. But I don't believe that could have happened."

"No, neither do I."

"Then how did he paint it so accurately?"

"There are only three possibilities."

"And they are?"

"Either he had seen it – perhaps not by the means he described; or someone told him about it."

"Who?"

Coward shrugged. "A nurse perhaps? If not that then, as I recall, service life has its communal moments. Billets are not the most private of places."

"True enough. And what is the third possibility?"

"A photograph."

"I was not in the habit of posing with my clothes off."

"Oh yes you were."

"At the cottage. After he'd already painted the scar."

"Well before that."

"When? Where?"

"On the roof of Woburn Abbey."

Her face shocked to the stiffness of parchment. "I did not tell you it was at Woburn Abbey."

"My wife did. She worked it out from the evidence you provided."

"Vera did not have a camera and there was no-one else on that roof."

"The roof is overlooked."

"No it is not. That's why we chose it."

"It is overlooked."

"By what?"

"By the sky."

"What?"

"Your lover was an airman. He had a camera. A very good camera."

"What?"

"It's one possibility. One of three. Would you like a cigarette?"

"Yes please."

Coward opened the maple cigarette case and proffered it to her. She took one and he lit it with his desk lighter of cut onyx set on a wooden pediment that was a close match to the cigarette case.

She inhaled a nicotine thought, held it, released it, and said, "Reconnaissance pilot."

"Not necessarily. Observer; or anyone based at the unit. Analyst, clerk, or even a dark room operative."

"Were there any such units in the right area?" It was more of a meditation than a question.

"The 'right area' being . . .?"

"Within half a day of . . . Woburn Abbey."

"That we can find out. But let's not completely rule out the other two possibilities."

"I'm sure he did not see my scar, until I chose to reveal it to him."

"Which means he lied to you."

"Mr Coward, your fee is for finding him, not passing judgement on him."

"I regret that the former may not be possible without the latter." His hand returned to the cigarette box and he selected one of the contents and lit it. "I think he lied to you."

She exhaled another grey cloud. "Perhaps - to cloak his true occupation? To preserve his anonymity?"

"Perhaps. Or to protect his source. Alternative two."

"Someone told him about the scar. Described it to him."

"How many of your comrades had seen it?"

"Not many. I can't be sure of any other than Vera."

"Vera Dalkandle."

"Yes."

"Uncommon surname."

"Dutch. She said. Though she was distinctly a Londoner. But she said it was Dutch."

"Did she?"

"Well isn't it?"

Coward shrugged. "We can check."

"And you think she's alive?"

"As far as we know."

"Do you have an address for her?"

"I think it would be unwise for you to contact her. Or attempt to do so."

"If she resides in East Berlin she may as well live on the moon. Do you think she might know where he is?" She inhaled smoke and tapped ash into the chunky glass receptacle on the desk.

"We are making inquiries."

"How?"

"My fee is for my efforts, not for my methods."

"I'm sorry. My question came from incredulity. I did not mean to pry."

Mr Coward smiled kindly. "I understand. Leave the prying to me."

"I will. Please pry very hard."

"I shall do my best. I'm going to eliminate alternative one. I don't believe he saw your scar before you permitted him to do so. So that leaves two and three. I shall discover what more I can about Vera Dalkandle, and we'll draw up a list of air reconnaissance units operational during 1943. If, and when, I have anything of worth pertaining to either of these two lines of inquiry, I'll drop you a note suggesting another meeting. I know it's something of a journey, but I feel it is preferable that we speak face to face than risk putting sensitive matters on paper."

"Sensitive?"

"I shan't ask you to travel unless I have something worthy to impart."

"This is all starting to sound rather ominous."

"It's too early to make assessments of that nature."

She stubbed out her cigarette. "However, if I may say so, you seem more earnestly engaged with my commission than when I first proposed it."

"It has its . . . intrigue."

"And dangers?"

He shrugged. "Who knows? But it is always advisable to proceed with caution."

"Yes, well, let's do that."

"And there is one other perspective we shouldn't overlook."

"And what is that?"

"Well if it was not Vera but your fiancé who triggered this whole enterprise then it seems that he was provoking you to find him."

"Seems?"

"We must not overlook the possibility that he – or someone – may have been actually trying to do the opposite and locate you."

"But he – or whoever sent the card – knew where I was."

"That's not what I mean by 'locate'."

"Then what do you mean?"

"I don't mean today," Coward said. "Persons may not know you are here today, unless you have told them."

"Persons?"

"But the first time you came, that presents other permutations."

"Permutations?"

"The initial post card was sent to a Post Office box. The sender did not know your home address, or even if you were still the recipient of the mail delivered to that box."

"By the sender you mean . . ."

"They could put a watch on the box. But that would be laborious and time consuming. And possibly fruitless."

"And who, are 'they'?"

"It would be much more efficient to simply watch this office, at the appointed time and date."

"I'm sorry . . ."

"That would not only identify you, but also confirm that you still harbour a desire to re-affiliate with your fiancé."

"Mr Coward, are you suggesting that the post card was sent by someone other than Vera or my fiancé?"

"No."

"Then . . ."

"But my wife raised that possibility. And she knows more about these things than I do."

"What – 'things'?"

In response to that question Mr Coward looked through his office window at the Town Hall clock. "I wouldn't want you to miss your train, though Mrs Coward has suggested that, under certain circumstances, you might consider doing precisely that."

NINE

Bright winter coats did little to lift the November gloom, and the soot-thickened steam clung to the station canopy. Door slams were dampened and failed to echo. The London train was late, adding to the sense of insecurity that Mr Coward had spawned. She had left the bank by the side door, because the side door was the way to access the staircase to the stockbroker's office on the top floor, but it felt as if she was evading someone.

It was difficult to miss a train that was more than twenty minutes late. Few persons disembarked and the surge of those desperate to board appeared even more determined than it normally was. Hoisting her shopping bag in front of her, she traversed three carriages. There were no vacant seats.

She stood with two men and a young woman in the lolloping lobby at the end of the carriage outside the toilet and where the footplates of adjacent coaches butted against each other beneath the canvas concertina. It was draughty. The other woman leaned against the door peering out of the drip-embossed window. One man read a folded newspaper, the other looked at the ceiling when she clocked him, and at her whenever she didn't. At least, that was her impression.

It was going to be a long five hours.

Mr Coward's closing remarks deeply troubled her. They had admitted her to a whole new world, but one founded entirely on speculation. She wanted to hold to her heart only one possibility - that her long lost love was trying to reunite with her - but Mr Coward, and his apocryphal wife, had suggested an alternative scenario. In that version she was a person of interest to devious, shady and dangerous individuals. Why? What possible value could she present to them?

Her work during the war had been confidential, but also mundane, laborious and banal. She had been an invisible cog deep within a clock tucked away at the back of a cupboard that few knew where to locate and even fewer knew what it contained. Locate. That word again. *They* might be trying to *locate* you. To place her. To position her. In some sort of danger? That's what Coward had insinuated, or at least he said his wife had. Mrs Coward – she knew of the clock in the cupboard. Perhaps she knew more of what went on at that place? Mrs Coward might be a person of interest. She might be worth locating, but as for herself, she carried no special knowledge, no sensitive information, and no recollections of value. Who would be interested now anyway? The war was a decade dead. As far as she knew, her place of posting had closed down, but even if it hadn't, she'd had no connection with it since she'd walked out of the main gate for the last time when she was demobbed in February 1946. All she'd done during her final six months was pack boxes or destroy record cards. She had never fully, or even partially, understood its purpose and still didn't but she had signed the Official Secrets Act and swore to adhere to it under pain of death. If anyone asked her about it she wouldn't be able to tell them, not because of her oath, but because she wouldn't have a clue about what they would want to know.

Ten years on, the world had a new optimism, or so she was led to believe. Many essentials were still rationed. Every city still had un-rebuilt bomb sites. Every family had memories, of airborne threat, of anxiety for relatives overseas or at sea, of bad news, very bad news, or worse. Some, like herself, harboured the nastiest bequest of all: a devotion to the unresolved absentee.

The woman opposite her, leaning right up against the door window, was incessantly chewing. She was, perhaps, ten years younger. She was dressed soberly, though her combed-back curls, and blusher-bruised cheek bones, hinted at a rebel within what was probably employer-imposed rigidity. She only lasted two stops, then she was off across a commuter-packed platform, pausing only to solicit a light from a man twice her age. Her place on the train was taken by a tall man in a raincoat and bowler and bearing a briefcase and furled umbrella. He took one look down the corridor of the compartment and settled for standing by the still open door. Bet you've got more confidentially in your briefcase than I have in my entire life, she thought. You should be *located*.

A guard slammed the door. After a short eternity, a whistle blew, the coach jolted and those left waiting slid away. Four hours and forty minutes she thought. The flat will be cold and dark, and undisturbed, I hope. The fact that she should think so, disturbed her deeply.

She understood how illogical it was to develop a paranoia based on the whimsy of Mrs Coward, but the notion had infiltrated her consciousness so much that she couldn't help it. Anyone could be tailing her. Any of the three others in the carriage vestibule with her might be on her case. The first two were unlikely, because they had been on the train before she boarded. Or had they? The tall person with the bowler hat was more suspect. He looked the type. Not that she knew what the type looked like. He didn't seem especially interested in her, unlike the lecherous specimen by the toilet door. This was absurd. The Cowards were reading too much into too little. It was her anonymous fiancé that had initiated her movements. He alone, was interested in her. She hoped.

Two stops more and the tall man advanced on her. She inhaled sharply.

He spoke curtly but with benevolence. "There's a seat," he said. Someone has vacated it."

"Oh, thank you," she said and eased past him to claim the only empty seat in the coach. She was grateful, after standing for almost an hour, but also felt a little guilty. She felt better, after the next stop when someone else left the train and her knight in black bowler claimed a place diagonally opposite her, and a few rows away. A gent, she decided. Nothing else.

Her seat was not particularly comfortable, which reminded her of the times she and her fiancé had shared coaches like this. Could this one be one of those? No it couldn't. Wrong pre-nationalised company. Wrong livery. Wrong line of thought. Despite the discomfort, the rhythmic motion nursed her thoughts from memories to fantasies and towards dreams. She did not want to doze off but the nurturing sway of the train

lulled her, and before no time had elapsed she was awake and a
third of the carriage had emptied. The bowler-hatted man had
gone and, unbelievably, so had the plump woman who had been
sitting between her and the window. She had no recollection of
being disturbed by her departure. She checked the shopping bag
that she had wedged between her feet. All seemed intact. She
must have woken, she must have moved it or the lady could not
have got off. The train was stationary. Beyond the window was
a lit platform but she could not see a station nameplate. More
people came on board, and she shifted across to the window
seat. In doing so she spotted that the tall man had not left the
train. He was now on her side of the carriage and two rows
closer than before.

Someone came to sit beside her: a stocky man smelling of
rain and a diet too rich with onions. By the time he'd settled the
train had moved off again, she'd missed all the illuminated signs
and the window was all raindrops and darkness.

She longed for her flat, whatever state it might be in.

"You understand, I'm sure, that the pre-Christmas period is our
busiest time of year."

"Of course."

"We have the highest expectations of our staff."

"I share and uphold those expectations."

"By example?"

"If you look at my record Miss Chisholme . . ."

"I have done that."

"There have been only two instances this year."

Miss Chisholme's office was the antithesis of Mr Coward's.
It was bright, and airy, with uncompromising southerly daylight
washing all surfaces from double-height frosted-glass windows.
Pristinely tidy, it's one desk, two chairs, three filing cabinets, and
one coat-and-hat stand, stood defiant, ready to repulse any
invaders.

"As third floor manager you are vital to our efficiency and
the reputation that rests upon it."

"I'm never ill."

"But you were yesterday."

"Yes."

"Without warning."

"Illness, doesn't sent advance parties, Miss Chisholme."

"But it frequently leaves signs of damage in its wake. You don't look ill today."

"Just tired."

"We are never tired. You know that."

"Yes."

"And we do not allow absences without notice."

"No, Miss Chisholme."

"If you are not well enough to be at work, I will send you home."

"Yes, Miss Chisholme."

"And I don't tend to do that."

"No, Miss Chisholme."

"We cannot allow a manager of your standing to set that kind of example."

"Of course not."

"If this were a quieter time of year, I might be at liberty to take harsher reprisals. But it's on your record. Remember that, the next time you feel too unwell to report for work."

"Yes, Miss Chisholme."

"Oh dear."

"Well, could have been worse."

"You be careful, won't you?"

"That day was interminable. As was the rest of the week; and this week is no better."

"The steak is fresh. I saw it being delivered."

"This is extraordinarily kind of you . . . Alice."

"I get discount."

"You are working tonight, aren't you?"

"You think I wear these bleedin' lashes for fun?"

"Compared to mine, your job is fun."

"That's as maybe. Appearances deceive. And it sounds like you're in danger of losing your bleedin' job, so I'll put a good word in for you, and you can find out for yourself."

"I haven't got the figure for it."

"We've got contraptions back stage that can fix that for you."

"Not when everything comes off."

Her hostess clicked her false nail extended fingers to summon the waiter. "Everything never comes off."

"Never?"

"Not on me."

"I thought it was all right so long as you didn't move?"

"Nature sometimes needs a little help. It's amazing what a Basque or a jewelled belt can do. Like hide a bleedin' appendectomy scar." The waiter, in bow tie, tails and pencil moustache attended them. "Two steaks. Medium, but bleedin' quick, because I'm on at nine and my guest needs a good night sleep. And a bottle of house red – the *real* house." He inclined his head in an affirmative manner and shuffled a balletic slalom between the tables and back to the kitchen. "So you think this Coward fellow is getting carried away?"

"He's been consulting with his wife."

"His wife!"

"I think she must have . . . government connections. She knows about Hut Six."

Their mutual stare solidified. "Blimey!"

"Exactly."

"What she look like?"

"I've no idea. She's the one that thinks I may be of interest to some unscrupulous other."

"I'm sure you would be, but you have too many scruples."

"I didn't when I knew him." She glanced across the cabaret tables towards the stage. The dowdy deep blue house tabs were in, masking the set behind. Christmas paper-chains lay along the edge of the stage apron.

Vera leaned forwards exposing the thickness of her make-up to the scrutiny of the table lamp. "Why don't he just come and find you?"

"I don't know. Maybe he can't."

"Then he should tell you that."

"Maybe he can't do that either?"

"Why ever not?"

She shrugged. "I don't know."

"It's all very - cloak and dagger."

"Says you!"

"Steady on now."

"Not sure about the daggers but that's a well-worn cloak you're wearing."

"Careful darlin', careful."

The waiter brought the wine and their conversation was paused while he pulled the cork. "It's fine, just pour it."

He inclined his head, half-filled their glasses, positioned the bottle centrally on their table and withdrew."

"Coward told me that, according to his wife, you are living in East Berlin."

Vera paused, pre-swallow; then swallowed and said, "do you mean me; or do you mean – me?"

She mouthed, "Vera Dalkandle."

"Well that's alright then ain't it?"

She spoke very low. "Have you ever lived in East Berlin?"

"Are you joking? Must be someone with the same name."

"Unless someone has stolen your identity."

"They're welcome to it. I left it on a bombsite in 1944. You know that."

"I do. Alice."

Vera visibly stiffened. "You didn't say nothing did you?"

"Of course not."

"Right" said Vera. "So back to your problem and my question."

"What question?"

"Is he worth it? Your man with no name."

"Yes," she said. "He's worth it."

"There are all kind of things might have happened, you know. He might have been injured in the war, he might . . ."

"I know, I know, I know. I've been through all that. Look, I'm not going into this blindly or irresponsibly . . ."

"You did that in 1943."

"I was young, it was wartime, I was bored and he was . . . he was lovely."

"And in your mind he still is, ain't he?"

"Why would he be other?"

"Because he wouldn't tell you his name, he left without a word and he ain't been in touch for ten years."

"Until now."

Vera sighed. "If it is him."

"Not you as well!"

"It's all a bit bleedin' strange. You ain't heard no more?"

"This morning. That's why I had to see you. Put me right . . . Alice, tell me what to do."

45

"What's the latest?"

"I received a communication from Coward's office, saying I am to come and collect all that they have. Soon as possible."

"And . . ."

"That's it."

"That's it?"

"Yes."

Vera screwed her top lip. "It's a bit vague. A bit brief. To the point of, being, well, curt."

"It was a telegram."

"A telegram?"

"Six thirty this morning."

"God."

"I need to leap on a train – tomorrow – but how? I cannot fake another sudden illness. I have to do six days a week until Christmas. Going on a Sunday would be unthinkable, and pointless, because Coward's would be closed."

"Have you tried the telephone?"

"Can't get through. Tried all the way through my lunch – almost getting lynched by the lady waiting for the box – and tried again on my way here. There's no point after six, but I tried anyway. It's like the bloody war again."

"Try again tomorrow."

"I'm desperate."

"Don't do anything rash."

The waiter brought their steaks. Another served vegetables. When they were alone again, she said, "Do you think she'll sack me?"

"Nah."

"Then I'll go tomorrow."

"But I think she'll hand you your notice. Make you work until the January sales."

"I'd just leave."

"No job, no wages, no references and no bleedin' fairy tale."

"I have savings."

"And how long will they last?"

"Could you make me look ill? Really ill. Stage make-up?"

Vera sipped her wine. "Stage make-up is for the stage. It don't work close-up." She leaned forwards again and pointed at her face. "Look."

"Well I am ill, but not in a clinical sense."

Vera spoke very slowly. "It won't get you a day off."

"I know."

"Send Coward a telegram. Ask him to put all they have in the post."

"It would take too long, and besides, I'm not sure they'd want to commit it to paper."

"Why ever not?"

"Because they could have done that already. Instead – a telegram. A telegram that tells me nothing."

"Irritating man, your Mr Coward."

"It wasn't from Mr Coward."

"What?"

"It was from his assistant. Mr French."

"Makes no difference . . ."

"Makes every difference. Mr French is a stockbroker. That's the capacity in which he works for Mr Coward. As far as I am aware Mr Coward was not confiding in him, with respect to my affairs."

"Well he was probably just delegated to send you the telegram. That's all."

"But Mr Coward has only communicated with me via my post office box. I did not tell Mr Coward my home address. Yet it was on the telegram delivered to my door this morning."

"Well, he's obviously a lot bleedin' better at detecting than I was giving him credit for. Perhaps he will find your man for you."

"And there's every chance he may already have done so. And told him where I am. And that's not the way I want to play this game."

"Then you don't need me to tell you what to do. You're going north again aren't you?"

"I've got to. You understand don't you? I'll go in the morning. I may even get the midnight train."

"And what will you tell Miss Chisholme?"

"I'll think of something."

"And, there is one other thing to think about."

"What?"

"What will you tell your husband?"

TEN

She did catch the midnight train. It was rash, impulsive, and foolish to the point of verging on the self-destructive. Or it might have been the making of her. Time would tell.

It was a sleeper train but she did not have a reservation, nor would she have wasted money on one. She did have an overnight bag. She'd thrown it together that morning after receiving the telegram. She'd deposited it at the station left luggage office, and consequently been late for work. The clocking-in machine had stamped her eight minutes into red time. She'd waited for the summons to Miss Chisholme, but Miss Chisholme had been absent. Her deputy, Mr Grainger, should have sent for her, but he didn't. Mr Grainger was more lenient, or at least he was towards her. She knew things about Mr Grainger.

Before she and Vera had parted, they'd finished the wine and downed whiskey chasers. She was drunk. There was no turning back. To do that she would need to be sober and that was many hours away. By five past midnight, she was snug in the intestine of a smoky serpent slithering out of the city and panting its way northwards. She was very, very happy.

The train was quiet, and she even found a compartment to herself. She stowed her overnight bag safely overhead and she was soon asleep. She awoke frequently, and slept fitfully and only for an hour or so. Ironically she felt the most inclined towards sleep when it was necessary to stay awake so that she would not miss her stop. Her head was heavy but not painful, and she found herself amid an icy wind on a dark and freight-littered platform at quarter to six in the morning. She navigated a delicate but irregular path to the ladies' rest-room and then set off to find the station café, with three hours to kill before Mr Coward could be visited.

Mr French stood before her on the platform.

She caught a glimpse of him over the lower crescent of her eye whilst avoiding what she presumed to be a child. The child was not a child. It was Mr French. His black worsted overcoat was tailored impeccably to his modest dimensions and he sported a matching Homburg hat.

"Mr French!"

"Miss . . ."

"I was on my way to see you."

"The office is not open today."

"I've come on the overnight train; I'll go in the café until nine."

"Not at all today."

"Why ever not?"

"I'll explain in due course. Not here. Not now."

"No. Very well. What shall I do?"

"Come at four pm."

"Four!"

"Come as discretely as you can. Don't linger outside or anything."

"What?"

"Promptly at four. I'll be there." With that he was gone. For a man with such a short pace he could move at a remarkable speed without appearing to hurry. By the time she'd gathered her thoughts he was half way up the ramp from the platforms to the ticket office and main exit.

She felt cold, bewildered and suddenly very tired.

She didn't know what to do. Her intoxicated bravado was still on the train, heading for Scotland. It had slipped away as she had washed her face in the ladies' rest room. She had a sudden hunger for the secure normality that she had so recklessly abandoned. One thought of the artist put paid to that. The ache to find him over-ruled all other feelings. Her chance meeting with Mr French had both heightened and dulled that drive. His mysterious instructions supported the notion that he needed to meet properly and pass something on, but his manner added to the sense of a furtive and possibly unsafe dimension to her destiny.

To begin with she simply adhered to plan A, and went to the station café. A cup of caffeinated gruel did little to raise her spirits or her temperature so she didn't stay long, and soon she was walking the streets much slower than the swelling workforce making its way to shops and offices. Seasonal window displays thick with synthetic snow and wooden Santas lined the main street, the length of which she covered in something short of fifteen minutes. She couldn't do that all day. She went into an hotel, *The Clarion* but the receptionist insisted that they would not have a room until two in the afternoon, it would have to be booked for at least one night and she'd need to enquire again at noon. She suspected the rebuttal was based more on her solo status and pathetic demeanour than it was on clerical fact. She had better luck at a smaller coaching inn, *The Dickensian,* where the proprietor took pity, took her money, and showed her to a room in keeping with the hotel name in spirit and in decor, and she locked the door, lay on the bed and slept until noon.

She had a steak and kidney lunch in the restaurant of the inn, and then passed two torturous hours not reading the newspapers that she hid behind in the lounge. At three-thirty, she collected a small clutch bag from her overnight case, deposited the key to her room at the unmanned counter, and stepped out into the December high street. It was bitterly cold, there was a peppering of sharp sleet and daylight was already in full retreat.

To her dismay she found that she was barely ten minutes from the bank building beneath Coward's Stockbrokers, and in order to comply with Mr French's instructions, she set off back along the high street and wove in and out of stores sardined with seasonal shoppers, and every step, squeeze and sham browse, reminded her of where she ought to be.

Mr French let her in, unlocking the door so swiftly that he must have been waiting behind it. He locked it again immediately and invited her to take her usual seat before Mr Coward's desk, while he went to fetch "some items". He still wore his overcoat, though it was now unfastened revealing a sharp three-piece suit, white shirt and black tie.

She knew immediately that something was badly awry. She could sense it. Somehow Coward's office had shed its sepia membrane and replaced it with a cold, ebony miasma. Something had stopped.

Coward's desk looked precisely the same yet entirely different. She could not reconcile that contradiction any more than she could dismiss it. She wondered if she was still hung over, or developing flu, or a nervous complaint. There was a thick silence disturbed only by the sound of the invisible Mr French taking short steps and moving wads of paper. He returned with a slender buff folder, and expertly hitched himself up onto Coward's chair. He opened the folder. Inside was a thin, sealed, buff envelope and two sheets of foolscap paper, one of which she recognised as Coward's handwritten notes, the other comprising a list in a more florid style and pale blue ink.

French splayed his child-sized hand on the papers and slid the envelope to one side.

"I regret to tell you," he said, "that Mr Coward is deceased."

"What? When?"

"Some ten days ago. Shortly after your last visit."

Her mind was fuzzed. She fished for a sentiment, any sentiment, but none would come. "Oh," she said. "Oh."

"We laid him to rest today."

"Today?"

"This morning, at nine."

"I'm so sorry," she said at last.

"It would have been sooner, but we had to wait. Post mortem."

"Really?"

"Heart attack."

"Oh dear."

"Motor accident."

"Which?"

"Chicken and egg I'm afraid."

"What?"

"The coroner can't say which came first."

"I'm so very sorry."

"Yes. So am I." He meant it.

She felt suddenly very alone.

"Was anyone else involved?"

"Well," said Mr French, casting his eyes over the list before him, "that's not for me to speculate."

"I mean – in the accident."

"Oh – no. Rural road. On his way home."

"How's Mrs Coward?"

"Stoic. Strong. She's that kind of stock."

"I see. Well, would you convey my condolences?" Mr French looked bemused. "We may be acquainted," she added.

"Yes," he said. "You may." He turned his attention to the list before him. "I have a number of things to tell you."

"Very well."

"This envelope contains certain information. Please do not open it in my presence. I have no desire to glimpse the contents." He held it towards her.

She took it and softly snapped it into her clutch bag. "Thank you. There are names and there are addresses and there is a schedule of specific squadrons in the Royal Air Force and their wartime bases."

"That will . . ."

Mr French raised his palm. "Please!"

"I'm sorry."

"I am to inform you that the names may not include the one that you most desire to know. I'm afraid that has not been determined."

"I don't desire to know the name; only to find the person."

"Be that as it may, I'm simply informing you that the name may not be there."

"I'm glad to hear that."

"And hence, neither are his whereabouts. But hopefully the other information might support your further inquiries."

She doubted it. "Thank you."

"The envelope also contains our cheque for a partial refund of your deposit towards Mr Coward's fee."

"There's no need . . ."

"There's every need. Our accounts are unimpeachable."

"I'm sure so."

"Finally, I am to invite you to a meeting."

"A meeting?"

"With Mrs Coward."

"Mrs Coward?"

"You are at liberty to decline."

"I do not know how long I will be staying . . ."

"This evening."

"This evening?"

"Yes."

"But the funeral . . . was today."

"Yes, it was."

There was a hiatus whilst the room tolerated gravity.

She said, "I would like to meet with Mrs Coward."

Mr French slipped from the seat and began to fasten his overcoat. "We will leave immediately, by the rear exit."

"The rear exit?"

"The service lift. Follow me."

Mr French secured the office, pausing only to make a brief internal telephone call. The twin-grilled rudimentary elevator took them through two floors of the banking branch to where a gentleman with a grey crew-cut and a watch-chained waistcoat was waiting with a triad of clusters of keys. He unlocked a small pass door and they were out into rain and onto greasy cobbles. Five minutes later she smelled steam and saw the railway station, but they did not enter it. Mr French summoned a taxi and they jostled through the burgeoning rush hour to follow the rural road that, ten days earlier, had ended Mr Coward's life.

"I must offer my heartfelt condolences."

"Thank you."

Mrs Coward stood illuminated from one side by a heavily tasselled standard lamp and from the other by brightly burning coal fire. She had a military bearing, a classically chiselled face, defiant and severe, but fixed with resilience rather than remembrance, or loss.

"I believe we were . . ."

"We'll not speak of that," said Mrs Coward.

"No."

"Save to say I have no recollection of your being there."

"Nor I of yours."   That was a lie. She did recognise this person, but only as a face in a crowd. She wondered if they were both disguising the truth.

They were alone, as Mr French had been directed to the

dining room where he was in conversation with another visitor.

"You asked to meet me."

"Would you like to sit down?" she said, indicating the end of the sofa closest to the fire."

"Thank you."

Mrs Coward sat in the armchair opposite.

The lounge was very well appointed. It was up to date without being fashionable, expensively furnished and, despite the day, felt very cosy. Mrs Coward's plain black dress was cut to lower calf. She still wore the sensible shoes that had seen her through the ceremony. There was a sliver of sandy soil along the side of one. "I think you may have killed my husband," she said.

Suddenly all warmth went.

"What?"

"Unwittingly."

"Mrs Coward, I . . ."

"We're still awaiting the full police report. And then it will be down to the coroner I suppose."

"The coroner?"

"The inquest was suspended. He's happy that the cause of death was from heart failure, but whether that caused the crash or vice versa, we may never know. There is some inference of a brake failure. There may have been tampering. It's hard to tell. Even harder to prove, I expect."

"And do you think I tampered with the brakes?"

"Of course not. But if someone did, it might have been because my husband was making inquiries on your behalf."

"How can you think so?"

"Well I do. And that's why I asked to meet you. Because you need to understand the depth of the danger you may be in, and the immediacy of it."

"Immediacy?"

"Whilst you were billeted at Woburn you had an operation."

"My appendix was removed."

"Where did you have that operation?"

"In the sick bay there."

"Do you remember the surgeon?"

"I can picture him. I don't remember his name."

"Dr Stonorowich."

"Yes, I think that's right."

"He was a refugee."

"Really?"

"From Poland. It is our understanding that he returned there after the war, or maybe even before the end of it."

"Did he?"

"Possibly to Poland, possibly to Russia. And he took certain things with him."

"What kinds of things?"

"Of that we cannot be certain."

"Forgive me, but who exactly is 'we'?"

Mrs Coward took a breath. "Mr French will have given you an envelope?"

"Yes."

"Have you opened it yet?"

"Not yet."

Perhaps you would like to do so now. May I offer you a sherry?"

"Well, just a small one."

Mrs Coward went to a sideboard and returned with a silver letter knife before retracing her steps to fill two small sherry glasses as the envelope was opened. It contained two folded pieces of typewritten paper and a strip of three identical photographs, printed in a single band no broader than a standard post card. She had never seen the image before but recognised it immediately, in spite of its peculiar perspective. It was a naked woman, in a deck chair, on the roof of Woburn Abbey. It was not perfectly sharp, and looked as if it had been both cropped and enlarged, but nevertheless she could make out her appendectomy scar.

"The list of squadrons is self-explanatory. The second is a list of personnel from the one that took those photographs. 541 Squadron based at RAF Benson, Oxfordshire. The schedule is not exhaustive, and though your fiancé may be listed there, we simply don't know. I cannot say that his name is on the list. Sweet sherry all right?"

"Thank you," she said, taking the small schooner and sipping from it straightaway. "I'm not sure I want to know his name."

Mrs Coward resumed her seat and downed a quarter of her own glass. "I don't see how you can find him without doing so."

"It might be better if I stopped searching."

"That's for you to decide. The other paper contains the last known addresses of Dr Stonorowich, and Miss Vera Dalkandle. They are both on the wrong side of what we are obliged to call the Iron Curtain."

"How did you obtain them?"

"You will understand that there are questions I cannot answer."

"Of course." She sipped more sherry. Her gaze kept being drawn back to the photographs. The scar was there all right, but not in crisp detail. It could not be accurately replicated from these pictures, though it could have been precisely located. "Are there more photographs?"

Mrs Coward shrugged. "I don't know."

"How did you find them so quickly?"

"Serendipity. When Conrad told me of your inquiry, I remembered seeing them some years ago. And that was a stroke of luck too. The first time I saw them it was because a former colleague from . . . another place . . . knew of them from his war service. Once again your abdominal repair was the culprit."

"How?"

"We were responding to a request for information on the wartime activities of Dr Stonorowich. The inquirer wanted to know how many appendectomies he had carried out at Woburn. By a miracle, I was able to track down the medical records of the operating theatre. There were six in total. All of them were on women. The six women are listed on the third sheet."

She looked at the list. There were six names. Three were followed by the word *deceased* in parenthesis. The final name, inconsistently spaced from its predecessors above, was her own. "Three of them are dead," she said.

"The first, Ann Clark, was from natural causes."

"And the other two?"

"Were shot." Mrs Coward drank more sherry, leaving only a golden meniscus in her schooner. "That's why I had to see you."

ELEVEN

She sat alone, chilled, damp, anxious and hungry in her Dickensian hotel room. The taxicab had waited. Mr French paid the bill but she suspected that Mrs Coward had footed it. The parting request from each of them had been that she should not contact C. E. Coward and Co. again regarding her predicament. She was overwhelmed by their generosity on such a difficult day and simultaneously overwrought by their abandonment of her.

She was so disturbed by the thoughts that Mrs Coward had planted in her mind that she barely dare leave her room, and had declined the invitation to eat in the restaurant as she reclaimed her key from the hotel reception. Extensive elaboration by Mrs Coward had been impossible, or avoided, and so she had only a limited understanding of why Dr Stonorowich's medical log had been sought, why two of his six appendectomy patients had been shot, or by whom. Both crimes remained unsolved, each of the women had been assassinated whilst alone. There were no witnesses, no subsequent arrests and nothing to link the two women other than their wartime surgeon - a surgeon that they shared with her.

The other great puzzle was how this all related to the artist and to the photographs that he supposedly took, or at least subsequently saw. She kept looking again at the pictures. The three images were either reprints from a single negative, or taken in rapid succession, because there was no difference between them as far as she could see. The harder she stared the more convinced she became that, while offering a general and very feint impression of where her scar was, the reproduction was far too feeble to support the degree of detail she saw when the painting had been revealed to her. Or was she superimposing the memory of it once the portrait was done? She could not be sure.

What could she do now? She had burned her employment boat, walking out of a job that she had held for a decade into a vacuum devoid of any means of earning a living, and harbouring the prospect that she might not even stay alive.

Even slipping along the hotel corridor to the lavatory was nerve-wrenching. She slammed the door too loudly and bolted it too quickly, slicing a finger on the edge of the bolt sheathing. She ran back to her room, locked the door and made a pathetic attempt to wedge the chair under the handle. She decided to sleep in her clothes and on top of the covers but beneath the quilted eider down. Sleep she did not.

All through the night she churned the same thoughts. Multiple scenario emerged, deeply imagined, fantastically resolved, terribly concluded.

In the morning she was neither refreshed nor rested but her appetite had returned with a vengeance and against all expectations she devoured a very full English breakfast. She settled the bill and made for the station, deliberately making a detour so that she could stand outside the town hall and look up at the offices of C.E. Coward and Co. It was not contemplation, nor was it recollection, it was lamentation. She had liked Conrad Coward very much. He had given her hope, and in that moment of remembrance he patted the pocket in her soul where she had stored that hope. He told her not to lose it, and she remembered how to smile.

Down the side of the town hall stood a regiment of seven telephone kiosks, six of which were functioning. Even so, she had to wait her turn to claim one. She knew Vera would be sleeping, but she was able to get one of her neighbours in her block of flats to pin a note to the board by their shared telephone. She managed to get a ticket in time for the 'express' and consequently she was in London in just under four and half hours. It seemed like forty minutes, because she slept most of the way.

Vera met her off the train.

"You look like death," she said.

"I think you've mistaken me for my new travelling companion."

"What?"

"Get me some air and I'll explain."

"Are you going home?"

"Don't think I dare. Could I stay at your place tonight?"

"Course you can. I'll give you the key."

"Thanks."

"Come on, Let's go to the park."

They took two tubes, then wove through the sharp faces and wispy breaths of seasonal shoppers to the park. She told Vera all that she had learned.

"Christ," said Vera.

"So I have three lists, three photographs, and the grim reaper over my shoulder."

"But – why? And who? Who shot them? And why? Why?"

"No one knows. But there's one more detail of significance. Something Mrs Coward told me - in confidence - because the police have not made it public."

"Oh," said Vera.

"So I will tell you."

"You don't have to."

"That's why I will."

"Go on then."

"Once they had been shot, the women were sliced open."

"Yuk! Are you sure you need to tell me this?"

"Along the line of their appendectomy."

"Right. And?"

"And nothing. Nothing else was done."

"Why?"

They were drawing close to the Christmas fair, and took a detour alongside the aviary. Goldfinches bickered. Peacocks strutted.

"Your guess is as good as mine."

"And what is your guess?" asked Vera.

"Well, when I recovered from the operation the pain had gone, so I presume Dr Stonorowich had removed my appendix."

"I would hope so."

"What one can now speculate is that, as well as taking something out, he may have put something in."

Within the cage, a peacock splayed its tail fan. It was less than impressive in both span and condition.

"What – stitched something inside of you?"

"That's Mrs Coward's theory. It either wasn't in the two who were assassinated, or it was removed. If it wasn't in them, the chances of it being in me are somewhat increased."

"But – what? What would he put inside of you?"

"Who knows? It can't be very big. Or very heavy."

"Can you feel anything?"

"Don't be silly."

"But it's been there for ten years."

"If it is there."

The peacock tried again. The span was greater, the damage to its tail feathers even more apparent. They wandered away from the aviary. The sun was very low, and the air temperature much lower. Children had turned a puddle into a standing slide and were practicing their screams.

Vera thrust her hands deeper into her coat pockets and retracted her head into her scarf. "Why would anyone hide anything inside another human being?"

"To smuggle it somewhere."

"But you haven't gone anywhere, you're not going anywhere, and why would you? And - anything could have happened to you." Vera turned around to face her friend who had suddenly stopped. "What's up?"

"But I am going somewhere," she said, more in realisation than in information. "I'm going to find my artist." Way behind her, a merry-go-round struck the notes of *Winter Wonderland*.

Vera held the hiatus. She stretched free of her scarf, contorted her upper lip, and then scrunched her cheeks before saying, "Is that why he sent for you?"

More thinking time tinkled by.

"It could be why someone has. Because they want what is deep inside me. I'd like it to be him; but it could be anyone."

"He could be anyone," said Vera. "You've never known who he was, or is."

Shadows stretched. Soon they would be elongated beyond elasticity and into night. Vera waited. Her friend walked towards her, and beyond her.

"I'm going to find out," she said.

"I have friends in high places," said Vera catching her up.

"How high?"

"The Air Force."

"Tally-ho," she said.

"Chocks away!" said Vera.

She slept on Vera's floor for two nights. The offer to move in permanently was made. She declined. Vera had pointed out that the Cowards had soon discovered who she was and where she lived. In response, she pointed out how simple it had been, as Mrs Coward already knew of the list of appendectomy patients, only three of whom were still alive. They knew she lived and worked in London, and if the others didn't, then the process of elimination was fairly straightforward, especially as they knew she had a post office box in Twickenham. Those who might wish her harm were probably not privy to all that information, or surely they would have located her by now.

Vera said she couldn't be sure of that, and anyway, harm had been done to Mr Coward.

It might have been an accident.

It might.

Vera said it would be safer if she stayed with her.

Safer for whom? Anyway she wasn't going to stay in London long, as she soon would not be able to afford the rent.

She could contribute to Vera's rent. Vera could also get her a job at the theatre. She'd already asked Mrs Bartram, who was always looking for new girls.

She was not a 'girl'. Not anymore.

Some men liked the more mature ladies. All she had to do was take most of her clothes off and not move.

She was not of a mind to do either of those things.

Vera said that sooner or later she would need money.

She would get another shop job, with or without references; but not yet. First she would find her artist. She was a free agent. She would find him.

She popped into the theatre most nights. She became well known to the performers and the weary backstage crew and Imo, the laconically witty West Indian stage door keeper.

She went back to the department store. Miss Chisholme was off sick and had been so for a week. Mr Grainger conducted a meeting with multiple levels of awkwardness. He'd like to reinstate her, he said, but it was really out of his hands. The decision had been taken. He hoped that she understood.

She understood.

Christmas was only four days away. As a gesture of goodwill they paid her three weeks' wages from her final month's salary. Under the company rules that was more than the amount to which she was entitled. He hoped she appreciated that.

She appreciated it.

The store was bursting at the seams that day, and she had to force her way through the multitude. She did so with an unexpected sensation of glee. She had rarely felt so confined, or so free.

Great news, Vera informed her. Gloria Fanfare was not appearing that night, and Vera had claimed her dressing room, and someone would descend from high places to join them in the cleavage between the twice nightly shows.

The dressing room was small and cluttered with the personal paraphernalia of the self-styled top of the bill, but with only a single dressing table, two chairs and a mirror, it offered a degree of confidentiality.

"Who is it?" she asked.

"A friend of a friend," said Vera as she smeared on numbers five and nine greasepaint.

"What's his name?"

"Mr Tinker. Formerly Flight Lieutenant Tinker. Evidently everyone calls him Tinky."

"Tinky?"

"Tinky was his nickname during the war."

"Do we call him Tinky?"

"You should call him Father Christmas. He was in 541 squadron. And he's bringing photos."

"Photos?"

"Do me a favour, wait for a big number and nip next door and nick another chair."

Tinky was due to arrive at nine but came at eight-thirty while the first house was still in full swing. She heard a contralto "This one?" followed by something indecipherable from Imo the door-keeper, and three rapid raps on the door. She opened it, and in he blustered, shaking a spray of raindrops from his gabardine coat and fawn trilby.

"Alice from Wonderland, I presume?"

"No, she's still through the looking glasses I'm afraid."

"Then you must be . . ?"

"I'm the person you've come to meet."

"Aha! Alice didn't mention your name."

"No, I asked her not to."

"Most wise, my dear, that way no one can forget it." He raised his hat, put his briefcase on the floor, and began to unfasten his coat. "Now – no names, no pack drill, that's fine – but how shall I address you?"

"You decide."

"Well, if she is Alice, you can only be . . . the hatter!" He put his trilby on her head.

She laughed and took his coat to hang behind the door. She retained the trilby. She had instantly warmed to this somewhat rotund package of exuberance. His three-piece suit was tweed, his shirt had a Norfolk check and his tie was evergreen. "Tea, coffee, or sherry?"

"Oh gosh, is there sherry?"

"There's sherry." She poured him one.

Vera burst in and without the slightest hesitation commenced a quick change from a dishevelled Lewis Carroll lead, into the kind of Christmas fairy of which only grown men dream.

"You must be Tinky."

"And you are the wonderful Alice, I presume."

"That misapprehension has been made from twenty yards or more." Her transformation necessitated ten seconds of total nudity. As she squeezed between them it was Tinky who received the full-frontal display.

"Good heavens," he said. "Weren't you The Seaman's Mate?"

"You've a good memory for faces," said Vera stepping out of an elaborate suspender belt, bejewelled with paste gems.

"I love burlesque," he said. "It masks so many hypocrisies."

Vera wrapped herself in a sparkling silver Basque. Her female friend helped her to fasten it. "There you are - new career as a bleedin' dresser. Love the trilby. See you in ten." And then with silver stilettos in one hand, and tinplate halo in the other, she was gone.

Tinky chuckled, and then all was strangely quiet, with everyone gone from the dressing rooms for the yuletide-themed finale.

"Take a seat," she said. "Here's your sherry."

"Too kind. I understand I may be able to offer some information regarding my mother squadron?"

"Could I show you a list of names?"

"Please do."

She produced the paper that she had been given by Mrs Coward.

"Ah yes," he said. "I remember many of these. They didn't all survive, though we did fare better than most, because we shot film, not bullets. However, it also meant we couldn't defend ourselves. No guns you see, to make space for the cameras, and speed us up. Oh look – there's me."

"Were you a pilot?"

"Hard to believe, I know. Put on a few pounds since then. And why not? I shat enough of it out in those days. Bloody terrifying, I can tell you."

"I can imagine."

"Oh, please don't. Not a happy time. Not at all. Not when we were above cloud nine. Mind you, we made up for it when on *terra firma*. You know, there's at least three people I can remember whose names are not on this list."

"Did you know any of those men well?"

"Oh yes." He sniggered indulgently. "In which are you particularly interested?"

"The problem is; I don't know his name."

"Ah!"

"He was a painter. In his spare time. An artist."

"Well there were quite a few arty types. They didn't all let on, of course. Some liked to keep their predilections private. And that is often a wise course of action."

"He was the introspective sort."

"No harm in that."

"He was tall. Five ten or eleven. Something of a

Mediterranean look to him."

"Hmm. Fits a few of these. Shall we look at my photograph albums?"

"Yes, I think we should."

She sat by him and he opened the first of three small volumes, and began to name those captured within.

"Box Brownie, I'll have you know. A king of a camera. Well, here we are. Lots of partying at the pub, messing around outside the mess and a few naughty ones I was not supposed to take. Classified backgrounds and all that." He chuckled.

After three or four pages, there was a growing rumble beyond the door as the cast returned. Vera came in, clasping her shed Basque to her belly. She wrapped herself in a scarlet dressing gown and collapsed into her chair. "Thanks for coming over. Jinty said you would."

"When Jinty commands, Tinky jumps. Glad to be of service."

"Any luck yet?"

The hatter smiled and shook her head. "We've only just begun."

From time to time, Tinky pointed out someone whose name was on the schedule, but the majority of people in the photographs were not listed there, as Vera remarked.

"Yes, my darling," said Tinky, "because what you have here is a list of flyers with some - notable – omissions. Lots of people in the pictures were ground crew or admin staff. Some were friends of friends, or people who had dropped in for one reason or another. There were a couple of flights that spent most of their time at our satellite field – chaps such as him. What was his name? Edwin. Edwin Heap. Well-to-do type. Nice chap, though. Very nice."

She suddenly felt compelled to take the trilby off. "Edwin?" she said, and leaned over to get closer to the picture.

"Edwin. There. In the deckchair."

"And who is that standing behind him?"

"That I do not know. Could have been a friend of Edwin's I suppose. Don't know who he is."

"I do," she said, unwittingly crumpling the trilby in her grip. "That, is my fiancé."

TWELVE

The Austin rocked around wooded lanes.

"This is unbelievably generous of you Tinky," she said. "Thanks."

"Piffle!" he replied, jiggling what seemed to be a far too loose steering wheel. "What else would I be doing?"

"Don't you have family?"

"My dear hatter, the very worst people to be with at Christmas are family. Don't you agree?"

"Sometimes," she said.

"Always," he replied, swerving slightly to avoid a pot-hole. "I suppose it depends on the family in question. I imagine I'll go over at New Year, though term starts two days after – on the Thursday, God help us. So I'll have to be back in harness by then."

"Science, isn't?"

"Physics mostly. And – you won't be surprised to hear – the photography club!" They came to a three-spurred junction. "Now, how's your memory?"

"Nothing yet," she said.

"Hmm. Left, I think."

"Why left?" she said as they set off again.

"Because I feel sorry for it. There's a lot of prejudice against the left."

She gripped the door handle to steady herself as they took the turn. "Well, I've never spent a Christmas Eve like this one."

"We'll need to find it pretty soon or we'll be looking for rooms in an inn and ending up in a stable."

"Are you remembering anything?"

"My dear girl I was pissed as a newt. But as soon as you described it, everything came flooding back. When I say everything, I mean something. Not very much actually. We stayed the one night. Two car loads. Edwin said the whole estate had been his, or was going to be his - but not anymore. His father had cut him off. He called it *untitled*."

"That's what the painting was called," she said.

"By the time he brought we flying boys here he was already persona non grata. That's why we couldn't stay long." They crested a hill and Tinky lifted his foot from the accelerator. "Ah!"

"What?"

"See that wall?"

She peered into the hazy December mist.

"Yes. Yes I do," she said.

"So do I," he said. "So do I."

She had confided in Tinky all she could without compromising her official secrets oath. She told him she had been billeted, but not stationed, at Woburn. She could tell him no more about her war service. Tinky accepted that. She could reveal however, that her work had been mundane and repetitive, and that she could not imagine that what she had experienced would be of any value to anyone, especially so long after the end of hostilities. She told him all that had happened since. The postcard out of the blue, her interactions with the Cowards, and what she had learned about the other women with a similar medical history. Tinky was excited and intrigued, but his overwhelming emotion was one of empathy. If he could help, then of course, he would. He had asked more about her love affair. She told him about the lodge in the woods and his face burst into radiance. He'd been there, he said. He knew where it was. It had belonged to Edwin Heap's family. Could he help her find it? He was fairly confident he could take her there – but why? Because it was the only place she could look for her paramour's paintings.

The gate was chained but not padlocked. Tinky pushed it open.

"Think we should?" she asked.

"As I understand it, it is passing into public ownership. We're public."

"I don't think that really holds water," she said.

"It's Christmas Eve. I doubt there's anyone here. What's the worst they can do? Throw us out."

"Lock us up for trespassing."

"On public property? Anyway, from what I've been able to establish the place is derelict. There'll not be anyone here."

They drove to the lodge, which was in a dilapidated state.

"Oh," she said as she stepped out of the car.

The surrounding ground was thickly overgrown. It may have been impassable if they had found it in high summer. The tangled growth had died back, but even so, they had to negotiate woody brown strands and a weave of weary grasses to fight their way to the door which pushed open with very little persuasion. The door frame was severely rotted and the securing latch and lock had nothing with which to engage.

Inside it was damp and smelled heavily of saturated decay. She recognised a great deal, as did Tinky, because the furnishings were still there, though everything was pockmarked with mould and putrefaction. The scent of sweet vinegar and sour citrus made her scrunch her nose, but it was the memories that made her eyes moisten.

Tinky tried to open a drawer in the sideboard, but none would yield. Rodents had made nests in the cupboards. He gingerly pulled part of a magazine from one. "March 1947," he read.

"Is that when the family left?"

"Edwin said it was on the cards even during the war. Mind you, I used to think it was wishful thinking on his part."

"Because they'd ostracised him?"

"Other way round I think. He hoped to see them homogenised. Bit of a socialist was dear old Eddie. Shouted his mouth off once too often, if I remember rightly. Did a couple of other things that scandalised his poor papa, and that was enough to get himself disinherited."

"Even while he was fighting for his country?"

"My dear mad milliner, we didn't fight. We just took pictures."

"Surely you trained as fighter pilots. Or bomber boys."

"Of course. On photo ops, while we didn't shoot others, they certainly shot at us. So it was lives on the line for the motherland." He shut the cupboard and slipped into the kitchen. She followed.

"Surely his father could have waited until after the war?"

"You would have thought so."

The utensils and pans were on the floor. Segments of broken plates snapped underfoot. She recognised the fated lovers' willow pattern.

Tinky squeezed past her. "Of course being a dyed-in-the-wool socialist, there was nothing Eddie liked better than to fight the National Socialists of the Rhineland. Strange how people label things isn't it? Do you think we should risk the stairs?"

They looked at the treads. One was missing. All were blackened.

"Ladies first," she said and set off warily selecting the steps that looked the most secure and solid. The room in which her artist had slept was open, but the one in which she had used, the one in which painting had been created, was padlocked. "That wasn't there in my time," she remarked.

"I would hope not. Who puts a padlock on a bedroom door?"

"It was his studio."

"Do you want to force it?"

"I have to. I'll get something from the kitchen."

It didn't take very long or a great effort. She managed to prise the rounded handle of a serving spoon between the hasp and the door frame, and following a few levered twists from each of them, the screws shredded the rotten timber and wrenched free, and they were in.

This room, though weather stained, was by far the least damaged and disturbed. It was clear that other people had been in the cottage since it was abandoned, probably children, but this bedroom had escaped their attentions. It was damp and lined with the detritus of natural deterioration, and bird droppings suggested something had roosted there, but the window was intact and there was a sense of stasis. Things had not been moved. She recognised it all. The bed, the bedside table, the chair, the easel.

"Aren't we the lucky ones?" said Tinky.

The easel was empty but several canvases were stacked against the wall, many more than she could remember seeing. She flicked through them. Some were landscapes, others still lifes, and just two were portraits, one was a middle-aged woman in a green skirt and cardigan, and the other a man with a rifle standing smiling amid the rubble of a rural building in a country more arid than was found in the United Kingdom.

"Is this Edwin?" she asked.

Tinky came to look. "Oh I'd say so. Spanish Civil war."

"Was he there?"

"Claimed to have been. Said he met Lorca – the poet. Lucky sod. Edwin that is. Lorca is dead. Shot for being on the wrong side."

"Have you seen any of these paintings before?"

"No, we were here a year or so before you came, and your fellow wasn't on the scene then. I barely remember seeing him at all. I cannot put a name to him."

"Me neither."

"He certainly wasn't in our squadron. Edwin brought him here about the same time as he met you I suspect. Looks like he came quite a bit after that."

"It also looks like he took any post-operative portraits with him."

"It seems so."

"Why padlock the room? There's nothing of real value here," she said.

"Well, we haven't looked everywhere yet. And value is very much in the eye of the valuer."

She was opening drawers in the little dressing table. "There aren't even any paints. Or brushes."

Tinky was viewing the space through a frame made with the forefingers and thumbs of his hands, as photographers sometimes do.

"What are you doing?"

"Enlarging the room. Old snappers trick. Pulls out the detail. Saves wasting film."

She checked the portraits again, making sure that none were double-sided, and that none had been missed.

"You did say that he said Edwin had sold your portrait."

"He implied that he'd done others of me. I only ever saw one. And . . ."

"And what?"

She was reluctant to speak, but sighed it out. "I just had the feeling, that I wasn't the first."

Tinky backed off until he was tight into the darkest corner of the room. He knew what she was thinking. "The holy grail would be one of the other appendices. If we can call them that." She formed an inverted smile and nodded. He viewed the ceiling though his finger frame. "Ah!" he proclaimed.

"Found something?"

"Perhaps."

"Where?" she said, looking at the ceiling.

"Here," he said emerging from the corner and looking down at the floor. "The skirting board moved when I put my heal against it."

She manoeuvred around the bed until she was behind and above Tinky's crouching form. He jiggled a section of skirting board, and with a little persuasion it lifted clear of the wall exposing a narrow cavity.

"Anything there?" she asked.

"Bit of wall," he said.

"Hmm!"

"Can't really see. Hold on." He rooted in his trouser pocket, produced his petrol lighter and after three grates of the flint, ignited a flame. She saw only plaster and rubble, but Tinky saw an opportunity. He found that by slipping his hand where the skirting board had been, he could reach under the floorboards into the cavity there. "Tra-la!" he said, awkwardly producing a black package about ten inches in length and six in width. He tossed it onto the bed. It looked to be wrapped in rubber and was held tightly closed by several elastic bands.

"Merry Christmas," said Tinky. Neither of them did anything. "Are you going to unwrap it now, or wait until after midnight?"

She picked it up and began to remove the elastic bands. Two of them snapped as she stretched them, and some had bonded to the wrapper, but soon all were free and she was faced with what appeared to be a rubber envelope.

"Save me," said Tinky. "I haven't seen one of those since the war."

She slipped her hand into the opening and gripped what felt like a book. She pulled it clear, lifted the patterned but untitled cover and drew a sharp breath.

"What is it?" asked Tinky.

She angled the page towards him, showing him a pencil drawing of the face of a man. "It's him," she said. She began to flick through the other pages. "I think it's his sketch book."

"Is it a self-portrait?"

"He told me once. Said it was a way of identifying ownership without using your name."

"Sure it's his?"

"Oh yes," she said. "I'm certain."

"How so?"

"Because here am I." She showed him a pencil study of a nude.

"Ah," said Tinky.

She turned the pages, moving backwards through the book. "Here's another. This one's not me. But the scar looks just the same."

THIRTEEN

They drove back through the overcast darkness of Christmas Eve, to Tinky's rooms in the precinct of a public school which he assured her was within sight of Ely Cathedral. He gave her toast with honey, and cocoa, a blanket and a hot water bottle, and hence she slept remarkably well on his sofa.

The next day he served her duck, vegetables and Christmas pudding, and plenty of sherry. They walked around the precinct while his little kitchen range did the roasting, and there, deep in the damp haze of flat distance, was the ship of the fens, ecclesiastical Ely.

She had the sketchbook with her. It was not going to leave her person. They had shared every page and ostensibly there was nothing drawn or written within that would lead to any assumption that it hid anything of value. But it must do, or it would not have been hidden. There were, in fact, several sketches of her including a head and shoulders study looking out of a railway carriage window.

It was the images of her fellow surgery recipients that troubled her the most. Tinky pointed out that their presence had answered one of the conundrums they faced. Every surgeon had a signature style. If the artist had seen two previous examples of the surgeon's stitching he would be able to estimate the positioning and pattern of a third patient's scar. That was how he had painted her wound so well prior to seeing it.

She concurred but asked if he thought there were more aerial pictures, and might they be more detailed? Tinky said it was possible but he did not feel the artist would need them to depict her as accurately as she had described. Tinky didn't pursue that line of discussion. She knew he could see the resignation in her face. Her fiancé had painted at least two other naked women, and probably done so in that cottage. What else they may have shared under that roof could only be mused. She was not unique.

All in all, this was starting to look less and less like a love affair and more and more like some kind of underhand undertaking. The no names business, the naked art, the nights at the lodge, the succession of scarred women, the friendship with Edwin – was it all some immature masculine challenge? She may have been prepared to dismiss it as such, were it not for what had transpired, and what she had learned in the previous three months. Mr Coward had died. The two other women in the sketchbook had died, and their wounds reopened. The sketchbook had been hidden.

It was dark again by the time she and Tinky had cleared up after their meal. Could she possibly face another night on the sofa? Of course she could. He would drive her back to London the next day, he promised. There was no need. The nearest railway station would do. Nonsense. On Boxing Day? What was she thinking? Besides they should both report back to Alice. She'd squeeze them in to see her show. By all accounts it was a riot. She acquiesced and Tinky stoked up the fire and uncorked the brandy. He enraptured her with tales from his days with the boys in blue. He talked more and more freely, and her appreciation of him turned from a curious study into a tender portrait. The more she gleaned, the safer she felt, and the sorrier. He held secrets. He held them very warmly.

Suddenly he said. "It may have been only a joke, but I swear Alice said something to you about your husband."

She made the brandy sting her tongue.

"It's a euphemism," she said. "He is 'my husband' but I'm not married to him."

Tinky caught on straight away. "He's your lover."

She nodded.

"How much does he know about all this?"

"Nothing."

"Nothing?"

"I can't trust him."

Tinky uncrossed and re-crossed his feet, wriggling the slipper on the upper one loose. "It that a wise choice for a lover?"

"He chose me."

"How long?"

She thought for a moment. "Four years."

Tinky nodded slightly and smiled slightly more.

"How did you meet?"

"At the shop. He was a customer."

"How does he earn his living?"

"He's a driving instructor. Our meetings always fit into sixty minute slots."

Tinky beamed more broadly.

She said, "Sounds sordid doesn't it?"

"That's not the word I would have chosen. Regulated. Ordered. Almost military. Have there been any other romances?"

She shrugged. "One or two."

"Proposals?"

"Turned down two."

Tinky pushed his bottom lip forwards to signal his salutation.

"Both from him. So he married someone else."

"Because you were waiting on your artist?"

She nodded.

"Did you tell him that?"

She nodded again. "That's why I can't tell him any of this."

"He knows none of it?"

"He knows some of the war-time stuff. Less than you."

Tinky smiled wider.

"But until September he was the only other person who knew of my post office box."

The brandy sustained Tinky's smile for a moment, then it faded. "That could be significant."

"I know. That's one of the reasons I didn't confide in him. To test him. But he hasn't changed. I'm sure he's ignorant."

"How sure?"

"He's a child. He likes his games. He couldn't sustain this

one. And he's not capable of killing living women, and even less capable of cutting dead ones open."

"Did you tell him the artist's code? Reversed phone numbers and all that?"

She shook her head. "I let him use the P.O. Box so there was no chance of his wife ever finding my address. And it gave me a reason to keep checking it. I was about to give it up."

"How often do you see him?"

"Varies. About every two to three weeks. He lets me know what evenings and I make sure I'm in. Usually."

"Usually?"

"Recently I've been out. I imagine he's not thrilled."

"No."

They fell silent. Tinky used the tongs to put more coal on the fire. Then he said, "What will you do with the sketchbook?"

"Do you think there is any way I could get photographs of the women who were killed? To see if they match the sketches?"

"Not easy and may even not be possible. Who would we ask? Mrs Coward?"

"I think not. I promised Mr French I would leave well alone. You don't recognise either of them do you? From your Benson days?"

"Let me have another look."

She produced the sketchbook from her bag and handed it to him."

"I took rather more notice of the men than the ladies."

She smiled and his knowing glance locked their confidentiality. "There are male studies as well. That's Edwin isn't it?"

"I'd say so."

"How well did you know Edwin?"

"Not as well as I would have liked. He was based at our satellite field a few miles away - Mount Farm. When the new squadrons were formed in forty-two he remained there and I went to Lossiemouth in bonny Scotland, with the Mossies."

"Mossies?"

"Mosquitos. Wooden wonder. Twin-engined marvels."

"Ah yes. What did Edwin fly?"

"Spitfires. Mark ones or PR nines, or elevens later I think."

"PR being *photo reconnaissance?*"

"Indeed."

"What rank was he?"

Tinky turned the pages of torso studies slowly. Most were of men. "You are thinking of the uniform you saw at the lodge."

"Flight Lieutenant."

"Well I'm pretty sure Edwin Heap was a Pilot Officer when I was there, but he may have been promoted."

She nodded. "My fiancé may not have been a flier."

Tinky ran his fingers slowly around the margin of the page. "He may not have been a flier but he was a very fine, fine artist." He carried on moving his fingers slowly forwards through the book, turning the pages with tenderness.

She said, "You don't think those sketches alone could justify his hiding the book?"

"Not for an artist. Life drawing – that's all." He sipped sherry. "And life affirming."

Both he and she knew he was going the wrong way to find the female nudes. He was about to flick back when he suddenly stopped.

"What is it?"

He turned the page to face her. It was a simple but surreal sketch of tears arranged on telegraph wires or similar.

She shrugged. "Just experimenting, isn't he? Messing about?"

He angled the page so that it was between her and the fire. Despite the thickness of the cartridge paper, she could make out the sketch on the reverse of the page beneath the tears drawn on the side towards her. It was a pencil study of her head and shoulders. The combined effect was of her face melting into tears.

Tinky was looking to see if she had spotted the effect.

"Accidental surely," she said.

"Five lines."

"So?"

"Musical stave. Do you read music?"

"No."

"Neither do I. But we both know someone, who will know someone, who does."

By six pm on Boxing Day they were back in the company of
Vera. She took them along to the tiny orchestra pit where she
persuaded the pianist to tap out the pattern of tears. He
recognised it immediately. It was a phrase from Cole Porter's *I've
Got You Under My Skin.* Furthermore, the pattern, when
translated into notes, fitted precisely to the final three words of
the title.

Vera poured a trio of brandies in her dressing room, a little
unsteadily. "Well, it looks like your fears are justified. Whether
or not your bleedin' surgeon removed anything, I think it's
bloody bleedin' likely he also stitched something in."

"And," said Tinky, it's equally likely that your fiancé knew
about it."

FOURTEEN

If there was something inside her she could not feel it. Once the initial soreness had diminished there had been no discomfort following the operation. She had occasionally felt the stitched flesh pull but that was all. She detected no extra bulk, no internal weight or any sense of a foreign implant. Now, she probed from the outside, pushing around the scar with firm fingers, hoping against hope for an unexpected sensation within, or the sense of an object resisting her searching. Anything to progress the uncertainty towards confirmation would help.

Nothing.

Tinky pointed out that it might be something very small, very light and impossible to detect. She wondered about x-rays but knew that if it was tiny, or of low density, and not metallic it would be unlikely to register on the negative. What about an exploratory operation? Vera had cautioned against that. How could she arrange such a thing? Privately? Think of the expense and could she really imagine explaining her reasons? Apart from that, all operations carried a – bleedin' - risk. Was it worth it? Yes, was the reply, if the alternative was a post-mortem. Tinky quelled that thought, even though she knew that they all assumed it was not just likely but almost inevitable based on what they knew had happened to her predecessors.

But what could it be? And why was it inside *her*?

Two days later she handed in her notice on the flat. She would need to pay another month's rent, but had no intention of remaining there that long. In fact, she only visited during the day and in the morning so Vera could go with her. She off-loaded many of her possessions to the Salvation Army, sold others to neighbours, and moved in with Vera, making it crystal clear that it was only going to be a very temporary arrangement. She had made up her mind. She was going to see this thing through. She would find her fiancé if only to formally break off the engagement. Only he could shed light on her predicament.

Tinky said the horse's mouth was to be found on the surgeon, but she reminded him that Dr Stonorowich had gone behind the Iron Curtain, and she certainly wasn't relishing going there. She was no wiser as to the whereabouts of her fine artist than she had been when the card came from him the previous September. If indeed, it was from him. There was one thing she had learned, and that was the alleged address of Vera in East Berlin.

Alleged address stressed Vera.

It was all she had to go on. It was the only line of inquiry.

Was she seriously contemplating traveling to Berlin?

Yes, she was. She was decided on it.

"What's the bleedin' point?" demanded Vera. "I'm here!"

"But someone with your name is there. And according to Mrs Coward, so is the veritable Dr Stonorowich."

"You can't go off to East Berlin looking for a bleedin' crackpot surgeon."

She stared into mid-distance, or it could have been an uncertain future. "I've got nothing else to go on. There's no alternative."

"Yes there bleedin' is!"

"No," she said. "There really isn't."

"Well," said Tinky. "We should have a farewell dinner."

"All right," she said. "That would be lovely."

By late afternoon on the final day of 1956 the flat was almost bare. The rudimentary furnishings remained. Her suitcases had gone, bar the final one, which was now tucked neatly by the door. Whilst waiting for Derek, she had unzipped it and taken the sketch book from her clutch bag and buried it inside the case. It was bulky and she wanted to avoid any possibility of Derek noticing it and wanting to see it. Two tea chests stood beneath the window, but they contained only rubbish. Her heels knocked against the floorboards, as she checked the empty shelves for the umpteenth time.

Derek was catapulted into a state of shock from the moment she admitted him. His tie was already off and half coiled around his hand. He stepped into the flat mouth gaping, hands still, head slowly scanning the bare surfaces as a child studying the syllables of an unfamiliar word. The letters were there, but they made no sense.

"I'm going abroad," she said.

"What do you mean, you're going abroad?"

"You understand English, Derek."

"Where abroad?"

"I can't say."

"Why not?"

"It's confidential."

"You're going to him, aren't you?"

She flicked up the collar of her overcoat and thrust her hands back into its pockets.

"I don't know where he is, Derek. I don't even know if he still exists."

"He does in your mind."

"Yes, but that doesn't mean he exists in reality."

"So what are you going for?"

"I don't know that either."

"God's shit!" he said, turning away from her and taking in the emptiness of the flat. "Well it looks like you've made your mind up."

"Yes," she said. "I have."

"That's me back on the scrapheap then."

"If that's what your marriage is." Hearing her own words made her both haughty and regretful. She was pleased by the sarcasm but regretted the sharpness she'd suspended in the gap of air from her to him.

His voice carried heightened vibrancy. "You know full well I would have married you."

She softened hers. "And you know full well why that couldn't have happened."

"Because of this fantasy fella of yours."

She looked through the airborne dust at him. "I think I'm the fantasy, Derek. He's the mystery."

"He's a bloody mystery all right. Why have you even bothered to tell me? Why didn't you just go?"

"Because I don't want anyone chasing after me."

"Bit hard that. If I don't know where you've gone."

"I don't want any questions. I don't want any fuss. And for God's sake - no *missing person* nonsense. Just let me go."

"How will I know if you are all right?"

"You won't."

"Shelagh . . ."

"And just for the record," she said.

"What?"

"That's not my name."

He hadn't tried to kiss her, and surprisingly, she was glad of that. Their kisses had been affirmations of sensuality, not of affection. She had made love to him many times, but loved him never. He knew that and hated it. He desired her deeply and she had satisfied that desire a hundred times or more, but she had never voiced precious sentiments, no matter how hard he had tried to trick them from her.

He had yielded to the dissolution of their relationship astoundingly easily. She thought it likely that her recent reticence had forewarned him of her desire to terminate their arrangement. She had sent a coded message via his work, by telephoning his home, and speaking to his wife who had the efficiency of a secretary and the voice of a child. She had used the code they had agreed by giving her name as Miss Culpeat, which was an anagram of Capulet, Juliet's surname. She'd given a false address, but the correct time, which is why he had turned up when he did. He may have had a prior booking, but she knew he would cancel it.

His final farewell was through the door, framed by the architrave, one hand on the door handle, his cap in the other. He had held her eyes long, stinging them with a watery steel stare. "Be seeing you then."

"Well . . ."

"In my mind's eye."

She nodded and half smiled.

He shut the door.

She harboured many layers of guilt about the way she had

used him. Vera was not critical, at least not in a moral sense. Vera rejected morals and adopted personal standards. Vera had a monolithic ethic, carved in stone and applying only to the sculptor.

She admired Vera's behavioural pragmatism, but her own morality was by no means as clearly justified. She had not made choices. She had simply responded to whim, or been restrained by the bonds that had been tied into her peculiar personal history. She had loved her artist, and still loved him, even though Derek was right, she was enamoured by the imaginary future of someone who may not even have survived the past.

Derek had been a distraction, but the artist was her muse. She thought about him every day and most nights. She had even thought about him when she had been with Derek; especially at the most intense times. She had long admitted that the man she adored had become an icon rather than a reality. Like so many of those who had not been seen since the war, he remained as he was when last she saw him, even though she knew that, in reality, he must be quite different. She frequently feared that if she saw him again she might not recognise him. Even worse, she might have already seen him and not known it. How terrible that would have been, especially if he had recognised her.

She lingered, partly to make sure Derek had plenty of time to drive away, and partly to savour the features of the flat for one last time. It was a home she had tolerated rather than celebrated. It had been convenient financially and for transport to work. The neighbours were nosey but that gave a sense of security. They had not been nasty or especially inconsiderate. The water pipes had been problematic in harsh winters and she'd heard the occasional mouse at night, but all in all it had served her well enough. She opened the door, and the architrave framed her fiancé.

"Hello you," he said. He looked exactly as she imagined, except slightly older.

She stared.

He removed his Homburg hat and extracted two train tickets from behind the band. He held them up and smiled.

"Second class," he said.

FIFTEEN

Merry was a word that originally meant 'contented'. That's what Tinky had told her. It was what the lyricist intended when he penned in the carol *God Rest Ye Merry Gentlemen.* Let nothing you dismay. The streets shouted *merry* at her from every shop front, from domestic windows, from scraps of red and green litter. Be merry. Be contented. She was far from contented. She was deeply dismayed. Her heart ran at double speed. She needed two hearts, and twice as many heads.

The artist was at the wheel. There were six wheels: one at each corner of the car, one strapped to the lid of the boot, and the one in his hands. It was a small car of the type she'd seen in some of Tinky's photographs. It might even have been the very same car. It had only two seats and a soft collapsible roof. It was cold, and he wiped the windscreen furiously and frequently to remove their condensed exhalations.

She was exhilarated and exasperated, elated and dismayed, triumphant and crestfallen, victorious and disqualified. The puzzle was over but it was not resolved. The hunt was concluded but the quest was just beginning. She was safely in deep danger. She was overwhelmed with happiness, but the one thing that she was not, was merry – except in an intoxicated sense. She was drunk with delirium.

He had closed her gaping mouth with a continental kiss

that went on for ever and lasted no time at all. In answer to her first question he had confirmed that it was really him, but there was no time to lose. She had to be protected.

He grabbed her case, took her hand, and led her down the stairs at full pelt, as if he knew them a hundred times better than she did. She heard a neighbour's door open as they left it behind. The car was on the street, and in a doorway close to it, stood the tall man from the train; the one who had pointed out the vacant seat to her. The artist put her bag in the boot and told her to get into the car. It took three attempts to start. He revved the engine and switched on the headlights, then accelerated towards a silver-grey cone of after-dark December. She watched her home territory shrink in the wing mirror.

"How did you find me?"

"I never lost you."

"Where have you been?"

"To the place where we are going."

"Where's that?"

"A place of safety."

"Why do I need a place of safety?"

"We all need a place of safety." He glanced from the headlight cone to her. "You're twice as gorgeous as I remember."

The indoor trees wished her merriment from behind urban glass. The outdoor trees were naked, lost among a damp dark haze and imprisoned by railings. She studied his intermittently streetlamp-lit profile. He seemed merry.

"I'm staying with a friend," she said.

"Yes," he said.

They came to traffic lights, which changed just in time to preclude their stopping. He turned left. She would have preferred right.

"I can direct you," she said.

"No need," he said. He glanced at her and grinned more broadly than she could remember him ever doing. "Don't worry."

"I'm not worried," she said.

"Of course you are."

"I'm perplexed."

He nodded, slowly, once. "What did you tell Derek?"

"You know about Derek?"

"He didn't look too happy as he was leaving."

"What do you know about Derek?"

"Enough."

"How . . . why?"

"All part of keeping you safe."

"Why do I have to be kept safe?"

"Because you're precious."

"The flattery is all well and good . . ."

"It's not flattery." The car decelerated, though the carriageway ahead was clear. He looked at her again. "You are precious, but not priceless."

She became more merry, but even less contented.

He returned his focus to the road and his foot to the accelerator. "You are very, very valuable. And there are people prepared to pay."

"Pay for what?"

This time the lights were red. He had to stop. If he didn't turn at this junction, they were leaving London. He met her eyes, then diverted his towards her tummy. "I thought you might have worked it out by now."

"There's something stitched inside me isn't there?"

"Not something. Everything."

"How can it be everything?"

"Depends on your perspective."

"It's not possible to have a perspective when you are blindfolded."

He declined to reply, turning his attention to a dog-walker on the far side of the road.

She said, "What exactly is inside me?"

Still watching the man and dog he said, "Something that will do no harm at all, as long as it stays there."

The car behind blasted its horn. He threw their vehicle into gear and drove straight ahead. She saw the turning that they should have taken slide away and felt a surge of desperation. "Can we call on my friend? She'll be worried if I don't show up."

"What did you tell Derek?"

"About what?"

"About me."

"That you exist. Existed. That's all."

"That's all?"

"There's not much else I could tell him. There's not much else that I know. He wanted me to marry him. You were the reason I wouldn't. I told him that. Because of your promise."

He nodded, and drove a little faster.

She said, "I need to call my friend."

"The stripper? Alice."

She hesitated, then breathed, then spoke. "Yes."

"She's been taken to hospital."

"What?"

"A stage light fell on her."

"When?"

"This afternoon. During the matinee."

"How do you know?"

"I was informed."

The road was clear. He increased the speed of their abandonment of London.

"You know Alice?"

"It wasn't fatal, not as far as I am aware."

"Oh God. Can we go to the hospital?"

"No time, I'm afraid."

"Why not?"

"Because we have a deadline to meet."

"We need to stop. And you need to explain everything."

"We can't stop."

"Why not?"

"Because we have to keep moving."

"I need the toilet."

"You'll have to contain yourself."

"Something has happened to Alice, someone else I know was killed, and you have swept me into a nightmare, telling me I'm in danger, and you expect no physical reaction?"

He looked in his mirror and studied the road ahead. "Do you really want me to stop?"

"Yes."

"I'll have to watch you."

"What!"

"I can't let you out of my sight."

"Just stop as soon as you can, or I'll turn your car into a cowshed."

"All right. Hold on for twenty minutes. Until we are rural."

Their conversation stalled. She breathed deeply and tried to contextualise what she had been told. She wondered whether or not to believe it, and decided she would not have done so, were it not for what had happened to Mr Coward, and for the unmistakeable fear beneath the faces of his widow and Mr French. Worse than all other considerations, was the anxiety she felt for Vera. Was it an accident – a cruel coincidence – or were all her acquaintances being targeted? The suburbs slipped away and she recognised the road as the same one she and Tinky had taken on their return from Ely.

"How did the stage light fall?"

"I don't know, I wasn't there." He pulled into a layby. "Can you scramble over that wall?"

She looked at the chest-high structure, and then extracted a bunch of tissues from her clutch bag. "Are you really going to watch?"

He opened his door. "I'm going to keep watch."

Behind the wall was a hawthorn hedge. She pushed through that into a field, and hitched up her skirt. She heard him flick open his petrol lighter. It sounded just like the one he'd used during the war. She scented the smoke and recognised the brand.

She pushed back through the hedge slightly further along and in front of the car. He'd turned the lights off but left the engine running. He saw her and drew three rapid, but deep, drags on his cigarette. By then she was already round on the driver's side of the car. She twisted the keys and snatched them clear. The engine died. He advanced towards her but she backed against the wall holding his keys high.

"Stop," she said. "Or I throw these as hard and as far as I can."

He held his ground, then eased back to lean against the side of the car. "Listen," he said.

"I'm listening," she said. "So explain."

He coughed once, then breathed deeply, then coughed twice more. He cleared his throat. "Do you know what you were doing during the war?"

"Thinking of you mostly."

"What you were really doing. For the war effort."

"Boring myself stupid, losing weight, and being rubbed raw by that bloody uniform."

"What you did was vital. It won the war. That's what I've been told."

"I don't see how."

"Code cracking."

She thought, remembered what she knew, remembered what she had signed. "I didn't crack any codes."

"Yes you did. You and hundreds of others. Mostly women like you."

"I don't see how."

"That's the irony. Tiny cogs. But take the tiniest cog out and the whole machine stops. You didn't know it, but without you the codes could not have been cracked."

"And what's that got to do with what's happening now?"

"It's the same thing. There are codes. They can't be cracked without you."

The keys in her raised arm suddenly seemed weightier. She lowered it. "You mean - what's inside me?"

He wriggled a little more snugly into his overcoat. "That's right."

"But it's been there for thirteen years."

"Correct. But now someone's started using it."

"O God. Do you want this code?"

"I want to stop other people getting it. Because to them, you are everything, but also nothing."

There was a sudden gust of a bitterly cold breeze and the skeletal branches of the hawthorn bush rattled. This new night air had a damp caul. She threw the keys. He caught them.

At the fifth attempt, the car started.

She recognised the premises as being of wartime vintage.

They drove through an open gate past three or four small buildings, and parked the car outside a prefabricated hut. The icy yuletide air seared across the emptiness that she sensed as she got out of the car. He took her suitcase and another from the boot, then locked the car and patted it.

They were greeted by an elderly man in a duffel coat. The artist gave him the keys to the car. His every utterance and demeanour signalled decades of military service.

"Would you like some cocoa, sir? For you and the lady."

"Thank you, Warrant."

There was a small toilet compartment with a cold tap and cracked sink. She tidied herself up. There was no towel so she rubbed her hands dry on her worsted skirt. When she emerged she gravitated towards a room which had an electrical hum, but the artist came from it and shepherded her away from that and towards the other half of the hut where their suitcases stood side by side. He unfolded a wooden chair and indicated that she was at liberty to sit.

The room was inadequately lit by a hissing Tilly lamp, and inadequately heated by a paraffin stove. She could smell the paraffin, but of even greater pungency was the unmistakable aroma of mothballs. Space was at a premium due to rows of cupboards that lined the walls. She strongly suspected that she was in a store room, probably containing uniforms. A single window held back a vista of nothing, but she sensed a wide open space beyond it.

The Warrant Officer brought mugs of cocoa, superbly sweet and lip-burning hot.

"Thank you," she said.

"You're welcome," said the Warrant. He had the face of a kindly grandfather. "Would you like a rich tea biscuit?"

"Yes," she said. "Yes I would."

"I'll bring you some."

He disappeared and she heard crockery, and the cackle of what might have been radio static. He returned with a saucer with four biscuits splayed on it.

"Thank you."

"You're welcome, Miss."

The artist took one and nibbled it standing by the window and looking higher than the horizontal. "E.T.A. Warrant?"

The old man looked at his watch. "Twenty minutes at the most, sir. Fifteen."

The artist nodded. "Keep an ear out will you."

"Certainly will, sir."

The Warrant Officer went.

"I take it this is not the place of safety?"

He leant against the window frame and put his focus on her. "Correct. It's not." He placed the last of his biscuit in his mouth.

The memory of their meals together came back to her. "It's an airfield isn't it?"

"It was."

He sipped his cocoa, she sipped hers.

"Where will the plane take us?"

"Somewhere much safer."

"What if I don't want to go?"

"Then you won't go."

She smiled. He didn't.

"But your cargo will."

The heat of her mug was scalding her finger. She let it. "What do you mean?"

"I think you know what I mean."

"I thought you loved me."

"You thought correctly."

"Then why are you doing this to me?"

He sipped and swallowed, and considered. "Because I loved you."

"Loved?"

"Loved."

"Not anymore?"

"Ten years is a long time."

"Thirteen."

"Even longer."

"I still love you," she said.

"At this moment?"

There was a hesitation. She put her mug on the floor, and massaged the sting in her finger. "Yes."

He cupped his mug with both hands and drank, and then said, "What you love is the memory."

"Have you changed?"

"The memory of a fantasy," he said.

"Fantasy?"

"I didn't let you know me. I don't let anyone do that."

She became more insistent, stressing each syllable. "Did you love me?"

"I loved my fantasy of you. I still do."

"Then you have to reason with me."

He shook his head. "Love has no need of reason."

"Then what does it need?"

"Nothing. Nothing at all. Love is need."

"A need to intimidate? To threaten?"

He readjusted himself against the window frame. "I didn't

threaten you."

"Tell me where you are taking me."

"To a place where you might save a lot of lives."

"Even if it costs me mine?"

He leaned forwards slightly "Even if it costs me mine."

He drained his cup and left the room. She continued drinking and considered her limited options. She could make a run for it. Where to? Which direction? How far would she get? She studied her suitcase. It contained the final dregs of her belongings. It was the least useful collection she could take with her. She could abandon that. It contained nothing of value.

She could leave a note. In her clutch bag there was a notebook and pen. She could scribble a message. Saying what? She had no idea where her fate lay, or who would even know that she had been here. The Warrant Officer would be most likely to find it, and what would he do? He was subservient to the artist, and most likely on the inside of what was happening to her.

Dialogue was patently not going to work. This night she had seen a new aspect of her artist, and she didn't like it. She didn't like the cold determination she sensed, and she didn't like his deception, and most of all she didn't like the truth he told. Love was a need. The need of a memory. The need of a fantasy.

She heard a drone. It had the swaying resonance that her war service had taught her meant two engines. It drew closer, then faded away entirely. Then there was a mechanical stutter. She stood and went to the window. A twin-engine monoplane was taxiing towards her, its green and red navigation lights wobbling as the wings dipped and rose in response to the uneven turf. Then it was on tarmac and the movement was smooth as it swung around to face away from her. She recognised the type. The propellers still span, as the door opened and the pilot emerged and came towards the hut.

"I'll take your cup, Miss."

The Warrant Officer had made her jump.

"Oh – thank you." She drained the cocoa. The Warrant Officer and she were alone in the room. "Do you know where we are going?"

"Thank you, Miss," he said, and took the warm mug away.

She returned to the window. The pilot and the artist were

side by side now in deep debate. She watched them draw near and heard their steps as they came in and then the voice of the Warrant Officer greeting the new arrival. "Evening sir."

"Hello Warrant."

"All in order, sir?"

"Mostly. This the lav?"

"Yes sir, through there sir."

She heard the lavatory door shut. The artist came in and positioned the suitcases nearer to the door and then he calmly closed on her, paused, and put his arms around her waist. "You have to trust me."

He kissed her. She let him.

They broke. She looked at his lips.

She kissed him. He let her.

They broke and briefly hugged, head to head, she drinking a scent she couldn't name, but that cut through the mothball bouquet of the store room and stirred thoughts of trains, and rains, and damp bedrooms deep in woodland.

They separated. She said, "Are we going abroad?"

He studied her, and then gave the slightest of nods.

"I haven't got my passport," she said.

"You won't need it."

The Warrant Officer came in. "Shall I take these out to the plane?"

"If you would, Warrant. Then stay with it. The Flight Lieutenant's left it running."

"Right, sir." He took the bags.

She had found a new calmness from the kiss. She was not settled, far from it, but she was enlivened. "Flight lieutenant?" she said.

"Our pilot."

She heard the toilet flush and the water pipes complain.

"Plenty of hours under his belt I hope," she said.

"He knows what he's doing."

The door unlatched and he came through, shaking his wrists. He was smaller than the artist and sported a trimmed beard. There was a vague familiarity about him. "No towel," he said.

The artist opened one of the cupboards to reveal a row of greatcoats. In the dimness she thought them grey or air force blue. The artist peeled the front flap of one out and the pilot dried his hands on it. "Hello?" he said chirpily. The voice had notes that she recognised.

"This is Heapy," said the artist.

"Heapy."

"Edwin. We spoke about him. In fact, I think you spoke to him, on the telephone."

"Ah yes," she said, and held out a hand. Now the face beneath the beard was identifiable. She had seen it, clean shaven, in Tinky's pictures.

He made doubly sure his hands were dry before taking her proffered grip. His was firm and friendly.

"I believe we are going flying?" she said.

"That was the idea," he said.

"Was?" she said.

She was looking for an answer but so was Edwin, for he was focussed on the artist, who now put his hand firmly but with tenderness on her upper arm. He squeezed gently through her coat, through her cardigan, through her blouse. "Have you been back to the Lodge?"

Her mind whirred as she realised that she might have a place of purchase for leverage. "Kendal's Lodge?"

"Yes."

The wheels in her head spun with smooth precision finding an answer before she even looked for it. She heard herself saying, "Whatever makes you think I might have done that?"

He held her gaze but did not answer her question. She preserved the pause. He said, "Have you been back? Recently."

She studied him, and then gave a slow, slight, nod.

He relaxed his grip then reapplied it. "Did you take anything from there?"

She looked quizzical. It felt forced and artificial, but she liked that. "Paintings you mean? Nudes?" He smiled slightly then quickly annulled it. She stabbed. "With scars?"

For the first time the artist seemed uncomfortable. Edwin was edgy too and swaying slightly.

The artist said, "Heapy went there. Something is missing."

"It was in a state," she said with a calmness that caught her unawares. "Children may have been in."

The artist let go of her, and involuntarily slid his fingers over his cheek and chin.

"Pic," said Edwin, nodding in the direction of the aircraft.

"She's still turning over."

"I know," said the artist. "Warrant's with her."

"Shall I shut her down?"

"No." He put his hand back on her arm, this time higher up. He ran it over the rim of her shoulder feeling the roundness through the layers.

"I need my sketchbook," he said.

There was a palpable vulnerability in his bearing. She felt it through his grip on her shoulder. In it she found firepower.

"I have it," she said.

His face brightened. "With you?"

She made him wait. She thought. She made him wait longer. "It's at Alice's."

His face darkened. The two men inclined towards each other.

"Leave it," said Edwin.

The artist shook his head.

Edwin went to the window and looked out to where the plane softly chugged. "Forecast isn't great. We need to go," he said.

"I need the book," said the artist.

"We need to keep ahead of the front," said Edwin. "We need to go."

"I need the book," said the artist.

"You need to decide," said the woman.

SIXTEEN

The Avro Anson scudded through the broken cloud over Scandinavia. She knew it was Scandinavia because she had spent numerous idle hours scrutinising her atlas when a child. She knew it was an Avro Anson because the hut in which she had worked during the war had sported aircraft recognition posters on the wall. The first poster was dedicated to allied aircraft manufacturers starting with the letter A: Airspeed, Armstrong and Avro. There were no photographs, just technical drawings in silhouette, with some features, such was weapons, edited out. The drawings were a kind of map. She cherished maps.

The decision had been made, and they had taken off into the night and flown north-west keeping ahead of the cold front sweeping in from the Atlantic and bringing rain, sleet and some snow. The sky behind was stacked with cumulus but ahead there was only celestial cirrus high above. The coast, when they came to it, stood out in contrast to the sea, and she knew it was Norfolk. Soon after leaving that behind they descended to fly low, very low she thought, though gauging height above open water was not easy. They remained at what she estimated to be less than a thousand feet of altitude, and the ride was turbulent and felt erratic due to Edwin frequently making small adjustments to the airborne attitude of the Anson. The artist, occupying the right-hand front seat, had an air map folded open before him, and he scoured the seascape, glanced at the stars, studied the gyroscopic compass and issued occasional corrections to their course. Eventually they began a steady climb and she identified the bunched fist and pointing finger of the topographical cartoon of Denmark. Edwin maintained the same heading continuing on a north-west bearing to cross the Baltic and make landfall over what she knew must be either Norway or Sweden and most likely the latter.

It was Sweden. It was almost another hour before that fact was confirmed. They landed on a snow-dressed airfield in the small hours of the first day of 1957. Although the ground was comprehensively covered, she found on disembarking, that the snow was not as thick as she had imagined as they had made their final approach. No radio communication had been conducted at any point in the journey, and she knew that to be not only unusual, but in contravention of international regulations. Its absence may have explained the very low altitude they had adopted over the sea. That, in turn, had made demands on their fuel supply, and by the time they landed there was no discernible reading on the gauge on the control panel. The men had inadequately masked their concern from her, and were visibly relieved when the aircraft touched down.

A set of headlights bounced out of the distance and a military-style truck eventually materialised out of the night. Her companions left her in the lee of the Anson and went to greet the driver. Loud voices conversed cheerfully, though she could not make out what was said. She could see that it wasn't just conversation that was being exchanged.

Eventually, the artist returned, extracted their bags from the aircraft and said, "Right, all aboard the limousine." They climbed into the back of the truck. She was helped up by a tall masculine bulk, grinning through a bearskin beard and steaming breath from beneath a what she worryingly thought to be a soviet-style fur hat with tied-down cheek flaps. They jostled over frosted ruts to arrive at the far side of the airfield where there were hangars and parked private and commercial aircraft, most of which had tarpaulins over their windscreens.

They had breakfast – of sorts – in a hut not unlike the one she had occupied just prior to her departure from England. The coffee was stewed but hot. The bread was hard and gritty, but did not taste stale. Their host – the truck driver – said nothing to her except very basic pleasantries, and very little else to her companions. His English was basic, but efficient.

"Please tell me this is not the Soviet Union," she said when he left the room and the three of them broke bread.

"No," said the artist. "It is not the Soviet Union."

"If this was the Soviet Union," said Edwin, we would most likely be spread over some field like strawberry jam."

"Sweden," she said.

The artist nodded. "Your favourite subject at school," he said.

"What was?" asked Edwin.

"Geography," said the artist.

"Who told you that?" she asked.

"You did," he said. "Whilst sitting for your portrait."

Once again her instinct kicked in and she seized the moment. Fixing Edwin with an Olympian gaze she said, "Did you take the photographs?"

She was unlucky because he'd just taken a mouthful of bread and his mastication gave the artist a chance to interrupt. "Which photographs?"

"The ones I unwittingly sat for on the roof of Woburn Abbey."

Neither man spoke.

She continued, "The ones I could have returned to you if we had gone to Alice's flat."

"We had to come tonight," said the Artist.

"Why?"

"Do you still not realise how narrowly you have escaped?"

"Escaped into what?" she snapped. "Captivity?"

The artist sat back in his slightly unsteady seat. "Freedom is impossible without captivity. Those who are free have to be kept safe."

"And where will I be kept captive?"

"Here," he said. "In Sweden."

"For how long?"

"I don't know," he said.

"Yes," said Edwin.

"Yes – what?" she asked.

"I took the photographs."

"Why?"

"Testing the camera."

She fired a look which said she doubted his justification, and didn't regard it as an excuse, even if it was true.

"Sorry," he said.

The artist leaned forwards. "But where could he find a prettier subject?"

"Among the first five?"

Both men contorted their brows. "Five what?" asked the artist.

"Women to have their appendix removed by Dr Stonorowich. And their portraits painted by you. Scars and all."

For a moment there was only the sound of Edwin chewing and the distant throb of a lorry engine. Then the artist said, "I only painted two others."

She fixed his eyes. "Really? Is that all you did?"

Edwin swallowed.

The artist broke their eye connection and took a packet of Churchman's from the pocket of his flying jacket. He extracted a single cigarette with his lips. He returned the pack to his coat and found his lighter. Without removing the cigarette from his mouth he interlocked with her eyes again and said, "I didn't ask them to marry me." He pushed his chair back, lit the fag, and sent the smoke towards the apex of the cabin.

Edwin drained his mug, stood up, and announced that he should, "Check that they're putting the right petrol in the plane."

She stopped him. "I think I want you both here while I get a full explanation."

Edwin grimaced a grin. "That's not something with which I wish to be acquainted."

"You must be more than acquainted," she snapped, "to have done what you have done."

He shrugged. "These days I'm a commercial pilot."

"Did you fly to Kendal's lodge?"

"What?"

"To look for his sketchbook."

Edwin shrugged again. She raised her eyebrows to signify that it was an inadequate reply. He slinked away to lean against the partition door. The artist recovered his cigarette packet again and offered her one. She shook her head.

"Why have we come to Sweden? Why didn't we fly straight to the Soviet Union?"

Edwin sniggered, and the artist smiled. "Because, my

muse, we are in search of safety, not danger."

"Safety for what? Me, or my cargo?"

"You."

"Because of this code that's inside me."

"It's not a code, well, in all likelihood only a partial one. More like a key or diagram legend."

"Explain."

The artist looked towards the door behind which the Scandinavian bear with the beard was chinking cooking utensils. He edged his chair closer to the table, leaned in towards her. "This is not the best place."

She said, "I'm sure it will suffice."

He spoke softly. "The code is known. It's been known for some time. But part of it is missing. An additional part. An addendum."

"And I've got it."

"Safely inside you."

"Safely?"

"That's our aim."

"And what exactly is this addendum written on?"

"Nylon."

"Nylon?"

"A square of Nylon. About the size of a postage stamp. Rolled into a tube and stitched to your intestine where the appendix used to be."

"And who wants it?"

"Everyone who knows of its existence."

"Including Stonorowich?"

The artist shrugged.

She snatched the packet of Churchman's from the table and extracted a cigarette. "But why? Why plant something so small inside another living human being? It was wartime. Anything could have happened to me. Apart from which I just don't see the point. Nylon you say? Stitch it in a jacket, under the lining of a shoe, in a pair of tart's knickers, anywhere. Why inside some ignorant woman in the middle of England in the middle of a war?"

He flicked his petrol lighter into flame and lit her Churchman's. "You'd have to ask him."

"And how do you know it was done?"

"An appendectomy is not a one-man operation. There was

an anaesthetist, and a theatre nurse. Brenda."

"Brenda."

"Brenda Beasley. A sweet old lady who lived in a nursing home on the outskirts of Bedford. Lost her mind, poor dear, or parts of it. One missing component was her discretion."

"You said 'lived'."

"I did."

She drew on her cigarette again. "Did she die recently?"

He flicked the wilting finger of ash from his onto the floor. "I believe so."

"From?"

He shrugged.

"If no one believed her . . . why do you?"

"Because Stonorowich had paid me to paint portraits of his patients."

"You knew him?"

"It was arranged by post."

"And was I part of the commission?"

"No."

"Why not?"

"That poser was precisely what procured my interest."

"Why, then, did you paint me?"

"Because I wanted to."

"Did Stonorowich know about my portrait?"

"Not at the time."

"And since?"

He glanced at Edwin who flicked his eyebrows in reply. "I believe so. It's changed somewhat since you last saw it."

"Where is it now?"

"In a day or so, you can see it."

"It's here – in Sweden?"

He nodded. His untipped cigarette was almost singeing his fingers but he drew hard on it making the stub fiercely glow.

Her eyes swelled slightly. She consciously narrowed them and stabbed towards him with her cigarette. "How did you know he had stitched something inside me?"

"I told you. Brenda Beasley. Things started happening a few months ago. Stonorowich came back on the intelligence radar. His wartime records were unearthed. The theatre staff were traced."

The poser wasn't satisfied. "You knew during the war."

The artist squeezed even more nicotine from his fag. "Why do you say that?"

"Because I've seen your sketchbook."

He breathed out grey smoke. Edwin shuffled his feet. The two men exchanged looks. Edwin said, "I knew the anaesthetist."

She said, "So you always knew what had been done. You didn't need to wait ten years to talk to nurse Brenda Beasley."

The artist said, "We discovered that others had done so recently. That's why we had to find you first."

Edwin gasped as the door behind him pushed open. The burly Swede came in. "So sorry."

"No, no, my fault entirely," said Edwin.

"The fuel is almost in. Are you flying again, or shall we get a cover on the cabin?"

"Do you have a weather report?"

"Not good I'm afraid. Heavy snow."

"I suspected as much. I should, perhaps, sit it out."

"That would be wise."

"Yes," said Edwin. "That's probably the best thing to do."

The Swede glanced at the artist. "Your car is ready for you."

"Thank you."

The Swede left. The two Englishmen shook hands. "Thanks," said the artist. "Safe journey – eventually."

"And you." He turned to the poser and held out a hand. "Good luck."

She switched her cigarette to her left hand and returned Edwin's gesture. "Sounds ominous," she said.

"Well, that's not quite what I intended . . . but . . . good luck."

"Thank you. And thanks for the flight. It was my first."

Edwin paused by the door. "Get him to paint you again. Might actually do you justice next time."

She sniggered. Edwin edged away and raised a hand in farewell. She raised a hand in reply.

"Just going to see him off," said the artist, and she was alone again, but this time it felt much more intensely isolated. New Year's Day had never had more meaning. Once again she stared out of a window upon an airfield, but this time it was not just unfamiliar, but foreign. She had offloaded almost everything and found herself facing the unknown, but, she mused, wasn't that true of every New Year's Day? In fact, wasn't it true of every day? She had spent a decade of new years imagining herself with the man she loved. Now she was with him, but not in the way she had imagined. She was glad to be with him, and she undoubtedly loved him, but she didn't trust him. Not at all.

Despite her predicament, she felt strangely empowered. She had not been abducted. She was not here against her will, though neither was she fully in control. She was at the mercy of events, and perhaps even of plots and people of malicious intent. She didn't care. It was supremely superior to managing New Year sales.

She had value, even if that value endangered her. She was precious, she was sought after and she was treasured, and perhaps all these attributes were horribly artificial – imposed upon her, hijacking her, enslaving her – but that was something she had seen burden others a hundred times. No one actually carved out their careers, their loves, or their lives. Everyone simply wrangled their way through each day in spite of set-backs, in spite of misfortune and in spite of spite. She was simply facing up to a more extreme experience. And face it she would.

She sensed the pearl inside her like an unplanned pregnancy. She believed that it was there but could not accurately imagine it, nor truly know if it would ever be safely delivered, and what it's impact might be. For now, she would bear it. She needed to learn more. From what she had learned so far she knew that she might discover that it's cost was too high to contemplate.

She might have to destroy it.

SEVENTEEN

She was surprised that not all of Sweden was covered with snow. In her mind Scandinavia was always entirely draped in white during the winter. They drove away from the airfield through slushy streets and out along roads that, although intermittently treacherous with ice were, for the most part, wet tarmac. After twenty minutes or so, the snow on the landscape lay only in patches. Fields and forests of fawn and evergreen lay beneath a clammy damp hood, but as the short day drew on, the air cleared and the wind that followed them brought sharp sleet. Later still, they climbed to higher ground and the green was banished beneath layers of white, stratified in bands of increasing thickness.

The artist struggled a little with the car, not because of the road conditions, but because he was unfamiliar with the vehicle. It was an ex-military machine, not unlike a Jeep or Land Rover, and had a coarse clutch and gutsy engine that seemed reluctant to change its rate of rotation smoothly. Tiredness was overcoming her. She hadn't slept at all during the night and had been pumped with anxious adrenalin which drained away soon after daybreak leaving her weary and sullen. She was constantly jostled due to the faltering nature of the ride.

From time to time they would pass through a small town or village, but the names on the roadside signs meant nothing to her. Their route was clearly familiar to the artist who drove without reference to maps, and took each turn with confidence. They journeyed almost entirely in silence, which was ironic as he was now at liberty to speak freely. She didn't press him because she was just too tired, and because she suspected the answers she sought were not going to be volunteered without extensive persistence on her part. He had granted her the primary reassurance that she required of him, which was that they were not heading to either a coast or a border. They were staying in Sweden.

Despite the discomfort of the cab, she grew drowsy and at times even nodded off. Dreams and thoughts became intertwined. In light sleep he was her hero, lifting her from the mundane and moribund life of a department store spinster into an idyllic existence amid shared seclusion. In deeper sleep he was a diabolical deceiver, handing her over to Soviet surgeons who removed her hidden appendage without anaesthetic, and then left her to wither from infection. When she was awake he was close and distant, benevolent and menacing, familiar and strange.

Just before dark they pulled into a layby alongside logging trucks and he took her into a simple but snug café where he spoke Swedish to buy coffee and sweet pastries.

"I didn't know you were bi-lingual," she said as they climbed back into the even colder cab of their vehicle and he swore at the engine as it refused to re-start.

"I know a few words," he said.

A few Anglo-Saxon words later the engine obliged. He rooted beneath the dashboard until he found the cloth there and then vigorously rubbed the frosted condensation from the inside of the windscreen. The sudden darkness of winter nightfall was in place and it started snowing thickly.

"Are we going to get through this?" she asked.

"It's only about nine miles now," he said.

She snuggled down into the collar of her coat, hoping that somewhere in her third choice suitcase, behind her in the car, was a thicker scarf and a pair of gloves. She doubted it. He revved the engine, prised it into gear, and lurched them into motion.

Her dreams banished into rationality, she began to plot her way through the unknown. She must first discover where precisely she was, and then as soon as she could she would somehow let someone know that she was there. The best someone would be Vera, but she had no knowledge of her condition following the stage light incident. Nevertheless, she would attempt to make contact with her. In addition, having stayed with Tinky, she knew where he lived and worked. She would contact Tinky as well. She would do all this surreptitiously. She would have to be patient and she would have to be cautious, but do it she would. What on earth either Vera or Tinky could do in response she couldn't imagine, but that wasn't the point. Someone should know where she was, even if, by then, she wasn't anywhere at all.

He said it was a fishing chalet. Even in the dark she could see it overlooked an expanse of openness. It appeared grey and flat but it was too dark and her view was too obscured by falling snow for her to see properly. They had not passed another settlement since leaving the café, and she could not confidently recall seeing a single roadside property. Visibility had been poor, but even so, she speculated that they were somewhere very remote. She felt very safe, and very vulnerable.

The cabin was utterly unlike Kendal's Lodge. It was entirely timber, and in very good order. It was cold inside, but not damp. There was a stove, ready prepared with paper and kindling, and the artist wasted no time in lighting it. Meanwhile, by the light of one of the two paraffin lanterns, she unpacked her case, her heart sinking further as she sifted through her least favourite skirts and blouses and thin cardigans, all of which were far better suited to summer in central London than midwinter in northern Europe. She hastily wrapped his sketchbook inside an underskirt which, in turn, she buried beneath a pair of thin blouses, and then locked that pile back inside the suitcase. Everything else went inside a dresser in one of the two efficiently stark bedrooms.

The stove, which was central to one side of the main room, drew strongly and the sight of the blaze through the tiny cracks around the door offered a slither of comfort as she huddled close, her head slowly thumping. The artist crouched alongside her. "Shall I make up one bed or two?"

"Just one," she said. "I'll make up the other."

He didn't object to that, in fact he persuaded her to bring the mattress though and put it on the floor next to the stove, which she did. He bedded down in one of the rear rooms but came back through a couple of times during the night to feed the stove. She slept beneath four blankets and in her clothes, including her coat. She still felt cold, though she knew that was probably down to exhaustion. She slept thinly and fitfully.

In the morning he produced dried sausages which he sliced and fried on the stove as she remained snuggled in her bed on the floor at last feeling warm. He sliced bread and made coffee with hot milk. She sat in her bed to consume it. He perched on a stool close to the stove.

"Where did all this come from?"

"From Klas."

"Where?"

"Not where – who. Klas. Santa Klas." The artist giggled, something he hadn't done since England. "Klas was the man at the airfield. He put some supplies in the car."

She felt fragile, shivery and sad, but was determined not to let him see that. She ate and drank, knowing and hoping that the food would boost her. "Where are we?"

"Safe."

Daylight was arriving tardily. Through the main windows she could see a roofed veranda. From her floor-level perspective she saw laden conifer branches and a heavy sky. Snow was no longer falling but the clouds looked pregnant with a weight they didn't want to carry.

"I don't feel safe."

He looked hurt. "Do you think I'd go to all this trouble to put you in danger?"

"If you thought it was your duty."

"Is that what you think I am doing?"

"I don't know what you are doing." She finished her sausage slices, slipped out from the covers and took her crust to the window. She saw a great expanse of water, very still close to shore, but with crested waves in the distance. "I don't know what you are doing. I don't know who you are." She turned towards him. "I think it's time you told me your name."

He looked crestfallen, and due to the shortness of the stool, a little pathetic. "Can't we continue with our pact?"

"What pact? I do not believe for one minute that you do

not know my name."

"Believing or not believing doesn't make something true or false."

"You couldn't have executed this operation without knowing who I am."

"I know what you are, but not who you are."

"And what am I?"

"An ignorant mule."

"Thank you very much." She chewed the last of her bread.

He put his plate down, collected her cup from the floor and brought it to her. "They were not my words."

"Edwin's?"

He shook his head.

"Edwin knows my name doesn't he?"

"He hasn't told me."

She gave him a disbelieving sneer. "Have you got a cigarette?"

He left the room. She took in the view. A very large lake. Or it could be an inlet of the sea. Close to the shore the surface was paved with broken slabs of ice.

The artist returned with a fresh pack of Churchman's No 1 and his petrol lighter. They each selected a stick and he lit hers first. "The only name of yours that I know is your code name."

She exhaled over her right shoulder. "And what is that?"

"The poser."

"I don't believe you."

"Not believing doesn't make it untrue."

She undid her coat. "I don't believe that you've done everything you have knowing me only by a code name."

"It suits you."

"It's not something I've chosen."

"Neither is your real name."

"I'm tired of that game."

For the first time ever, she heard real anger in his voice. "Then choose a name. Any name that you want. But not the one you already have."

She turned back to the view. "For God's sake . . ."

"For my sake."

She studied the horizon trying to see land, and sucked on her cigarette. She blew the smoke against the window then refocused on the faint reflection of his face. "I want to know your name."

"Well I'm not going to tell you."

"Edwin called you Pic."

"That was my nickname during the war, and before."

"Why that?"

"Picasso. It was schoolboy sarcasm."

"Right. I'll use that."

"Please don't." He turned away and left the room. She heard him putting on boots and then leave the chalet. He passed the window wearing a heavy jacket and she watched him walk a few yards to a shed which he unlocked. From it he produced a woodsman's axe and began splitting logs from a lean-to wood store. She washed up the breakfast things, returned her mattress to the bed in the bedroom, and once more rooted through the inadequate clothes she had brought.

She washed using a bowl and water from the kettle, and changed into the thickest blouse she had unpacked, and put on two cardigans and a pair of slacks beneath a worsted skirt. She went to the toilet which was also out of doors, in its own free-standing cabin with a slightly rotten wooden door. Her period had started. She would have to improvise some sanitary supplies.

She then took in a quick tour of the chalet and its environs. At first glance it seemed they were entirely isolated. It was enclosed on three sides by forest and on the fourth by the water. The track they had followed terminated here and after a brief walk she could see no sign of the road that they had turned off. The building itself, though spacious, was not large and comprised only three rooms and the vestibule.

She found more food supplies that Klas had put in two sacks in the rear of their vehicle. She took them to the chalet and began to unpack them. He saw what she was doing, but did not interrupt his labours.

There were a lot of vegetables, a small amount of fresh meat, and a good deal of tinned fish. There were several cans she could not identify from their labels. It all looked rather utilitarian and she wondered if that was the Swedish way, or if it was ex-military stock. Appraising it all she considered that the artist was planning for an extended stay, though they would soon run out of bread and milk. There was a large tin labelled 'Mjölk' which she thought might be powdered milk. She added wood to the stove and put the kettle on the hotplate topping it up from a jug of water which, she suspected, the artist had brought from the rivulet that cut through the woods a short distance away. When it was hot enough, she would brew some more coffee. Whilst waiting she began to reassess her predicament.

There were a few books in the chalet, stacked neatly on the dresser in the corner. She flicked through them. None contained maps, or any indication that she could decipher as to where she was. She visualised as best she could the peninsular that was Norway and Sweden. She thought it unlikely that their combined journey had taken them very far north. She could only remember one Swedish city – Stockholm – and was confident that it lay on the coast to the south and east. She reckoned she was probably in the same quarter of the country as the capital, but even that could mean she was hundreds of miles from it. If she was in that lower 'toe' of the peninsular she knew that to the north and west were vast expanses of mountains and wild forests and to the east and south was the Baltic. Beyond that was the Eastern Bloc. Why had the artist brought her there?

Thankfully, her suitcase had contained a pair of gloves. They were knitted and quite thin, but very welcome. She pulled them on, donned her coat and took two mugs of coffee out to where he was breathing and sweating clouds. He grinned his appreciation and for a moment all was surreally normal. He perched on a pile of logs. She put her cup down and took up the chopping maul. She balanced one of the un-split logs on its sawn end atop the tree base that he'd been using as an anvil.

"Have you done that before?" he asked.

She hoisted the axe high and brought it down sweetly, splitting the target log in two. "What do you think?"

"Looks like it."

"You clearly don't know everything about me."

"I've only ever claimed to know virtually nothing about you."

"But you know far more about me than I do. Because you know why I'm here."

He wiped the back of his sleeve across his brow, and ruffled his hair. "You're here to keep you safe."

"For how long?"

"Until it's safe to move on."

She positioned another log. "To where?" She split the log.

He went on: "This place isn't ideal in winter. It can get a lot worse than this."

"So why stay here at all?" She selected another log.

"We need to be confident that we've gone off the radar."

"And how will we know that?" This time she hit the log with a glancing blow. A sliver split off but the bulk of the log went tumbling towards the lake. He recovered it and stood it back on the chopping base.

"Word will come through."

She swigged from her coffee. "Which means someone knows we're here."

He nodded towards the car. "Klas will want his car back."

"Is this Klas's place?"

The artist shook his head. She swung the axe and split the log perfectly. "Don't tell me it's yours?"

He shook his head again. "It belongs to a Stockbroker. In Stockholm."

She looked askance.

"Seriously," he said. "I rented it for a couple of summers. I'm renting it again. It's very cheap in winter."

She chose another log, with a larger diameter. "And who's footing the bill?" She hit hard. The log did not split but the axe sank deep and stuck in the centre. She lifted axe and log together, and let it fall back twice. The second time the log split. With two further swings she sliced each half in half. She let the maul topple over and took up her cup.

"I'm footing the bill."

"And how do you earn a living?" He didn't reply. "The question is allowed," she said. "It's not about your past."

"I have income."

She went over to stand close to him. "The thing is, I now know about your past. In particular one week in June 1943."

"I remember it with affection."

She raised an eyebrow. "Really?"

"I think it's affection."

"Or affectation?"

"How about you?" he said.

"Do I look like I'm pretending?"

"How do you reflect on what we did in June 1943?"

"As a deception."

"You're right," he said.

She finished her drink and returned to splitting logs.

He said, "You don't have to do that."

She said, "It's warming me up."

He watched her for a while, then wandered closer to the water and scanned the expanse. The short day was brightening but an insipid greyness persevered and invisible damp sparks spoke of more snow to come. After another dozen splices she walked over to join him. Thin slabs of ice nudged each other as slight waves rippled in.

"Will you please tell me precisely where we are?"

"You are on the western shore of Vättern; the second largest lake in Sweden and the sixth largest in the whole of Europe. We're about a hundred miles east of Gothenburg. Two hundred west of Stockholm."

She instantly felt much happier, simply because she could visualise herself on the map in her memory. "Why here? And please don't say because it's safe."

"Well, that is the primary reason, but also because I know it."

"And you can speak Swedish."

"I can get by."

"I can't."

He prized a pebble from the glazed beach and sent it skimming across the ice of the lake. It skidded swift and free until it hit a raised fracture and went arcing through the air in a fan of frozen debris. "If we hadn't found you when we did I suspect you'd be getting by even less well by now. Perhaps you wouldn't be getting anything again."

"There you go again, with your 'we'. Who is 'we'?"

"Heapy and me."

"Just Edwin and you?"

"Yes just Edwin and me."

"Why?"

"Let's put that down to affection shall we?" He found another stone and hurled it skywards. It smacked down hard on the lake ice, but by then he was on his way back to the chopping place. She called after him.

"How did you know to intervene?"

He shouted, "Because Heapy told me to."

She caught him up. "And how did he know?" The artist

picked up the axe. She grabbed his arms. "Listen," she said. "I'm 'safe'. I'm here. With you. With very little else. Without a passport. And with somebody else's secrets stitched to my stomach. Don't you think I deserve something more of an explanation?" She moved her hands down to find his, gripping them through the gloves her godmother had knitted.

He surveyed the sky. "As soon as this weather blows through Heapy will sneak the plane he stole back into Britain. He might get away with it; he might not. He's risked more than anyone dare ask for an old friend of dubious loyalty." He looked down at her. "I don't usually do loyalty."

She detected something. She could not locate its nature. She gently unfurled his fingers from the axe and tipped it to one side. Then she took hold of his hands properly. "Well I've done a decade of loyalty. Not to you, because I don't know you. Loyalty to a fantasy, that has become a quagmire of treachery. You might think you've been loyal, you might think you've 'saved' me, but you haven't done either of those things. I want an explanation. A full explanation. And I want it now."

"The winter days here are very short. I'll tell you what I know tonight." He made to release her grip and continue chopping, but she held firm.

"It has to start with you," she said. "No more mystery. I want your history. It doesn't have to include your name."

Ice slabs moaned.

"All right," he said.

She kissed him, briefly and gently on the lips. Then she let him go, and turned back to the lake. "And tomorrow you can start teaching me Swedish."

"Ja," he said.

"That will impress Alice. I do hope she's all right."

"You can never go back to Britain," he said.

"Why not?"

"Because it's the British who want to cut you open."

EIGHTEEN

"I knew Edwin Heap before the war. We went to the same school. Chance brought us back together. One day he walked into the annex where I was working."

"At Benson?"

"Nearby."

"You were in the Air Force?"

"No. I was not in the military."

"Then what were you?"

"An interpreter."

"Of which language?"

"Of chiaroscuro."

"I'm sorry?"

"Of photographs. I interpreted photographs."

"Aerial photographs."

"That's right."

The fishing chalet was surprisingly warm. The stove had burned fiercely all day, and now, in the quick depths of the premature evening the timber walls of the chalet swelled to make a tight shield against the snowstorm outside. The snow, already thick on the roof, added to their insulation. She had concocted a warming, and surprisingly tasty meal from the tinned stock. They'd had pork and fresh vegetables, with tinned pears to follow. The supper was done and he'd opened a bottle of vodka. He drank it neat. She poured some in her coffee. They slouched in a pair of wicker chairs, not overly comfortable but more relaxing than the upright ones at the table.

"I know that Edwin was based at Mount Farm. Is that where you were?"

He shook his head. "Benson had its own interpretation unit but I wasn't part of that. Anything of particular note was brought to my department by dispatch rider. That's how Heapy and I met again. One day the regular dispatch riders were under-strength for some reason. Heapy stood in. We met socially after that."

"He brought you the picture of me on the roof of Woburn Abbey."

"Artist's models were not easy to come by during the war. He knew I was looking for someone willing to sit nude."

"So you set out to locate me."

"He did that. He knew people at Woburn."

"How? He went around waving the photograph?"

"He had the negative. He enlarged it and cropped it to a head shot and posted it to his contact. Took a couple of weeks but eventually he had your name – which he has never divulged to me. Not even to this day."

"Really?" she said sarcastically.

"Yes, really. Edwin Heap is perhaps the only human who understands my . . . peculiarities. I wanted my muse to be untitled."

"So he knew who I was and where I was stationed."

"And hence which railway services you were likely to use."

"Then you must have always known where I worked."

The artist took the vodka bottle from the floor and refilled his glass. She noticed the label. The lettering didn't look Swedish. It looked Russian. "It was hard to avoid knowing that. But I didn't know of the work that was done there until long after the war was over. Most people still don't."

"So you had a grainy picture of a woman who chose to sunbathe naked, and some sketchy information about which railway station she might frequent and off you went."

"You make it sound very simple."

"I don't believe you for a minute."

"It was my fifth attempt."

"I don't believe any of it."

"Why not?"

"Because you painted two other women before me. Both of whom happened to have been patients of the same surgeon."

He swallowed half of his drink. "That's why I had to find you. To see if the scar was the same."

"And did both of those women sunbathe on the roof of Woburn Abbey too? Just when Edwin happened to be testing his camera?"

"I doubt that very much."

"Then how were you introduced to them?"

"I never met them. Their portraits were painted from photographs."

"Aerial photographs."

"No. Pictures taken of them on the operating table. I suspect there's one of those of you too, but I've never seen it."

She took up a tea towel and, using it to protect her hand, removed the enamel coffee pot from the stove and refilled her cup. He added more vodka to her drink. Her mind was whirring. "Where did you get those photographs from?"

He took the tea towel from her, used it to open the door of the stove and added more of the logs that they'd split that morning. "There's only one possibility isn't there?"

"Dr Stonorowich," she said.

He secured the door on the stove and returned to his seat. "The pictures arrived by post with a down payment and a written commission. I did as was requested. No one ever collected the finished works."

"How do I fit into this?"

"Exactly as I have described. It was chance. But when Heapy showed me the picture of you, my interest was aroused on several levels. I wanted to meet you because I genuinely wished for an untitled model. I also wanted to meet you because . . . well I just wanted to meet you. Thirdly, that scar could not be ignored. Even with the poor resolution it looked to have been done by the same hand as the others. Eventually, I knew for certain it was the same surgeon."

"Just by the scar?"

"You must remember that the wound was only a few months old. And for those in the photographs, only minutes. In each case the final stitch was actually a close band of several closely grouped stitches. The first picture I was sent had three, the second four, and you had five."

"But I was his sixth patient."

The artist shrugged. "For all we know you were his sixtieth. You were the sixth at Woburn, but that may be of no significance. I think what matters is that you were the third of a group of three."

"Then why didn't he ask you to paint me?"

"We may never know."

She remembered something about the sketchbook, but decided not to mention it. She decided that she believed him, but she was not at all sure that she had the full story yet.

"You and Edwin were school friends."

"I said we went to the same school. Leave it at that. The pre-war stuff is still off the agenda."

"And will it remain so?"

"It's not a matter for negotiation."

"Then let's move forwards. After the war. The end of the war. The last time I saw you was quarter to seven on the evening of Wednesday 22nd September 1943."

"Closer to five-to, I think. The train was late."

"At least it came back again."

"So did I."

She gave him one of her withering looks. "We'll come to that. Let's keep it chronological."

"I worked on your portraits. Plural. Painted over a couple of them. Started a fourth. Tried to get you out of my system."

"Thank you," she said sarcastically. "Meanwhile I was going crazy trying to contact you. Did you send messages?"

He shook his head. A new darkness veiled him. "Heapy was missing."

"Oh."

"Shot down. He spent two years in the camps. Of course I didn't know that at the time. It was almost a year before we heard."

"How terrible."

"Sounds cruel but, thoughts of you were always intertwined with thoughts of him. I can't really explain that."

She felt guilty. She had no reason to feel guilty, but guilt was what she felt. "Perhaps I could have helped?"

The veil became a shroud. "No one could have helped."

"No."

"I could not go back to Kendal's Lodge. I did not know your name. And while I knew where you were billeted and had an idea where you were posted, finding you would have been a very peculiar process. Apart from which, it might have put you in danger."

"How?"

"I did not know why I'd been asked to paint your predecessors or why I hadn't been asked to paint you, but I was convinced that there was a connection. If my patron had known what I had deduced, he might have taken action against one or both of us. I tried not to think about you, or Heapy. I got on with my job. Then I was posted."

"Posted? You said you were not enlisted."

"I said I was not in the military."

She only needed a moment's thought. "The Intelligence Services."

He kept his head very still.

"You still work for the Intelligence Services."

"It was August 1944. I was posted overseas. Following the Allied advance. I ended up in Berlin."

"For how long?"

"Six years."

"That still leaves a gap."

"More postings. Including Sweden."

"Is it really necessary to send spies to Sweden?"

"There's only one way to find out. And I never said I was a spy."

She stood up and went to the dresser and opened a cupboard. She selected a packet of biscuits and studied the wrapping. "You were though, weren't you? You still are."

"I was a civil servant."

"What's kokos?"

"Coconut."

She sliced the wrapper with her thumbnail and extracted a coconut crusted biscuit. She took a bite and proffered the pack to him. As he reached towards it, she suddenly angled it away from him. "That's how you knew they were looking for me."

"I got a tip-off."

"Then you must have known more than my codename. You must have known it was me."

"The tip-off came from Heapy."

This time she only needed half a moment. "He has the same employer."

"Heapy's business is Heapy's business."

She proffered the pack again and he took a coconut biscuit, but she didn't move away. She was locked by a thought.

"But you said it was the British who were trying to find me."

He nodded. "Heapy's courage is only surpassed by his loyalty."

"But he's been disloyal."

"Not to me."

"And so have you."

"Not to you."

She gripped the biscuit packet more tightly. "Berlin has four zones," she said.

"That's right."

"In which one were you based?"

NINETEEN

She thought that she was in for a long stay on the shore of Vättern, but she was wrong.

The main room of the chalet was cosy, lots of vodka had been consumed and many questions remained unanswered, but she agreed that it made sense to bring the two mattresses through to the floor close to the stove and for them to share the soft space. The blankets were big enough to cover them both. He had pyjamas. She had not packed any nightwear but changed into one of his shirts and they brought blankets from both beds. They could not make love because her period was underway, but they shared an intense intimacy. Her body seemed untroubled by the unresolved concerns in her mind.

The second day there was not dissimilar to the first in that they spent time making the accommodation more serviceable. They cleared away the bed and unpacked the remainder of the stock of supplies from Klas's car. They heated water and washed themselves thoroughly, after which she felt much better. She sorted through her clothes once more, which depressed her again. It was virtually all summer wear. Both pairs of shoes she had with her were ill-fashioned for the conditions she now faced. The pair she had worn the previous day was severely dilapidated by exposure to the snow. Nevertheless, she put in her stint of log-splitting again. No more probing conversations took place.

They each seemed silenced by the general weariness that follows prolonged exposure to adrenalin. He made the main meal – a fortifying corned beef hash.   They rebuilt the bed by the stove again, as the bedrooms still seemed uncivilly cold.

The next morning, they remained cocooned, waiting for the lazy dawn but before it arrived they were startled by the sound of a vehicle. She had never seen the artist move so rapidly. He was out of the covers and peering through the window shutters in what she perceived to be a single move. She drew a sharp breath. Even the feeble light was sufficient to show her that he clutched a handgun.

"What . . .?"

"Shh!"

They waited.

His silhouette against the shutters became more defined. A pyjama-clad male, lithe and sinuous but strong, poised and locked with elastic energy, focussed at two points of potential: a forehead and a muzzle.

The sounds continued. The vehicle was manoeuvring. She hoped it was an error; someone had lost their way. It stopped again. It moved again. It stopped. She could hear the engine idling. Then a hammering on the door, and a deep-throated shout.

"Pic! Pic!"

The artist launched himself back towards the bed. He grabbed his clothes and began to wrestle his way into them. "Stay there," he said to her. It's Klas."

"Pic! Pic!"

"One minute!" he shouted.

She heard the visitor shout again, but could not distinguish what had been said. The vehicle drove away. She reached to find her clothes. The artist slid the gun beneath the mattress, slipped on his shoes, and struggling with his sweater, headed for the door.   She pulled her skirt on, tucked his shirt into it, and wriggled into her cardigan, hastily doing up the buttons. She quickly wrapped her scarf around her neck and let its length further shield any betrayal that she was not wearing a bra. She tucked that, and her underskirt, out of sight beneath the blankets. She considered moving the bedclothes, pillows and mattress but realised that in doing so she would reveal the handgun, so instead she just cursorily tidied them.

The door was unbolted. Greetings were exchanged. The artist stepped outside and pulled the door closed behind him. The two men conversed in a blend of Swedish and English. She couldn't decipher the substance but the mood was clear. It was urgent and nervous. There was agitation. Sentences were short.

They came in. Klas, with his face sunken deep within the bulk of his winter coat and hat, nodded a greeting.

"Miss," he said.

"Hello Klas."

He volunteered an awkward and short-lived smile. The artist followed him. There was something overwhelmingly wrong.

"Pack everything," said Pic. "Everything. Every last thing. Every hint of you."

"What is it?" she asked.

"Tell her," said the artist. Then he disappeared in the direction of the bedrooms. She heard desperate thuds and scrapes and scuffles.

"What is it Klas?"

He removed his hat and passed his hand through his hair. "The Flight Lieutenant," he said.

"Flight Lieutenant Heap? Edwin?"

The Swede nodded; then shook his head.

"What happened?"

"He was taking off. He didn't. Not properly. He just never gained any height."

"How?"

"We don't know."

"But . . .is he . . .?"

Klas shook his head again.

"But . . .where . . . what are we . . .?"

"An investigation is starting. You need to get away from here."

"Why? We're miles away."

"Questions will be asked."

"Here and in the UK," said Pic darting back in and making no attempt to mask his recovery of the hand gun, which she now saw clearly for the first time. "There must be no trace that you have been here."

"Pic . . ." she heard herself saying. She had never called him that. "Are you . . .?"

No reply came. Klas shook his head again. "I will help you."

They folded the bed sheets. She gathered her underclothes and took them to the bedroom that she had not used. She shut the door and leaned against it as she quickly undressed and dressed again. Good sense began to kick in and she added nylons and an extra cardigan. Meanwhile she heard the men talking, but could not interpret the sounds. Klas brought the mattress, knocking politely on her door. She helped him slot it onto the bed then went to help him transfer the other to the artist's room. Pic was immobile, sitting on the bare bed boards staring at the woollen sock in his hand. The sinews in his neck were taught. His eyes were locked in a redundancy as he saw with his memory.

"Pic," she said again. Somehow it seemed right. Klas had called him that and it was the way that Edwin had addressed him. She laid her hand gently on his. "I'm so sorry."

She considered the artist would crumple, but he didn't. His form was sculpture hard. She felt deep sympathy but also a strange superiority. For the first time, she was in command. She was the agent of calm and the angel of urgency. She understood what needed to be done even if she didn't fully comprehend how it could be achieved. "I'll get all my stuff sorted, then help you with yours."

It took them an hour, during which she scoured the chalet for every last trace of her occupancy. The artist regained his proclivity for action, though his communication remained restrained and terse. Their task, he said, was to remove any clear indications of recent occupation. She felt they made a decent job of that. They loaded their luggage into the car that they had borrowed from Klas, and locked the chalet. The artist opted for the rear seat, as this time Klas was going to drive.

"One thing, before we leave," said Klas. "Stand there please." He positioned her with her back to the lake then, from his pocket, produced a compact camera.

"What are you doing?"

"Don't worry," he said, crouching a little. "Behind is just the clouds."

She contorted her face.

"Relax please," he said. "It's for your passport."

He took four photographs. She got into the car while Klas

conducted a final external inspection of the property and its surrounds. Pic was sealed in silent contemplation. She knew that nothing needed to be said.

Klas climbed in and after three attempts, the engine fired into life. "It will snow again tonight," he said. "Should cover everything. Including our tyre tracks."

This time she saw the wider locality in daylight. They were truly remote which begged the question as to why they should move, but she understood that if the artist was known to spend time there, then they would be safer elsewhere.

"Where are we heading?" she asked.

"I'm going to put you on a train," said Klas.

"That'll be nice," she said. Her apparent nonchalance surprised and delighted her. She was acclimatising to adventure. "And where will we get off?"

"Stockholm," said Klas with a smile.

"It's lovely at this time of year," said Pic suddenly.

"Wonderful," she said.

Klas eased the car around an uncomfortable corner. She kept the mood light. "And what will you do, Klas?"

"I will get my story straight."

"How straight?"

"Smuggling," he said with a smile.

"Smuggling what?"

"Vodka. There was a crate on the Anson, so they might find some bottles among the wreckage. That would help to . . .validate . . .things."

"But still cause trouble for you?"

"All I did was sell him petrol. I never saw no one. Not Pic. Not you."

She put her hand on his arm. "Thank you."

He negotiated another bend which excused his lean towards her. "My pleasure."

The lake vanished from view. The road was Roman-straight through white-dressed woods. "You mentioned a passport."

Klas fumbled in his jacket pocket and produced a film cartridge. "Give that to Pic," he said.

She took it and passed it back to Pic. "Is it for a Swedish passport?" she asked.

"I don't think that would work," grinned Klas.

"We'll find you a new name," said the artist.

"Good," she said. "I'm tired of hearing my old one."

"We have various passports. British, Irish, Canadian."

"Canadian?" she said. "Not sure I can do the accent."

"British would be best," said Pic. "If we can find the right one."

"Genuine then? Not fake?"

"Just a question of finding the right person. Your gender, roughly your age, and dead."

"Dead?"

"All the best people are."

Just over an hour later they arrived at the railway station in the city of Jönköping. Klas bought their tickets and he also purchased pastries and coffee and three packets of Swedish cigarettes. "It's better that you do not use the British ones," he said. "Attracts attention."

After they had eaten, she said, "I'm sorry, but I really need a ladies' convenience."

Klas craned his neck and indicated the sign. When she returned Klas was alone. He said Pic had taken all his change and was making a phone call.

"Wonderful," she said. "Where is the phone box?"

"Over by the main entrance," said Klas.

She could just make it out beyond the jumble of customers and the glass of the café window. "What exactly happened – with the Flight Lieutenant?"

"The weather was too poor, so I put him up overnight. The next day it improved. We cleared the snow and ice from his plane. I watched him. He accelerated along the runway as usual. The tail rose. He rotated very late. Didn't climb properly. He clipped trees beyond the end of the runway, through the fence, across the road, into the field and a mushroom of fire and black smoke. That was it."

"Why?"

"Who can say? Maybe he didn't have the speed? Maybe something didn't work? A malfunction."

"We'll never know."

"I doubt we ever will."

A question came into her mind. She held it there for a

moment, then said, "Did it look deliberate?"

"What does deliberate look like?"

"How well did you know him?"

"Not at all. We only met three days ago."

"How well do you know Pic?"

Klas stretched his beard with a smile. "Even the people who know Pic, don't know Pic."

"Don't tell me – but do you know his real name?"

"I thought Pic was his real name."

She rubbed a small irritation from her left eye. "What do you know about me?"

"I know that you are having a baby."

She burst out laughing. "Who told you that?"

"Flight Lieutenant Heap. Are you having a baby?"

"Just the opposite."

"Oh. I'm sorry."

"That's all right. What else did he tell you about me?"

"Nothing. I know nothing about you. Except that you are very brave."

"Very foolish."

"And that Pic loves you."

"Did Edwin tell you that as well?"

"He didn't need to."

She saw Pic leaving the telephone kiosk. "What were his exact words?"

"He just said Pic was very much in love with you. In-something. In-fat-something."

"Infatuated?"

"Could have been. Could have been that."

"What were his exact words about the baby?"

"He said you were pregnant."

"Pregnant."

"Pregnant."

Pic re-joined them. "Sorry Klas. I used all your money."

"That's all right."

"Did you get through?" she asked.

"Not really."

"Can I ask who to?"

"Not really."

She pierced him with a cynical stare. He rebuffed it with a glare.

The two men then spoke in Swedish. She picked up her handbag. "I'm going outside for some fresh air, and a smoke." She left them and stepped onto the crisp and slightly damp atmosphere. The platform was long but there was no corresponding one on the opposite side of the tracks which edged the shore of the great lake. Snow was evident everywhere, except on the water, but she considered the coverage less dense than at the fishing chalet. This part of the lake was not frozen. The cigarette cut her throat more sharply than usual. It lifted her spirits.

She wished she could make a call. Most of all she wanted to hear Vera's voice. She dearly hoped that Vera was on the mend. She allowed herself a wish that she had not been injured at all, and that Pic's story had been a fabrication. It wasn't just the nicotine that prompted that thought. So much about Pic was smeared with deception. Part of his artistry was in painting over the truth to render it less visible. He was a man of layers, and despite the dangers and strangeness of her predicament, she felt excited by the prospect of peeling them away.

Klas found her. "I've come to say goodbye."

"Where's Pic?"

"Making another call. Or it could be the same one."

"I thought he'd used all your change."

"I got more. From the girl at the café."

"Listen Klas. I don't know you, I don't know really what you do, or why you've done this for Pic, or for me, but I really like you; and I thank you."

"My pleasure."

"I doubt that, but I hope it doesn't turn to any kind of unpleasantness. I hope no bad things happen as a consequence of this. Of me."

His eyes twinkled. His beard broadened. "I talk well. I'm just so sorry for Pic's friend. And for Pic."

"I expect he'll pull through."

"You know him better than I do."

"I somehow feel that's not true."

"Well, I don't know. I wasn't meaning to lie to you."

She swivelled her shoe on the tip of her cigarette. "Will you tell me one more truthful thing?"

"If I can."

"Is Klas your real name?"

His beard stretched even wider. "Yes," he said. "Klas is my real name."

"Thank Christ for that."

The train to Stockholm was much more comfortable than the post-war rolling stock she was used to in Great Britain. They had a compartment to themselves. She travelled with her back to the engine and he sat opposite her. He was still deeply immersed in his thoughts and she avoided looking at him, choosing instead to watch her ghostly reflection skim across the landscape as it stretched and slowed and became the land they left behind. She was right about the snow coverage. As they curved around the toe of Vättern and then eased away from the eastern shore of the lake the snow coating became thin and translucent and then vanished altogether. The clouds were broken, the sky ice-blue, and the boundary of the canvas of her perspective was a band of evergreen. Her reflection became both more distinct and more captivating as it cut through, over and under, the foliage. Then she looked a little higher and saw a second ghost. This must have been the image of something else in the train but she could not discern what, and she didn't try, for in her mind's eye it had a form and that form was her. It was her torso. Headless and limbless and white and not mirrored but correctly oriented opposite her. It travelled independently and separately but was inextricably tied to her, matching her in speed and following every slight curve in the direction of travel. She knew it was imagination because it couldn't be anything else. She knew it was her, because there was her scar, not on her left side where she saw it in the mirror, but on her right, where he had so appositely painted it.

He shocked her out of her daydream by asking her what she was thinking.

She told him.

He told her he'd sketched out that scenario over a decade before. She didn't believe him, but then remembered she had seen a drawing of it in the sketchbook she had hidden.

TWENTY

It made no sense to travel to Stockholm. The artist said he had an apartment there. She was incredulous when he told her in their room at the Hotel Drottning Kristina. She was furious that she would be spending a good deal of time there by herself.

His apartment, he explained, was elsewhere in the city. Their hotel was much more central. They had checked in as Mr and Mrs Colin Proctor. He had filled in the registration card with an address in Sweden, though she noted, not in Stockholm. He told the receptionist they intended to stay for one or two weeks. They had a plain room, curiously triangular in plan, at the rear of the hotel. He told her he would spend one night there and then leave her. They would meet back at the hotel every other day.

She was aghast. Why had they left a remote location for a much more obvious one where he had an apartment? He said that following the crash someone may be sent to check on him. If so, they would find him where they expected him to be, in his apartment. Yes, she said, and then they'd follow him right to her. He said that he wouldn't let that happen. He had methods.

"And what am I supposed to do? Sit in this Pythagorean prison all day and all night?"

He said she could come and go as she pleased. He would write a list of places she could visit.

"And get snatched by the Soviets?"

"The Soviets are not interested in you. They already have what's inside you. That's why the Brits want it."

"And they're going to come and get it."

"The British don't know you are here."

"Then why can't you stay with me?"

"Because if they check on me I want them to find me alone."

"Check on you? They'll do more than check on you!"

"Why should they do that?"

"Because . . . because . . . because of all this!"

"They don't know about all this. There's been a plane crash. It's a British plane. Privately registered. Heapy borrowed it from a friend. He's going to be pretty upset, but he's no idea why Heapy wanted it, what he did with it or who was with him. When the police quiz him it cannot possibly shed any light on us."

"Then why did we have to come to Stockholm?"

"Do you know what MI5 is?"

"Secret Service."

"They know that Edwin Heap and I have history."

She stared at her beloved stranger. "You work for them don't you?"

"No. But Heapy did."

"What?"

"His loyalty to me was the ultimate betrayal. He's paid the ultimate price."

"Are you saying the crash was punishment?"

He considered before replying. "I think it was probably an accident."

"Probably?"

"Probably. I expect they'll put a check on me. They might just watch me. I'm going to have to appear ignorant of Edwin's demise. And if they make contact and tell me what's happened, I'm going to have to get very upset."

"I don't think that will be difficult for you."

"No. It won't."

"But if they know you are with me . . ."

"Why should they know?"

"Everywhere I've gone I've left a trail of disaster. Mr Coward, Alice, . . . they must have been watching me."

"If they were watching you, why didn't they just snatch you?"

"Then why was Coward killed?"

"Because his brakes failed."

"How do you know that?"

"Because you told me."

"I don't think I did."

"Well let's agree to differ on that shall we?"

"I don't think I was that specific."

That evening they had dinner in the hotel. He reiterated that she should not feel confined. She could use the hotel facilities. He suggested she remained indoors for the first forty-eight hours, but after that she could come and go as she pleased. She, in turn, pointed out that she had three problems: she didn't know Stockholm, she had no money, and she couldn't speak Swedish. He said that within two days she would have money. He would bring her some. Stockholm was a cosmopolitan city. There were plenty of English speakers and visitors from the UK and the United Sates were common. She may not have a passport, but she did have an identity. She was Mrs Colin Proctor, the wife of a dealer in art, antiques and curios.

"On the subject of passports – you've still got the film with my pictures on it?"

"Yes."

"Do I have a Christian name?"

"Christina. That's what I put on the hotel registration card."

"Why did you choose that name?"

He hesitated. "Same as the hotel. Spelt differently."

She had a remarkably good night's sleep. It was the most comfortable bed she'd slept in for years. Fortunately, new concerns and old were shelved behind dreams she could not remember when she woke. After breakfast he slipped away, promising to return in the evening of the following day. She retired to her room, hanging the 'do not disturb' sign on the door. She sat on the bed and took stock.

Once again her mood took her by surprise. She was alone, with very little money – all of it English – and with a completely inappropriate collection of clothes, in an alien city, in a foreign country, and with a price on her intestine. She was elated. She should have felt despair but instead was exhilarated. She couldn't understand why. It was as if the fusion of anxieties had formed a spiritual adrenalin. She was not overawed by her predicament; she was enthused by it. Even so, she was not in denial of the danger. She embraced it. What was going on in her head? Was this the nourishment needed for martyrdom?

For the first time in a long time she recalled her childhood. There had been freedoms but not from frugality. Somehow her mother and step-father had sent her to what was ostensibly a decent school. She now had her own opinions about decency. The convent school had given her what she needed: good grammar, meticulous arithmetic, conventional deportment and a deeply disguised cynicism. Home life became less comfortable. The war came in the nick of time. She enrolled, had an income, had a roof, had a uniform, had a purpose. That purpose had been uninvited and unexplained, just like her current one.

That evening she dined alone. Her husband was doing business she told the waiter. He served her additional charm. She relished it.

She did not sleep quite so well the second evening, but at least she was warm and comfortable. She was not as elated as she had been on the previous morning, but neither was she unduly apprehensive. She resolved to venture out after breakfast but there was a heavy snowfall in progress and she was entirely unequipped for that kind of weather, so she perused the somewhat overbearing life-size statue of Queen Kristina on a prancing horse in the foyer, then went to sit in the hotel lounge where she found a copy of the London Times. It was three days old, but nevertheless, it centred her sense of being at least tenuously connected with a place she knew. She scoured it from cover to cover. There was no mention of aeroplane accidents or mishaps in London theatres.

She took coffee while she read. It was the best coffee she had tasted since before the war. By the time she had finished the paper the snow had stopped falling. She resolved to go out, walk the streets and get her bearings. Her shoes were not the most suitable, one pair was cut too low to cope with the city slush, and the other damaged by the snow at the chalet, but she had no other option. She would take what money she had, find a bank and exchange it for krona. Then she would buy new shoes, and if she could afford it, a much more robust winter coat.

Within moments of leaving the hotel she realised her mistake. It was Sunday. No banks would be open. No shops would be open. Still, she could do her reconnaissance. She took careful note of the frontage and location of the hotel and set off along the street. A ten-minute walk took her all the way to the harbour. There was little activity. A few public transport launches chugged about, but most vessels were tied up and silent. She did, however notice a large ocean liner berthed some distance away on the far side of the dock.

She retraced her steps and took minor detours to take in the window displays still very much in yuletide mode. The street layout seemed strongly linear to her and hence she did not lose her way. She was at liberty for less than an hour and with damp and frozen feet returned to her hotel. The twenty-something female receptionist confirmed that there were no messages for her, and handed over the room key with respectfully disguised dubious looks. She took the tiny caged lift to the second floor and put her shoes and nylons on the radiator in her room.

He was supposed to join her for the evening meal but he did not appear. She dined alone and checked again for messages at the reception counter. None were to be had. She imagined the receptionist's facial expression to be doubly dubious having no doubt noticed her less than pristine and totally unseasonal attire. Her nylons were dry but her shoes were not, and looked dreadful. She ordered a Scotch and soda and sipped it in their room. Thoughts regarding his whereabouts began to gather and swarm in mind. An hour and an empty glass later the thoughts were less about what might have befallen him, and more about what he might have decided to do.

She took towels to the nearest bathroom. She ran the bath, and soaked in it for less than fifteen minutes. Upon returning to her room she telephoned for another Scotch and enquired again for messages. She tried to not apply perceived conceit to the tone of the negative reply, but failed. She sipped the second drink slowly, locked the door and retired to bed. The alcohol worked for the first part of the night. She was awake from three a.m.

The counter staff had changed by breakfast so her enquiry was easier to make. This new clerk, a young man, was amiable but negative. She asked that if a telephone call was received, she should be brought from breakfast and after that it should be put through to her room. He said of course. She made sure he saw her return to the elevator after breakfast, but to her agony, he made no attempt to summon her. She locked the door of her room and sat on the chair that, as a consequence of the irregular rear geometry of the hotel overlooked the windows of the restaurant. She watched the diners as isolation descended. Slowly the breakfast traffic dissipated and the waiters tidied ready for lunch. Then all fell motionless.

What was he up to? Where was he? Who was he anyway? She searched for the elation she'd felt the previous day but could not find it. She was tired and dejected. She set aside her personal situation and instead forced herself to re-evaluate her understanding of the man that had dominated her consciousness for over a decade. He was not the person he had been during the war. She questioned if he had ever been that person or was that collection of impressions simply the fabrication of idealised memories? Certainly he'd been enigmatic, unique and fascinating, but all of that was a blatant fabrication on his part. He'd constructed an artificiality by making the artifice the actuality, and the pretence the truth. That had been mesmerising, and when he had combined it with an intensely deliberate fixation on her, the combination was compelling. She had thought he'd loved her but in the cold light of mellowing, it may not have been love at all. It may not even have been affection. It was passion, but passion is never permanent, she mused. Its transient expression need not be symptomatic of any other condition. It had been passionate. In truth it had not been affectionate. It had not been romantic, except when she had amplified its meaning in her mind.

Since their reconciliation he had never resumed the degree of fondness that she recalled him exhibiting in their wartime heyday. Her period had precluded full consummation, but even without that, she perceived his embraces to have been less frequent and less intense than she had expected. His general demeanour was distanced, his touch pragmatic, his kiss restrained. Or was she expecting too much of him? Their flight to supposed safety had seen him under stress, but even during the two days at the chalet he had taken few opportunities to signal joy at being in her company. Then the news of the demise of Edwin Heap had broken him.

She was being unfair.

She went to her suitcase and recovered the sketchbook. Flicking through it she relocated the faint and quick cartoon of herself sitting, clothed, looking out of a railway carriage window. It was closer to the middle of the book than the more detailed drawings of her, and there was no direct representation of a train compartment, but there were pencil marks that generated electric jolts as she looked more closely. There, in the plane of the window pane were just six or seven curves that could be interpreted as a torso, complete with the hint of a surgical scar. Or was she reading too much into it? Had she seen that detail before without consciously classifying it in her mind? Was that why she had imagined the torso in the window on the train to Stockholm?

Was this man manipulating her to a level she hardly dared to contemplate? Had he steered her mind as well as her physical self? That thought led her down the soft vortex of uninvited daytime sleep.

The phone in her room, jangled. She looked at her watch, it was just after eleven. Shaking off the bewildering sleep shroud, she stumbled to pick up the receiver.

"Yes?"

"Mrs Proctor?"

It took her a moment. "Oh – yes."

"There's someone to see you in reception."

"Someone?"

"Yes."

"Who?"

"They didn't give a name."

"Well who is it?"

"They didn't give a name." It sounded like the counter clerk who she imagined had sneered at her behind her back. "They said to say it's a second class delivery."

"What does he look like?"

"It's a woman."

"A woman."

"Yes."

"Very well. I'll be down directly."

"Thank you."

She hung up the receiver, but her hand remained glued to

it. Her feet wanted to probe roots into the floor. Who knew she was here? Who knew where she was? Could it be Vera, miraculously healed, and with sufficient skill to have sought her out? Ridiculous. Vera would have given her name or her Alice pseudonym. Could it be someone from the UK Secret Service? Did they deploy women? She thought they did. Could it be someone from the Soviet Secret service? Did they deploy women? She was sure they did. Second class. That was their code. Hers and his. She even entertained the thought – or hope – that it might be him in disguise. Absurd. He would have come straight to the room. For a moment, everything seemed so bewildering that she considered that she might still be asleep. She let go of the receiver, inhaled the aroma of the room, heard the detail of muffled movements. She wasn't asleep. She needed the toilet.

She took her clutch bag, locked her room, and went to the toilet. That gave her time to think. She thought she ought to go back to her bedroom and get her coat. She decided the most likely scenario was that she was about to be escorted away. She didn't go back to her room. She didn't take the elevator. She descended the stairs that snaked around it. Slowly.

As she approached the reception desk she heard voices. The receptionist saw her and sent a knowing sneer. Perhaps she always sported a knowing sneer? A clutch of three bulky figures were grouped facing inwards and talking in guttural syllables that carried no meaning for her. Two were men and one was a woman. They wore identical buff greatcoats. The woman had her back to her and did not break her monologue. Both men saw her and inclined their eyes but not their heads in her direction. She steadily approached them. She positioned herself just over the shoulder of the woman and waited for her to stop speaking.

She didn't stop.

"I'm Christina Proctor," she said.

The woman turned her head and uttered unfamiliar words. She looked to be fifty, and had a Slavonic fleshiness to her features.

"I'm Christina Proctor," she repeated.

The other woman made sounds.

Silence.

"Mrs Proctor?" said the receptionist.

"Yes?"

The receptionist nodded to a couch that was partly obscured by the statue of Queen Kristina on her horse. There she saw the boots and leggings of a slender young woman. Relief came as a cold blush. "Oh – I'm so sorry."

The buff trio resumed their conversation.

She made her way to the couch. Before she could speak the elfin face exploded into a grin. "Are you second class?" she said. Her accent was Scandinavian, her articulation was metropolitan, with a hint of Brooklyn.

"I have been."

"So have I. I have a parcel for you." By her fawn, wool-trimmed boots, was a red and white knitted carrier bag. She wore a duffel coat with the hood down, but her head was scarfed in deep scarlet.

"Is there somewhere we can go?"

"Let's go to the lounge."

They found a green leather sofa in one corner of the lounge. There were only two other individuals in there. He read a Swedish newspaper, she a hard-backed book.

"I'm Emira."

They shook hands.

"Christina."

"For now."

She hesitated. "Yes."

Emira chuckled. She appeared all of twenty-five but may have been more. Her duffel coat was black with wooden pegs stitched on with red cord. The same thread made piping around the opening of the hood. "Pic sent me," she said.

"Is he all right?"

"He's fine. He sent this." She produced a thick medium-sized envelope from her bag. "You can open it, but perhaps, discreetly."

She took the parcel, slid her thumbnail under the seal, tore the end open and peered inside. There was a stack of banknotes and a blue booklet, that she instantly recognised as a UK passport.

"Fifty krona," said Emira.

"For me?"

"For you."

"From?"

"From Pic, of course. He said he promised you it."

"Where is he?"

"At home. He can't move. He's being watched. If he came here he would be followed. He sent me."

Suddenly she felt vulnerable again. "Were you followed?"

Emira chuckled again. "Why would anyone follow me?"

"Because you've come from him."

"No I haven't. He sent me. I don't live with him."

"Of course not."

"Not anymore."

She selected the next question from a number of more tempting alternatives. "Then how did he send you?"

"Telephone."

"Ah."

"And then some written instructions that I collected from . . . a place. He asked me to bring you the second class delivery."

Her hand was in the parcel. She didn't want to extract the contents, it felt too brazen. The man with the paper looked on the edge of dozing, the woman with the book was preparing to turn a page. She peered into the envelope again and angled the contents to see them better. She lowered her voice. "This is a passport."

Emira grinned. "Check it."

She extracted the passport and opened it. It contained the photograph that Klas had taken, and the name Mrs Christina Proctor. There was a London address. Kew. The date of birth was within two years of her own. "What exactly am I checking?"

"That you are happy with it."

"Happy?"

"Note the stamp. You flew into Stockholm on January 4th. From London Heathrow. Arrived just before midday. British European Airways. Vickers Viscount aircraft. Your journey to the city centre was by bus. It is just conceivable you would check in here when you did."

"Why do I need to know all this?"

"To be consistent. With Pic."

"Has he been questioned?"

"Not as far as I know. Just in case. Are you happy with the stamp?" Emira pointed to the Stockholm ink imprint.

She was puzzled by the question. "Well . . . yes."

Emira beamed broadly. "I did it. And the London departure."

"This is a stolen passport?"

"Stolen?"

"How did you get it?"

"From Pic."

"He said he chose the name because of this hotel."

Emira shrugged. "It was already in the passport."

She held the moment and considered carefully. She'd had enough. "What is Pic's full name?"

Emira's grin had a sad-clown quality. "Colin Proctor." The tone was confirmatory but the associated facial expression was inquisitorial.

"You said you lived with him."

"You need thicker fabrics to keep out the Swedish winter. Let me take you shopping."

"Would you?"

"Pic asked me to."

"Come to our room. I'll just freshen up and get my coat."

They went via the elevator. To her horror, when she opened the bedroom door, she saw that she'd left the sketchbook on the chair by the window. She immediately sat upon the chair, scooping the book to one side in the feeble hope her summer skirt might hide it. Placing her clutch bag on top of the book she took out her compact and lipstick and reinforced the coverage. It matched Emira's headscarf, which she had now removed. Her hair was straight and auburn but perhaps not naturally so. There were lots of burning questions to be asked but the thought of new clothes that were appropriate to the climate overrode all other priorities.

When Emira went to the mirror to needlessly adjust her hair, the poser managed to slip the sketchbook beneath the cushion on the chair. Before they left the room, Emira donned the scarf again. As they handed the key in, Emira exchanged a few words in Swedish with the receptionist.

The excursion was very successful. New winter boots, a new coat, three thick skirts, a pair of slacks, two blouses, a sweater, a woollen scarf and a pair of leather gloves. Both women enjoyed the experience and their combination of retail know-how and local bargain locations made for a satisfying expedition. As they made their way back to the Hotel Drottning

Kristina, Emira became more open. She said she and Pic had co-operated on many tasks. This was not the first time she had 'adjusted' a passport for Pic. By profession she was an artist, but found it difficult to carve out a living from painting. Things were better during the summer when she could sell her work to tourists.

"How did you meet Pic?"

"Modelling," said Emira. "I sat for him."

"Me too."

"I know; I've seen the picture."

"Which one?"

"On the train. Looking at your nude reflection."

"I haven't seen that one."

"It's how I was sure that you were the second class lady." Emira was holding half of the store-branded paper carrier bags. She bounced them playfully off her knees as they strode along.

The muse felt able to try one of the suspended questions. "You don't live with him anymore?"

"Not anymore."

They walked a little further, still casually window shopping as they went. A patent leather handbag took their attention. Emira said, "How about that Mrs Proctor?"

"I'm not married to him."

"I know that."

"He told you?"

"He didn't need to. You couldn't possibly be married to him."

"Why not?"

"Because I am."

TWENTY-ONE

She reported the theft to the receptionist.

"A sketchbook?"

"My husband's." She wondered if she should say that, but she was in a state. She'd checked the chair as soon as she'd got back in the room. Then she'd searched the room. Then she'd raced down to reception in hope that Emira was still there. They'd said farewell at the ground floor door of the elevator. Emira wasn't there.

She remembered the exchange Emira had had with the receptionist when they'd deposited the key. There'd been another, also in Swedish, when they'd reclaimed it. It was the same receptionist to whom she was now reporting the theft – the young woman that she presumed to have a disparaging perspective.

"Nothing has been handed in."

She suddenly remembered that she'd left the room key in the bedroom and had not locked the door. "I need to speak to the manager."

The receptionist summoned a middle-aged man, who had been rifling through papers at the far end of the counter. "Herr Lund?"

She doubted he was the manager.

He strolled over to them. Hair slicked, moustache combed,

three-piece suit and bow tie. "Is there a problem?"

"A sketchbook has gone missing from my room. While I was out. This morning, or this afternoon."

"A . . . sketch . . . book?"

"A book with drawings. My husband's."

The man looked mildly confused and artificially concerned. The conversation continued. Was she sure? Had she looked everywhere? She should look again. They would check with the maid. They would telephone her room.

She returned to her room, knowing that there had now been another ten-minute period during which the room had been unlocked. She searched everywhere again. The book was not there. The telephone rang. It was the senior staff member. They had asked the maid, and she had not seen a book, but they would continue their inquiries.

She put on some of her new clothes and while doing so, she focused her memory on the conversations between the receptionist and Emira, as if by trying hard she could in some way make sense of the Swedish words they'd used. She couldn't even remember the sounds. The tone stood out. It was hushed and confidential. Or was that simply her imagination taking control?

Once she was dressed, she sat on the bed and reviewed the conversation she'd had with Emira at the end of their shopping expedition. Following her revelation regarding being married, they'd diverted to a café not far from the hotel. Emira led her to a table in the corner overlooking the January street as dusk settled and the street lights came on. "I modelled for Pic," she explained. "We got on really well despite him being . . ."

"Evasive?"

"What?" asked Emira.

"Evasive. Not telling you everything."

"Yes. But I quite liked that."

"Me too," said the poser.

"Before long we were dating. Then he asked me to marry him. I said yes. Two artists in love. Why not?"

"Then he must have told you his name."

"His name is Colin Proctor."

"Then you must be Emira Proctor."

"I was for two years."

"Was?"

"I moved out. So I'm using my maiden name again."

"Is that legal?"

"Artists don't care about laws. If we did we wouldn't be artists. An artist is a rule-breaker."

"What made you move out?"

"In Sweden separation is straightforward if both people agree. It's better if they first live apart."

"But why?"

"In Sweden we have a 'no fault' divorce. That's what we're applying for." Emira's eyes said more than her mouth did. "It's simpler. Less painful."

"In theory."

"In practice."

"So you're saying there was 'no fault'?"

"That's what we're saying."

"But in reality?"

"Artists are rule-breakers."

"His fault?"

"We paint the rules. We paint the breaks. We paint over the breaks."

"I'd like to see some of your paintings."

"I'll take you to my workshop – at home and show you. Another day. Not today." She produced a pencil, tore a tiny strip of paper from the wrapping around the skirts they had bought. "I'm going to give you my telephone number."

"Could you also give me Pic's number?"

"He doesn't have one."

"You said he'd called you."

"From a telephone box."

"Oh. Could you give me his address?"

Emira shook her head. "It's being watched. You'd be seen. You would be followed."

"Are you not watched? Are you not followed?"

Emira added a little swirl beneath the number she had written. "Well, if I am, I expect one of us will soon find out." Emira looked at the poser and the poser scanned the café. Any one of the other customers might be trailing them, and so might the man standing waiting across the street. Emira slipped her the scrap of paper. "It is my mother's apartment. If you telephone, she might answer. I'll be in touch with you again in two days if Pic is still tied down."

"The photograph."

"Which photograph?"

"The passport photograph. How did you get it from Pic?"

"There are places where we leave things, for the other one to collect."

"Including the money?"

"I made the money."

"It's your money?"

"It's no one's money. I made it."

"You mean it's counterfeit?"

"It's a work of art. Not original. Reproductions I'm afraid."

The muse was now less comfortable about visiting Emira and viewing more of her artwork. "You make money?"

"Literally."

"And passports."

"I didn't make the passport. It's genuine. I simply retouched it. A few stamps, and swapped my picture for yours."

"Your picture!"

"It was my passport. I was Mrs Proctor. I still am."

"But Emira – not Christina."

"When we travelled I became Christina. Just like you have done."

Her mind was whirring, juggling, sorting, finding links, finding gaps. "But this is a British passport."

"Of course. So was the first Christina Proctor."

"The first?"

"Pic's first wife."

She dined alone again that night. The waiter remarked on her new clothes. She joked about finally getting around to winter shopping. He laughed. He was slim, average height, white shirt with detachable collar, black waistcoat, black trousers, bow tie. She asked his name. He said it was Torn. She asked him how long he'd worked at the Drottning Kristina. He said almost nine years. Quite the expert she said. She could tell. He thanked her. She asked his age. He was twenty-four. She squinted endearingly. A good age. Still plenty of time for adventures. He said that service was an adventure; and also an honour, especially when the guests were as gracious as she. What else did he do apart from waiting at tables? All kinds of things. The bar, room service, and a lot of stock control. Special tasks for guests.

Room service. Would he bring her a Scotch and soda at about nine-thirty?

He would.

She thought a great deal about Christina Proctor. She had bequeathed a floating identity that had been deposited on a succession of women. So what had happened to the original Christina?

Emira said that Pic had told her that Christina had died during the war, in England, during an air raid.

When?

1944.

The date had stunned her so much that Emira had ordered more coffee. When did Pic and Christina marry? Pic would not talk about it, but they were not married for very long. Less than a year Emira thought.

Had Pic been in love with Christina?

Emira said that Pic's love was a peculiar thing. He claimed to love lots of people but she thought that ultimately he was in love with himself, or some construct of himself, something shapeless, without physical form, without a label.

Untitled.

Yes.

Did Emira believe Pic's account?

No, but neither did she disbelieve it. Ultimately Pic was fascinated by façade and delusion.

Smoke and mirrors.

Emira was not familiar with that expression, but yes, Pic was a person who liked both those things. She looked injured.

Why was she helping Pic?

She wasn't. She was helping Christina.

What was Pic playing at? Was he really Colin Proctor? It seemed a far too ordinary name. According to Emira the 'Pic' moniker was a contraction of his schoolboy nickname brought about by his painting prowess: Picasso Proctor. This fitted with what Pic had said.

Her esteem was mortally wounded to discover that he was already twice-married. She wondered if that, despite his assertion that the first Christina had died during the war, the duality could be a bigamous one. The greatest wound was delivered not by the fact of his matrimony – if it was fact – but by the date of it. If he married Christina in 1944 he had done so while she – his 'adored' muse was aching for news that he still breathed.

She no longer doubted that he loved her; she knew he did not. Here she was in a loveless cold war cul-de-sac. To begin with she thought he had saved her from an untimely autopsy, but the more she reflected on the unfolding facts the more she became convinced he had simply placed her, as a detached grand master might move a chess piece. She kindled a cruel strand of suspicion that he would never return to the hotel Drottning Kristina, or to her. She had been moved to queen's knight four: a sacrificial square.

Methodical, logical, meticulous. Those were the qualities that had resulted in her wartime posting. That's what she was eventually told. Certainly they had always been the triad of her default modus operandi. They had solicited praise from the nuns and spinsters who supervised her studies at the convent school. They had attracted approving murmurs from the officers and civilian academics at her base. They had gone unacknowledged but not unnoticed during her post-war decade at the department store. Now they would serve her and her alone.

She had other qualities, assets and abilities that had largely gone unrecognised hitherto, and had reposed dormant within her like once and future acolytes perpetually awaiting their summons. She summoned them now. She was patient, she was astute, she was calm in a crisis – even when her mind stalled and her emotional aeroplane fell into a flat spin. She could recover. She always recovered, and while she recovered, she saw clearly the causes of the trauma and the potential balm she could apply. She had the head to analyse carefully, the heart to empathise pragmatically and the courage to cope hopefully.

She remained puzzled as to why she should have been chosen to be the courier of the code within her. She was still at a loss to know exactly who had selected her. It might have been her surgeon, it might have been his superiors, it might have been his paymasters. Whoever it was, they had chosen the wrong person.

She considered the possible sketchbook thieves logically. Most likely was the chambermaid, but why would she feel especially covetous of a sketchbook and why risk her job by removing it? Unless, of course, she was acting under instruction.

The second candidate, perhaps acting in cahoots with the maid, was the receptionist. She recognised that this suspicion was founded entirely on the hushed conversation she'd had with Emira who, distasteful as the thought was, must line up as the third suspect. Pic's current wife could not have removed the book while they were both in the room, she would have noticed, but she may be the next link in the chain. From chambermaid, to receptionist, to Pic's current wife to . . . Pic? If Pic had suspected the sketchbook was there he had had a hundred opportunities to secure it for himself. After all, it belonged to him.

The logic of her reasoning led her straight back to the most likely explanation being an opportunist theft by the maid, yet in her analysis it was also the least probable. In trying to solve one problem she had exposed another, not only must she wrestle with the problem of who stole the book, but also the conundrum of why they thought it was worth taking.

At precisely nine-thirty Torn knocked on the bedroom door. She summoned him in and he entered expertly balancing her drink on a small silver salver. He did not shut the door, but neither did he leave it wide open. She was sitting in the chair by the window, but rose to meet him. She took the glass and slipped a krona into his hand, making a firm and slightly prolonged contact with his flesh. He thanked her, and she saw that he noticed that she still clutched one of the new silver five-krona coins.

"Will there be anything else, madam?"

She held the moment and took a step closer to him. "Yes."

He studied the third button from the collar of her blouse. "How may I be of service to you?"

"Have you heard about my theft?"

"Theft?"

He was feigning ignorance, but she didn't mind that. Sometimes deception was discretion. He seemed skilled in discretion. "A sketchbook was taken from that chair while I was out today."

"Are you sure, madam? Could I help you to search . . .?"

"It was taken." She slipped the five-krona coin into his waistcoat pocket, but did not withdraw her fingers. Instead she used them to exert a little pressure as if she was about to tug him closer. "Could you make some – careful – enquiries for me?"

"Careful?"

"I would be very grateful."

"Of course."

"But, Torn, this is just between you and me. You do understand, don't you?" She applied slightly more tension to his waistcoat, peered into his pupils, sipped her drink, and partially pursed her wetted lips.

"Of course."

"I'd be grateful for any information you might discover."

"I'll make some careful enquiries."

"Thank you." She released him and for another silent moment neither moved nor spoke. She knew what he wanted to try. He was too well trained. Too disciplined. Too discrete. That was good, though she really wouldn't have minded, in fact it would have hooked him more securely.

"Will there be anything else?"

"Yes." She collected two envelopes from the dressing table. "Could you post these for me?"

"Of course." He offered his salver, but she moved it aside and slipped the envelopes inside his waistcoat, pushing them down until they were out of sight, and ensuring that he felt her fingers against his chest through his shirt.

"No – could *you* post them for me. You."

"Of course."

She drank again. "Thank you." She stretched a downturned hand in the direction of his mouth.

He took it, kissed it, released it, made a flustered turn and grasped the door handle.

"I shall report back as soon as I have anything to disclose."

"Thank you, Torn. I will be deeply obliged."

He closed the door gently, but the sound of his receding footsteps had an unsteady urgency. If he was loyal, or sufficiently mercenary, she may have made progress, if he was not, she may have hastened her demise.

TWENTY-TWO

7th January 1957

Dearest Wonder Lady,

I'm so sorry, my dear Alice, that I had to do a Cheshire Cat departure, but trust me, I could not discern an alternative. I'm sure that the address on the hotel notepaper must have caused you some surprise. I was somewhat surprised too, I can tell you, and totally unprepared, having picked up the suitcase containing only summer outfits mindlessly packed in the panic to not miss our plane! Thankfully a most kind Swedish lady by the name of Emira Proctor came to my aid and helped me to secure something more suitable for this delightful, but rather chilly, city.

I do not know when I'll be able to see you again, but I doubt it will be nowhere near as soon as I would like! Please give my regards to T, along with my apologies for not being able to tell him I was flitting. I do hope that I find you well, and that soon - vice versa.

Much love,

Christina Proctor (Mrs)

7th January 1957

Dearest Tinky,

I must apologise for the sudden break in communication and I do hope that you do not take it personally. It was neither intended or expected. Events overtook me. It was all a bit of a flap, but actually went like ABC or as we used to say Anson, Benson, Christ! The boy will not be back at Mount Farm ever again I'm afraid. I hope that I will be able to explain myself to you sooner rather than later. I would find it most agreeable if that process could be accelerated. Please be aware, however, that those you might imagine would be most suitable to assist, may provide the greatest peril. Anyway, at least now you know where I am – or by the time you read this – where I was.

Tally-ho!

The Mad Hatter.

It was a horrendous risk writing the letters. She imagined Torn taking them straight to the receptionist who would slice them open without hesitation and then make a telephone call that would seal her fate. She knew, however, that she had to start taking decisive action. The very least she could do would be to make the two people that she most trusted aware of where she was. It would be days, perhaps even weeks, before they received the letters and by then she may have moved, or been moved, or not even be at all, but she would have left a trail.

It was all very tenuous. Vera was allegedly severely injured, but the poser had her doubts about the veracity of that anecdote, mainly because she had learned to doubt all of Pic's words, and especially his promises. By also writing to her new ally, Tinky, she doubled the chances of someone being aware of her unfolding difficulties. There was little they could do. She had desperately wanted to write more patently but something told her she should be obscure. She hoped that they might be resourceful enough to do something to help, but if they couldn't, they would at least have some hint about what might have happened to her.

The next morning Torn was not on duty at breakfast and the receptionist, about whom she had suspicions, was not behind the desk. She went to the hotel lounge again and found a copy of *The Times* dated Saturday 5th January 1957. She consulted the Swedish papers to confirm that it was, in fact, Tisdag - Tuesday - 8th. Once again she looked in vain for any column inch that might in some way relate to her adventure; a plane crash, a stolen or missing Avro Anson, or a tragic accident in a London Theatre. All the while she kept her eyes open for Torn but he was nowhere to be seen. She was not going to sit around and stew all day waiting for either Torn or her alleged husband to put in an appearance. She had a plan. She thought of utilising the number that Emira had given her, but decided it was a little soon to do that, and she was wary of trying the Swedish telephone system, instead she went to the reception desk and asked Herr Lund if there had been any progress regarding her missing property. He regretted there had not. She asked if she might consult a copy of the Stockholm telephone directory, and he obliged by handing over a well-thumbed volume. She turned to the pages listing surnames starting with P and to her shock saw Proctor, Colin, leaping out at her with not only a telephone number, but also an address. 57 Upplandsgattan.

"Excuse me, Herr Lund?"

"Madam?"

She thought he perused the page flattened before her. "May I have a pencil and paper please?"

"Of course."

She noted the number and the address, then closed the directory and returned the pencil.

"Thank you, Herr Lund."

"Madam."

She was instantly energised. She knew the dangers but was determined not to sit and wait to see what transpired, but instead she would gain as much understanding as she could and then apply it accordingly. That was the logical thing to do. She had the clothes, she had the confidence. She went straight to her room, which had already been cleaned and tidied. She adjusted her hair, added more lipstick, then put on her new coat and boots. She slipped her clutch bag inside one of the store bags she had acquired the previous day and took a cursory glance around the room before departing.

She froze.

There was a slight bulge under the topmost bedcover.

She snapped the sheets back, and there, protruding slightly from between the pillows was the sketchbook.

She felt completely alone and entirely surrounded. She heard the whispering of a thousand invisible gargoyles. A rivulet of sweat rippled down her spine. Her underwear stuck to her by using perspiration as a paste. She felt it adhere to the contour of her appendectomy scar. Disbelieving what she saw she dropped the store bag and pounced onto the bed. It was the book. No doubt about that. But was it all there?

She flicked through the volume, quickly scouring the spine for any tears. She found none. She turned the pages more slowly, pausing longer on the pages with her own image. Everything was intact. She sat and thought, imagining who had returned it, how and why. Once again the chambermaid was the most likely. In probability she would be close at hand, still at work, but which person was she, and how well might she speak English? Could anything be gained by tackling her? Was it better to not even let it be known she had the book back in her possession? She checked her watch. Ten minutes to eleven.

She buried the book among the summer clothes in her suitcase and snapped it shut, and locked it. She put the suitcase at the rear of the wardrobe, checked how much money she had in her purse then locked the room, handed in the key, and set out across damp Stockholm streets.

A dressing of white edged the carriageways but there had not been any recent falls so in the main thoroughfares, tyres and shoes had worn it away, but outlines remained where pavements met walls, along window ledges, balconies, protruding architraves and, of course, on all the rooftops.

She had memorised the way to the harbour. It was simple from her hotel, turn left out of the door and stay on that main road – Birger Jarlsgatan. She wasn't going all the way to the harbour, she was going to a specific shop where she had spotted tourist maps for sale. Having purchased one, she moved half a block away and consulted the index. Upplandsgattan was in square D1. A quick reference to street signs enabled her to determine that she was in square G4. There was a distance to cover, but the scale suggested it was by no means onerous. She didn't set off straight away, instead she retraced more steps from the previous day and found one of the department stores they had visited. She bought a red and white knitted hood of the traditional Sami style that covered the ears and had long side straps. She bought a white headscarf also. Before leaving the store she donned both, hiding all of her hair inside the scarf and putting the knitted hat over that. She used the clothing department mirrors to check her appearance. It wasn't a disguise, but she estimated that, in profile, she was almost unrecognisable. She checked the map and set off for square D1

As she made her way she reviewed her plan. Heeding Emira's words that Pic's place was being watched, she would begin by walking straight past the address on the far side of the street. She would gain a first impression, but also assess the danger by scrutinising the street for suspicious persons and the places from which they might be watching the property. She would continue for a block or two, take a right-angled turn, pause somewhere, then make a return journey but this time taking a closer look at the address by going down the pavement on the side where it was. She had no other intentions but if, as with many of the buildings she passed, it was an apartment block with a common entrance she might risk going in and trying to ascertain on which floor he resided. She would do no more. She would not surprise him and present herself. Not yet.

The walk to Upplandsgatan took twenty minutes. Had she been in England she would have described the street as Georgian. The thoroughfare was wide, the buildings mostly five stories. She found number fifty-seven. It was an impressive stone structure in clean pale grey and with arched windows on the ground and top floors, but rectangular ones on the three stories between. Each window had a decorative keystone above and the central column of the building protruded in relief. It bore an ornamental panel with the date 1902 embossed, so her architectural appraisal was wide of the mark in time, but not in style. The clean perpendicular lines and spare décor were, to her mind, distinctly Georgian in appearance. The entrance was narrow and tall, but it was the main ground-floor window that made the greatest impact. At the pavement level the property was, without doubt, a commercial outlet. It was an art gallery.

High in the window a painted board shouted the words *Colin Proctor* and *England*. Beneath that a number of easels were visible supporting what looked from across the road to be cubist works. But one picture had deliberate prominence. It was not cubist. It was far more realistic. She'd seen it only two days before in the sketchbook. It was a portrait of her.

Her calm plan evaporated. She was already crossing the road, and she hadn't even checked for traffic. If anyone was watching she was walking straight towards their focal point, but she could not help herself. As she drew close to the façade a passer-by faltered in his step, uttered what might have been an apology but was more likely a profanity, and danced past. She made no response. She was transfixed.

The portrait was beautiful. The facial detail was impeccable, save for the fact it showed her as she was a decade earlier. Her face had lost some of that tautness of youthful maturity, but there it was, preserved in paint, exactly as she had forgotten it. There was the velvet crimson lipstick she favoured during the war. There, on the right side of her face, was the way her hair naturally curled when springing from wet to dry, but on the left side was where the ultra-realism melted into something more, as ringlets of hair ran into rivulets of paint. The base of her neck did the same. Down in the bottom right quadrant of the picture the three-dimensional doppelgänger flattened into two-dimensional signifiers. She studied to see if the drips formed the pattern she'd discovered in the sketchbook, but they did not. The torso reflected in the window was ghostly white just as she'd imagined it only a few days previously. How could he have known? The background imagery was coniferous and Scandinavian, just as it had been on their journey, except that it appeared less wintery. The aqueous green of her eyes sparkled joy but stared at imagined terror suggesting that the torso was a daydream rather than a reflection. The scar was fierce and fresh. Five stitches.

She had no idea how long she stood looking through a window at the painting of herself looking through a window, but there came a moment when she was aware that her own reflection was superimposed on the reflection in the painting and that behind her, across the street, were half a hundred windows, any one of which might hide a person spying on her. If that person had a telescope he must surely see her resemblance to the reproduction, despite her attempts to change her appearance. Within the same moment she noticed the gallery attendant, a female, glance away. She could not fail to have perceived the similarity. The woman turned and moved deeper into the store.

The muse returned her troubled attention to the portrait. It was so different from the one she had seen in Kendal's Lodge. He'd moved closer, cutting off her torso and placing it in the window, where it could not be a reflection, but instead stood as a symbol of her imagination. Or as a sign to an informed onlooker. She was clothed, and this was principally a head and shoulders study and as such it was superb. He had every surface, every highlight, every freckle, every manicured eyelash. He had the line of her lips, and the unwitting gap of worry trapped between them. Most of all, he had the fear in her eyes, a fear she did not have when he knew her during the war. It was the fear she had found after he had relocated her just over a week ago. She felt a different fear now, but this fear was not generated by her portrait, but by the more abstract work positioned next to it. That work was a collage in the style of the early cubist artists. It was mixed media with gouache, charcoal, pasted paper, newspaper cuttings and pasted card. There was a medical theme, with hand-drawn surgical instruments and receptacles, but also pasted sections of printed material which she could not read, though some looked to be newspaper advertisements for surgical procedures. One detail was at odds with the rest and it drew her cornea with a tangible suction. That component she could read. It was a business card, for the hotel Drottning Kristina where she was saying. The juxtaposition of the two paintings rang a peal of alarm bells in her head. Her picture next to her address in the window of his gallery. This was more than betrayal. This was taking aim. Despite those thoughts she discovered that she was already making her way into the shop.

The woman came to meet her. Forty, she thought. Very smart. Black skirt, black cardigan, blue blouse, mid-denier nylons, glossy shoes with delicate silver buckles. The smile was flawed. It failed to disguise recognition. She spoke a greeting in Swedish. The poser replied in firm, almost aggressive English.

"I'm looking for Mr Colin Proctor."

The attendant's English was calipered but clear. "Oh, I am afraid he is not here at the moment."

"Not at home?"

"At home?"

"This is where he lives."

"This is his gallery. Do have some interest in his work? Or is it a personal inquiry?"

"I'd just like to speak to him."

"He is abroad at the moment."

"Abroad?"

"That is correct."

It was not correct. It sounded like a standard deflection. "Could you make sure he is not here?"

The attendant looked bewildered. She executed a half twirl with open palms. "You can see. Today there is only me."

"Does he live over the shop?"

"I'm sorry?"

"Does he have an apartment here?"

She sniggered. "Not here."

"Not here."

"No."

"It's in the telephone book. Under his name. Here."

"This is his gallery. Mr Proctor does not live here."

"Where does he live?"

The attendant clasped her hands and rubbed them slowly together. "Do you know Mr Proctor?"

"We've met from time to time."

"Ah!" She gave a half laugh. "Professionally?"

"I sat for him."

"Oh – I see." She faked a gasp of uncertain identification, and looked askance. The poser waited for more, but it didn't come.

"Well, if he's not here . . ."

The attendant made a dart for the desk. "Let me note your name."

"No, it doesn't matter."

"I'm sure he'd like to know you called."

"He's abroad?"

"He went home for Christmas and the New Year."

"Home?"

"To England."

"I thought he lived here."

"He doesn't live in Stockholm."

"In Sweden."

"Oh yes, he lives in Sweden most of the year."

"Where?"

"Where?"

"Where does he live?"

She turned a leaf of the notepad. The pencil was perfectly sharpened, and poised just above the third line. "What name shall I say."

"I don't have a name."

"Oh."

"I'm untitled." She smiled, swirled round, surveying the easels and walls in one continuous swoop. She saw no more portraits, no other scars, and strode out onto the many-windowed street.

When the shop door closed and she stepped from the foyer she was vividly aware of all the panes of glass facing her. As she set off southwards, a figure in the corner of her eye, stepped out of an apartment doorway across the road, and strode in her direction. She knew better than to look back and knew also that his movement was almost certainly coincidental to her own. Nevertheless, she increased her pace. She hadn't fully registered him, other than his overcoat was black and he wore a squat fur hat that she associated with soviet leaders.

Her route was simple. She had memorised it from the map. Passing the sacred edifice of Gustav Vasa Kyrka she need only remain on Upplandsgatan for its entire length to arrive at a square very close to the railway station. She would then turn left and head eastwards across the city to arrive at her hotel. She would need to consult the map again once she had left the station behind. The sun was sinking beyond the buildings on her right and only the top two storeys of the blocks across the road caught its feeble and hazily frosted light. The effect was to render those buildings even more sinister, with their upper-most windows becoming even more eye-like. The urge to turn and see if she was being followed was overwhelming. She resisted for several blocks, but Upplandsgatan had many shops and there came an opportunity to step into the recessed doorway of what appeared to be a pharmaceutical store and by doing so she could seem to look in the window whilst actually looking back along the road. There he was. Still on his side of the street, still walking in the same direction as she, and looking towards her. She peeled out of the doorway and swiftly shuffled for several yards in an attempt to regain the ground she had lost by stopping. She knew that the next test would be to turn off and risk losing her bearings to see if he followed, or better still if she could lose him. She might lose herself, but Stockholm had a relatively simple grid-pattern street layout, and she had her map. The traffic was intermittent, and she took advantage of the end of a busy spurt to dash across the road and then take the next left away from her planned path. Ironically she noted that she was now on a street named Observatoriegatan. The day was fading fast and the light spillage from the shops was already competing with the sun which barely touched the tops of the naked trees that she could see populating the parkland at the end of the street ahead of her. She found another window at which to wait. This shop sold shoes and other leather goods. The window display was decorated with seasonal electric lights and the suggestion of snow made from what she first thought was straw, but then determined that is was thousands of curled strands and shards of leather. She glanced towards Upplandsgatan and there, less distinct than before in the chilled backlight, but unmistakeable, was her pursuer.

He had gained on her. He had flicked his coat collar up, and with hands in pockets and taking stretched strides, he cut a determined figure. She ran.

When she reached the garden space she ran right across the roads almost causing car accidents at each side. She strained for breath but ploughed on taking random twists and turns and alternating between running and a hurried walk. Soon she had to stop, but she'd gone so far she felt confident she had shaken him off. She took one last bearing as the sun finally went and found her orientation. She was on Eriksbergsgatan. She unfolded the city map beneath a streetlamp and to her relief saw that she was close to her hotel.

The sight of the Drottning Kristina was both reassuring and forbidding. It was the safest place for her in Stockholm, but knowing what she now knew, it was also the most dangerous. This place too, might be under observation. She checked her step as she approached. She had never arrived from that direction before, from the north, and she instinctively veered off

as she arrived at the triangular block in which it was situated.
The east window of her bedroom faced the rear of another
block which comprised living apartments and offices. She
wondered if she could find entry to the gap between it and the
hotel and hence locate a service entrance. She was brazen
enough to enter that way, but she could find no such opening
and was soon approaching the main entrance again. She pulled
her new hat tight over her brow, buried herself amid a bustle of
folk hurrying along and darted through the door at the last
minute.

Thirty seconds later she had removed both hat and scarf,
buried them in her bag and was at the reception desk, and Torn
was handing her the room key.

The reception area was busy. A group were checking in.
The receptionist she didn't trust was dealing with them. A
couple were boisterously checking out. They didn't sound
Scandinavian. The man sounded drunk, the woman less than
sober. Herr Lund was falsely laughing and raising his voice
cheerily repeating something which made the grateful intoxicated
one contort and wheeze. Torn held onto the key when she tried
to take it.

"Half an hour," he said. "Room service."

She was still slightly panting from her exertions. "All right.
I'll ring down."

He nodded.

She took the elevator. The cage it made overwhelmed her
with warm safety.

"An accident."

"She is very sorry," said Torn

"Who is?"

He moved her Scotch and soda from his salver to the
dressing table. "Astrid."

"Who is Astrid?"

"The chambermaid."

She took the Scotch and sat on the edge of the bed. "Close
the door Torn and sit down."

He closed the door and sat on the chair by the window,
after first closing the curtains. "If I'm seen sitting I'll get into
trouble."

159

She got up and drew the curtain at the other window then returned to sit on the bed, but closer to where he was. "How was it an accident?"

"First you must understand that Astrid is very sorry. . ."

"Yes, alright, but how did it happen? What happened? How did the book disappear?"

"Second, you must appreciate that she is very frightened. She could lose her job."

"Did she take the sketchbook?"

"It was an accident. It got mixed with the laundry."

"How?"

"She doesn't know, but when questions started being asked she remembered moving it from the chair to the bed, and she realised it must have got gathered up in the sheets. Fortunately, the laundry had not been done and she went and searched and found it."

"Why didn't she just say so?"

"She would have got in trouble. She might have lost her job."

"I wouldn't have let that happen."

Torn smiled indulgently and shrugged. "They can be very strict and. . ."

"And what?"

"It's not the first mistake Astrid has made. She has been warned before."

"So she put it back."

"Today. This morning. You found it?"

"I found it."

"It is . . . all right? Not damaged."

"It is not damaged."

"Good." Torn leaned forwards in the chair. "I need to ask you."

"It's all right. I won't say anything."

"Will you say . . . will you say that it was your mistake? That you found it where you hadn't looked."

She studied Torn. She wondered if his attitude to Astrid was more than just sympathetic.

"For example," said Torn, "it might have slipped down between the top of the bed and the wall."

"It might have."

"Could you say that?"

"Did you post my letters?"

"Yes, I posted them myself." He slipped his hand into his trouser pocket. "I got extra stamps for you. And these." He passed her two small perforated rows of stamps and two airmail envelopes. "You should send airmail. It will be much quicker. Look, just one of those stamps."

That small act of thoughtfulness lifted the tension that had been in her solar plexus since arriving at the gallery window, and diluted it. "Thank you, Torn."

"You are welcome, Mrs Proctor. Astrid is very sorry."

"Will you do one more thing for me Torn?"

"Of course."

"Will you look at Mr Proctor's registration card, and copy me the address that he put on it?"

"It won't be easy. I'm not often assigned to the reception."

"You mustn't be discovered doing it."

"I think I will be able to."

"Thank you. I think I may be able to eventually find the sketchbook between the bed and the wall."

"Thank you."

"Or better still Astrid could have found it there this morning, when she changed the sheets."

"I'll get you that address," said Torn.

She dined alone again that night. It was now three full days since she had spoken to Pic. He had not been in touch since leaving the hotel after breakfast on the previous Saturday, except indirectly via Emira. There were several dimensions to the worry caused by his absence. She had rapidly learned to question everyone involved, and she had her doubts that Emira was being completely honest, but as yet she had no proof to the contrary, so the preferred scenario was that Pic was indeed lying low, and unable to return to the hotel for fear of betraying her. It was entirely feasible that if he suspected his telephone was being bugged, then he might not feel he could even risk a call to the hotel. He could, however, make one from a call box as Emira had claimed he had done to her with instructions for the passport and money. But what if Emira's phone was also bugged? They – whoever 'they' were – must be aware of his relationship with her. Unless he had spoken to her in some sort of agreed code. That was entirely within Pic's palette of curious techniques. Another terrible possibility was that something had befallen Pic. He may have been taken. The possible consequences of that were too distasteful to contemplate. He may, at that very moment be drawing on all his resilience in order to keep her safe. Another alternative was that he was no longer alive. She preferred that scenario to any in which he was in pain. There was one prospect worse than all the others, however, and that was the one in which he had quite simply abandoned her.

Torn appeared at the table and presented her with the menu. "Good evening, Mrs Proctor. Just yourself again this evening?"

"I'm afraid so, Torn, unless you have heard anything to the contrary?"

"I'm afraid not, madam. Shall I give you a few minutes to decide?"

"Oh I don't think so." She opened the menu. Paper-clipped inside was a strip of plain notepaper, bearing an address. "Oh," she said.

"There was no telephone number," he said.

She peered closely at Torn's handwriting. "Where is . . . Mariefred?"

"About fifty kilometres away."

"In which direction?"

Torn thought for a moment. "West."

"Fifty kilometres?"

"About that."

"Thank you, Torn." She carefully scrunched the slip of paper into her palm and returned the menu. "I'll start with the salmon, and then have the beef."

"Madam." He inclined a slight bow and went about his duties.

Fifty kilometres? He had given an address fifty kilometres away. It must have been a cover. After all, it would look odd to record an address in central Stockholm. Torn's risky work may have told her nothing, or something very unsettling indeed. Was her 'husband' fifty kilometres away? For all she knew he might be fifty thousand kilometres away. She was alone. It was a familiar feeling. She had been alone since she had left home mid-way through the war. For a fleeting few weeks in 1943 Pic had promised companionship. That promise had become a dream, and then a memory, and then a myth. Now it was a carcinogen. With each second that elapsed the notion that her artist had abandoned her grew tighter strands within her. They competed for the soil of her soul with the even more pernicious tendrils that told her she had been set up. She felt more and more sure that she was contraband about to be collected. She needed to get out of that hotel and she needed to do so that night.

Torn's service through the meal was civil and efficient. There were things she wanted to ask, but the restaurant was busy and all the tables were taken making conversation unwise. Some faces she knew, many she did not, and all were now suspects in her head. She consumed all that she could, for she wasn't sure when she would eat again. She lingered over her coffee, but Torn ceased to emerge once the restaurant began to empty, so eventually she folded her napkin, checked that the smuggled slip of paper was safely inside a pocket with her clutch bag and headed for the elevator.

As she passed through reception, Herr Lund summoned her.

"Mrs Proctor?"

She went to the desk. "Yes?"

"Herr Berndtsson tells me you have found the missing book."

"Herr . . ?"

Her Lund nodded in the direction of the statue of Queen Kristina on her horse where Torn was tidying the small table in front of a sofa. "Herr Berndtsson."

"Ah yes. It had been left for me on the bed."

Herr Lund looked disapprovingly perplexed. "Oh!"

"I think it must have slipped between the bed and the wall. The chambermaid must have found it this morning."

Herr Lund looked relieved. "Ah. Good."

"Yes. Thank you. So sorry about the fuss."

"There was no fuss."

"Ah well. Thank you."

"Thank you."

"One other thing . . ."

"Yes?"

"Could you possibly show me how to operate the public

telephone?" She inclined towards the kiosk in the corner of the reception area.

"If you wish we can make the call for you and you can take it in your room."

"Not if I'm not in the hotel. I've never used a Swedish call box you see."

"Ah." He called, "Herr Berndtsson?"

Torn left what he was doing and approached with a slightly suppliant air. "Herr Lund?"

"Would you show Mrs Proctor how to operate the public telephone?"

"Of course."

They squeezed into the mahogany kiosk together. He showed her which coins to use, how to operate the coin buttons, the order in which to do things and very simple instructions in what to say to the operator. She repeated his actions whilst ensuring that her thigh was pressed between his and that he had to brush against her blouse front as he made his demonstration.

She practiced the procedure while he watched. She didn't actually dial, but pretended to speak into the mouthpiece. "Torn, I need you to do one more thing for me."

He put his hand over the receiver. "What?"

She hung up, taking his grip and interlocking it with her own. "Does the hotel keep the daily newspapers?"

"For a few days."

"Could you scour the Swedish ones for me?"

He struggled with the word, "Scour?"

"Look through them. For a story. A mention of something."

"Of what?"

"An accident. A plane crash."

"A plane crash?"

"In the south or west. Perhaps near Gothenburg."

"I will look."

"Don't tell anyone. Just me." She tugged his fist tighter against her bosom.

"Of course. How many papers – how long ago?"

"Oh – a week? Well from the start of the year."

"Very well."

"Thank you."

Back in her room, one of Torn's comments from earlier in

the day annoyingly repeated in her mind. "Not damaged?" She took the sketchbook from its hiding place and positioned it directly under the bedside lamp as she inspected every page. One of the pencil-drawn surreal tears-notes on the telephone-wire stave looked odd. It was the note corresponding to the first syllable of *under*. She couldn't really tell, but the cartridge paper looked as if it had been sliced very precisely with a scalpel and then pasted back down. She turned the page to Pic's first working of his initial nude study of her. From that side the paper looked untroubled, but the place where the cut may have been made was unnervingly close to her appendectomy scar.

TWENTY-THREE

"I need you to level with me, Emira."

"Level?"

"Be completely honest."

"I have been."

It was the next day. Wednesday 9th January. Still no Pic. Still no calls from Pic. She telephoned Emira from the hotel call box as soon as her breakfast was done. Initially she had a fraught conversation with a person that she presumed to be Emira's mother. Her English was very limited but eventually she got the message and a sleepy sounding Emira came to the phone. They arranged to meet an hour later and now were heading along the northern quay of the harbour area close to the railway station.

"Where is Pic?"

"I told you. He's at home. I think."

"Four days. Not a word."

"I told you. He is being watched."

She stood still, making Emira overshoot her. "By whom? By whom is he being watched?"

Emira stopped, came back, stood close. "Look, I'm not involved."

"Not involved? You gave me money. Fake money."

"Sshh!" Emira looked around scanning the passers-by and

the moored ferryboats. Some had their motors running. Others were silent, nonchalantly listening.

"And a fake passport."

Emira gripped the poser's arm gently but firmly. "Please. Don't shout."

"I'm sorry."

"Don't even say those things. I did them for you, you know."

The poser gathered herself. "Well I think I need you to convince me of that."

"That's why I'm taking you to my house. All this is very risky for me."

"It's even more risky for me."

"Yes. Come on."

They started walking again.

"Why didn't you tell me about Pic's gallery?"

"It was better that you didn't know."

"With my portrait in the window."

"That was for my benefit."

They walked under the railway bridge that took the tracks from the island of Gamla Stan into the southern approach of the central station.

"For your benefit?"

"So I could recognise you and also locate you."

"Locate me."

"The mixed media collage next to it . . ."

"I know, I know, I saw it."

"Pic's gallery is close to a dead letter box we sometimes use. I collected the film that had your photo on then went past the gallery when it was closed. Pic did not say on the telephone where you were. It's safer that way. That's why he arranged to put the poster and the collage in the window."

"But if you had my photograph, why did you need to see my portrait?"

"Because the film had not been developed. For all we know it had not been exposed."

"Do you not even trust Klas?"

"Pic only trusts me."

"And Edwin Heap."

Emira's head fell slightly and her pace shortened almost imperceptibly, but the poser noticed it. "Pic doesn't trust

Edwin."

"Not anymore."

"I don't think he ever did."

There were more ferryboats here. Some rattled their diesel engines. Most were silent. The poser read the name of one boat and stopped in her tracks. The boat was called *Mariefred*.

Emira swung around and saw what she was looking at. "What's the matter?"

"That's where Pic lives."

"What makes you think that?"

"He put it on the bloody registration card. At the hotel"

"Why would he do that?" The question sounded more rhetorical than inquisitive.

"I thought he lived in Stockholm."

Emira was already on the move "Pic lives in many places. Some are in Stockholm, some are not."

The poser caught up to her. "Why is that boat called *Mariefred*?"

"Because that's where it goes. Every day in summer."

They walked past the City Hall and into the Kungsholmen district. Soon they had slipped into an apartment block and were heading downstairs. Emira explained, "We live on floors three and four but I also have the basement." The studio was simple but filled with painted work, some of which the poser recognised.

"I know this."

"Goya," confirmed Emira, slipping off her coat and switching on the array of unshaded ceiling lights. There were canvasses stacked along all four walls. Most were unframed. They varied in size from four or five feet down to a few inches. The floor was paint-spattered, as was the old sofa in the centre of the room, and the half a dozen easels regimentally lined up by a door leading into another space.

"And this?"

"Rembrandt. Those two are Mondrian and that one is Kandinsky. They're easy."

"They are forgeries."

"They are replicas."

"Replicas."

"Yes." On the floor by the easels was a single hob connected to a gas tank and kettle. Emira, lifted the lid to check the water level, lit the hob and put the kettle on.

The poser unbuttoned her coat. "What's the difference between a forgery and a replica?"

"A replica isn't pretending to be what it represents."

"But they are not prints."

"No, they are originals."

"Original copies."

"Exactly. My best work is through here."

The muse followed Emira into the back room which was lit by natural light from a rank of frosted windows high along the far wall and which bounded an interior courtyard, at what she thought would be floor level, or a little higher. Along that wall was a workbench bearing the scars of many labours, and its own multi-coloured rashes, but in much more delicate patterns than those adorning the main studio. There was a pair of angle-poise lamps and a similar device that positioned a large magnifying glass over what looked to be a miniature cameo portrait, part completed. Emira unlocked a cupboard and produced a tray of a dozen brooch-sized portraits. They were exquisitely painted and pristinely mounted in tiny metal frames.

"Are these – replicas – too?"

"Mostly. That and that are entirely original, and this one is my own work from a photograph."

"A photograph of who?"

"Pic's first wife."

"You mean . . ."

"Christina Proctor. It's from her passport photograph."

The muse looked at the image adorned with high powdered hair, and generous décolletage. "But this lady is . . . I don't know . . . eighteenth century?"

"It would have amused Pic. It was going to be a birthday present for him but . . ."

"But what?"

"The day after I finished it, I arrived back at our apartment and found him in bed with someone else."

The muse waited a moment, then said, "Who?"

Emira waited a longer moment, then said, "Edwin."

"Edwin?"

"Edwin. Edwin Heap."

The muse was caught in a pincer of shock. Emira's assertion applied one pierce but it was matched by another. At first she couldn't speak, simply because she wasn't breathing. Her lungs had locked at half inhalation. She freed them with a surge and then turned the exhalation into an exclamation. She was processing what she had just heard, but could not detach her focus from the cameo she held.

Emira said, "Is something wrong?"

"No, no. It's just that she looks remarkably like someone I once knew."

"Christina Proctor?"

"Someone who was killed by an unexploded bomb in London in 1944."

"Actually Pic said that was what had happened to Christina. She died in an air raid, but her passport survived."

"Is that was he told you?"

"That's what he told me."

"And all the while Pic was in love with Edwin Heap?"

"Since they were at school."

The muse unwittingly sucked in a sharp breath. "Since school?"

"That's why they were both expelled. That's why Edwin was disowned."

"Disowned?"

"By his family. By his father. Completely cut him off. Lost everything. Including his title."

"Title?"

"According to Pic."

"I didn't know you could lose a title."

"It all hurt Pic very badly. I didn't realise how badly until . . . until I came home when they were not expecting me."

"And that's why you left Pic."

"It wasn't the only reason. No one ever marries the person they marry. They marry the one they think they're going to be married to."

The poser had already mused on that. She moved the conversation on. "I need money. More money."

"I've been making you some." Emira went back into the main workshop. The poser followed. Over in one corner, a tarpaulin covered a hidden bulk. Emira lifted one edge and revealed a small printing press. She removed a cardboard box and opened it to expose three neat bundles of banknotes. "I had a problem with the machine. The quality was not good. They're not perfect even now, but it's the best I can do at the moment. Three hundred krona."

"I thought I was going to have to threaten you."

"And how would you have done that?"

"It doesn't matter."

Emira fixed her with a malevolent smile. "Yes it does."

"Why?"

"Because I need to know how ruthless you are. I need to know the strength of the woman I am working with."

"Working with?"

"Yes."

"Why do you desire to work with me?"

Emira laced a hard stare with a soft smile. "Because I honour my contracts." In the room next door, the boiling kettle was rattling its lid. Emira set off in that direction. "Would you like some coffee?"

"Yes please." The poser followed her through. "I was going to threaten to reveal your money-making hobby."

Emira produced coffee and a filter from among a nest of paint pots. She spooned the powder into a cafetière and poured in the hot water. "And how easy would it be for me to deal with such threats?" Hardly anyone knows you are in Stockholm. Nobody knows who you really are. Nobody knows you are here with me."

The muse watched as Emira depressed the plunger on the cafetière. "I put your name and telephone number into an air mail letter, which I posted on the way to meeting you."

Emira looked genuinely disturbed. "Posted to who?"

"A friend. In England. Don't worry they won't do anything. As long as I send a telegram within a day or so."

"Did you tell them where you are? I mean - the name of the hotel."

"Of course."

"We must move very quickly."

"To where?"

"To Copenhagen."

"What?"

"Come here."

They left the filtering coffee and went back to the workbench. Emira selected one of the miniatures. "Maria Feodorovna. Wife of Tsar Paul of Russia. Paul the Mad.

Originally painted by Janez Herrlein." She positioned the magnifying glass over it. "Look at the decoration on her hat. The pendant."

"What about it?"

"The elaboration in the centre."

"Well?"

"It's not painted like the rest. It's been printed directly on to the silk. Do you know what a microdot is?"

"I've heard the term."

"They can be printed about the size of a full stop but contain a great deal of information only visible when enlarged many times."

The poser stared intently through the spy glass. "Are you telling me this is one?"

"You'd need a microscope or special viewer. Pic reckons there's a bunch of those stitched to your intestine."

She pulled back from the bench. "Printed on silk?"

"Possibly. More likely on nylon."

"Why nylon?"

"Much more resistant to the fluids in your insides and won't show on x-rays."

"Pic told you a lot."

"We still have a working relationship."

"Working for whom?"

Emira replaced the portrait in the tray then said, "For each other."

"That can't be very profitable."

"If I need a profit, I just print it. What is inside you isn't just a threat to you, it puts other people in danger."

"And in which country do these people live?"

"All over the world. What you carry is a code. A cypher. Codes don't discriminate. People using them do. There are two ways of making those people safe. One is to destroy you. The other is to remove and destroy those microdots inside you. In Denmark there is a doctor who will do that. She won't ask any questions that do not need to be asked. She is a very good surgeon and she works in a very safe and very discrete clinic. You could never afford her services, but we can." Emira led the way back to where the coffee was brewing.

"Are you telling me that Denmark was always my destination?"

"It's a bit like bomb disposal. If we can remove that cipher from your tummy we can make you safe. And lots of other people. The surgeon is not Danish, she is Swedish, but her surgery is in Copenhagen. Pic brought you here to give you a cover identity and a passport to go with it."

"Why didn't he tell me that?"

Emira shrugged and found two mugs among the jam jars of paintbrushes.

"And where is he now?"

Emira took the mugs to the sink and rinsed them under the tap. "I don't know."

"You said he was at home. Why don't you telephone?"

"I told you. He lives in several places. They don't all have telephones. And anyway it would be too dangerous." She dried the mugs with a tea towel.

"Who is watching? The British? The Soviets? East Germans?"

"Any of those. All of them. Who knows? They all want the unexploded bomb in your belly."

The muse fiddled with a bouquet of paintbrushes. "So how do I get to Denmark?"

"By ferry. In two days. I will go with you."

"You will?"

"If Pic has not turned up by then."

Emira handed over one bundle of the counterfeit krona, then insisted escorting the poser to a post office where the promised telegraph was dispatched. The poser filled in the message first and showed it to Emira before shielding the form from view while she filled in the address. She handed it over to be transmitted to Tinky. This enterprise redefined the relationship of the two women. They now shared a mutually respectful distrust but, nevertheless, there was a special bond between them. It wasn't just the fact that they had fallen for, and been deceived by, the same man, it was also an admiration of spirit, of independence, of resilience. The poser was in awe of the artistry of her new associate. She was, without doubt, a highly talented painter, but she was also a wickedly enterprising individual. There was a glow that emanated from her stratified fraudulence. She could create incredibly truthful counterfeit reproductions of the works of great masters, and do so on large or miniscule scales, and was equally proficient at producing fake currency. At face value she had been brazen in exposing her methods and products but, if anything, that added to her allure. The fact that Emira had let her into her secret world ironically made the poser less likely to betray her. She felt a layer of unease about the imposing of the threat that led to the telegram, but was glad that she had done so.

"I will bring more money before we sail. We will need to change it. I have no template for Danish banknotes." She then led the way into Gamla Stan the oldest part of Stockholm. "You should be a tourist for an hour." They arrived at the Royal Palace in time to see the daily charging of the guard. The traffic was halted as smart blue-clad soldiers with steel helmets blew regimental tunes on silver trumpets, whilst riding impressive horses that trotted over the bridge and into the palace precinct. For a few moments she was back in London. The colours and the melodies were different, but the patriotic sentiment was the same.

They wandered the narrow tall streets of the island at the heart of the historic archipelago, with no particular purpose, but Emira had been wise. An hour of doing something that she might have done under entirely different circumstances somehow settled her and cleared, if not reassured, her thought process. Suddenly Emira terminated the distraction. They stood at the foot of a statue of St George slaying a heavily spiked dragon. The beast held the knight's broken lance in its claw but George was unshaken by that setback, and with his broadsword already swung high, there was no doubt that the final blow was imminent. The poser reflected that her confidence came not from the prowess of the protagonist, but simply from knowing how the story ended.

"Which one am I?" she asked.

"Which?"

"St George or the dragon?"

"Neither."

"Neither?"

"You are the horse," said Emira.

The poser studied the scenario and found that she agreed. The horse was caught between the combatants, stamping with its hooves, it unwittingly added to the fray, but from the fear in its face it undoubtedly did not want to be there.

"I'm going to leave you now," said Emira. "You mustn't follow me. I'm going to see if I can check one or two of Pics places."

"Don't end up the dragon," said the poser.

"I won't take any risks."

"But you are worried."

"Yes. I am worried. But don't you worry. If Pic can't take you to Denmark I will."

The poser put a hand on the forger's arm. "I'm sorry I threatened you. I'm sorry I endangered you."

"Don't be. If you hadn't have threatened me, I would have abandoned you."

The poser withdrew her touch and frowned.

Emira said, "It's just the way my mind works."

"Very well."

Emira nodded towards the statue. "That wasn't the only horse in the stable. George chose it for a reason. It doesn't want to face a dragon, but it's not afraid to kick out."

"Is that why you brought me here?"

Emira laughed. "Pic told me that George is your patron saint."

"That's right."

"Represents all that is English."

"So they say."

"He's a fraud."

"St George?"

"He was born in Cappadocia. Today it's part of Turkey."

The poser regarded the statue again, smiling at the almost nonchalant expression on the fighting saint's face, and when she turned back to comment to Emira, there was just a vacant space.

When she emerged from the elevator Torn was waiting. Without speaking, she led the way to her room, admitted him and shut the door. His aftershave was cinnamon and pine.

"Nothing," he said.

"Nothing?"

"I have looked at all the papers we have from the second day of January. Two Stockholm papers and GT from Gothenburg."

He was standing very close to her, leaning his shoulder against her bedroom wall. She didn't move away. She also leant against the wall and then rolled her shoulder blades to it. She fixed her focus mid-way to the embossed light fitting and adopted an expression of mildly concerned contemplation. She let him peruse her profile.

"It was an unusual request," he said softly.

"I'm an unusual person."

"Yes," he said. "You are."

She waited a moment to see if he would make a move. He didn't. She went over to the bed where she'd thrown her bag and extracted a packet of cigarettes. By the time the tube of tobacco was between her lips he'd struck a match torn from the hotel's branded flip that he'd produced from his waistcoat pocket.

"Thank you."

He wafted the match out, picked up the packet from the bed and examined the contents. "English cigarettes."

"What did you expect?"

"There's only one left. You'll have to buy some Swedish ones."

She exhaled towards the light fitting and offered him a slightly condescending expression. "I already have."

"You haven't been in Sweden long."

"That's right. I haven't been in Sweden long."

"Your husband has been here much longer?"

She didn't flinch but knew her brow had instinctively tightened. She took another bellyful of smoke, held it, exhaled it from her nostrils and turned to face him head on. "Why do you say that?"

"Because I'm concerned for you."

"Are you?"

"Yes."

"Why?"

"A woman whose husband has . . . disappeared. Who asks me to check the address on his registration card. Who asks me to look in newspapers for crashed aeroplanes. Who arrived in January but with only summer clothes."

"I'm an unusual person."

"Very unusual."

"That's my problem."

"I didn't say it was a problem."

"I did. And it is."

"Let me help."

"You have done."

He took half a step closer. "Can I be of further assistance?"

She stood her ground and drew again on her Churchman's cigarette, fearful that its glow might ignite the cinnamon and pine carrier spirit. She exhaled to one side then changed her weight from one foot to the other, allowing her knee to touch his. "How do I get to Mariefred?"

"It's where your husband lives."

She blew smoke to one side. "It's where he says he lives."

Torn smiled smugly and edged closer. "Train."

"Do they have second class tickets?"

Torn frowned. "Second class?"

"I'm a second class woman." She slipped her arms loosely around his neck. "Wouldn't you say?"

"No, I wouldn't."

He put his hands on her hips. She looked at his lips, and then she kissed them. She allowed her mouth to open just enough for the tip of his tongue to find the head of hers. She broke gently from him and extinguished her half-cigarette. He went to door and locked it from the inside. She removed her coat and cardigan. They lay on the bed. Their mouths locked more. She let him unfasten her blouse and nestle his mouth in her cleavage and cup her nipples with his palm. She slipped off her skirt but did not allow him to remove her nylons or her knickers.

She made sure he saw her appendectomy scar.

The train to Läggesta station took an hour and forty minutes. A local narrow gauge line provided the final few miles to Marifred. The town was utterly unlike Stockholm. It was dominated by the historic Gripsholm Castle which fronted onto a great expanse of forest-lined water that looked like a lake, but was in fact, another corner of the meandering rim of the Baltic sea. A taxi took her to a street that was tucked just a few minutes away. The property was in two storeys, detached, timber clad, and painted pastel blue. The watery winter sun, slung low in the unclouded quarter of the sky made the paintwork glisten, but something foreboding spoke to her.

She paid the taxi-driver with one of the fake banknotes and, much to his joy, waved away the change he offered. He drove off, the blue fumes from his exhaust dancing behind. The road was quiet. Three parked cars and a pedestrian walking a dog. She pushed the picket gate which held firm until she found the slightly awkward latch. All the windows were shuttered and there was no smoke from the chimney. The main door was at the side. The knocker was in the form of a fish. She hammered four strokes. No movement. No sound. No one came. She hammered again. Five smacks this time.

In the thin distance, a dog barked.

Another five knocks. No response. She walked round to the rear of the house. Here the window shutters were fastened open. The window was tall, and seemed too big. It was French in style, fastened centrally, and sat awkwardly on the façade, but it overlooked a long garden so she could see the architectural sense in it. As she drew near her spirits lifted for she could make out easels. North-facing window, she thought. The best light for painting, Pic had said. Two easels were stacked, but a third bore a mounted canvas, the rear of which was towards her. It looked a little odd as it was adjusted to a low level, and then that conundrum was resolved as she saw that just beyond it was an armchair. The main bulk of the seat was obscured by the shadow cast by the painting, but she saw shoes and trousers that she recognised. By squeezing herself tightly to the edge of the window she saw much more that she recognised. She rapped on the window. The feet did not move. She hammered harder, hurting her knuckles through her gloves. The feet did not move. She hammered again, and shouted.

"Pic! Pic!"

The feet did not move. She squeezed even more tightly up against the window frame and brought her hand to the side of her head to shield the light. She could then see much more clearly into the shadow across the chair. She saw enough.

She scurried further along the rear of the house and found the back door. It was locked. She put her shoulder to it, to no affect.

She ran back to the window and banged persistently at the central join where the interior handle was. She set off across the garden and found a tool shed. It was padlocked. She ran back towards the house, heading for the side she had not yet explored. She found a lean-to wood store, and there, bellowing memories of the chalet at Vättern, was a chopping maul.

Three strikes and she fractured the frame of the back door. She pushed it open scratching her face on a splinter, ignored the sweet damp smell that knocked at nauseous memories from the war, and wriggled through the kitchen, to the hall, to the room, a room of easels, and canvas and oils, and rags, and still life.

He was slate. From head to foot he was slate. It was the suit he had been wearing when he had left the Drottning Kristina, but it was dressed with filigree dust and bore a war paint of splatters and drips. His shoes, she could now see, were drip-scarred too, as were his hands and even his face, but all his flesh was slate.

His eyes were open, his head lodged in the wing of the armchair so that unseeing, he stared at the painting before him. Brushes criss-crossed the floor beneath his right hand and among them, on its side, a glass tumbler.

All was still.

She looked at the painting. It was the one she had first seen at Kendal's Lodge, but it had been extensively, though not completely, painted over. The last time she saw it, it was a depiction of her nude self in a first-class railway carriage. Parts of the train remained. The lower half of her torso, complete with scar and pubic deltoid were unchanged, as were her legs. Her chest and head were gone, replaced by a naked masculine frame and her face had been replaced too, by a face she knew.

The painter looked at his painting, and looking back at him was the painted gaze of Edwin Heap.

She gently laid a hand on her former lover's arm.

She knew.

There was a shadow of movement at the edge of the French window, followed by the sound of scraping gravel from the direction of the back door.

TWENTY-FOUR

An evasive instinct had kicked in. Even before she acknowledged that she had seen the key in the French window, she found herself turning it, squeezing out though the cavernous gap, wedging behind the tool shed and somehow forcing herself through the hedge there onto the adjoining land. She galloped the width of that garden, scaled the fence before her, then pelted past the property to emerge on the road perhaps fifty yards from the house where Pic was. She recognised the vehicle there, or thought she did. It was the truck they'd borrowed from Klas. Or was it? Yes, it was. Even so, the person in the property might not be Klas. Even if it was him, she wasn't going to risk it. Her aim had been realigned.

She moved fast, keeping close to the line of houses, she lost herself in the interlaced streets and fading light. She was able to use the concentrations of street lighting to make her way to the market square and from there to the railway. She had the sense not to enter the station precinct until she saw the train pull in. She had a return ticket to Stockholm and the line was a simple branch link to Läggesta so there was no need to make a purchase. She remained hyper-alert whilst boarding and throughout the ride, but none of the other passengers paid her more than passing attention.

Läggesta station was bleak. A dank freezing fog

materialised as she made her way up from the branch line halt below to the long and largely exposed mainline platform. The express, was more comfortable, but crowded, and she was grateful for both those things. A tall, red-bearded business man vacated his seat for her, and she was pleased to take it, for he then stood close by in the aisle making an excellent masking screen.

She was back in Stockholm by six-thirty. The winter fog was there too, in fact, it seemed even more dense. She had used the rail journey to settle her shock and begin to think through what to do next. Her rationality was now in overdrive, and she was ready to weave. When she collected her room key she made sure she asked, as per usual, regarding any messages from her husband. The supposed cynical receptionist, responded with a good attempt at a cheerfully polite negative. The poser did even better at faking her controlled disappointment. She looked about for Torn but he was not in evidence. She went to her room and checked that all her essentials were safely still with her; her money, her passport and Pic's sketchbook. She took all those things to the bathroom where she ran a supremely hot tub. After her soak, she changed for dinner. Torn was not on duty in the restaurant, which meant she would not have to play conversational chess regarding the traumas of the day.

That night she not only locked her bedroom door but did her best to jam the wicker chair under the handle. She slept well, despite dreams that were very dark indeed.

Torn was conducting service at breakfast, but the room was busy, and they exchanged nothing more than a polite greeting, though he added a flash of raised eyebrows.

Back in her room she wore double layers of clothes, packed all other essentials into two shopping bags, left all her summer clothes in the wardrobe, put a generous, but fraudulent, gratuity under her pillow, left the room key on the lock on the inside of the door, took the staircase around the elevator and, without visiting reception, left the Hotel Drottning Kristina.

"I don't live here all the time you know," said Emira.

It's funny, thought the poser, that there comes a point in

any interpersonal reaction when true colours flash through. She surmised that the tone Emira employed would be utilised in a domestic altercation. All civility had been suspended. They were standing at the door of the apartment above the forging studio. Emira's mother was hovering in the hall. It had taken some persuading to get her to fetch her daughter from the basement.

"There's something you should know."

"What?"

"Are we to have the conversation here?"

"I'm very busy." Emira wore an artist's smock. Her sleeves were rolled back revealing paint-freckled forearms. Her stare was steely but wavered a little when she saw her visitor's bulging baggage.

The artist glanced at the older lady, but this was no time for niceties. "Pic's dead," she said.

"What?"

"That's a curious hue of grey," she heard herself say, inclining her focus to the painter's hands.

"What?"

"You needn't bother with the divorce. You are a widow."

"What?"

"Haven't you heard?"

"What are you talking about?"

"Has Klas not been in contact?"

Emira's mother said something in Swedish. Her daughter snapped a sharp reply and the old woman went muttering up the stairs. "Come in," said Emira and led the way to the basement. She hurried ahead and insisted that the poser waited at the door while she went in and cleared some things away. Eventually they sat on bespattered chairs near the gas ring. Emira's complexion turned ashen, but it may just have been the poverty of light in the room. The poser recounted her experience from the previous day. Her lover's lover listened with her hands resting in the fold of her lap, her shoulders sunken, her head cocked back. The poser had seen this manifestation before, during the war.

"Was it Klas?"

"I didn't wait to find out. It was his car."

Emira was motionless and silent for several moments, then lifting her head but not breaking her mid-distance stare, said, "This was not supposed to happen."

"I think perhaps it was."

"What?"

The poser shook her head dismissing that line of enquiry. She breathed deeply and felt her face sharpen. "Tell me what was supposed to happen."

"You were to go to Denmark."

"Why?"

"Pic was selling them your cargo."

"Why Denmark?"

"The Soviets see Denmark as a bridgehead to the Atlantic. Their fleets sail through the straits, but Denmark is part of Nato. If tensions grew it would be high on Soviet priorities. Denmark is always nervous. Having the code you carry would make them feel a little more secure."

"Then why bring me all the way to Stockholm?"

"Pic ran here when things went wrong with Edwin. Vättern is much closer to Gothenburg. Pic knew he could put you in my care, while he took the heat off."

"Looks like it didn't quite work."

"You're still here."

"Not for long."

"What will you do?"

"The surgeon you spoke of – is she the Danish contact?"

Emira's breathing pulsed unnaturally. "I think so."

"I want her details."

She rubbed at the drying paint on her hands. "I can't come with you."

"I'm not expecting you to. Just give me her address or anything else you have."

"It's upstairs. Wait here."

Before she left, Emira went to a drawer and rooted for a key with which she locked the door to the smaller studio. "Wait here," she said again. Part way to the exit she stopped. "What did you mean? A curious hue of grey."

"The paint on your arms. On your apron."

"Pic got me to mix it for him. I've been using it up."

"He won't be needing anymore."

"No."

She floated from the room, but was fully absent long before she got to the door.

She changed the currency in three different locations; two banks and a travel agency. She then caught the train to Malmö, where she lodged overnight in a small guesthouse close to the harbour. She caught the ferry to Copenhagen the following morning. No one questioned her passport.

She turned up, unannounced at the private surgery of Dr Signe Nyström which, to her relief, did exist at the address she had been given by Elmira. Her Englishness caused some consternation but an appointment was fixed for one pm. She killed time in a café overlooking the waterfront.

Signe Nyström was a tall, ash blonde, with a pale complexion warmed with only a hint of blusher, and no mascara. Her eyes were dull blue and accusatory by default. Her tone was professional but sharp. Her English strong.

"How can I be of service?"

"I am going to be completely honest with you."

"Good."

The consultation room was small but bright, with tall windows, obscured by horizontal white cellophane blinds. The desk was bare apart from a blotter, a notepad, a pen holder and a white telephone.

"During the war I was given an appendectomy. Recent events have led me to believe that microscopic information was stitched to my intestine. Persons may be interested in that information, including my own countrymen. I want that information removed. I believe you can do that." She opened her purse and pulled out all the notes. "This is all the money I have."

Signe twiddled the pencil above a blank notepad. "I see. And what exactly is the information?"

"I have no idea. It is probably some sort of cipher."

"Printed on what?"

"Nylon, or silk. I don't actually know. I don't even know if it is there."

There was silence. Signe put the pencil down. "That would not even cover the cost of the anaesthetist."

"Then keep me awake."

Signe smiled. "Why, and how, did you come to me?"

"I was in Sweden. I was given your name by someone who

helped me. My husband was killed."

"How?"

"By suicide."

"Strange choice of words."

"We have to ask what drove him to it. Or perhaps it just looked self-inflicted."

Signe made a steeple out of the forefinger of each hand and kissed it. "Can you tell me the name of this person who sent you to me?"

"Emira."

"Second name?"

"I don't know."

"How did you meet her?"

"Through my husband." A sea breeze pushed at the window pane. The celluloid blind moved slightly. "I'm on the run, if you understand my meaning."

"Yes, I understand your meaning. I lived in the United States for two years."

"Well, that's what I'm doing. I'm tired of it, but if you can help me, I might be able to at least catch my breath. I can't pay you any more than this, but I promise to settle any debts provided I live long enough to raise the funds."

Signe spread her palms flat on her desk. Her nails were short but perfectly manicured. "And what am I to do with the . . . foreign body . . . inside you, if there is such a thing?"

"I would want to take it with me, but I would have no objection to you making a copy of it, if that were possible and perhaps that, in some way, could be used as some sort of surety." She glanced at the minutely dancing blind, then pierced the surgeon with a stiletto stare. "I understand it may have international value."

The women meshed their stares. There was a very long period during which neither of them spoke. Signe studied her prospective patient, then scrutinised the blank notepad on her desk. "Tell me more of your story."

Before committing, the poser weighed up her prospects. It didn't take long. "I thought my husband had died during the war. Some weeks ago I discovered this was not so. We were reunited and he enlightened me regarding my particular pregnancy. With help from his friend we fled England and went to Sweden. Unfortunately, his friend had an accident and did not make it back to England. My husband left me in an hotel in Stockholm. I eventually traced him to a house in Mariefred where I found him dead. He'd swallowed something I think. He was an artist. He'd painted over a portrait of me with the face and torso of the friend he'd lost."

"How did your husband know about what was inside of you?"

"I think he was a spy."

"For which sovereignty?"

"I don't know. But I think his friend worked for the British Secret Service. If so, by helping me he was being treacherous. That might explain his 'accident'.

"What kind of accident?"

"Aeroplane."

Signe sat back in her chair and the chiaroscuro caused by the window blind picked out strands of grey among the ash-blonde. "All medical procedures contain an element of risk."

"Do you carry out abortions?"

Signe did not flinch. "Why do you ask?"

"Because if you do, you will know desperation when you see it."

"If I remove your problem, it will not stop them looking for you."

"But I might be able give them what they want without paying for it with my life."

"But then it might have less value because someone else has had sight of it."

"I'll let you know if that happens."

"Considerate of you."

She uncrossed and re-crossed her legs and leaned towards the desk. "Listen, you'll be the one who'll be conscious. You'll be the one with the blade. If you want a guarantee you know what to do."

Signe smirked. "Who is travelling with you?"

"No one."

"You are completely alone?"

"Yes."

"Who knows you are here?"

"Emira."

"And whoever she has told."

"What difference does that make? I'm here. In your

hands."

"Why isn't she here?"

"I'm learning not to trust anyone. Not even you."

Signe ran her fingers through her hair, gathering it behind her head before releasing it again. "After all that you've told me, you really don't have a choice, other than to trust me."

"I know. But I don't. Sorry."

Signe stood and drew a nylon curtain to reveal a medical couch. Take everything off except your underwear and lie on here." She then spoke two unintelligible sentences.

"I'm sorry?" said the poser.

"You don't speak Danish or Swedish."

"I only understand English."

"While you get undressed I'm going to make a telephone call. Don't worry, I'm not putting you in any danger."

"Very well."

The call lasted five minutes or more, then Signe came behind the curtains and saw the extensive pile of clothes on the chair. "You find Scandinavia very cold I see."

"Yes."

"So are my hands, I'm afraid." She examined the appendectomy scar and pushed and prodded the abdomen. She took a reading of the poser's pulse, and listened to her heartbeat and lungs. She unhooked and applied an inflatable cuff to measure blood pressure. She made notes. "You can get dressed again."

The muse put all the clothes back on and emerged from behind the curtain.

"Have you eaten today?"

"I had a cake in a café."

"Don't eat anything else. I'll operate in the morning."

"Thank you."

"Where are you staying?"

"I'm not."

"Well that makes things even simpler. We can accommodate you in the clinic overnight."

"Thank you."

Signe looked at the cluster of bags by the door. "This is all you have?"

"All I have with me. I have a friend in England who is looking after other things for me."

"Can that person be recorded as your next of kin?"

"There are two names I can give you for that purpose. Two friends."

"Thank goodness for friendship," said Signe.

"Yes," said the muse, and held out a hand for the surgeon to shake.

The test-tube took her back to her schooldays, though she didn't remember seeing one that small.

"I believe it is nylon. Or something very similar."

The curtain around her bed had been drawn. Signe had then slipped the tube from the breast pocket of her white laboratory coat. The poser twisted it between her forefinger and thumb.

"Have you photographed it?

"I've looked at it under a microscope. There are twelve clusters of print."

"Microdots."

"In themselves they don't seem to make any sense. Are you very sore?"

"Yes. And rather groggy?"

"Groggy?"

"Sleepy."

"Ah yes. Well you will probably sleep quite a lot for a couple of days. I expect you will want to keep that very close to you. Here's some surgical tape. Perhaps inside your upper right arm. The tube will not break. Not easily."

"Thank you."

"You will stay for another two or three days, while we make sure there is no infection and the wound is healing. I opened you very close to the original incision. You now have a railway track across your abdomen."

"I won't be going back to nude modelling then."

Signe smiled indulgently. "It was a very straightforward procedure."

"Good."

"But it wasn't attached to your intestine. It was just under the skin, on the inside where they had opened you up. I almost missed it."

"Under my skin?"

"And yes."

"Yes?"

"We have photographed it through the microscope. I should be able to give you a print before you leave."

"That might be dangerous."

"You can always burn it."

"I will never forget this. And I will pay my debts."

"There is no charge."

"What?"

"A gift. From the people of Denmark."

"I'm very grateful."

"So are they. Where will you go, when you are discharged? Back to England?"

"Eventually, I expect. If I can be sure it will be safe. Paris perhaps."

"Why Paris?"

"Why not?"

"I will ask the nurse to keep the curtain drawn for a quarter of an hour, while you sort yourself out." She nodded at the test tube.

"Thank you."

"I'll see you tomorrow."

After Signe had gone she studied the test tube for a long time. Inside was the tiny mega-magnet that had drawn so much danger towards her. It looked so flimsy, so feeble. Pink in colour, it could have been a sliver of flesh. She surmised it was probably originally white but had been discoloured by a decade of biological staining. She could just make out a pattern of dots, four columns and three rows all fitting within the diameter of the shaft of a goose quill. The relief she felt to not only know it did actually exist, but had also been removed was somehow more palpable than the object she held. Except, of course, she didn't know that. She could feel the discomfort, but once again everything had to be taken on trust. What she held in her hand might be a total fabrication. It may never have been inside her. It may not enlarge to reveal a cipher. The Swedish surgeon may have betrayed her and the good people of Denmark may have gained nothing. Everything had to be taken on trust. Everything might have changed or it all might be the same. Once a mule, always a mule.

She was grateful to be alive, but knew that every slip into

sleep might be her last. She would leave Copenhagen as soon as she could. Paris did appeal, even though she'd only suggested it to put up a smokescreen to shield her subsequent movements, but the more she thought about it, the more it attracted her. Might be wise to select an alternative. Amsterdam? Berlin?

She taped the test-tube to the inside of her right thigh. Having it there amused her, as if it had slipped out from its hiding place and been caught in a fairy bottle suspended by a strand of sprite-spun web. Before the bed curtain was drawn back she was asleep.

Alice was looking down at her, but Alice was damaged said her memory.

"God, Alice. Vera. Alice."

"Hello 'atter."

It was three days later. She had been sleeping.

"What the. . .? I thought you were . . ."

Vera smiled broadly. "It's been worse. The swelling has almost gone, but I'm still a bit bruised. How are you?"

"I'm, I'm . . . I don't know where I am."

"In a very smart clinic in Copenhagen."

"What are you doing here?"

"Visiting." She pushed a bunch of purple flowers between the poser's face and the edge of the pillow. "How the hell do they get such terrific blooms in January? I think they must be from bulbs."

"What day is it? What date?"

"Wednesday. Seventeenth."

She grimaced a little as she pushed herself up in the bed. "What the hell are you doing here? What happened to you?"

"Bit of a scalding."

"What?"

"I've never been on a plane before. Didn't know what to do. Lucky I had a bleedin' passport from working in France five year ago."

"You didn't need to come!"

"Oh yes I did. And Tinky agreed. He was going to come himself but I told him not to be so bleedin' stupid. He has a job to do, and at the moment – I don't. Which is why I'm here. You need an ally. I need revenge. I do like Denmark. The people are so kind."

"But how did you know I was here?"

"Your surgeon telephoned Tinky. Doctor Nice . . . something?"

"Er, yes. Sorry I'm not . . . I was in such a deep sleep."

"Very concerned she was, evidently."

"Was she? She operated on Sunday."

"Sunday – I know!"

"Convenient, she said."

"For who? For what?"

"Let me show you something. Draw the curtain around. Give me those, they're gorgeous."

Vera handed over the flowers and got up to draw the curtain, hiding the bed from the glazed door of the private room. The poser peeled back the covers and lifted the hospital gown to show the test tube taped to her thigh. "That's it," she said. "They got it out. It wasn't on the intestine. It was just under the skin."

Vera bent over and peered, slightly wincing, not from the sight, but the action. "Whooey! Little rascal. Source of so much bleedin' upset."

"What happened to you? Pic said a stage light fell on you."

"Pic?"

"That's his name. Well it's not. It's what we call him."

"We?"

"His friend - late friend - Edwin, his wife - former wife - who was never his wife, and me – also his wife but not his wife."

"I was hoping things had got simpler. Is there writing on that?"

"Microscopic. What happened to you?"

"Well," said Vera pulling the bedclothes back over her friend's legs. "You was correctly informed. A stage lantern did fall. That's what they do if they are dropped."

"Dropped?"

"During a bloody show. Most dramatic thing ever happened to me. Had to bring the house tabs in. Some bastards asked for refunds. Off I went to Chelsea and Westminster in a bleedin' blood wagon."

"But what actually happened?"

"Little cunt."

"Who?"

"Harry Shepton. Up in the gantry. Flickering he said. Unsafe he said. So he unplugs it, unhooks it and ceremonially drops it on yours truly twenty feet below."

"Deliberately?"

"Who knows?"

"Right on you?"

"Not exactly. He ain't that good a shot thank god. Landed on the rostra but the lens and the bulb shattered. Bleedin' red hot shards everywhere, but mostly on yours truly. Geoff Bickerstaff chucked a bucket of water over me but by then the damage were done. I'll not be doing no encores on that stage, unless they do a back to the bleedin' Blitz tableau."

"Oh Vee, I'm so sorry."

"Ah - things happen." She leant forwards and lowered her voice. "And, er, it's Alice."

"Sorry. This didn't just happen though did it?"

"Who knows? She sacked him evidently, but by all accounts, he weren't over bothered. Which suggests he got a fair handout from someone somewhere."

"This is all such a bloody mess."

"Which is why we're going to put it right. We'll get the bastards. Unless it's your – what's his name – Pic fella."

"Not so easy if it was him."

"Why not?"

"I'll explain, but not now. Who knows who might be around."

"Well I'm around. How long are you going to be in here?"

"Another day or two. Now that you're here, I might be able to get out sooner. Then we need to leave Copenhagen and not tell anyone where we are going."

"And where will we go?"

"I can't go home. Not yet. This little roll of nylon is still very much sought after, and for all the seekers know it's still stitched inside me."

Vera kept her voice low. "We could go to Paris. I know parts of Paris. I worked there for a summer after the war."

"It's the one place I've mentioned to the people here, which means it's not ideal, but we could make it our first stop."

"We could go to Lourdes."

"Where's that?"

"It's a shrine where Catholics go to get cured."

"I'm not a Catholic."

"Technically I am," said Vera cheerfully. "It's a place full of damaged people. The bleedin' Virgin might even cure me."

"She might."

The poser grinned, the maimed model grimaced. "But perhaps we should start with Paris?"

"Let's do that."

Four days later they checked in to a hotel in Gothenburg, Sweden.

TWENTY-FIVE

'Alice' had visited the hatter for three more days, before the clinic staff were happy regarding the state of the lesion beneath her latest set of stitches. They did not discharge her because they stressed that she had never been admitted or treated. Signe Nyström had checked on her each day but all conversation had been restricted to purely medical matters, until the day before she left.

"You can leave after breakfast in the morning," she had said. "Your friend will collect you?"

"Yes. I can't thank you enough."

"You already have. Sorry we had to keep you so long. The incision would have been less if we had known exactly where to look. It seems you were somewhat misinformed."

"Yes. I'm getting used to it."

"I'm sorry?"

"Oh, not on your part. I meant with my life in general."

"I see. Well I hope things become more straightforward. You must understand that we cannot acknowledge what we have done for you."

"I understand."

"But you only need to expose your injury to show there has been a second intervention."

"Yes."

The surgeon produced a buff envelope. "This is the photograph I promised. It makes no sense to me, and probably won't to you, but I thought you deserved to see it. Nobody – and I mean nobody – knows that this copy is in your possession." She handed it over. "And now perhaps it should not be so for very much longer. We all might be safer that way."

"Yes. Thank you once more."

The poser had used Vera's visits to bring her up to date with the particulars of her escapade. She omitted the details of the conversation regarding the miniature Emira had based on the passport photograph. Vera had been gripped, but also angered, by the story of Pic's demise. As a consequence, she was even more determined to see the whole thing through to some sort of resolution. "What was the point getting you to bleedin' Sweden just to drop you and do himself in?"

"The turning point was the crash," she explained. "I saw a different Pic after that. I had my suspicions when Emira told me her story. And then there was the confirmation in the last painting he had done."

"Another untitled one?" said Alice.

"I'm collecting a gallery of them."

It was nine o'clock on the morning of Saturday 19th January 1957 when Vera and the poser stepped down the smart white steps of the clinic to be smacked in their faces by a blast from the Baltic. They called at Vera's hotel in order to collect her luggage and then took a taxi to the rail terminus.

"We need to go to Munich first," said Vera.

"No we don't," said the muse. "We need to mingle in this crowd a good deal then catch a tram to the harbour."

"What?"

"Trust me." She swayed a little unsteadily but shrugged off Vera's concerns. "I've only walked to the bathroom and back for the last week. I'll be fine once I find my feet."

Two trams later and they were purchasing ferry tickets.

"Right, my little wounded chick, I think I should be enlightened before I offload my breakfast over the side of that beast," said Vera as they stood in the ferry terminal and watched the ship tie up.

"You'll be fine. It's only a short crossing and the swell doesn't look bad."

"It never does in the bleedin' harbour in my experience.

Now – explain!"

"Ever seen a dead body?"

"Several, during the Blitz."

"I've only ever seen three; my parents and one grandmother."

"And Pic."

"No. I've only ever seen three. Pic wasn't one of them."

"What the hell are you talking about?"

"I grabbed his arm. I may or may not know a dead body when a see one, but I've worked for ten years in a department store. I know a shop mannequin when I feel it."

Soon they were in Sweden and on a train to Gothenburg. Only when they were safely in their hotel room did they dare to open the envelope Signe Nyström had handed over. They could not make any sense of the writing on the enlarged photograph it contained for one simple reason – it was in the Cyrillic alphabet. Other than that it looked reasonably logical, with each of the twelve blocks of text listing the letters with corresponding letters and numbers alongside them.

"Looks like a calendar to me," declared Vera.

"Could be. Different code for each month. The Nazis used to change theirs every night if you remember."

"Well thank god the Soviets don't or you'd have had a roll of bleedin' wallpaper inside of you."

"How trustworthy is Tinky?"

Vera contemplated. "He came to see me as soon as he knew you were missing. Came again when he'd heard from you." Her pupils narrowed. "We talked deep." There was calm iron in her tone. "Trust him with my life. He's trusted me with yours."

"We'll send this to him."

Vera gripped her friend's wrist. "I'm not saying he's nothing to do with – you know anything. For all I know he could be in cahoots with, well anybody. I just don't think he'd betray us."

The poser considered Vera's vocabulary. Betray *us*, she'd said. "I don't care who sees this now as long as they understand that they don't need to look for it inside me."

"Then what are we doing in Sweden? Why don't we just take it to Tinky?"

The muse stared past her friend through the hotel room window and to the grey undulations of the North Sea. "Because nothing's changed, nothing at all. I'm back to where I was last September. I have no idea where the man who asked me to marry him is, and I'm determined to find him."

"Why?"

"The whole parade makes no more sense than that pernicious piece of nylon. But unlike that, it hasn't been removed from within me. And it hurts a hell of a lot more."

"Do you still love him?"

"He fascinates me and frustrates me in equal measures, but those measures are very weighty. I've carried them far and for a very long time. Someone needs to pay for their passage."

Vera took half a sidestep and obstructed the poser's view. "Just because you didn't see him dead, doesn't mean he's alive."

"Why else would you fake a death?"

"Sounds to me like they didn't do a very good job."

"Oh they did an excellent job. I was entirely convinced until I touched him."

Vera shrugged and sat down on one of the beds. "Then it wasn't a very good job was it?"

"Not if you were in the room."

"You mean you'd have been fooled if you'd have stayed outside? But you said you couldn't see him properly through the window."

"It was Klas's car outside."

"So?"

"He made no attempt to follow me or chase me."

"Good for you. He must have thought whoever had broken in had scarpered. For all he knew, hours before."

"Could be."

"Well then? What's your point?"

"Why was he there at all?"

"God knows."

"What was the last thing he did to me?"

"Did to you," said Alice. "I don't know do I?"

"Yes you do. I told you."

"Oh yeah. Took your picture. For your passport."

"If he took a picture in that room, that picture would persuade anyone that Pic was dead."

"You mean the whole thing was like a window display?"

"Exactly that. I mean, the colours weren't quite right, but on a black and white photo . . ."

"Well, it's a theory," said Vera. She lay back on the bed and stared at the ceiling, while the poser watched the Atlantic. Then she sat up, began to speak but checked herself."

"What?" asked the poser.

"It just crossed my mind . . ."

"What did?"

"If Pic's not dead . . . then . . ."

"Then Edwin Heap might not be dead either."

"Makes no sense does it?" said Vera.

"Makes a lot of sense to me," said the poser. "That's why I've brought you here. We're going to find the crash site. So first we need to find the airfield. We need an air navigation map."

"Well that's tomorrow's first job," said Vera.

Fortunately, Gothenburg had a selection of very good stationers, unfortunately it was Sunday and they were all closed. First thing on Monday morning they discovered most of them supplied nautical maps and one even stocked air charts, albeit used ones. The one they bought covered the whole of Sweden and Norway, though the poser was insistent that they could not have ventured further north than about fifty-eight degrees of latitude which would put them on a level with the lower regions of Vättern lake. She knew their journey to the chalet had been northerly and possibly also westerly. It wasn't long before they located a prime airfield at Jönköping.

"Christ," said the poser, "I went there to catch a train to Stockholm."

"Let's hope the line stretches this far," said Vera.

It did, but despite being energised by the progress they were making, they were also jaded, especially the poser, so having noted the location of the station and the times of the trains, they returned to their hotel and relaxed for the rest of the day.

They each took a bath. Vera redressed the poser's wound which was healing well, and for the first time, she showed her friend the extent of her own injuries. She peeled open her bathrobe to reveal a pair of silk French knickers. She carefully eased down the elasticated waist to reveal the full extent of the bruising on the left side of her torso. There were two burn scars, one extending from her lower ribs almost to her left hip bone, the other, a flat-iron shaped one, on her left breast. They looked more like bruises than burns and the discoloration was more muted than she had expected. According to Vera they had been much worse initially and she always plastered them with talcum powder to soften their appearance and because she thought it helped them to heal.

The poser looked horrified but Vera told her to snap out of it in her usual ebullient and pragmatic manner. "Show business is show business," she ejaculated. "If I can't show my tits I'll have to use my tongue."

They laughed and hugged. Vera winced but laughed away the poser's apology and hugged her friend more tightly. The tender warmth of unharmed skin spoke a two-way code that was completely undecipherable and entirely understood.

The poser was a few inches taller than Vera and as she snuggled into the embrace she shifted slightly to one side to protect her operation wound and her upper thigh slipped between Vera's legs and pressed against the silk of her knickers. This exploded a jolt of joy and shock in her. Her thigh could feel something through the silk. Each of them craved this cuddle and rejoiced in it but she could not ignore the irregularity she could detect low on Vera's torso, and she was confident she knew what had caused it.

The hug persisted with neither woman signalling the need to break, meanwhile a myriad of thoughts surged through the poser's puzzled cranium. Her mind was machine, and some components sang whilst others grated. She heard noises from the war; secret rattles fighting hidden battles, losing tirelessly until they won.

Her hands were beneath Vera's robe, sliding softly over new touches, finding contours, donating tenderness, delivering affection. When they eased apart it was impossible to know who had retreated first. A brief kiss was the only natural punctuation. Several unspoken answers were sealed with that kiss, but one answer was a super-loaded query. What had she felt through the silk, and was the cause as hazardous as she suspected?

Vera handed her friend a delicate golden chain with a small and understated crucifix sliding freely along it. "Fasten this for me will you?"

"Never knew you were religious."

"Isn't everybody?" asked Vera turning her back. "When they are desperate."

"Never known you desperate. There."

"Thanks." She turned back. "I'm not. It was my mother's. She said it would protect me. Pity I didn't wear it when I was on stage."

"Then you wouldn't be here now. With me."

"Oh yes I would."

Vera kissed her on the lips.

The poser smiled and returned the favour.

"Now what about your jewellery," said Alice.

"Jewellery?"

"You can't keep walking around with a test-tube in your knickers."

"Why not?"

"Could do you yourself a bleedin' injury. I have a much better idea."

"What?"

Vera went to her suitcase and produced a small sewing kit. "Let's stitch it back in," she said, and threaded the needle.

After dinner they learned from the concierge that Jönköping did not have an airport but there was talk of one being built soon on the site of a field that had been used for flying since before the war. They were even more encouraged by learning that it seemed to fit well with the muse's memory of her impressions of the site. They checked out the following morning and caught a train. Four hours later they had a new base at the foot of lake Vättern. By the time they had settled into their new accommodation the afternoon was aging so they decided to wait until the next day to begin their exploration. Their intention was to get a bus to the field and walk right around it. Klas had said the Anson had failed on take-off, so they should see signs of a major incident somewhere close to the perimeter.

She could not be sure that she recognised the airfield. Her arrival had been early morning at a time of year when daylight was at a premium, but the two hangars and their adjacent huts looked very familiar as did some of the parked planes complete with tarpaulin blindfolds. The more she studied the site the more confident she grew that this was the place where she had landed three weeks earlier. The airfield looked to be fairly limited and probably only used for recreation and light commerce. The covering of snow meant the majority of the tracks and runways could only be discerned by ruts and wear rather than by concrete or tarmac. It looked like there was one runway aligned roughly north-south and a shorter one almost at right angles to it, and possibly a third, but it was difficult to tell. They'd found a slightly elevated vantage point close to the edge of woodland, which appeared to bracket the site on both flanks, and that observation fitted the impression she had formed on final approach. There was no obvious disruption to the field surface at any point. There may have been snowfall in recent days but they doubted it could have disguised such traumatic disruption as would have been caused by a crash. Furthermore, they could see no sign of impact damage to the perimeter fence in line with the ends of the runway, nor any indication of burning beyond the boundary.

Their reconnaissance therefore provided them with several scenarios. The first was that this was the wrong site, and other alternatives being that the crash may have been cleared, or Klas may have been inaccurate in his description of what had happened. The Anson may have got into the air but failed to climb and come down somewhere in the woods. Their chances of finding evidence of that were slim. Alternatively, Klas could have been lying and the take-off might have been successful. Vera pointed out there was yet another possibility: there may have been no attempt to take off at all. Faced with that prospect, they decided they had to pluck up the courage to walk onto the business end of the field and get a closer look at the types parked there. The poser remembered they had disembarked some distance from the dispersal point, but there were no signs of aircraft elsewhere on the field.

It took them almost an hour to work their way around to the main gates which were open. They wandered among the huts most of which showed little signs of recent occupancy.

"Christ!" said the poser suddenly.

"What?"

She nodded towards a hut with un-shuttered windows. "That's where we had breakfast. And that's the truck that brought us from the Anson."

There were few persons in evidence and no one challenged them. They walked confidently towards the dispersal point and

201

on to where the parked craft stood. There was no sign of the Anson. By this time the short day was starting to fade and they were thoroughly chilled.

"I'm freezing," said Vera. She certainly looked ultra-pale.

"We ought to look in those hangars."

"You're kidding!"

"In for a penny."

"You are bleedin' insane!"

"The worst we can do is get arrested. Then we can ask about the crash. That should clear it up one way or the other." She strode ahead.

They did not get arrested. They were not even accosted. The nearest hangar was completely secure and they couldn't see in except via a very narrow aperture at the edge of the sliding door, but that showed them nothing of value. The second hangar also had its main doors closed, but the small pass door in one of them was not locked. They secured each other's eyes, synchronised inhaling, and edged it open.

"Christ on the toilet!"

"What is it?" whispered Vera.

"That's it."

They both looked. There stood the Anson. It had not crashed. The engine cowls were off exposing the finned cylinders and their attendant pipes and cables. Its propellers were in place, and were perfectly formed. A toolbox stood, open on the floor.

"Someone's working on it."

"Yes. But I can't see a scratch of damage."

They heard the sound of a spanner on concrete, softly closed the door and hurried off towards the perimeter fence and the dispersal area where they calmly but determinedly made for the gate. They walked briskly back to the place where they had disembarked from the bus. They interpreted the timetable displayed in the shelter correctly and thirty minutes later they boarded the bus back into the centre of Jönköping. They found a cosy café and drank chocolate infused with schnapps which inflamed their constitution but clouded their thinking.

"What now?" asked Vera.

"If we had a car, a map, and summer conditions, we'd go in search of the chalet."

"Why?"

"Just a gut feeling."

"Well we ain't got any of those things."

The poser inhaled the sweet alcoholic aroma. "Mariefred then."

"Mariefred?"

"We don't need a car, a map, or summer conditions for that."

"And what do you think we will find there?"

"What you always hope to find in the home of an artist."

"And what's that?"

"Inspiration."

The windows of the house at Mariefred were entirely shuttered. They made their way around to the back, where the French windows were completely obscured. The damage that the poser had done to the back door had been repaired with a new door and frame.

"We need to get inside."

"You're not going to bash the bleedin' door in again are you?" said Vera.

"There must be a key somewhere."

"In Pic's pocket."

"Or with a neighbour."

"Why would he do that?"

"People do."

"Pic doesn't sound like that kind of person to me," mused Vera.

"We could ask. After all, according to my passport, I am his wife."

"Do they all speak English?"

"Some might."

"You're going to need a bleedin' good reason and be out of this world at explaining why you ain't got your own key."

"People hide them under plant pots. Under stones."

Vera looked at the snow covered path and garden. "Do you want me to start looking for stones?"

"Had a thought!" said the poser suddenly and dashed off to the wooden lean-to where she'd previously found the maul.

Vera followed. "Don't break the bleedin' door again," she shouted when she saw the axe, but the poser was calmly running un-gloved fingers along the inside edge of the front rim of the roof. She produced a key.

"No need," she said triumphantly.

"Bugger me," said Vera.

"Same place as at Kendal's Lodge."

Everything had been tidied. They opened the French window shutters to let in plenty of light. The armchair was there, but no sign of a human, fake or deceased. There was other furniture that the muse had not consciously noticed on her first visit, a second armchair, two small tables, a standard lamp and a sideboard. There was no carpet and the floorboards were peppered with a myriad of paint speckles, as were the three easels and, to a lesser degree, the armchairs. There were a dozen or so completed canvasses. She had recalled seeing those the first time, but now they had all been neatly stacked along wall.

"Just like Kendal's lodge," she said.

"What is?" asked Vera.

"The way these paintings have been arranged."

"Anyone could have done that," said Vera selecting the nude that had been overpainted with Edwin's torso."

The muse was at the sideboard where the oils and brushes were laid out in spectrum and size order. "Pic's done this," she said. "He always kept his brushes in order."

"This is well dry," said Vera. "It was done weeks ago."

"It's two weeks since I was here."

"It's oils. Takes longer than that," said Vera. "I know a lot of painters. Takes weeks and weeks. I'd say this was done years ago."

The muse came to look. She had to agree. She took it from Vera and stared at it for some time, not absorbing the image, but scrutinising the brushstrokes. Meanwhile Vera disappeared into the other rooms. When she eventually came back she expressed the opinion that the house had not actually been lived in for some time. There were few food supplies none of which were fresh. The kitchen looked undisturbed and the two beds she had found were not made up except with a layer of dust.

"Supposing it was him," said the muse.

"Supposing what was?"

"Who was on his way in, when I was here. Supposing he'd come in and found me here?"

"He wouldn't have been happy about what you'd done to his door."

"Do you think it was him?"

"How am I supposed to know?"

"Could have been him and Klas I suppose."

"You think he set up the whole caboodle? The whole painted corpse malarkey?"

"Having seen the work at Emira's studio, it was either him or her, and she was three hours away." She was running her hand around the edge of the canvas and sliding her fingertips over the ridges of paint. "It's all pre-planned isn't it?"

"What is?"

"Everything. His fake death, Edwin Heap's fictitious fatal crash, and me being here to bear witness."

Vera cracked open a new pack of cigarettes, handed one to her friend, slipped another between her own lips and lit both. "You can't think you were supposed to come here?"

"It wasn't hard to find. And Emira didn't stop me."

"She didn't know you were going. And you said she was genuinely shocked when you told her what you found."

"She was stressed. But she looked stressed even before I said anything. She didn't want me to see what she was working on, and her arms were splattered with exactly this hue of grey." She rubbed a drip on the floor with the toe of a boot that Emira had helped her to buy. "She admitted she'd mixed it for Pic."

Vera dragged on her fag, considered, exhaled. "She didn't encourage you to come."

"She didn't need to. And if she had, I would have insisted she came with me. I kept it from her because, kind as she was, something told me not to trust her. Not to trust anyone."

"Except me."

The poser didn't reply but remained blatantly focussed on her line of thought. "Bit of a coincidence that whoever it was arrived here just as I was taking in the exhibition."

Vera said, "Who did know you were coming here?"

"No one. Except . . ."

"Except Torn. The waiter at the hotel."

She nodded, savoured nicotine, and thought. "I had to use somebody to get a foothold. I was a stranger in a foreign land. It's possible he was primed. He was keen to make a connection with me. He helped. Emira helped. She got me the money and she promised to get me to Denmark for the operation."

"She succeeded in that."

"Dangerous to let me out of her sight, if I was all part of some grand plan."

Vera blew a tumbling grey-brown cloud. "You don't know that you were."

"I think I was."

"You don't know that you were out of her sight. She sounds like a crafty little cow. She might have done a costume change, or sent a swing."

"A swing?"

"Someone in her place. Theatre term, lovey."

"Think about it Vera. If Pic was in the pay of the Danes, they've got their desired merchandise. Pic's not only not involved with the delivery, he's even apparently dead. And so is his main partner in crime, Edwin Heap."

"But someone's going to want their plane back, and if Edwin's employed by Her Majesty, then someone will be looking for her missing spy. And aren't the same people supposed to be looking for you and your nylon baby?"

"The problem is; I've only got the word of people whose stock-in-trade is distorting the truth."

Vera wandered over to the window and surveyed the snow garden. "Well if you ask me, what you've just said makes a lot of bleedin' sense. And if Pic and Edwin are in a deal with the Danish, they'll have to avoid the Downing Street cloak and dagger brigade as much as you have to. Hence they do one and disappear."

"We're not at war with Denmark."

"Maybe not, but the boys back home are still going to be miffed that they ain't got what they wanted and somebody else has."

"That somebody doesn't have to be the Danes. The only person I dealt with was the doctor and she's a Swede."

"According to your little miniaturist who is all-knowing on things like microdots and the fraud trade."

"Oh Jesus!"

"Well your vanishing man ain't here is he? Still want to find him?"

"More than ever."

"Revenge?"

"Much more than that."

"Meaning?"

The poser took a final drag and twisted her cigarette butt beneath her boot and between two splats of grey paint. "Retribution."

"What - you going to bleedin' well cut him open?"

"Quite possibly."

Vera finished her cigarette extinguishing it by squeezing it between the nails of forefinger and thumb and slicing off the smouldering shard. It may have been the poser's imagination, but there was a tiny tremor in her voice. "Listen, if everything up to Copenhagen was in the plan, they must have kept an eye on you there. They'll know about me being with you."

And now the tremor was in Vera's hand. The poser took it and steadied it. "That's why we had to lead them a merry dance at the railway station."

Vera was nodding sagely, but looked more optimistic than wise. "Pic wanted you to run for home. He doesn't care if you hand over the microscopic polka dots so long as you say he's dead and gone."

"And Edwin Heap too. I think they wanted to disappear together."

"How romantic."

"Thing is, the powers that be won't let him disappear if he is a secret agent. Who knows where he might have gone?"

"Well we could just let them go and get on with whatever they want to get on with," said Vera.

"We can't. If they work out what we know, who knows what they'll do?"

Vera bunched up her cheeks and gave a childish grimace. "So - where next?"

"Stockholm."

"Stockholm."

"You're going shopping."

"Loverly."

"For a portrait of me."

TWENTY-SIX

Pic's art shop had completely closed down. All that remained was the signwriting on the painted board that had hung inside the window *Colin Proctor, England* but it was standing on its edge and leaning against the rear wall. Vera and the poser stared through the glass. The latter had come to see for herself after Vera had reported back. This time they had selected a hotel close to the harbour and the station. They had wanted to avoid being seen by staff at the Drottning Kristina, or the staff at the shop, or Pic or Edwin themselves should they be frequenting the premises. It was Friday 27th January.

They'd not found anything of significance at the house in Mariefred. They'd secured it and replaced the key in the wood store. Fortunately, they had sufficient time to catch the connecting train to Stockholm though it was well after dark when they arrived and selected where to stay. Vera had been dispatched after breakfast the next day. The poser accompanied her part of the way, but then sent her on ahead using the same street map she had utilised three weeks earlier. They arranged a café rendezvous but Vera was there well before the appointed time as all she could report was that the gallery had gone.

They considered investigating the apartments above, and questioning neighbours but there seemed little point. Two tentative enquiries in nearby shops resulted mostly in shrugs.

The gallery had closed suddenly, about a fortnight ago. No one offered anything more.

The twosome took stock. Their options were limited. The trail had run dry. Who knows where Pic was? There were only two possible threads to tug on. They knew where to look for Emira, but they'd need to think through what to do if they confronted her. Their other alternative was the Drottning Kristina. They considered blustering into the hotel and catching Torn or the receptionist off guard, or alternatively implementing a plan by which Vera checked in and made more subtle inquiries.

"And what's my story?" asked Vera. "How many single women go gallivanting around Scandinavia? And why?"

"You're a showgirl. You're here on business."

"And what exactly am I supposed to say to him?"

"The truth, in part. Say you've come to Sweden in search of me. You don't have to tell him you've found me."

"And at that point he just opens up and bleedin' well admits everything. Presuming there is everything to bleedin' well admit to."

The subway train swayed vigorously then suddenly decelerated into a station. They lowered their voices further. "He supplied the address in Mariefred. And I think he knew more about the theft of the sketchbook than he implied."

"But that was returned intact."

She thought for a moment, holding the silence until the train restarted. "Not quite."

"What?"

"Remember the musical notation that you got your pit pianist to play?"

"What about it?"

"One of the crotchets looked damaged to me."

"Damaged?"

"Hard to tell. But knowing what we now do about microdots, I think one might have been removed and a pencilled replacement pasted in."

"Well," said Vera, "I'll give the hotel a go, if we still draw a blank after we've taken a peep at your little elfin forger. I'll make out I'm a wronged showgirl hunting a lying sailor."

"What?"

"Every sailor loves a showgirl, and vice versa."

Putting a watch on Emira's home was not easy. Although central to that part of the city, the street was mainly residential. There were no shops or cafés close in which they could linger. All they could do was walk slowly past several times, but that was both unproductive and pointless. The poser then had a moment of inspiration. She remembered that Emira's workshop had frosted windows at a high level but which appeared to open onto a rear yard, and at the same time recalled her attempts to find access to the courtyard at the Drottning Kristina. That search had been fruitless, but this time she was more successful and they negotiated an arch via an unlocked gate and found themselves in what they were sure must be the right enclosure. There was a row of mottled and frosted windows perhaps a foot from the floor and protected by metal grilles. All of the windows were closed tightly shut and almost completely opaque. It took nervous minutes to calculate which array would belong to the basement of interest, and to whisper out the risk of discovery from one on the dozens of apartment rear windows above their heads. They summoned recklessness and crept closer. Despite the daylight an interior bulb burned in the basement room, but all they could make out were very general slabs of shape. Then there was a smudge of movement and they quickly retraced their steps and returned to the street where they put a block and a half between them and the apartment door before daring to slow and talk.

"Well that told us nothing," declared Vera. "Except that she's in there painting her pretty like fake portraits."

"No she's not."

"How do you know?"

"Because she's right ahead walking straight towards us."

"Christ!" said Vera. "Turn quick!"

They turned linked arms and hurried back the way they came taking the first junction that they came to and dashing forty yards to flatten to a doorway recess.

"Did she see us?"

"I don't think so. If she looks this way, we'll know she did."

They tensed and waited.

"There!" whispered the poser, as Emira crossed the end of the street. She did not look in their direction and as soon as she had passed the poser set off in pursuit.

"What are you doing?" protested Vera, but her friend did not falter.

"Come on!"

They reached the corner just in time to see their quarry insert her key into the door and disappear inside.

"Definitely her?"

"Definitely her."

"What now?"

"Back to that yard."

"What?"

"Come on!"

Vera caught up and held her back. "Too risky," she said.

"I don't see why it's any riskier now than before. Wait at the gate if you want."

Vera lurked inside the ginnel while the poser crept close to the window again.

A sentence was shouted.

The poser turned to see an elderly man in waistcoat and rolled-up sleeves waddling across the yard towards her. He shouted again with increased aggression. She had no idea what he was saying.

"Sorry," she said. "Sorry, I was just . . ."

She ran out of words but he had plenty and projected them with power.

"I'm very sorry," she said, "I've, I've . . ."

"It's here!" yelled Vera from behind the man. She held her hand high and when she came closer, it was clear she was holding her fine golden necklace. "Found it!" she said. "It was over here." She indicated the paved floor by the ginnel arch.

"Oh wonderful!"

Both women smiled and threw joyous thanks in the direction of the angry man. It seemed to placate him, at least partially, and they hustled each other back to the street.

"That was brilliant thinking," said the poser when they were striding back towards the harbour.

"It was acting not thinking," said Vera. "I'd done it before I'd thought about it. Lost the bleedin' cross though."

"Oh no! Shall we go back and look?"

"Don't be stupid. Told you we shouldn't have done that."

"There were two people in there," said the poser.

"Doesn't mean a lot. Are we walking or taking the metro?"

"Walk. It's not far. I want the air, and I want to show you something."

The *SS Mariefred* was in steam which the poser thought strange, because she understood that it did not operate out of season. There were people in the wheelhouse and some on the lower deck.

"Very pretty," said Vera with some sarcasm. "But why do I need to see it?"

"You don't. And neither did I, but Emira made sure I saw it."

They set off towards their hotel.

"What are you getting at?" asked Vera.

"She didn't have to bring me this way. It could all have been part of ploy to persuade me to go there."

"Bit subtle."

"Not at all. And it worked."

"You're reading too much into it."

"Maybe. But there's someone other than Emira in that back studio in the basement, and I'm beginning to think he may have been in there the last time I called. I told you, she looked uncomfortable and locked the room when she went upstairs."

"You think it could have been Pic?"

"Or Edwin. Or both."

"Christ, this is getting complicated."

"I don't think so. I think it's getting simpler."

They walked along the quay and under the bridge that carried the railway from the island of Gamla Stan.

A bag crushed over her head. She heard a muffled scream from Vera and drew breath to do the same, but by the time she'd found the volume to power it, she'd recognised the stab of the hypodermic needle in her side, and all sensation slipped away.

TWENTY-SEVEN

What followed was a series of excerpts from an abstraction. It was not possible to partition time. She had no idea how long had elapsed before she was aware that chronology had continued, but a broken narrative began to whirl. There was swaying. There was noise: mechanical, rhythmical, loud and persistent. There was a vehicle. She understood the jostle and the stiff pendulum of balance within motion. She smelled leather. She felt the shock of cold. She smelled petrol fumes. She felt hot. She sweated.

Blankness.

Cupboards. Woodgrain. Magnified woodgrain. She studied the sliced contours exposed in the timber, veneered with polish and elbow grease, and looking like the outline of Norway.

Blank again, but this time the dark was ash in tone and made of powder. She could smell mothballs.

She caught sight of faces, but the heads were enormous and formed like faces in seaside postcards and newspaper cartoons – made from papier-mâché, and far too big for the tweed-clad bodies on which they sat. Then they were gone and the dark returned, cloud-like and funnelled horizontally and shaded patently as in a woodcut print.

Then time. Lots of time. Paused but passing.

Then she was tussled. Too many hands. Straps. Fabric webbing. Thunderous clicks. Contractions of torso. A soft but heavy thudding against the backs of her thighs.

Fuel. Aviation fuel. The torrential swatting of airscrew propellers. The noise of angry internal combustion.

The shout of air. The shock of typhoon.

She tried to raise her arms but she could not even lift her eyelids.

She came and went between worlds of rubberised beings comprised entirely of gas masks and clad in laboratory coats and multitudes of magpies whose flapping caused kerosene-scented winds. She was turned and jostled. Her arms and legs were prised into tinplate crevices. She glimpsed standard issue fabric webbing and quick-release buckles. She was smothered by having her face clamped inside a latex breast. The magpies' wings flapped so fast they sounded like wartime aero engines.

The next she knew; they were bringing her round. Restoring her to communication. Introducing her to the familiar. And everyone was speaking English.

Captain Lilley, she decided, should surely have been a schoolmaster. He had that air about him. He would have been a popular sort, she thought, not that she had any experience of schoolmasters. Every single teacher she had known had been female, or least they had dressed that way. The room could have been a schoolmaster's study. It wasn't. She didn't know what it was, but it was cosy and warm, thanks to the spitting solid-fuel fire growling in the small hearth. It was a corner room with windows on two aspects, through which she had surveyed the grounds. Not school grounds. Whose grounds they were she had not been told. Whose house it was she had not been told. The nation's in all probability, though the nation probably didn't know it.

She had been loaned a simple frock and a plain brown cardigan, some underwear that was slightly too generous for her, and a pair of slippers. A military nurse had escorted her down from a bedroom on the floor above, where she had been for three nights and two days. Her sense of self gradually returned and it was only during the previous afternoon that she found coherence in her awareness of her circumstances. Her questions had been politely deflected and buried beneath the kind of reassurance that only military authority would regard as sufficient.

She occupied one leather armchair, Captain Lilley the other. He was not uniformed. White and green checked shirt. Bottle green tie. Faded and much-worn mustard waistcoat. Tweed jacket and trousers to match. Brown shoes both polished and scuffed. In his youth his hair had certainly been curled, but now it resigned itself to unruly waves. His vaulted temples formed a forehead that stretched over a demi-cranium that hadn't rooted hair for some time.

"Mount Farm," he said peering amiably over half-moon spectacles.

"Mount Farm," she said.

"It's an airfield. Strictly speaking it's an adjunct of . . ."

"I know what it is. I know where it is."

"Oh you do?"

"I do."

"You remember that."

"I remember that."

"But you do not remember your name?"

"I cannot recall it."

"But you do remember that you are not Christina Proctor?"

"I am not."

"As it says in your passport."

"She is not me."

Captain Lilley removed his glasses and sucked on the ear flange. "So what are we to call you?"

"Miss Poser perhaps?"

"Well you certainly are that. What did they call you on the ward?"

"Mrs Proctor. But that I am not."

"You are not married."

"No. I am not."

"Spinster of this parish."

"Not of this parish. I don't know where this parish is."

Lilley adjusted his posture, shifting into a more upright shape, but still adopting a relaxed attitude, leaning to one side against the generous arm of the much-utilised chair. He resettled his notes on his knee and stroked the shaft of his fountain pen. "Well you are safe, that's the first thing. Secondly, you are nestled in the very heart of England which makes you all the more secure."

"Except for the fact that I am surrounded by the English."

"And are you not English, Mrs Pro . . . Miss Poser?"

"I was born in London."

"To English parents?"

"I only have their word for that."

"Mr and Mrs . . .?"

"My father was not married to my mother."

"I see."

"I never knew him. And neither did she for very long. He's in a trench, somewhere along the Somme."

"I see. And you can't recall his name."

"I was never told it."

"What about your mother? What was she called?"

"She was called mother."

"I see." Lilley toyed with his fountain pen. She noticed that the insides of his fingers were stained with old ink. His countenance was losing tenderness.

"Listen Captain, I will tell you all I can. But I cannot tell you my name, and when you have heard all I have to say, I think you will understand why."

"Very well."

"In return I do not expect you to tell me where I now am, but I would very much value your opinion as to how I got here."

"Well that's easy. You were found in the middle of Mount Farm airfield shortly before nine o'clock in the morning of Sunday the twenty-ninth of January. Three days ago. You'd been there probably since the small hours. You were lucky not to have suffered frostbite. There was no wind to speak of but your parachute covered you."

"Parachute!"

"You don't recall jumping out of an aeroplane?"

"I don't recall being in an aeroplane. But . . ."

"Yes?"

"Let's start at the beginning."

"Yes. Let's do that."

She recounted her story, but selectively. She spoke of the war and of her anonymous friendship. She spoke of the postcard from abroad over a decade later. She mentioned Coward, but not what happened to him, except to say that she had been informed that he had passed away, and been presented with a dossier of his findings on her behalf. She did not mention Mrs Coward. She told of her further inquiries aided by 'Alice' and Tinky and of her unexpected reunion and the subsequent night flight. At no point did she mention her fear that it was the British authorities who posed a threat, instead she suggested she was motivated by love. Captain Lilley appeared entirely convinced by that. She then implied that Pic's concern was that her hidden cargo was being sought by the Soviets. She wanted to avoid bringing Edwin Heap into it, but he was too integral to leave out. Lilley seemed impressed that she specified the aircraft type as an Avro Anson. He probed her on that, but she once again said that she could not reveal the nature of her war service. He seemed even more impressed. She spoke at length about her adventures in Sweden but reported what she thought she had been intended to see, not what she actually perceived. She implied that both Pic and Edwin were dead. She told him what had happened in Denmark and said that she and Alice had gone back to Sweden to try to connect again with Emira.

"Why?"

She thought fast. "We were running out of money. We thought she could give us more."

He didn't seem convinced.

"And I wondered that she might know what happened to Pic. After his death I mean. Where he might be buried."

"And did she?"

"I didn't manage to re-establish contact. I was attacked, pretty much in public, on a quayside path beneath the railway bridge to Gamla Stan. I was drugged. I felt the needle. The next thing I knew I was in your bed."

Lilley shuffled uncomfortably. "Not exactly."

"In a military bed. Not a civilian hospital."

"No. Well, you were in uniform."

"In uniform?"

"Women's Royal Army Corps."

It was her turn to shuffle uncomfortably. "Ugh."

"From that reaction I suspect you were a Wren during the war."

"Suspect as you wish."

"I have no wish to suspect. Only a desire to be of service. As I believe you do."

"You don't have my clothes?"

"I'm afraid not."

"Or any of my belongings?"

"Your, or rather – a – passport, was in the breast pocket. That's all."

"All?"

"We do not have the item that was allegedly inserted and subsequently removed from your abdomen."

"Oh. Well easy come, easy go."

"Hardly easy."

"No." She didn't ask about the sketchbook, because she had excluded it from the account she had given. She had reasons for that. Neither had she said anything about the enlarged facsimile she had posted to Tinky or about their expedition to the airfield at Jönköping or her return visit to the house at Mariefred. "What about Alice?"

Captain Lilley shrugged. "No sign I'm afraid."

"Oh god."

"Best not to presume, until such time that presumptions have foundation."

"No."

"Well, all that was very interesting."

"What now?"

"Is there anything that you have omitted to tell me?"

She faked thinking. "Not that springs to mind."

"There's a lounge along the corridor. I'm sure a cup of tea could be furnished."

"But – what now? For me?"

"We'd like you to stay for a few days longer. Just while you fully recover, and in case anything else occurs to you that you think it would be useful for us to know."

"You being what exactly?"

Lilley smiled as if to say you are an intelligent woman and I think you know the answer to your question. "The civil service. And we're nothing if not civil, so let's sort you out some tea." He started to get up.

"And after a few more days – what then?"

"Well – you can go home."

"I don't know that I have a home to go to."

"I'm sure we can sort something out."

She learned that the house was referred to as *The Manor* which didn't help very much, but she observed that, irrespective of Captain Lilley's reference to the civil service, they were situated in a military establishment. Everyone held a rank, including all the medical staff, though not unlike her wartime posting, there was a mix of the armed forces. She was informed that the grounds were secure. Military police patrolled, and manned the gate.

She could see little from her room as an arc of woodland embraced the estate on three sides, and while the fourth aspect was open, all she could see was arable pasture and a farm in the distance.

She was intensely concerned about Vera, to the point of entering the kind of suspended mourning that she had seen drain so many during the war. She had no feelings regarding her material loss of the clothes she had bought in Stockholm and the few personal items she had left there. Not even the separation from Pic's sketchbook bothered her. She had worked out its purpose in a super-secret theory that she had shared with no one, not even Vera. Page by page the geography of the atlas of her escapade was falling into place. The latest chapter had been the most disturbing. To enter unconsciousness intravenously and to awake in a different country and be told that she had arrived by parachute in the middle of the night, required a comprehension of cavernous proportions and a mental stability to match, were she not to lose her sanity. To her joy she found not alarm but calm. It fitted with her thesis. Of course she had to be sent back to England, how else could she recount the story with which she had been infested?

She thought it likely that she had been trailed all the way to Denmark and that Pic's people had been kept fully informed of the medical procedure. She even thought that sending for 'Alice' was most likely part of the plan. It had probably been the hope that her friend would have persuaded her to go straight back to the United Kingdom, but that had not happened and the scheme may have been spoiled when they behaved unpredictably at Copenhagen station.

It seemed risky, but parachutes that were properly packed did not fail, and it was her guess that in order to ensure she landed on target, she most likely fell from a relatively low altitude. Being drugged, her landing would surely be relaxed and likely to incur little harm. Even if she had not survived her corpse carried enough clues to commence inquiries. The passport was fake but inside there had been placed a business card for Pic's Stockholm gallery and another for the hotel Drottning Kristina.

Of course she wondered who had handled her in her unconscious state. Who had dressed her? Who had pushed her from the plane? Probably Pic. It had most likely been the Anson, which had most likely been flown by Edwin. The door just aft of the wing trailing edge was ideal for shedding unwanted cargo. It would have been the final embrace from Pic.

She was pleased that she had been faithful to him. She had told Captain Lilley that Pic was dead. She had told him that Pic's lover was dead, but she hadn't enlightened him as to the nature of the relationship between the two men. She did not report what Emira had said about finding the two men in bed, but she had accurately described what appeared to be Pic's last painting. Lilley had carefully noted that. She saw his unspoken deduction. That was good. That painting had been displayed to her for that reason. It gave vitality to the reason for Pic's 'death'.

Although she still didn't know who Pic was, she suspected that Captain Lilley did. There was an assuredness to his inquiry that suggested he knew even before he introduced himself. He was by nature, and perhaps by culture, a calm and unflappable character. Nothing had surprised him, but she suspected that may have been because a good deal of it was already in his knowing. He did not appear astounded by the Danish connection. Perhaps they had even passed on the codes? They may have done, but not the additional one: the appendix to the appendix. She had an idea where that was.

Captain Lilley questioned her twice more, but by then she was almost entirely recovered and even more careful about what she said. She was the one holding all the strings. She knew which she wanted to pull tight. She continued to foster the opinion that Lilley actually knew quite a lot about Pic and Edwin, but she felt equally secure that he had not put a name to her.

"Well, there seems little point in detaining you any further," he said on the morning of Friday 1st February. "But it wouldn't be prudent just to let you loose, as it were. No name, no pack drill, nowhere to stay."

"I have things in London. I know people there."

He looked over his half-moon lenses. "And they will – er – recognise you will they?"

"Oh I expect so."

"You can tell us, you know."

"I wish I could. But I have no desire to."

He suppressed a squirm. "Well, we can't force you."

"I suspect you could." She had caught him off guard and the suppression lifted. "But how would it help?"

"How are we to contact you?"

"Why would you wish to?"

"We may discover something. About your friend Alice, for example."

"Then let the theatre know. That was the closest she had to family. And I've told you about Tinky, and where he teaches. I shall keep in touch with him."

"Yes. I think you should."

"I will."

"Well, a rail warrant. To London then."

"Yes please."

"We'll see if we can sort you out some more clothes."

"These will suffice. But a coat and some shoes might be beneficial."

"Old WRAC Standard issue I'm afraid. Ex war stock. But they should keep the rain off."

"Thank you."

"Oh and the first few miles will need to be, obscured, as it were. Blindfold, I'm afraid."

"That's fine."

The greatcoat was a size too big but the regulation shoes fitted. Her nurse also provided some stockings. The blindfold was surprisingly comfortable being more akin to a sleep mask than the bandage she had expected. She was assisted into the rear of a canvass-covered Land Rover and guided to sit along the longitudinal bench, at right angles the direction of travel. After quarter of an hour or so, the accompanying military policeman removed the blindfold but she remained ignorant as they were completely shrouded by the fastened canvas. She could not even see the driver or his companion as the front seats were cordoned off. The driver and passenger chatted a little. The latter had a Scots accent, and an irritating cough.

Just before they reached their destination the driver stopped and the passenger said his farewells before getting out. Only a minute or so later they drew to a halt, the engine died and the driver, who turned out to be another military policeman untied the back flap of the canvas and lowered the tailgate before helping her down to the pavement outside Oxford railway station.

Her rail warrant was made out for Marylebone. She didn't have long to wait for the train. It was long enough to hear the Scotsman's cough again. And she heard it several times more on the train.

TWENTY-EIGHT

It didn't take long to persuade Vera's neighbour to hand over the key to her flat, after all, the poser was known to her and had got on well with her. Deidre, who had the adjacent room on that landing, was immediately sympathetic. She'd known that 'Alice' had gone looking for her friend but hadn't been told where. She seemed understanding when the poser said they had met up but declined to say where or why Alice was still there. She inquired regarding her injuries and was reassured to hear that they were healing at least in terms of the severity of their appearance. Deidre was intelligent and wise enough to grasp the context without needing to probe further. Like Vera she worked in the theatre, hence her way of life was rooted in deception, which made her all the more genuine. She knew when the mask should not be lifted. She was satisfied, but not relieved by the truth that she was given: Alice was in Europe but her well-being was not known. She smiled thinly and handed over the latch key. It was somewhere to stay and at last the poser was reunited with the bulk of her belongings and with her genuine passport.

She commented on the key. It looked newly cut. Deidre confirmed that it was. When Alice had returned from the hospital she did not have her key. She thought she must have left it at the theatre, but when she visited to see her colleagues, she hadn't been able to find it. Evidently a relative had taken her belongings from her dressing room to the hospital, but the key wasn't among them. Alice lost keys quite regularly according to Deidre. A new spare had been cut from the previous one. This was the first time it had been used and it was a little stiff, but it worked.

The first thing she did was use the shared bathroom and have a good bath. She'd had one whilst in detention at *The Manor* but now she was able to savour it more, she was, at last, on home territory and at liberty, though she had reservations about the latter. She also carefully washed her hair, tenderly touching the strands that Vera had stitched together beneath the bulk at the back of her head and close to the base of her skull.

Only after that did she experience a slight stun. The two locked suitcases she'd left in Vera's flat had been opened. The keys that she'd hidden beneath the wardrobe had not been used. The locks had been forced. There did not appear to be anything missing, but her belongings had been disturbed. She reasoned through this and the stun faded. She understood what had happened and it complied with her emerging thesis.

She dressed in her own winter clothes. She selected the best quality underwear that she'd normally reserved for nights out, a thick underskirt, a cotton blouse, a finely woven A-line skirt and a highland pattern knitted cardigan. She rooted through Vera's stock of tinned food and concocted a mashed potato and tinned fish dish, which she found to be surprisingly tasty. It was the flavour of the England she'd forgotten. She also raided Vera's liquor supply, treating herself to a small sherry as the February evening fell. She wondered if Deidre would call, but then realised that she was probably at work. She planned her next moves. Tomorrow she would telegraph Tinky and hopefully arrange to meet with him, then she would travel north. She'd uncovered two fake deaths, and needed to check a third. She snuggled down in Vera's bed and imagined there was some trace of her friend in the scent of the sheets. There was. She slept soundly and did not remember the dreams that infused her.

She could not determine whether the office was still in use or not. Paul enlightened her. He was the caretaker who had unlocked the rear entrance to the bank when Mr French had slipped her out that way on the day of Mr Coward's funeral.

Someone must have alerted him when she was heard knocking repeatedly at the stockbroker's top floor door. Perhaps the banking branch staff on the lower levels had seen her ascending the staircase, or it might just have been a coincidence, but even if he hadn't have materialised it was in her mind to seek him out.

"Oh aye, they're still trading," said the security man, his colloquial inflection slightly at odds with his formal attire she thought. His three-piece pinstriped suit, winged collar and bow tie together with his weary pessimistic expression gave him the air of the former prime minister Neville Chamberlain, but the timbre his accent was more that of a factory shop steward. His suit was highly maintained but low quality. "But not every day. Not today."

"Bit risky for a stockbroker," she said.

Paul raised his eyebrows. "It's just Mr French now," he said.

"It was Mr French I was hoping to see."

"Well, you'll not see him today, I fear."

"I want to pay my respects to the late Mr Coward."

"Cemetery would be best place for that."

"Which cemetery?"

"Th'old one."

"Where's that?"

"Next t'new one."

"And where will I find them?"

"You'll want number thirteen bus."

"Thirteen?"

"Unlucky."

She smiled thinly, briefly. "Is it a large cemetery?"

"Oh aye. There's a lot of dead folk live there."

"You wouldn't know his grave?"

"Not intimately." Her smile thickened. He continued, "I haven't presented myself to it as yet, but I'm told his name has been added to t'tombstone. Quite a grand affair, according to Mr French. Longstanding family grave. Still room for one more I believe. That'll be Mrs Coward."

"She's not . . ?"

Paul shook his head. "In the fullness of time."

"Ah yes."

Paul fingered his keys. "There's an office. At the main gates. They have charts. Records."

225

"Ah yes. Number thirteen bus."

"Lucky for some."

"Thank you." She looked once more at the faded gold lettering on the glass of the door.

"Shall I tell Mr French? That you were here."

She considered. "No. There's no need. I've found out what I wanted to know. You've been most helpful."

"Right you are."

The gravestone was grand. It had a plinth and column base that would have graced any Roman forum or Norman church. The rectangular body was carved with gothic frames and bore inscriptions on two sides. It was topped by an impressive granite cross, plain in style and elegant in proportion. Conrad Coward's name was freshly imprinted towards the foot of the rear, something that could only have done by the mason working in situ. Inspired by Vera's Danish gift, she had purchased a potted hyacinth. She placed it reverently beneath his name then stood back in the manner of a cenotaph contemplation.

She had warmed to Conrad. He had somehow managed to combine the considerate geniality of a well-liked uncle with the restrained optimism of a reassuring general practitioner. In return she had brought about his death. There was no fighting the guilt. There was no denial of it. Had she not entered his life it would not have ended prematurely. The sadness she suffered was redoubled by this concrete confirmation of his passing. Unlike Pic, unlike Edwin, this demise was not a disguise. The grave had recently been excavated. The soil was disturbed, the spoil stood proud of the surrounding earth. The name was newly carved. This was consequence. This was collateral. This was cruel.

The east wind cut at her cheeks and her eyes ran wet.

"Sorry Mr Coward," she said out loud but inaudibly to anyone except herself and the magpie pecking at the periphery of her field of focus. She crouched down and adjusted the plant pot, swivelling it so that the proudest of the stacked buds faced the observer.

"That's lovely," said a voice from behind her.   Mrs Coward stood a dozen yards away beneath a yew that formed an umbrella over un-aligned headstones tilting around a curve in the graveyard path. She wore a black overcoat and hat and carried a grey furled gamp and matching leather handbag.

The poser shivered, partly at the sight, partly with shock, and partly with shame. "Mrs Coward."

"Miss A."

"I'm so sorry, I had no intention of contacting you."

The widow walked towards her. "I didn't think you would. That's why I tracked you down."

"How?"

"Mr Lonsdale."

"Who?"

"Caretaker at the bank."

"Oh."

"He telephoned me this morning. I came directly. I have a chauffeur." She inclined her head in the direction of the cemetery gate. The poser fancied she could see a human jackdaw pacing beyond the yew. It could have been the driver; it could have been another kind of anthropological corvid. "I enquired at the cemetery office. They said you were here. It's a pretty plant."

"Yes. I hope it survives." She hadn't meant to say that. Mrs Coward was now alongside her.

"Nothing does. Not for ever."

"I really didn't want to . . ."

"It's all right. I knew you to be a woman of your word, but I wanted to see you."

"This is my fault."

"Hardly."

"Oh yes, it is."

"I know I may have asserted that at our first meeting, but the passing of time brings perspective. All you did was what you were asked to do. And also that which you were not asked. You received a postcard and you followed the request. You unknowingly carried a precious cargo. Do you still have it?"

She had to think rapidly. This was not an exchange she had anticipated or rehearsed. "I've had an operation. The cargo was removed."

"Do people know?"

"Which people?"

"Her Majesty's intelligence."

"Yes, they know."

227

"Then you can relax. Are they in possession of the cargo?"

She hesitated, considered, decided. "I don't know. When you have an operation, you are not aware of all that takes place."

"Hmm." Mrs Coward used the tip of her umbrella to spear a small paper bag that had fluttered onto her husband's resting place. She strolled a few yards to a litter basked and scraped the bag into the receptacle.

When she returned the poser said, "Why did you want to see me?"

"Why did you come all this way?"

To satisfy myself that your husband really is dead she thought, but said, "To pay my respects to your husband. His passing played on my mind. I feel I brought about his death, albeit indirectly. He had been trying to help me. And so did you."

"Did you find your elusive paramour?"

"Yes. Or rather he found me."

"And is your friendship enduring?"

A real corvid croaked somewhere in the foliage.

"It seems he committed suicide. In Sweden."

"Oh dear."

"Possibly as a consequence of the loss of his close friend in a flying accident, also in Sweden."

"What kind of close friend?"

"A school friend. A wartime friend. Fight Lieutenant Edwin Heap."

"Ah."

"You've heard of him?"

"He worked for military intelligence during the Berlin Airlift and after."

"Until this day?"

Mrs Coward shrugged, rebuffing the east wind. "Clearly not, if he is deceased."

"You still haven't told me why you wanted to catch me."

"I'm not demonstrably sentimental as you have no doubt observed. It's all down to one's upbringing I suppose. But this place fails to induce any feelings of attachment for me. Would you like to see the bridge?"

"What bridge?"

"The one that Conrad partially demolished when he died. Do you have time or are you rushing back to London?"

The chauffeur was of a similar vintage to Mr Coward, the car, a Bentley, was new. "Simon cannot hear us speak unless we open the glass," said Mrs Coward as they glided through the suburbs, she then fell silent for some time. The roads were stark and spindly as February frugality locked their leafy ostentation firmly in waiting. Eventually they took a turning that she recognised from her taxi trip with Mr French, and the road was suddenly rural, narrow and with thick high hedges. "Captain Lilley told me most of what you told him," said Mrs Coward suddenly. "I didn't even tell him your name."

The Bentley slowed gracefully and took a tight turn without invoking any palpable centrifugal force. "Thank you."

"Of course he has no need to tell me anything. I'm no longer on the books so to speak. However, in the intelligence business no one ever retires. We rely on old heads for proverbial insight."

"I didn't tell him about you, or your husband. I didn't think it was relevant and I had promised to leave you in peace."

"I know and I'm grateful. I didn't confess any foreknowledge of you. I've kept your confidence too. Lilley telephoned me because you mentioned Lieutenant Heap. I'd enquired about him some weeks ago. Following my husband's accident."

"Why?"

"Conrad was an exceptional human being. He was the most tender creature I have encountered. This is the bend."

It was the most innocuous stretch of tarmac at first sight, however, once the chauffer had eased the car to a halt and they had stepped out she could see its deceptive severity. It comprised a double bend with the apexes separated by some fifty yards laterally but also by about thirty feet in height as the carriageway dropped to cross a stream. The bridge itself formed the lower curve. The parapet had been repaired. The car had not broken through, said Mrs Coward. The wall had held, though part of it had needed to be reconstructed. The car had crumpled selectively. The steering column had crushed her husband's breast. The dashboard had snapped his skull. She said all that without any emotional colour in her tone. She then led the way to one side and a little way up the hill. There, and some yards higher, the police had found spillages of oil. They speculated that it had sprayed from the front brake lines when the pedal had been depressed. The brakes would therefore have failed and the spilled oil may even have exacerbated the situation by spoiling the grip of the rear tyres.

He surely must have used the brakes before reaching that point?

Of course, but it was rush hour, so in town the traffic was slow-moving and this would be the first place where he would have placed them under high load. He was not a reckless driver but here the road would have been clear, he was going downhill and by now he may have already shed much of the fluid that should have been in the reservoir.

She wanted to know the coroner's conclusion.

It had been impossible to ascertain. Both front brake pipes had crimped as a result of the collision. Both had leaked where the crimps had fractured. They may have been weakened prior to the incident. They may even have been partially sawn through.

The recounting of the facts remained robust throughout Mrs Coward's description. Once she was done, a different demeanour descended. She observed the damaged wall with dejection, despair and envy. It had been repaired.   The poser did not want to break the contemplation with more questions. She wondered what would happen next. Mrs Coward still had not explained why she had gone to the trouble of this meeting. She had a train to catch. The afternoon was waning. She waited silently. Her companion took a deep breath, restored her robustness, and said, with just a hint of aggression, "May I offer you a bed for the night?"

The chauffer turned out to be an excellent cook. He served duck with citrus sauce and boiled vegetables. He did not eat with them, but Mrs Coward implied he had accommodation there.

"I imagine you would like me to fill you in on the details of my Scandinavian adventure?" she said.

"There's really no need. It's really not my affair."

"Then why am I here? Why did you go to the trouble of . . . intercepting me?"

Mrs Coward sipped the excellent wine. "It's not in my nature to simply let things lie. And I worked in intelligence too long to not sense the whiff of an underhand enterprise. Once the funeral was over and some sort of routine returned, I made discrete enquiries. I had copies of the information given to you. One name struck a chord. Edwin Heap flew many photoreconnaissance missions during the war and he remained in service for several years after. His work was always sensitive and so he inevitably moved in certain circles. Eventually he was recruited. He became a liaison person between the Intelligence Service and the armed services, in particular the RAF and the Fleet Air Arm."

"Is that still his function?"

"Still?"

Everything was motionless.

The poser clarified, "Until he crashed."

Mrs Coward resumed cutting her carrots. "Captain Lilley has had reservations about Heap for some time. He may have been a double agent. He may still be."

This time the poser paused, but her host persisted in eating. "Why do you think that?" She waited for Mrs Coward to chew her carrot.

"A crash can be used to cover a disappearance."

The ambience seemed supercharged with integrity. The poser was severely tempted to confess all she had discovered, but some even deeper instinct prevented it.

"From the description that I heard, those on board could not have survived."

"Those on board. Did you see Flight Lieutenant Heap board that aeroplane?"

"No, of course not. I was . . . miles away."

"Well he may or may not have been involved in that crash. And he may or may not have been involved in the one that instigated my widowhood."

"You think Heap was responsible for that?"

"I think it is quite likely."

"Just to stop your husband from helping me?"

"Why else?"

"But then he helped me. He flew me to Sweden."

"And – someone - brought you back. Who? And what was the point in that?"

"Heap was not operating in isolation."

"I have no doubt."

"His associates clearly wanted you to know my . . . artificial appendix had been removed."

"Very considerate of them. But there was no need to return you alive to prove that. What they wanted, my dear, was for you to tell us what you have recounted. Heap wants to be 'dead' so that he can live in peace."

"Heap?"

"Perhaps in Poland."

"Poland?"

"He has friends in Poland. And others with Polish connections."

"Connections?"

"Ancestry."

"Surgeons?"

"And painters."

Mrs Coward stared straight into her eyes. Each woman ate more slowly. Each waited for the other. Mrs Coward said, "Would you like me to tell you what I can about your paramour?"

"No," she said. "No I would not."

"As you wish."

"He's gone. He's dead. And so is Edwin Heap."

"Well, let us hope so; because if Fight Lieutenant Heap is not dead, he may not rest until you are."

TWENTY-NINE

Tinky was exuberant company. He immediately and persistently lifted her spirits. There was not a moment of silence during the entire weekend when they were in each other's company. She had travelled up on Friday 8th March, having spent all week back in London at Vera's flat. Deidre had remained discrete, but looked increasingly concerned as the week had progressed. She seemed to accept that there was more to be learned than she was allowed to know and did not pry. She did, however, help the poser with matters theatrical, bringing stage make-up, a trio of wigs and one or two items from her theatre wardrobe. In return she was promised to be made the recipient of any news about Alice that might transpire. The poser kept well clear of Vera's workplace, and moved about London constantly vigilant and hoping not to encounter any of Vera's colleagues. With Tinky though, she was completely open.

She had wired him before going north and she had telephoned him the previous Sunday from the station when she had arrived back in London off the slow train. It took two attempts to get through and an agonising wait whilst he was brought to the telephone. It reminded her of the awful wartime link-ups waiting to get to speak to cherished others. His voice suddenly bellowed its joy and arrangements were hurriedly made. She could sleep on his sofa.

They talked long into the night. She intrinsically trusted him. There was no logic to that judgment, but neither was there any niggling sprig of a doubt. He had all that she had dispatched to him from Sweden, very securely secreted away; the letter from the hotel, the airmail letter in case she disappeared, and the telegram to back it up. Most importantly, he had the facsimile of the enlarged photograph of Stonorowich's code safely stuffed in the rafters of his attic. All those things remained out of sight that night, as they had so much to talk over.

It was after midnight before they were in a position to review all that she had to report. Sherry had been consumed, but concentration was heightened rather than muffled.

"Well," said Tinky, stretching his spine convexly then collapsing back concave within the armchair, "where are we now?"

She rubbed her brow and slipped her hand through her hair, pausing when she found the stitched strands behind her head and close to her skull. "We are here," she said, and stood, stepping closer to him and bending before him to reveal what she was fingering. At first he was flummoxed.

"What?"

Then he saw the artefact she was trying to show him.

"My goodness!" he exclaimed. "It that it?"

"That is the question. It is certainly what they gave me in Denmark. You've got the copy in your attic and I've got the original in my hair."

"Good lord in heaven."

Tinky touched her locks and felt the flap of nylon that Vera had stitched into her hair. She said she wanted him to take it out, but it could wait until the morning. Then she wondered if the school biology lab might have a microscope they could use. Tinky said they most certainly did, and as lessons happened on Saturday mornings he would bring one back to his lodging at lunch time. They could then compare what was imprinted there with the enlarged photograph to ensure they matched.

"Even if they do," she said, "it doesn't prove this was inside me. I was not awake when they supposedly took it out. You can't do blood tests can you?"

"What - you mean see if there is any still on it? Unlikely, and far too small amount even for an industrial lab to deal with, let alone ours I should think."

"I suppose I'll never know. There is so much we have to take on trust."

"I studied the photograph. Twelve patterns. Meaningless to me, not being a linguist, but seems simple. The cipher doesn't look especially complicated, but impossible of course, unless you have the key and can read the Cyrillic script. And you think there was a thirteenth design?"

She sat down again and shook her hair back into place. "Something was removed from the sketchbook. I could show you the place but the sketchbook is still in Stockholm, depending on whatever they did with my belongings in the hotel."

"And of course there is the most disturbing question of all; what did they do with Alice?"

"You've heard nothing?"

"Not a peep dear girl."

"She would have contacted you if she could."

The room fell completely quiet.

"She would."

Quieter still. The poser was severely tempted to share the suspicions that had been generated by her intimate embrace with Vera, but held back.

"Very well," said Tinky at last, "tell me what you think. What's the plot of this tangled tragedy?"

She took a deep breath and another sip of sherry and then explained her grand theory. She was still puzzled by the very beginnings – the appendectomies – but she concluded that there was subsequently a connection between Stonorowich and the post-war Soviet Union. She guessed that his code was being used and that somehow the UK Intelligence Service had learned about it, but were completely unable to break it without the cipher key. They must have known where it was allegedly hidden and either they got to the other women or the Soviets beat them to it. She suspected the latter. She doubted, or hoped, that the British authorities would have carried out surgery rather than instigate a culling. Whoever killed those women either removed the implants or failed to find them because they were not stitched to the intestine. Or they might not have been there at all. She had become their last hope, but first they had to trace her, find her and abduct her. Prior to that being realised, Pic must have been brought into it all and he began the whole process of locating her first.

He was alerted by Edwin Heap whom, according to Mrs Coward, was inside the Secret Service.

Tinky concurred with her thesis thus far.

What she postulated was that Edwin might be a double agent who was worried that the code might in some way expose him. Pic was helping to prevent that.

Tinky's posture perceptibly tightened. That troubled her. She put it on one side and continued her hypothesis.

They had taken her abroad to protect her, and possibly also to protect Edwin.

"Or both of them," said Tinky.

Yes, she agreed, she could see that now. Pic might also have been implicated in espionage.

"Amongst other things."

"What?"

"Do you think Pic was in love with you?"

"During the war, possibly. His affections certainly felt genuine then. But he was different when we met again. The passion was not there."

"Not for you."

Her sherry was slowing her a little. "No."

"And why did he kill himself?"

"He didn't."

"I know. But at first you thought otherwise. And it made sense."

"He'd appeared so affected by the reports of Edwin's supposedly fatal crash. Emira told me she'd found them in bed together. I had come to the conclusion that Pic was in love with Edwin."

"I think you are probably right."

"So why fake the death?"

"What's your opinion?"

"So they can vanish and be together."

"It looks that way."

"And at the same time, shed all their former connections, responsibilities, allegiances. At least in this country."

"Yes."

"The whole plan may have been pretty much as it has panned out, except that I was not expected to arrange my own corrective surgery."

"Emira was probably assigned to that task. Could her reaction to Pic's supposed self-poisoning have been an act?"

"It's hard to say. It looked very convincing. But fakery is her stock-in-trade."

"I suspect your intended return to these shores may have been much more conventional business. If Emira had escorted you to Denmark, following your surgery, she would have reassured you that you were out of danger from the authorities here, and simply put you on a boat or a plane back to Blighty. The cipher they gave you might be fake and so it wouldn't matter if you handed it over. They may have swapped it. Or perhaps the only one that mattered was the one in the sketchbook."

"But they knew where that was – at Kendal's Lodge."

"However, we got to it first."

"Then why fly abroad without it? They didn't know I had it with me. The only people who could have known that were you and . . .

"Alice."

The new possible perspective on Vera's role was not the best thought to have in her head just prior to retiring for the night, but the sherry and the dinner had done their work and she slept soundly. When she awoke, Tinky was scoffing a hurried slice of toast and dashing off to take Saturday morning school. She rose, and washed and ate much more leisurely. Two slices of toast and some rather good tea. She wandered the school campus alone, enjoying the secure normality of the environment.

Tinky returned not long after noon bearing a wooden box with an integral leather handle. This turned out to be a microscope from the biology laboratory. He'd also been thoughtful enough to acquire pointed scissors from the same source and using those he was able to delicately cut the strands of thread with which Vera had stitched the nylon curl to the poser's hair. It didn't take long, and soon it was flattened between a pair of glass slides and clipped to the viewing plate of the brass apparatus. The microdots showed very clearly in most areas. Smudges that they had seen on the photograph were, in fact, replicated on the nylon, but they only partially obscured four of the twelve arrays. It all meant nothing to them, mainly because it was printed using the Cyrillic alphabet, but they were at least able to confirm that the photograph was a true replica of the synthetic patch she had been given, whether or not it had ever been sutured inside her.

"This is very technically sophisticated printing," said Tinky, "especially for 1944. I can only think Stonorowich brought it with him when he found refuge here."

"Unless it was sent to him."

"Possible. In either case he looks less of a refugee and more of an interloper."

"Still doesn't explain his bizarre choice of hiding place for it."

"What will you do with it now? I can darn socks but I wouldn't risk my attempts to stitch it back in your hair."

"I'll do the stitching," she said. "I bought a new shift last week, I'm going to stitch it into that. It somehow feels fitting."

Tinky returned the photo to his loft. She asked him if she could borrow the picture of Pic and Edwin from his wartime album and he cheerfully extracted it and handed it over. "Not borrow, my dear, have it. Have it."

"Thank you."

They talked more but without successfully extending their hypotheses. The following morning Tinky drove her to the railways station.

"What are your plans?" he asked as they jostled along the country lanes.

"Back to Stockholm."

He slowed as if on unsafe asphalt. "Seriously?"

"I have to find out what has happened to Alice."

"That might be very difficult."

She shrugged. "Difficulty has never been a deterrent. Alice came to help me. I can do the same for her."

"She might be beyond help."

"She might. But then there's the secondary objective."

"Which is?"

"To inform Pic that I haven't betrayed him."

"That might be equally difficult."

"I suspect it will."

He drove without speaking for a moment, then said, "So Pic is now secondary and Alice is primary."

She said, "Yes Alice is primary." She looked at Tinky who

smiled slightly, then he surrendered his lips back to gravity, and said, "Is she badly disfigured?"

"Badly enough to terminate her employment."

He nodded gently.

She said, "Do you think it is possible to live one's life without unwittingly damaging others?"

"That's what life does," he said. "Damage. Nothing can live without doing damage. And it cannot die without being damaged. Sooner or later whatever lives will be damaged."

She nodded not with consent but as a consequence of the motion. "Think I've had my share yet?"

"That suggests fairness is involved, which it most certainly is not. It all comes down to the cards we hold. Everyone fears the reaper, but the real threat lies with the dealer."

She tolerated more motion, thinking about cards and holding back the question that she had to ask, before very carefully enunciating it. "Do you curse the dealer, Tinky?"

"Oh god no. I just want to go to bed with him."

Tinky's magical honesty exploded the morose mood and they crumpled into giggling. Not long after that he pulled the car into a natural layby close to a stile in the hedge. She looked quizzically towards him.

"I suspected you might be going to throw yourself back into the fray," he said, "so I have something for you. Step out. It will only take a minute or two."

He took her around to the boot of the car from which he produced a brown paper package. She held it while he unfastened the string. It had substantial weight and rattled. "It's my old service revolver," he said, "and some ammunition. Don't ask how I snaffled it."

She looked alarmed but he maintained his chirpy pragmatism and took her to the stile where he demonstrated how to load and fire it. Then he made her try, putting two shots into the copse on the far side of the field. "Good," he said. "Now for Christ's sake be careful when you go through customs."

They got back in the car and he drove on to the station. They bid farewell and made promises to maintain contact as best they could, then they hugged and he drove off. She bought her ticket and went to await the arrival of anthracite steam. Her luggage was a little heavier, but felt much more so.

She showed the photo to Imo the stage doorkeeper. He nudged his multi-coloured cap back over his trimmed curls and leaned against the jamb of his kiosk. He peered through the dusty lenses of his spectacles, perused the picture and rocked his head slowly in confirmation. "That's him."

"Which one?"

He angled the photograph placing his thumb beneath Edwin's chin. "That's your man."

"You sure Imo?"

"Now Miss, you don't question Imo. Imo is not for forgetting a face. Your man said he was wanting Alice's things to take them to her at the hospital."

"Did he say who he was?"

"A friend of the family."

She paused. "A friend of the family," she echoed, slightly sarcastically.

Imo handed the picture back, and slowly slid the bridge of his spectacles higher up his nose. His weary deportment had a Caribbean warmth to it. He revelled in the authority his unflappability projected.

"So you let him in to her dressing room."

"That I did."

"Do you know what he took?"

"Her coat. Her clothes. Her bags."

"How many bags?"

"Both of them."

"Thank you Imo."

The doorkeeper returned to his high stool perch. "You're welcome Miss."

"Good bye."

"Good day Miss."

She turned to exit the theatre. He halted her with his call, which contained just a hint of urgency. "Miss?"

"Yes?"

"Will we be seeing some more of Miss Alice?"

"I really don't know."

"Should you be with her, say hello from Imo."

"I will."

THIRTY

It was only the third time she'd flown but only the second that she could remember. This time she flew in precisely the manner Emira had outlined as her alibi, with British European Airways aboard a Vickers Viscount aircraft from Heathrow. The flight was on Friday, so she had several days to wait, which only added to her anxiety regarding Vera, but she put the purgatorial days to good use by withdrawing some of her savings and, once again, replenishing her wardrobe.

She had fun. This time she was not dressing for who she was, but for who she was to become. One of the wigs that Deidre had sourced for her was blonde. She bought dresses, cardigans, blouses, skirts and a coat to complement her new hair. She was a chameleon, changing to blend in with the Scandinavian crowd. The Swedes were not all blonde, far from it, but there was a much higher proportion evident there than in the United Kingdom from what she had observed, and what mattered was a change in her appearance. She desired a disguise. The new clothes and wig helped. She also chose new make-up and experimented with that, retaining her pallor but easing it away from the porcelain paleness that she had previously favoured. She eschewed her usual scarlet lipstick and applied a softer rose hue. Similarly, she diluted the natural brunette of her eyebrows selecting an almond pencil to shape and colour them.

She then purchased a completely contrasting compendium of make-up and accessories to accompany an auburn wig. She also bought new shoes and a new small suitcase.

The experience of international travel was a touch bewildering but her years of dealing with all kinds of department store customers paid off. She had a particular regular patron in mind, and chose to imitate her enunciation, deportment and smugness but tempered it with false obsequiousness. That ensured the airline staff warmed to her and customs officials softened. She saw all persons as pawns; protectors that may be manipulated to enable her to move towards the endgame. She was not in any way intimidated, nor was she fearful. She knew what she wished to do and had a provisional strategy to initiate her campaign. She was concerned for Vera's well-being, but also that she might not succeed in her liberation, or in confronting Pic, but she was almost magically energised to attempt both. All that she had experienced thus far served to strengthen her. It had been a kind of metamorphosis. She had physically changed. Her body had opened twice, once during the war and once again in Denmark, and while each opening was small they each changed her conception of herself. She had been made the courier of a phantom. It was irrelevant whether or not she had harboured a physical artefact, or if evidence that had been handed to her was factual, her mind had been charged with the notion that she was a courier, and now it was infused with the peculiar satisfaction that she had navigated the route and delivered without handing over. She may not be pulling all the strings, but some she had plaited and others she had kept hidden. That felt empowering, but she wasn't done yet.

She went first to the hotel that she and Vera had shared, and asked about her own belongings whilst claiming to be her own cousin. Her pretence was not challenged and, after a short delay she was informed that her and Vera's luggage had been taken two weeks previously by a Swedish representative of an international shipping firm who produced signed affidavits and who had also settled the hotel bill. The representative had been female, and from the description, the poser strongly suspected it had been Emira.

She then had the audacity to present herself at the reception desk of the hotel Drottning Kristina. It was the ultimate test of her disguise and she knew it would fail, but that was the point. The subtly sardonic receptionist was on duty. The poser, with fake soft Scots accent, blonde wig, almond eyebrows, hay foundation and rose lips, gave the alias of Ruth McKean, the department store customer that she was imitating. She gave the correct address for Miss McKean, which she knew well because of several deliveries dispatched to her. The receptionist stared hard, barely attempting to disguise her suspicion, and gave the poser the key for precisely the same room she had vacated only a month earlier, at which point the poser smiled, said she had changed her mind and left immediately. She took her single suitcase across the road and into the café where she was able to secure a table with a view through the window but not too close to it. Peering over the menu she observed Torn as he emerged from the Kristina to look purposefully in each direction along Birger Jarlsgatan. She ordered fish pie and was just finishing it as Emira arrived wearing the same outfit she had worn when they first met - a black duffel coat with red piping. So the link was established. The hotel staff had a rapid method of summoning Emira. Pic had chosen that hotel. He knew of the network. He knew by then that she had not left the sketchbook in London, in fact he knew that before they had left England, because it was Edwin who had taken Alice's belongings from the theatre. It would have been he, or an accomplice, who had then used her door key, forced the locks on the poser's suitcases and searched in vain for the book. He knew she had it with her all the time they were together. He could have found it forcibly – so why didn't he? Because he didn't want her to know that the microdot it contained had been removed, and even if she discovered the damage and made the correct deduction he didn't want her to connect him with that removal.

Emira would now know the poser was back in town and have a description of her. That didn't matter. She had other clothes, she had other wigs, she had other make-up. She ordered coffee, she saw Emira leave. She waited, paid the bill, left the café and went to find another hotel.

The next morning, she emerged transformed into a burning redhead, with amber-fawn foundation, ginger eyeliner and burnt crimson lips. The counter clerks had changed from the night before, and the door porter was too polite or too ignorant to signal he'd noticed any alteration in her appearance.

She'd brought an old handbag from London, a little worse for wear, but still smart enough to employ, and into that she put Tinky's service revolver, loaded, but with the safety catch on and wrapped in a headscarf. She went to a hardware shop and bought a stout but short crowbar then made her way to Emira's workshop and forced the door.

She knew that the forger was out, because she'd already spoken to her that morning on the hotel telephone.

"Hello Emira, it's me."

"Me?"

"The third Christina Proctor."

"Christina!"

She allowed the phone line static to fill the cavity left by Emira's poorly faked surprise. "I'm back in Stockholm."

"You are?" Emira ought to stick to visual forgery, her vocal fakery simply wasn't up to scratch.

"We need to meet."

"Of course, I'd be delighted to." Now she wasn't faking.

"I'd like to repay you. For helping me."

"There's no need to do that, Christina. No need at all, but I'd love to see you. How are you? Did you have the operation?"

"We'll talk later. Meet me at the Drottning Kristina."

A tiny pause, then: "Is that where you are staying?"

"No, but I'm sure they'll serve us coffee in their lounge."

"I'm sure they will. What time?"

"Eleven, or just a little later. I have another appointment first."

"I'll be there at eleven."

At eleven the door jamb on Emira's workshop splintered and the poser slipped into the studio. She knew the residents sometimes left the street door unlocked during the day, but to her dismay she had found that was not the case when she tried to gain admission at ten forty-five. She had a plan, in this eventuality, to ring the bell of one of the neighbouring apartments, but held back from doing so, and her patience paid off. Just before eleven Emira's mother emerged. She did not lock the door behind her and as soon as she was two dozen paces down the street the poser went through the lobby to the basement room and set the crowbar to work.

It was not the first time she had forced a door. She'd resorted to it once during the London Blitz. This was just prior to her main posting and she was on leave. A stick of bombs fell in the suburb where her transit barracks was. Following the 'all clear' several damaged houses were thought to contain persons at risk or injured people and muscle power was in short supply. She and her fellow Wrens had been dispatched with jemmies to help with the search.

Her technique was effective, the Stockholm basement door not being especially robust. She wasted no time in repeating the process on the door into the rear workspace. It supported one of her fundamental suspicions. Over in the corner was a mattress. It hadn't been there the last time she was in the studio. It wasn't laid flat, but slanted against the wall, resting on its long side and with three folded blankets looped over it. A pillow was tucked on top. At the far end of the work bench a clutch of camping cutlery, a billy can, and an enamel plate and dish were stacked along with some half-consumed packets of biscuits, plus boxes of cereal and tinned vegetables. All the implements were clean and had the appearance of not having been used of late, but someone had stayed here in this subterranean space. That, in itself, was odd when there were apartments upstairs and the city was bristling with empty hotel rooms. Whoever had slept there had wanted to be well below the radar, and she thought she knew who that person might be. Finding those indicators pleased her, but it was only part of the reason for her forced entry. She searched for her primary quarry, doubting that she'd have the good fortune to find it, and all the while suppressing the shiver of anticipated discovery.

Periodically she would stop and listen hard for any hint that someone might be descending the steps and about to discover the damage she had done. She heard some movement and the opening and closing of the street door, and had heart-stopping hiatuses while she worked out which way footsteps were heading. She continued, knowing that the chances of her being disturbed were directly proportional to the length of time she remained, but she was driven to make her search as comprehensive as she could.

Two of the workbench drawers were locked. She left them until last, but not having found that which she desired, she put the crowbar to work again.

She was back on the street by twenty-past eleven and she was confident, but not certain, no one had seen her emerge. She went straight to a public call box and telephoned the Drottning Kristina. She spoke with her own accent and asked the receptionist to advise Emira that her expected meeting would be delayed but, she hoped, by not more than another half hour. She then went to the hotel Vasa, where she made a second call asking the receptionist to rearrange the meeting to the lounge of the Lady Hamilton hotel and as soon as Emira could get there. She hung up without waiting for a reply, went to her room, removed her red wig and auburn make-up before reverting to her usual appearance. She put the revolver in her handbag, ordered two gins with tonic and waited in the lounge. She was glad that there was no one else in there and hoped it would stay that way.

Ten minutes later the doorman admitted Emira. She sat opposite the poser on one of the matching leather sofas and accepted the gin. Gone was the confident cocky Emira of their early encounters, but missing too, was the apparently shocked recipient of the news of Pic's 'death'. Her sullen face was pale, with mild, but distinct, shadows below her eyes. Somehow her countenance seemed sharper and even more elfin, but joyless and embarrassed in a way akin to someone who has been caught but not yet reprimanded. She made a poor attempt at enthused enquiry.

"Did you go to Denmark?"

The poser sipped her gin. "Do you not know?"

"How would I know?"

"How would you not?"

She gave up on the enthusiasm. "Did you have the surgery?"

"I underwent an operation?"

"Was it successful?"

"I'm still alive."

"So I see."

"Just like Pic and Edwin."

Emira teased out a pause. Then she said, "What makes you say that?"

"The evidence of my eyes."

"You've seen them alive?"

"I haven't seen either of them dead."

Emira, crossed her legs. "The last time we spoke . . ."

The poser opened her handbag unobtrusively ensuring her

adversary saw the weapon within. She extracted a buff envelope and tossed it on the coffee table between them. "That's for you."

"You don't owe me anything."

"It's in sterling, but the exchange rate is good."

Emira ignored the envelope. "I didn't give you any real money."

"That's not what it's for."

"Then what is it for?"

"Where's Alice?"

"Who's Alice?"

"I think I know where she might be, but it would be quicker if you tell me."

"I don't know who Alice is."

"She's in one of three places; the first alternative being the bottom of the Baltic Sea."

Emira sipped her gin. "And the second?"

"You tell me."

"I don't even know what you are talking about."

"There's five hundred pounds in that envelope. That's pretty much all my savings. It's yours, in return for telling me where Alice is."

"Do you not want to know where Pic is?"

"He's not dead then?"

"I didn't say that."

"You didn't need to. And I know where Pic is."

"Where?"

"At the chalet on the shore of Vättern."

The ice in Emira's glass rattled as she took another drink. "Why do you think that?"

"Because the couple of days we were there he seemed to be preparing for a much longer stay."

"Well, of course he was, he thought . . ."

"Yet all the while he knew that Klas would come and with fake reports of the crash, and anyway it makes sense. It's the ideal place to hide away. I suspect that Alice is there too."

"You said there was a third alternative."

"The house at Mariefred. That's unlikely. Too suburban."

"I really don't know what you are talking about."

"I really think that you do. But I understand how frightened you may feel. The money is to make it worth the

247

risk."

"Why should I be frightened?"

The poser casually surveyed the lounge. They were still alone. "Because whatever Pic and Edwin are – or were – doing I think it affects people in powerful places."

Emira was drinking fast. Her gin was almost gone. "Why did you say 'were'?"

The poser considered. Emira seemed scared, but she also looked as if she might be sensing survival. "Because I think that Pic wants out, but in that business there is no way out. At least no simple way. That's why he and Heapy wanted me to be fooled into thinking they were dead. Through me they might convince the Brits, the Danes, Nikita Khrushchev and all."

"What?"

"Was Pic working for the Soviets?"

Emira drained all but the ice from her glass. "Alice is at the chalet."

"Thank you. Alive?"

"Alice? Or Pic?"

"Alice."

"Is she more important to you than Pic?"

"Pic was never important."

"I don't believe you."

"Neither do I, but it's true." It was the poser's turn to drink and think. It didn't change her mind. "Is Alice alive?"

Emira made the ice cubes in her glass swirl in a circle. "I don't know."

"What about Edwin?"

"I don't know where he is. Really I don't."

"But he was staying with you."

"How do you know that?"

"I just do."

"You saw him through the studio window."

"I saw something."

"And someone saw you."

"The man across the yard."

"Pic and Klas were already following you."

"Pic was?" That stung.

"Yes."

It was the poser's turn to drain her glass. "Was it Pic who injected me?"

"Injected?"

"I felt the needle. Then I didn't feel anything for a very long time."

Emira shrugged. "Him or Klas I suppose."

"Was Alice knocked out too?"

Emira shrugged again. "I wasn't there."

"What happened after that? Two unconscious women in the middle of Stockholm."

"Hardly the middle. You were under a bridge on the quayside."

"I thought you weren't there."

"I was told later."

"So what happened next?"

Emira tried to drink the ice cube meltwater, but did not say anything.

The poser suddenly said, "The *Mariefred*."

"What?"

"The *SS Mariefred*. It was in steam. They put us on the *SS Mariefred*."

Emira's response was slightly too slow in coming "Why would they do that?"

"Because it makes perfect sense. Perfect." She stared as if seeing the journey mapped out in Chinograph pencil on a Perspex screen in a war room. "It's a three-hour sail isn't it? Long enough to undress me and fit me out in my parachutist outfit. Then from Mariefred to Jönköping by car. How long would that take? Onto the Anson and off to dear old Blighty. The whole thing could be done in less than a day. It's a long time to keep someone sedated, and a terrible thing to throw someone out at three thousand feet and hope they bend their knees when they land, but then it wouldn't have mattered if I hadn't made it. They could always have cut me open and seen the nylon scroll was gone. But then how would her Majesty's men have been persuaded that Pic and Edwin were deceased?" No reply came so she added a layer of sarcasm. "Hold on one moment. You had a spare in Alice."

"I don't believe Pic was not important to you."

"Please don't tell me Alice is still sedated."

Emira glared and suckled iced air from the tumbler. "What kind of person do you think Pic is?"

"The kind who approves of dropping stage lanterns on

semi-naked ladies."

"I know nothing about that."

"And Conrad Coward?"

Emira's countenance signalled acerbity. "It's no use asking me about things that happened in England. I live in Stockholm."

"Is Alice all right?"

Emira shrugged, swirled the ice again and said, "What did you tell the British authorities?"

The poser kissed one of the ice cubes in her cocktail glass. She sipped a sliver of meltwater and swallowed. "I told them Edwin perished in a plane crash and Pic committed suicide. And yes, Pic was important. But life was different then. It was wartime."

"It's always wartime for Pic."

"And for Edwin?"

"When he's not with Pic."

The poser nodded in confirmation of her prior conclusion.

Emira said, "Will you stick to your story?"

"What story?"

"That they are dead."

"What if I don't?"

"Then you'll probably kill them."

"Explain."

"They have a chance now, to erase who they were, and become what they are. To un-title themselves and redefine their existence. To erase the counterfeit world. To craft new lifeworks."

"I'm not sure it will be that simple."

"Neither am I but I didn't say it was certain. Just a chance. It depends on you."

"And Alice. And someone else in the UK."

"Tinky."

"Yes."

"They know about Tinky," said Emira. "They think he will understand."

"Yes. He will. But I don't. Not yet."

"What do you need to know?"

"Why me? In the first place. Why stitch me up with a secret key? What was the code intended for?"

"I genuinely don't know."

"I need to find out."

"I can't help you with that."

"I think you can. But my priority is Alice."

Emira pushed her tumbler towards the middle of the coffee table and firmly placed the pack of UK currency next to it. "Alice wasn't insurance, she was an inconvenience."

"Was?"

"Klas took her to the chalet."

"Klas did?"

"Pic went with you to the plane, and to England."

"Did he indeed?"

"Edwin was the pilot."

"The Anson?"

"I think so."

"So it was Pic who pushed me out at three thousand feet."

Emira ran her hand through her hair and shifted her position as if readying to leave. "More like three feet."

"What?"

"They didn't push you out. They landed, laid you on the ground, put your parachute over you and took off again. They said the airstrip was disused. They thought they could get away with it. They did."

"They landed?"

Emira edged towards the front of the sofa. "I haven't heard from them in more than a week. I don't know what they decided to do with Alice. I wired Klas yesterday, to say that you were in Stockholm. I will try to telephone him tonight, to tell him what you have told me. I will come and see you again tomorrow, at the same time. By then I should know more." She stood up.

"Wait." The poser opened the envelope and also stood.

"I don't want money."

"And I don't want to be in debt."

"You are not."

She took out fifty pounds and pushed it into Emira's palm. "Thank you. And please stress to Klas – and to Pic – that I have been totally honest in what I have told you. Which is more than I was in England." She picked up her handbag and before Emira could object, turned away and left the lounge as if going into the body of the hotel, but simply went to the ladies' washroom. When she returned, as she hoped, Emira had gone. She summoned the waiter and settled the bill. He brought her coat, she tipped him and went straight back to the Hotel Vasa before once more adopting her redhead persona, prior to checking out. She took a train to Jönköping and checked into the Ericsson hotel using her real name and passport. Two days later she had secured the hire of a boat and crew of two with which to begin her survey of the western shore of Vättern. It was a small pleasure cruiser capable of travelling at eight or nine knots comfortably and the captain was willing to do a full day round trip, but he explained that would barely take them half way along the length of the vast lake. She was happy with that. Her story was that she was trying to locate a lodge her family had used on a childhood visit to Swedish relatives. She only had vague memories but felt she would recognise it when she saw it. The captain smiled indulgently. His English was limited, but she paid most of the fee in advance and they set out as daylight arrived on the third day of her stay. She wondered if Emira had organised a repair for her studio door yet.

The motor launch was noisy. The pounding of the diesel engine pressed not only on her eardrums but also on the soles of her feet. Conversation was non-existent but now and then the Captain or his mate would shout something and point to properties on the shore. Each time she replied with a shake of the head. There was a tiny galley from which she was furbished with coffee and, at noon, with a cheese sandwich. As the low-arcing sun started its downward curve, the captain announced he would do another hour or so and then they must turn back. She nodded and made sure he saw her consult her watch, something that she did every ten minutes subsequently. Shortly after her fifth check, the Captain cut the power, and the idling of the motor was a sweet caress of sound compared to the relentless growl of the previous four hours. He let the craft drift while pointing out the last pinpricks of habitation that they could survey that day. The furthest of them surged her heartbeat, and she asked the second sailor to pass the binoculars.

"That's it," she said.

"Sure?"

"Yes. No doubt. Can you put me ashore there?"

"Shore?"

"Yes."

"Land?"

"Yes."

"You want to go on land?"

"Yes."

"Get off the boat?"

"Yes."

"I cannot wait for you."

"Five minutes," she said splaying her hand and tapping her watch.

"Half an hour to get there!"

"She went to her bulging bag and took out her purse."

He waived it away and opened the throttle.

Twenty minutes later she was standing on the jetty close to a rash of the splinters from chopped logs. Everything was quiet apart from the gentle slow throb of the launch motor. The Captain stepped onto the jetty and wrapped the boat's cable around a post. There was no movement.

"Five minutes," called the Captain.

She ignored him and walked cautiously up to the chalet, reassured by the weight of the weapon in her bag.

Even on the outside there were signs of occupation with recent tyre tracks in the snow. The door was unfastened. She didn't knock.

The interior was not untidy but had neat arrangements of the detritus of lake-side living: opened cans, washed crockery left to drain, improvised ash trays. The stove was cold but dressed with burnt residue, a small amount of which dusted the floor beneath.

One of the two bedrooms told of recent use. The pillows, sheets and blankets were in place. The pillows were plumped and straight, the covers taut and neat. There was a suitcase beneath the bed alongside a pair of clean boots. She did not recognise them. She tested the case but it was locked. Its weight suggested it was full. There was nothing else in the room, but the way these few things were ordered spoke of a military regularity. The other bedroom was bare. The bed unmade, the blankets and pillows folded and stacked. She went outside.

The latrine shack door was unfastened. Boots had left their impressions and even at first glance she could tell more than one pair were involved. She scanned the woods and wandered into them. Something caught her eye. There was a scuffing sound behind her.

She whizzed around, her hand finding the opening in her bag and reaching to the cold metal within.

"We have to go back," said the Captain.

She took a breath. "You go," she said.

"But . . . we have to go."

"You go," she said again, swapping cold steel for warm leather, in her grip. She took out her purse and pressed money in the Captain's palm. He examined it. "Come back for me in two days."

"We have to take you back."

"Come for me in two days," she said. "Come back on Thursday."

He looked at the notes in his hand. "This is half what you owe."

"I'll pay in full," she said, "and double it when we get back to Jönköping. Thursday. Come for me on Thursday. Same time. Yes?"

"Thursday?" He glanced around sceptically. "You sure?"

"I'm sure."

He hesitated, backed off, then turned and walked slowly away, looking over his shoulder twice to check she had not changed her mind.

She went inside surveying the evidence of habitation again, and looking for hints of behaviours that she'd seen before, but found none. Someone had stayed here, and was probably still in residence, but she could not determine who it was.

The boat revved and pulled clear of the jetty. She watched it curve away and diminish in size. Keeping her bag with her, she went outside to the log store where she knew there was a spade. She took it to what she had seen in the woods.

She did not relish this task at all, but there was no alternative. Someone had recently been buried here, and there was only one way she could find out who that was.

THIRTY-ONE

She needed all of the afternoon and part of the night to exhume the corpse. The ground was hard, very hard, except where the more recently disturbed earth had been tipped, so she started with that. It wasn't long before she unearthed a hand. It was large and masculine. Once she saw the sleeve of the sweater she sighed relief because she recognised it as one that she'd seen Klas wear. She couldn't be sure until she found his head and was able to look at his face. She turned away, staggered a few paces, vomited, and then had to sit on the snow and lay back to be sure she did not faint.

She shivered and twitched but slowly regained a sense of stability and went back to look again. Although rigid and wax-textured there was no sign of deterioration. This, she deduced, was probably due to the cold.

She withdrew into the lodge, lit the stove and put a billy can of water on to heat. She then borrowed the boots from the bedroom which, although too big for her, offered more purchase on the blade of the spade than her shoes had done. Her labour was now intermittent as she was weakened, and kept returning to the stove to build up the fire and see how the water was doing. Three-quarters of an hour or so later it was hot enough to brew coffee. There was a tinned fruitcake in the larder. She opened it and ate half.

By the time she had rested the quick night was upon her. She lit the storm lantern and took it with her, though the night was clear and the moonlight was strong enough to see by, so she turned the lamp down low ready for when she needed to go back inside. Strangely, the darkness and the wind in the trees made her task more manageable. She had to get to the floor of the grave. That way she could be certain that it was Klas alone.

The most distasteful part was prizing the spade beneath him and lifting him to check there was nothing below. She could not see any sign of how he had met his death. He was fully clothed. She angled one of her borrowed boots alongside his and decided that those she wore were smaller. She was content that this was a one-person grave, but decided against reburial until the morning as she wanted better light to further hunt for signs of what might have ended his life. She left him lying face up, staring through Swedish branches at a Scandinavian skyscape, and then went walking through the woods with her handbag and spade. She could not see any more burial mounds but knew she must look more thoroughly when daylight returned.

She retraced her steps to where Klas was. He was still there, but the lantern was not.

She stood still, listening and looking. Her pulse was up but she felt no panic. She was alert and keyed. The only movement was by the branches bowing before the wind, the only sound was the lapping of the lake.

She stepped very slowly to one side and leaned the spade against a tree, then with one hand holding the outside of her bag and the other holding the revolver on the inside, she progressed step by step towards the chalet.

It was impossible to enter the cabin without making noise with the boots she had borrowed. She had no light to shine. She had shut the solid stove door so there would be no light from there. Stalemate.

She pressed against the door and hence managed to unlatch it silently. She drew it towards her. The top hinge protested, but it was a whisper of a whine. She stepped inside. Just one step.

Nothing.

She knew the door would swing back and slam but she cushioned it with the bag until it rested against the frame.

Nothing.

She was standing in the tiny vestibule between the bedrooms and the kitchen. She waited for her eyes to adjust. At first she could see nothing. Then she detected a slant of grey from the kitchen window slightly illuminating floorboards. She listened. She heard a log crack in the stove.

She took another step.

Movement. It sounded like cloth, but was already gone.

Half-burnt wood settled. Another sound – it could have been wicker being compressed.

She listened to her own breathing and heard it via her breastbone.

Nothing.

She'd had enough and was suddenly content. She strode swiftly in the direction of the kitchen.

Once inside she stopped and stood rigid. There was a form opposite her, filling the wicker chair. The lantern was beside it on the table, the flame so low it was but a bud of a glow. It grew and once it's radiance reached orange she saw the hand that adjusted the wick. Then she saw the other hand and the barrel of the gun it held. Then the light was yellow and the face was that of Edwin Heap.

"Quite the traveller," he said, without lowering his aim.

She kept her bag pointed at him. "When one is a go-between travelling goes with the territory."

He emitted an almost inaudible snigger. If it was the last thing she heard, she'd settle for that, such was the state of her heightened alertness. She was in a mystical place mentally. If he squeezed his gun hand, so would she. Nothing mattered; but it would be a waste.

She said, "You wouldn't shoot the messenger would you?"

"That might depend on the message."

"Where's Alice?"

"You mean Vera."

She didn't flinch.

"Where's Vera?"

"I'm afraid I can't answer that."

"Why not?"

"Because I don't know. Do you?"

She waited. She said, "The last time I saw her she was walking alongside me."

"The last time I saw her, she was with Klas."

"And when was the last time you saw Klas?"

"When I put him in the earth."

"When was that?"

"The ground is very hard at this time of year. It took a whole day."

She looked at her sometime lover's lover. "How did he die?"

Edwin twitched. It was more of a shirk than a shrug. "I found him floating face down in the lake. Beneath the jetty."

"Are you pointing that thing at me for a reason or does it just take you a very long time to aim?"

He put the gun down on the floor. "Would you like some more coffee?"

She let go of the weapon in her bag. "Yes, I would."

There were no easy conversations to be had and no simple ways of engaging. For a while they danced a standoff. It was both odd and yet automatically natural. While he poured the drinks, she examined the contents of the cupboards which had been re-stocked since she was last there. Though substantive in quantity they were rudimentary in variety.

She said, "Did you really think I'd be fooled by a mannequin made to look like Pic?"

He thrust his hands in his pockets and leant his buttocks against the edge of the kitchen table. "Well I was."

"Was it Pic's artwork or Emira's?"

Edwin passed her the mug. "I'm no connoisseur."

"So where was Vera when you saw her with Klas?"

"In his truck."

"About to drive here."

"If you say so."

"After dropping you, Pic and unconscious me at the airfield."

"If you say so."

"I do say so."

He put more logs in the stove. She selected a vegetable knife and toyed with it. "And where was Pic the last time you saw him?"

"Pic's dead."

She spoke flatly. "No he's not."

Edwin pushed another piece of timber into the flames.

"Pic's dead."

"Theoretically."

"Factually."

"And so are you."

He looked at her. His face was side-lit by the glow of the open stove. "Is that what you told Military Intelligence?"

She made him wait, then said, "The only people who know you are still alive are Vera and Tinky."

He snorted derisorily, "Tinky!"

"Tinky won't tell anyone."

"No Tinky will not tell anyone." Edwin shut the stove and stood up.

"How can you be sure?"

"Because he knows his name is on the list."

"What list?"

"The one that can't be read without the code."

She sipped her drink. "The code that was inside me?"

"You've had it removed then?"

"You know I have. What list is Tinky on?"

"A very precious one."

She put the knife down. "Don't tell me Tinky is a spy."

He laughed. "God help us if he is."

"Then what list?"

"Those naturally inclined to break the law."

She sighed. "Tinky does not go out of his way to hide his homosexuality. I don't think anyone is ignorant of his disposition."

"But they are probably not familiar with some of his previous partners. Some of whom move in very high circles."

"And is that also true of you?"

Edwin went to the window and perused the darkness over the water. "I've always moved in very high circles. It's called flying."

She brought her mug close to her face and gently blew the steam away. "How does Tinky know he's on the list?"

Edwin took three breaths, then he said, "Vera told him."

She let the coffee scald her tongue before swallowing. "And how is it that Vera knows about the list?"

"Because she's on it too."

The revelation that Vera had had numerous lovers was neither surprising nor shocking to her. Edwin said Vera had

259

been 'liberal' with her affections during the war and prior to it. Some of her encounters had enabled her access to the scandalous. She had knowledge of things sensitive enough to crush the UK establishment.

The atmosphere in the chalet was one-part stewed coffee, one-part split pine and one-part doubt.

"Why did you let me deliver the code?"

Edwin collected his automatic pistol from the floor and laid it on the table. "I think you have probably worked that out."

She said, "Because the cipher I passed on is not the genuine one."

"Isn't it?"

"Or it is not complete. Or not comprehensive. It can be extended. Part of the solution remains encrypted."

"Is that what you suggested to your compatriots?"

"No," she said.

He sank into the wicker chair. She sat down and propped her elbows on the table. The billy can of hot water still simmered on the stove, its lid rattled intermittently.

"Is it being used?" she asked.

"Who knows?"

"By the Soviets?"

"Why them?"

"Why else would it be of value to the British?"

He raised one eyebrow. "And the Danish?"

She didn't respond. The coffee tasted more bitter as less of it remained in her mug. She said, "If the British have an incomplete code it is of limited use. Unless . . .?"

He twisted the automatic until it was pointing towards the wall, and drained his drink. He looked at her as he swallowed. "Unless what?"

"Unless both sides have the incomplete code, and then one is offered the final instalment."

"And why would that be of any value?"

"Because then both parties would know some of the information, but one side would know more."

Edwin's tone was more that of a master than a pupil. "Explain."

"If the Soviets were in conversation with their . . . sympathisers, they could receive information in full, but not know what they had been told because part would still be encoded. If the British were listening in, they'd be in the same situation. Both sides would know everything but not fully know what they knew. Parts would remain encrypted because the code was incomplete."

"Go on."

"Unless they obtained the appendix."

He raised both eyebrows and softened his accolade with sarcasm. "Top of the class."

"But who is sending the information? And from where?" She leaned over and turned the automatic. He didn't flinch. She lined the barrel up with the window. "East Berlin," she said.

"Why there?"

She reached into her bag and took out a pack of Swedish cigarettes and offered him one. He declined. She struck a match and lit her fag and when she dropped the matchbox back in her bag it bounced against Tinky's revolver. She sucked the smoke, and as she blew it out, she unnecessarily tipped the first of the ash into a former sardine tin that already sported three stubs and their conflagrated residue. "Because that's where he is."

"Who?"

"Stonorowich."

He rubbed a thumb over a closed eye.

She said, "He's got the list hasn't he? He drew it up." She traced a pattern in the ash in the tin, twisting her cigarette and crafting a glowing nipple on the tip. "Was he spying for the Soviets during the war?"

"Why are you asking me?"

"Before the war?"

"For the Soviets? It's my understanding he went to Britain to avoid them."

It was her turn to raise an eyebrow. "For himself then. And for – the motherland."

"What motherland?"

She inhaled Swedish smoke and Swedish air, then sent both tumbling towards the ceiling. "Poland."

He shrugged.

She said, "Pic's Polish isn't he?"

Edwin didn't speak for a long time. The billy can lid rattled. Outside the west wind began to veer and a fresh percussion rose from newly-lapped surfaces. His eyes were focussed on the tail of smoke eddying from the sardine tin.

She waited.

He said, "Poland is permanently untitled. It is the perennial plaything of other powers. A country that does not exist cannot claim citizens."

"His mother or his father? Or both?"

"Britain entered the war because Poland was invaded. When the war was won, the lifeblood of Poland was transfused into Uncle Josef's foreskin. What kind of pact is that?"

She sucked another punch out of her cigarette and dashed ash into the sardine tin. "So Stonorowich starts sending information from Berlin to Moscow about high-profile homosexuals. London sees that. How does that help Poland?"

His mouth stayed shut. He looked embarrassed.

She answered herself with the solution she'd known long prior to posing the question. "Because of the final layer of encryption. The names remain obscure. London does not have the means to unravel them."

He stared at her but did not speak.

"And neither does Moscow. And that starts a bidding war. And Stonorowich discriminates between the countries that carved up Poland."

Edwin shifted in his seat.

She said, "But Moscow could get at Stonorowich very easily."

Suddenly he was too smug to hold his silence any longer. "As easily as you could get at Klas."

"He's dead?"

"He was when I buried him."

She didn't react but continued to apply nicotine to her nerve. "How many appendices are there?"

"He wouldn't tell me."

She didn't like the heavy flatness with which he had delivered that remark. It might have been for effect; it might have been bluff; or it might even have been a truth not even one tenth as sinister as it sounded. To press him on it would be to chew on his bait, so she veered. She had no idea if he was telling the truth about Stonorowich, or about Klas, or if he harboured any knowledge regarding the fatal crash of Conrad Coward's car, but his blankness further chilled her. "So if Stonorowich is no more, all you need to do is destroy the appendices."

He took up his automatic and toyed with it. "And why would I need to do that?"

"Self-protection."

"You seem to forget – like Pic, I am dead. Dead men don't need protecting."

"Neither do they need to kill."

"Are you suggesting I need to kill?"

"Why else would you carry that thing?" She swallowed more smoke and sent it back out through her nostrils. "But you are not dead are you? And you are far from at peace."

He ejected the magazine from the handle of his automatic and surveyed the top shell within. "Why have you come back to Sweden?"

"Why do you think?"

He reinserted the magazine and clicked the safety catch on the gun. Then he clicked it again, stood up, and dropped the weapon into his pocket. He walked over to the window and looked out. The wind was strengthening. "Pic went to great lengths to persuade you he was dead."

"No. He went to great lengths in the hope that I might persuade others that he – and you – were dead."

"Well, you've done that."

"You're welcome."

He sneered away her sarcasm. "Pic's interest in you was only ever as a muse."

"And where is he now? Looking for Vera? She needs to be dealt with, doesn't she?"

Edwin turned his back to the window and leant against the wall alongside it. "Pic's whereabouts are Pic's business."

"Perhaps she saw him coming and stopped him in his tracks."

He sniggered more in derision than amusement.

"If she dealt with Klas she could deal with Pic. *If* she dealt with Klas."

He took his gun from his pocket again and twirled it around his finger. He said, "Did you find any entry wounds on Klas?"

"No."

"Neither did we."

"*We* being you and Pic."

He reeled inside his eyes, then flattened his tone again.

"Pic's not here. There's no one else here." He clicked the safety catch twice again. "Just you and I."

"The boat's coming back for me tomorrow," she said.

"No it's not. It's coming Thursday, if you are lucky."

She squeezed another sting from her cigarette, buried the stub in the sardine tin, stood up, and opened the larder cupboard. "Shall I fix us some supper?"

They ate a very civilised meal of poached eggs and boiled potatoes. She asked him about his youth and, without romance or resentment, he described a privileged upper-class upbringing that had been brutally negated on the basis of his politics and his proclivity for unguarded displays of affection for males. She sympathised, but he was unmoved. He was what he was, he said. She then suggested that he was a traitor. He reminded her of his war service. Like Pic he was a pacifist, and while they had both contributed to the fight, neither had actually killed anyone during the war.

"Then what was the point of your aerial photographs?" she asked.

"To make targeting more accurate. To ascertain how precisely bombing had been undertaken."

"Precision is not impunity. People lost their lives as a result of your photography."

"Pacifists will kill," he said. The ice and steel were back in his voice. "If it is the most expedient means of bringing about peace. Expediency was our function. Peace was our objective. We achieved it."

"And now?" she said.

"Now?"

"What is your objective now?"

"The same."

After the meal she slipped on her coat and taking her handbag, visited the latrine. Instead of returning to the chalet she walked to the jetty and lit a cigarette. She heard his boots as they crushed the snow. He wore a thick duffel jacket, and was also smoking. His right hand dangled by his side, loosely holding his automatic.

She returned her attention to the moonlit expanse of Vättern and waited until he was alongside her. "What about since the war?"

"Since the war?"

"How many people have you killed since the war?"

"I've always believed in Socialism, but now it seems it cannot exist uncorrupted. At least not on a large scale. Left wing and right wing are misleading terms. They are not opposites at all. When wings flap hard enough they touch at the top. The place where they meet is called a labour camp." He threw his cigarette into the lake and toyed with his gun.

Watching this with the corner of her eye she used a drag on her fag to switch her cigarette into her left hand. She slung her bag over her right shoulder, then took it off again, to adjust the length of the strap. "The personal always overrides the political," she said.

"It has to," he said. "The political is not a person."

"And you just want to be a person."

"It's all I've ever wanted," he said.

She slipped her bag over her shoulder again. Now she was able to put her hand inside and find the trigger on Tinky's service revolver more naturally. She nuzzled the barrel tight against the lining. She would need to turn to face him and in order to do so she adopted a more assertive vocal thrust. "But once a spy, always a spy. Neither country is just going to let you slip away."

"Is that what Mrs Coward told you?"

"She said it applies to her."

He turned to face her. Both hands still toyed with his automatic. "Which it is why it is so regrettable that you told her we were still alive." His gun wasn't pointed, but his resentment was.

"I didn't tell her. She deduced. It's a suspicion. If anything happened to me, it would only serve to confirm it."

There was less toying. "She'll never know."

She held his eyes. "So what would be the point?"

"It's personal," he said. The beginning of an aim. "We have to shut all the doors. Tinky won't squeal because he's on the list. But you're not on the list."

Now the gun was level and she was looking at the black hole of the barrel. She tightened her grip and took up the slack on the trigger inside her bag. "And Vera?"

"One door at a time," he said.

Water lapped. The moon watched.

 She retained maximum stoicism and verbal calm. "Why will you not trust me?"

"It's not you that I don't trust."

"Who then?"

"Myself."

She angled her head. "Explain."

"Human triangles are not uncommon."

"So I am told."

"But I can't compete with a muse."

Her essence did not sink or leap; it imploded. "If Pic wants me – why did he let you fly me back to England?"

"To save you. To stop them looking for you."

"You could have done that by giving them my corpse."

"Pic wasn't in favour of that. He's a very peculiar person. And he is entirely infatuated by you. At the same time, he has no desire to be with you because he knows that will only destroy his conception of you. I can't trust him to refrain from finding you again."

"Is he looking for me right now?"

"And I can't trust myself from stopping him from doing that. But as you just intimated, there is one way."

The un-silence of the lake hammered against her ear-drums. She imagined his fist tightening against the trigger of his weapon, and felt hers doing the same.

THIRTY-TWO

She wasted no time in going to Gothenburg. It was the logical thing to do. She had kept good watch and been waiting on the jetty when the boat came to collect her. The sail back to Jönköping took four hours. She risked one more night there then caught a train for the coast. By the afternoon of the twenty-first of February she was in a very comfortable hotel close to the city centre, from where she sent a very simple, but veiled telegraph to Tinky: *The latest lodging of an insane milliner. Send any news by return.*

Her latest course of action felt both speculative and sure. By studying her map, she had made what she regarded as a good estimate of where the chalet was. She was acting partly on a whim, but equally strongly on what she considered was likely to have been Vera's logical pattern, if she had escaped from the chalet with a vehicle. If she had gone north she would eventually have met the highway between Gothenburg and Stockholm. Similarly, by driving south she would have arrived at Jönköping and been faced with the same dilemma, with the possible third option of continuing towards Malmö. Vera's instincts would surely have harmonised with her own in that, while the capital and the southern port both seduced with a sense of familiarity, each also held dangers. It would be safer to go somewhere new. Furthermore, something Vera had said stuck in her mind. *Every sailor loves a showgirl, and vice versa.* She didn't think the sentiment was entirely true but she understood what her showgirl friend meant. Seaports provided pent-up punters on the loose. That meant theatres. What Vera would have craved most would have been backstage amity. Theatre types were the kind of people most likely to come to her aid, and the ones with whom she could make an easy bond. It was a long shot, but worth a try.

Something seeded a deep doubt in her mind, however. She wasn't at all sure that Vera could drive.

Tinky's reply arrived the same day. *Nothing to report but glad to hear you have not copied the Cheshire Cat. Happy Hunting!*

It was not easy for a single woman to trawl the more salacious Swedish nightclubs but she did so on the pretence of seeking work for English artistes. She flaunted the name of Laura Henderson who had pioneered the Windmill Theatre in London, and while some of the Swedish managers had not heard of her or of that venue, one or two had and hence she wormed her way into four cabaret clubs on a complimentary basis, but neither her viewing nor her enquiries produced any results. Until her fifth night of trying.

She had exhausted what she thought were the most likely places but a waiter at Liseburg suggested the Sjöjungfru bar tucked away close to the cargo yards of the harbour. She was somewhat reluctant to venture there alone, but an instinct tugged with peculiar persistence, so ensuring she had Tinky's revolver, she followed the sketchy directions she'd been given, and was shown to a table in an unkempt corner.

The manager came to peruse her. He was smartly dowdy, sporting a heavily-brushed third-rate suit on a first rate posture. His English was efficient but stilted. Apart from his accent he resembled a French maître d'hôtel down on his luck and desperately trying to snatch respectability from the jaws of sleaze. She didn't think he bought her alibi, but neither did he challenge it. She drank two glasses of very expensive sour white wine and sat through three depraved pseudo-burlesque routines to show tunes from movies of Broadway stalwarts. She was about to leave, but sensed a building of anticipation among the now crowded club and so reluctantly summoned a third glass. Two Portuguese sailors still waiting to cruise out of their teens gate-crashed her table, and seized the other two seats, asking in a

language she could not speak, and not waiting for her consent.
She half-smiled while they established their nationality and their
fantasies by unambiguous gesture, winking and laughter. Other,
older wayfarers, emboldened by beer, edged nearer and declined
to avert their leers. She decided to jump ship, but then the out-
of-tune pit band burst forth, the house lights halved in intensity,
and two theatrical lanterns the size of dustbins spat thick
satsuma light at the tiny stage, and Vera strode on.

The effect was bizarre, because she was both instantly
recognisable and entirely alien.

She was wearing what was without doubt a genuine Second
World War Wren's uniform, but one that had undergone
extraordinary modification. The skirt was half regulation length
and had splits at each side right up to the waistband revealing
her fishnet-bound thighs. Her shoes were bizarre, being standard
service stock that had been brutalised to take extended heels and
fastened by laces woven to represent miniature marine cables.
Her jacket was fluted rather than fitted, and with extra darts and
stays forming a bustier superstructure that splayed into a gaping
collar. Her blouse was open to display a mammary deck edged
by the navy blue piping of the boundary of her underwear. Her
hair, recently peroxided, was pinned up and back in a style that
was neither prescribed military nor customary glamour but a
mule of the two.

She sang. Unbelievably, Vera sang. She was not totally in
key but vocalised with gusto and genuine joy. Even more
unbelievably, she was singing *The White Cliffs of Dover*. The
tempo was variable and the instrumental arrangement
mechanical but none of that mattered to the crowd who cheered,
whistled and joined in enthusiastically. She sang it through once
and then immediately started again, but this time removing her
clothes until at the end of the reprise she was down to shoes,
stockings, suspenders, bra and hat.

The applause was rapturous but the bandmaster did not let
it dominate, going almost immediately to the prelude of the next
number: *What Shall We Do with a Drunken Sailor?* Three verses
later Vera was entirely naked, but the act was not done. A host
of drunken sailors pressed against the stage apron holding aloft
glasses and bottles. After much teasing Vera lowered herself
onto the neck of one of the proffered brown ale bottles and
gripped it with her upper thighs so it became a drunken penis as

she waddled provocatively, singing all the while and laughing with her overjoyed audience.

It wasn't the audacity or obscenity that struck the stunned poser. Neither was it the ease and obvious delight with which her friend indulged the baying sailor boys. The thing that knocked the wind from her sails was that there was not a sign of the burn or scarring that had resulted from the falling stage lantern in London. It wasn't that Vera had hidden it. She was wearing nothing at all and the stage was so small and so close that it was clear that while her breast and torso may have been lightly powdered, there was no plastering of cosmetic there. A second blow was delivered by a tattoo, or what appeared to be a tattoo but, in all likelihood, was a painted design. It depicted a stereotypical anchor. It was in a position very close to the pubis, an area that had been shielded by a jewelled suspender belt in the London show, by her turned-away torso in the dressing room, and by French knickers in the Jönköping hotel. It was not the image that unsettled the poser, but rather the profile of the curving blade of the anchor. The stage lights cut cruel shadows, accentuated by the angle of observation and the proximity of the stage. The purpose of the anchor was to amuse, but also to mask. It confirmed what the poser had thought she felt during their intimacy. Vera had a scar.

As the song climaxed, Vera staggered back to return the bottle to its owner, who received it amid a tumultuous cheer. Without hesitation he drank from it again, even though the bottle was clearly empty. His shipmates squirmed and applauded with equal gusto as they hailed the chosen sailor.

Vera hit the high note at the culmination of the song and held it as she spread the searchlight of her smile around the auditorium, finishing with a professionally restrained, but visibly electrifying, stare of recognition as her eyes met those of the poser.

She took her curtain-call draped with a dressing gown that had been crafted by splicing two white ensigns and a union flag. As she did so she removed her Wren's cap and spun it with great precision towards the poser who instinctively caught it.

Several of the men close to her began speaking at her at the same time and she couldn't really understand or untangle what they were saying, until one recognisably north-east English sailor breathed brewed-oat breath at her and said, "Away ye go lass.

Hatch is over there."

As the manager unlocked the entrance to back stage and let her through he said, "She has already contract. With me. Understand?"

The dressing room was smaller than some broom cupboards the poser had seen. Vera was already fully dressed to the extent of a raincoat, and was fastening her hair in a plain brown headscarf.

"You're very popular," said the poser, passing back the sailor's cap.

Vera tossed the hat onto a hook over the dressing table and looked at her friend. "Is it really you?"

"I might ask the same thing."

"Oh!" said Vera, and dropped her eyes to the floor before grasping her guest in the tightest and most genuine embrace she'd felt since the end of the Second World War.

The poser hugged back with matching gusto and firmly kissed the scarf that bound Vera's bleached hair. "And – healed," she said as the hug slackened.

"Oh!" said Vera again. "What are you doing here?"

"What are you?"

"I think you've seen what I'm doing."

"Why?"

Vera held on firmly but sank back in the hug and looked into the soul of her companion with defiance and resignation, joy and sorrow, plea and persecution, all in equal measure. She shook her head, blinked back insistent tears, forced her lips into a crescent and softly inclined her forehead downwards. She breathed deeply and said, "I'm actually having the time of my life." She cocked her brow back and eradicated all distress with a genuine laugh.

The poser laughed too, then said, "But - why?"

"Why – what?"

"There's a hundred 'whys'."

Vera's face shadowed again, then brightened. "We'd better make a start then. But not here. I'd take you back to my digs, but it's a shithole."

"My hotel is rather nice."

"Your place then."

The taxi lurched. Its engine screamed. The driver had to double de-clutch to get it through the gears.

"How did you deal with Klas?"

"What?"

"At the chalet."

"What do you mean – 'deal with'?"

The driver cut the apex of the cobbled corner. The vehicle's springs did little to cushion the vibrations and the tightness of the turn pushed the poser into the flank of her friend. She decided to divert their discussion. "The last time I lay eyes on you we were walking along the quay in Stockholm. The next time I lay eyes on anything it was the ceiling of an ante-room at RAF Benson."

"Did they really do it? Did they really fly you back to bleedin' Blighty?"

"Well I got there somehow. But I don't remember anything about it. What happened to you?"

"A bag or a sack or something over my head. I fought and swore for a bit then felt a stab in the arm. Next I knew I think I was on a boat."

"The *Mariefred?*"

"Could have been. I don't know. Someone gave me something to drink and I remember sitting there in a daze. Then nothing until the house."

"Which house?"

"At Mariefred. The one we broke into."

"Who was with you?"

"Klas. There were others there too but I didn't really see them. I was still very hazy. He later told me they were your friends Pic and Heapy."

"'Friends' is not the most apposite descriptor."

"It's all something of a fuzz. I think we all crammed into Klas' truck. From what I can surmise we drove you and your – friends – to the airfield. It was night, or at least it was dark. After dropping you off, Klas drove me on. I still dozed a lot. We ended up in a lodge by a lake."

"It's the chalet where Pic had taken me."

"I was there for a few days and to start with I kept throwing up, feeling very cold and being a bit muddled, but once I'd sobered up Klas explained what had happened to you. I didn't really buy it, but – hey – it looks like he was on the level with me."

"What else did he tell you?"

"Quite a lot actually. We got on very well. All your adventures began to make much more sense."

"How did you escape?"

"Escape?"

"How did you get away from Klas?"

"He drove me to the main road and I caught a bleedin' bus."

"What?"

"We got on very well, Klas and me."

"But what was the point in doping you and taking you there if he just let you go?"

"I told him I wanted to disappear and this was my chance."

"Disappear?"

"He understood. He said he'd like to disappear with me. I said that might be possible but I'd need to disappear altogether first. He said he would help and he did. I said I'd go to Stockholm, get my things, go to Paris. I promised to meet him there on Bastille Day."

"And he drove you to the bus stop?"

"In a small town – Tibro – or something like that. Gave me the fare to get to Stockholm. Watched me onto the bus."

"You went back to Stockholm?"

"No. I took a leaf out of your book. Got off at the first stop and waited for a bus going in the opposite direction. That's how I got to Gothenburg."

The taxi lurched to a halt outside their destination. The driver leaped out and opened the cab door.

The poser said, "And will you be in Paris on Bastille Day?"

"I might."

"I wouldn't bother if I were you."

They sat side by side on the hotel bed drinking whiskey and smoking.

"Summer nineteen-forty-four I went to London," said

273

Vera.

"And supposedly died in an air raid."

"Yes, well we know about all that."

"Do we? All I know is that five years later I get a post card from you, saying you're in the West End with a new name and new occupation."

Vera laughed throatily and coughed out Benson and Hedges fumes. "Never could keep my kit on could I?"

They laughed together. When the laughter died the poser let the background hotel hum steady the ambience then said, "Did you really have a nervous breakdown?"

Vera drained her glass. "Of sorts."

"What do you mean?"

Her eyes glazed over with the memory. She toyed with the empty tumbler. "Yes, I went off the bleedin' rails. There were good reasons for that."

"Why?"

"Because of this." She patted her pubis.

The poser said, "That's not an appendectomy is it?"

"Wish it was. Your appendix is no use to you is it? Your womb bloody well is."

"Hysterectomy?"

Vera nodded.

"Why did you have a hysterectomy?"

"Because he buggered up the abortion."

"Who did?"

"One of the scummiest bleedin' saw doctors in the service of the military."

"Let me get my head around this. A medic tried to abort your child, messed it up and hence took away the whole womb."

"Baby and all."

"And why was a service surgeon carrying out an unlawful operation on a pencil-pushing Wren?"

Vera raised her glass. The poser poured a double-depth shot from the half bottle on the bedside table. "If you remember the Easter of forty-four I'd taken a week's leave."

"Portsmouth."

"Every showgirl loves a sailor. I knew a showgirl and she introduced me to a sailor."

"Who put the unwanted cargo in your hold."

"Correct."

"You were far from the first woman to face that voyage. But the Navy don't usually get a medic to carry out an illegal disembarkation."

"It's not illegal if the mother's life is in danger."

"And was it?"

"It was once he'd buggered it up."

"But why was he doing it in the first place?"

Vera sipped her Scotch. "Because I asked him to."

"It was a private arrangement."

"And he agreed."

"Yes."

"You had the money?"

"Not exactly. He didn't want money."

"Then – what did he want?"

Vera sipped again and licked her lips. "Information."

The poser held her breath; then exhaled in disgust. "You told him about Bletchley?"

"I got the impression he knew far more about the bleedin' Bletchley than I did. He said names of blokes that I didn't know were there."

"But what you told him was enough to settle the bill?"

"He said he'd took a shine to me. He talked about after the war. About going abroad with him. D-day had happened. Things were on the up. He talked about going home. To Poland."

A bell chimed in the depths of the poser's mind. "It was Stonorowich. You went to Stonorowich!"

"He'd done a decent job on you."

"And he risked doing an abortion?"

"He wasn't in the military if you remember."

"Wasn't he?"

"Did a lot for them but he wasn't enlisted. He was just about to move to London, where he was setting up a new practice. I had to wait three weeks. Probably not a good thing. Anyway he messed up. So he put me out cold and did the hysterectomy. I didn't know anything about it for three days, by which time I'd been gone so long I was officially awol."

"I remember that."

"I had some friends south of the river. They understood. It was time for a new life."

"You poor woman."

"Come on. Lots had a lot worse. I'm still here."

"What about him – Stonorowich?"

"We met up once. He'd changed his mind about me going to Poland with him. To be honest I'd never believed him. He had no eye for women. He batted for the other side."

"I think you could be right."

"I know I am. I've worked in the theatre my darlin'. I know a naughty boy when I kiss one."

"So why did he ever suggest it?"

"I dunno. Perhaps he wanted a costume wife? Lots of them do. Keeps them out of the courts. He went to France I think. After D-Day. Following the front line. Least, that's what he said he was going to do."

"He did." She waited. She was computing. She felt she loved Vera, but she didn't completely trust her. She knew that the truth for Vera was a cocktail; a mixture of two-parts fact and one-part fiction. Vera did seem to be loosening up however, and she half-formulated a theory regarding Stonorowich's interest in his hysterectomy guinea pig. Despite her doubts, she deeply wanted to help her friend, and to do that they must grip the stem of danger. "He has a list. You're on it."

"Yeah, I know."

"How do you know?"

"I couldn't possibly not be on it."

"Why?"

"I sold him passports I'd nicked from a house that was bombed-out."

"Christina Proctor?"

"And her husband."

"Colin?"

"Yeah. We were going to travel under those names. He even took my photo to put it in the passport."

"Stealing a passport isn't enough to get you on Stonorwich's list."

"Well, there's another reason."

"What?"

"I told him who was the father of the child he'd aborted."

"And who was it?"

"A Second Lieutenant about to take command of a ship for the first time."

"So what? I'm sure Second Lieutenants fathered their

share of illegitimate children during the war."

"The doctor's face lit up when I told him the father was royalty."

"Royalty?"

"Not British royalty. But not unconnected. And even less unconnected now."

The poser pondered and sipped. "Not British?"

"No."

"What nationality?"

"Greek."

"Greek."

"Or so he claimed"

"And now?"

Vera sipped and swallowed Scotch. "Now he's very close to Her Majesty. Couldn't get any bleedin' closer."

That night they shared the same bed.

Vera bathed at length in the en-suite bathroom and dried herself in full view of the poser. Yes, the tattoo was just greasepaint, and the bath diluted, but did not destroy, the colours. Yes, the shattering stage lantern had scalded her but the shards had bounced off her flesh so the discolouration had been superficial. She'd only been in hospital for one night. She had enhanced the burn with stage make-up to gain some time off from the show and in an attempt to shame the theatre into paying compensation. Unfortunately, her ruse had back-fired and they sacked her on the spot. The poser asked her why she hadn't admitted that to her when she came to join her in Sweden, but Vera had no reply other than a doe-eyed shrug.

They both slept naked and Vera had reached over for a hug. The poser had obliged. The snuggle suggested Vera wanted more affection, but the poser was unsure. Her mind was troubled by the permutations of what might have befallen Klas. She still withheld the fact that she knew him to be dead, trying to unearth any hint that her friend knew that too. If she had not curtailed his life, then who had? Edwin? Pic? Klas himself?

What should she do now? She had found Vera. The

biography she had related seemed almost too fantastical to be true, but if it was the case then her friend might be safe for now, but not out of danger. There was also a new tantalising thread: the passports that Vera had stolen had somehow travelled from Stonorowich to Pic, allowing the latter to utilise Proctor's identity. Vera, Emira, Klas, Edwin Heap and Pic were all bobbing in the same boat, and the hand on the tiller belonged to the Polish surgeon.

She had not located Pic, and while Edwin Heap had not confirmed her theory about who Pic might be, he had not denied it either. She was not at all sure she cared about that anymore. Pic was who he was, but he was not the person she had hoped he would be.

It could be that it was simply time to pack up, go home and start afresh. That sounded very tempting, but there remained the problem of the incendiary list that only needed an appendix to reveal the names of homosexuals and their high-profile peccadillos. She pondered what that might mean for Tinky, a person of whom she'd become very fond, and someone who'd leaped to her aid when she needed it. Vera's name was also on the list, if its secrets were finally made known, then so would the story of her illegally aborted child, and the name of its father. The scandal would sour the image of the monarchy but she didn't care about that. She cared about scores of people she didn't know whose lives may be ruined by Stonorowich's list. They would be mostly men, but there may be other women like Vera. In addition, there would be the people they had known, and their lives, too, might be torn open to satisfy the insatiable desire to feast on the salacious failings of others.

The security of her country may be compromised by unlocking the list. The Soviets could target the vulnerable, and coerce them to cooperate, and some of that cooperation could result in the transmission of information at the very core of the kingdom. On one hand the task seemed far too onerous for a floor manager of a department store, on the other hand, she felt she knew just where the final segment of the cipher was, and hence she may be the one person capable of keeping the Cold War cool.

She slept well, but Vera slept even better, and in the morning she left her snuggled beneath the sheets and went down to the dining room to eat her own breakfast and smuggle some back to the bedroom for her companion. Prior to doing that, she'd searched the pockets of Vera's raincoat. She found a chunky wallet containing a good deal of Swedish krona. There was no name inside, but several business cards, mostly to do with aviation, and there was a small photograph of four men. Putting all those things together, she had no doubt that the wallet belonged to Klas.

Vera paid for the largest magnifying glass they could find and they took it back to the hotel. Her room was east-facing and filled with slow February sunlight. The poser produced the miniature cameo from its hiding place among the knickers in her suitcase. "This is what I removed from Emira's studio," she said.

Vera sucked shock. "Shit on my head," she said.

"It is a terrific likeness."

"It's like looking at a bleedin ancestor."

"Unquestionably you," said the poser. "Done from a photograph. A passport photograph."

"You bleedin' housebreaker," said Vera. "That's another string to your bow. Making quite a habit of it aren't you?"

"I reimbursed her for the damage." She indicated a detail on the cameo. "It's her pendant we are interested in. Particularly the stone."

They took it in turns to focus on the microdot.

"It looks the same to me."

"The same as what?" asked Vera.

"The same as what was printed on my nylon appendix."

"You can't tell," said Vera. "It's too small."

"We could certainly do with Tinky's microscope, but it looks identical."

"Tinky has a microscope?"

"Tinky has everything. Which is far too much to lose."

Vera took the spyglass again and angled the cameo directly into the light from the east. "Why should Tinky lose anything?"

The poser flung herself onto the bed, sighed and stared up at the ceiling. "Oh come on Vera. You know all about Stonorowich's list, and you told Tinky he's on it too. At least that's what Flight Lieutenant Heap said."

Vera didn't stop staring at the cameo. "Heapy? When?"

"Last week. At the Chalet. You know – the one near Tibro."

Vera lowered the glass and the cameo and turned. There was trepidation in her glare but not in her voice. "At the chalet?"

"Yes."

"With Heapy?"

"Last week."

"What was he doing there?"

"Burying Klas."

A slight pause then, "Burying him?"

"That's what he'd said he'd done. And there was no one else there."

"Klas?"

She sat up on the bed. "You remember Klas, Vera. You purchased that spyglass with his money." The two women locked looks. "From his wallet. Which is in the pocket of your raincoat."

"Said he'd done?"

"Yes."

"How do you know he was telling the truth?"

"I don't."

"Then how do you know it was Klas?"

"Because I dug him up."

"What?"

"It wasn't the easiest way to spend a night in Sweden."

Vera adopted an expression suggestion that she was working something out. "Heapy killed Klas?"

"I don't think so."

"Why not?"

"Why would he?"

Vera stared, her eye sockets failing to repel a swelling. Her corneas glazing.

"Why would he, Vera?"

Vera threw the magnifying glass onto the bed, but remained hold of the cameo. "Because he wants to disappear without trace. With your painter. The two of them want to vanish down a rabbit hole together. They've had enough. They just want to grow cabbages and drink schnapps."

"Klas was helping them."

"Which means he knew their plans," said Vera. "He knew where they were. They knew where this was." She held up the cameo. "Klas must have got greedy – demanded more from Heapy. Heapy shut him up."

"That's not what Heapy said."

"Well what do you expect him to say?"

The two women studied each other's pupils and breathed the unsettled ambiance. Vera looked again at the cameo. "Why did the little rat paint this?"

"You have to remember," said the poser, "that when she painted that she had never set eyes on you. She was copying a photograph. She didn't know it was you."

"But why?"

"To carry the microdot."

"Where did she get the microdot?"

"From the sketchbook."

"And how did she know it was in there?"

"From the person who first pasted it in."

"Pic."

"Heapy."

Vera looked askance.

"I think it was his copy. His fee. To ensure his co-operation. For the last ten years Heapy and Pic have had their own copy of the code, they just didn't want anyone to get hold of the one inside me."

Vera's face told of realisation and puzzlement in equal parts. "So Heapy and Pic always had the appendix?"

"But just like me and the Danes and Her Majesty's Secret Service, they don't have the appendix of the appendix."

Vera shook the brooch. "But why this?"

"Heapy or Pic must have recognised the picture Emira removed from Christina Proctor's passport in order to paste hers in. Pic knew all about you when he turned up at my flat. They'd obviously been watching us in London."

The brooch still shook, but now it was involuntarily. "And?"

"And if they knew where the passport had come from they could have worked out the connection between you and Stonorowich."

"Are you saying they then got Emira to paint that?"

"I don't know. But she was very keen to show it to me."

"That was weird wasn't it?"

"She's a weird woman. She enjoyed my reaction I'm sure.

Perhaps she was hoping I'd confirm the identification of your picture? Perhaps I did. Part of me thinks she had her own plot. She didn't strike me as especially loyal. Perhaps she hoped to blackmail me, or you or Tinky, or someone else on the infamous list."

"Really?"

"Possibly. Or simply sell it – with the associated information."

"Who to?"

"I don't know. Someone who could find you."

"Me? Why?"

"To take care of you."

"What?"

"And hence obtain, or permanently erase, the appendix to the appendix."

"I haven't got that."

"I think you have, Vera. I think you have."

"Where?"

"Where your womb used to be."

It took Vera a long time to regain her composure. The poser ordered room service and they brought a brandy. Vera sipped it. She appeared a crushed woman, but slowly her strength returned and the tears stopped.

"He said the same."

"Who?"

"Klas."

"Said the same about what?"

"About what was inside me."

"How did Klas know that?"

"He worked it out the same way you did, by seeing me naked. We made love and he felt and saw the scar. It clicked in his head. He said the same as you."

"Klas and Emira could have been in cahoots. She's the one processing the photographs and forging the passport. Once she was privy to Heapy's identification of you, she could have told Klas who then sets about confirming it."

"He told me there was never any need to operate on you. But they didn't know that until after they'd extracted the bleedin' ribbon. Pic told him that the code was exactly the same as what they'd kept in Pic's sketchbook. The extra bit, he said, was inside me. That made me the most valuable woman in the world, as well as the most desirable, he said. We should go away together he said. We could make a bleedin' fortune, then have a fantastic life."

"So why didn't you?"

"Because I didn't believe him. I know love when I see it, and I haven't seen it in a man for a very long time."

"So what happened?"

"I found the syringe and the solution."

"What solution?"

Vera dabbed her nose. "The one they had used on us. It was with Klas's stuff. I worked out what they had done to us. Sent you back to England with incomplete cargo and kept the key for themselves. So what were they going to do with me?"

"The same as they did with me, I expect."

"I don't think so. I think they would just have sliced me open and taken what they wanted."

The poser shook her head.

"Well, you think what you like. But that's what scared me," said Vera.

"So what did you do with the anaesthetic?"

"I made him think I shared his vision of I future. I made him make love to me again, then when he fell asleep, I plunged two full syringes into his chest."

"Two?"

Vera nodded. She was shaking and failing to retain tears.

"Then a third."

"A third?"

"And two more."

"Then?"

"Then he stopped breathing."

The poser held her breath. She gripped Vera's arm and pulled her into an embrace. The cameo finally fell from her grip and bounced off the bed onto the floor. She got her to sip more brandy, and went to a drawer to bring a fresh handkerchief.

"Have you ever tried putting clothes on a naked dead man?"

The poser shook her head.

"Then I dragged him to the jetty and pushed him in."

They hugged again. She rubbed Vera's back and made her

drink the rest of the brandy. "How did you get from there to here?"

"I walked. I set off while it was still dark. In fact, it wasn't very far – only two or three hours and I came to a place called Hjo or something. Had a meal, and got a bus to Tibro then one to here. It wasn't difficult. And I had plenty of money."

The poser smiled.

Vera said, "But I was terrified."

"Because of what you had done?"

"And what I'd been told. To be honest, I'd had my bleedin' suspicions ever since you first confided in me. Once Stonorowich came into the discussion I began to wonder. The 'accident' at the theatre made me wonder more."

"I think that might have been more to scare me than you. To make me go with Pic."

"I was a wreck when I got the letter from you saying you was in Stockholm, and then when that Danish doctor telephoned Tinky wild horses wouldn't have held me back. It wasn't pure friendship. Sorry."

"I'm not sure there is such a thing."

"The whole business with Klas was just too much. I didn't know what to do. He said I shouldn't go back to London, I should stay with him, but just didn't trust him. So I . . ."

"What is done is done. And you're here now. With me." She dabbed Vera's eyes, smearing away trails of mascara, and then she kissed her, softly on the lips.

"What about you?" Vera asked. "You said you were with Edwin Heap. At the chalet."

"I was."

"So where is he now?"

"I expect he's still there."

THIRTY-THREE

On the thirtieth day of March nineteen-eighty-four she turned sixty-four years of age. On the twenty-seventh day of May that year she stood in the warm summer sunshine in the harbour in Stockholm, and with a score of other passengers, waited for permission to board the *SS Mariefred*.

She looked at her fellow travellers. She saw her thirty-year old self, economically smart and with a blend of expectancy and resignation ingrained in her face. She saw a woman who could have been a burlesque dancer, and another who could feasibly be the much older Emira, but almost certainly wasn't. She saw a brace of openly gay men, sharing a joke about something they'd spotted in a glossy magazine. There was no sign of the passenger she hoped to meet.

The party grew. She surreptitiously counted them. Forty-three. That had been a momentous year. She longed for that year again even with its rations, air-raids, depressing news, bereavements, and hidden horrors waiting to be uncovered. She longed again for the day when she could choose to keep, or not to keep, a casually-made appointment with a man who never wanted to know her name. She would tell him her name and not keep the appointment. No she would not. She knew what she would do. She'd do everything she had done. She'd do it all again. That's why she wanted it to be nineteen-forty-three again; so that she could relive that summer, and a winter over a decade later, and carry the consequences from then until now.

The boat made increasing internal complaints. Steam was rising. The vessel looked unchanged to her. Older. There were wrinkles in the woodwork beneath her painted make-up. She smelled the same. Carbonated steam.

More people arrived to wait. She hoped the number was now fifty-six -another momentous year - but she didn't count in case it wasn't. Two sailors appeared on the foredeck. They too, were joking. They joked with each other. They joked with the men who shared the magazine. A woman overheard and she laughed too. Then an instruction was passed from the wheelhouse and one of the sailors rolled out the gangplank and unhooked the safety rope. The passengers filed on board. She made her way swiftly through the lower deck to the staircase and climbed to the upper deck where she positioned herself on the bench seat that ran along the outside of the port side of the forward passenger cabin. She was in the shade but she knew the ship would turn when they set sail and she would be in the sun for the three-hour excursion. Just as importantly, from her vantage point she could now survey the quay and keep a lookout for him.

The departure time drew near, but he did not. The postcard had come to her home address despite bearing the details of the post office box that she had stopped using in nineteen-sixty-three. It hadn't been delivered there, however, but to Tinky at the Norfolk school where he was now Head Master and contemplating terminating his tenure in order to keep bees and collect World War Two photoreconnaissance memorabilia. Tinky had forwarded it to another part of Norfolk, close to the coast, where she and Vera had spruced up a splendidly preserved post-war prefab, and where they had lived in fractious contentment until Vera's departure last November.

To the intrepid first-class traveller in the second-class compartment the postcard said and then *Post Office Box 21, Tower Road, Twickenham, London.* It had been delivered in an envelope to Tinky who had placed it in another without opening it, and forwarded it at the school's expense. The postcard sported a photograph of the ship on which she now sailed. On the reverse was written a date and time. This date. This time.

There was a light onshore breeze, but she was sheltered

from it by the superstructure. The steamship *Mariefred* nudged the concrete quay, its paintwork protected by logs slung over the sides. One or two people were mooching about on the quayside, looking like they too were waiting for last-minute fellow passengers. Their companions came. Hers didn't.

Noises suggested the ship was being readied for departure. She couldn't see, but knew that the sound she heard and hated, was the withdrawal of the gangplank. She scanned the extremities of the passenger dock, slightly adjusting the spectacles she now wore as if moving them would bring non-existent figures into focus. The *Mariefred* lurched. Bells rang. The eighty-year-old steam engine raced. The ship began to edge astern and swing around, curving away from the quay. Still she looked. If he arrived now, she could at least wave.

More bells rang. The engine sank to a murmur. More bells, and it raced again and their aftward drift diminished until, for a moment they were stationary, as if the vessel was affording her one last chance, then the *Mariefred* leaned forwards and began the painfully slow arc taking the quay from sight.

It was not an unfamiliar sadness. She had known something similar for thirteen years prior to the nadir of the nineteen-fifties. She settled into the residue of the dissatisfaction that she had more than half expected. She found sangfroid in the confirmation that the suspicion that he would not come had proved to be correct. She would never know if the postcard had been a cruel trick, by him, or by another. She would never know if he had intended to be there but circumstance had crippled him. She would never know if something had befallen him in the intervening six weeks between the card's delivery and her departure. She would never know if he had ever seen the summer of nineteen-fifty-seven.

She sank slightly further back into the slatted yacht-varnished seat, and resigned to watch the far shore pass and recede as they steamed through the archipelago. It would be a lengthy sail, but not as long as the one she'd undertaken to find the chalet on the side of Vättern. No matter. Sailing was what she did, as Vera had often said to her. Vera, a showgirl who loved a sailor. Vera was right – the poser had been a sailor, rarely ashore, mostly at sea, not drifting but not knowing what lay ahead. She had learned to sail with expectancy but not with anticipation. She had learned not to hope. Without hope there could be no disappointment. She was not disappointed; she was confirmed in her usual state of sailing.

The other passengers began to move about. They went down to the tiny galley hatch and came back with drinks and snacks. They chatted in languages mostly alien to her. Her crumpled raincoat still reserved the space between herself and the wheelhouse access door and she hoped she would not have to release it. Her side of the ship was the more popular, because the passengers realised that for most of the voyage the port side would face south and hence harvest the sun. The water bounced brightness, and the breeze although stiffer now than when they were in port, was not sufficiently chilled to countermand the warmth from above. They began to pass islets, some no larger than suburban gardens, some more expansive, and just occasionally with chalets brightly painted in pastel shades of blue, or yellow, or pink, or green.

This was a nettle-balm trip; joyous to behold, woeful to bear.

The couple to her left chatted in a Latin language. Italian, she thought. They were of similar age to her, and luxurious in their enjoyment of the voyage. She did not envy them, but would have preferred not to be a collateral witness to their entrenched warmth, routine familiarity and evident happiness. She thought about moving to another part of the ship, but the sender of the postcard had drawn an arrow to the place where she was sitting and she was glad to have secured it. She had kept her part of the rendezvous and was not inclined to rescind it. She concentrated on the delectable panorama and tried to turn the sounds of her neighbours' shared joy into an inner score of what might have been, but need not be. There was no need. There was only she.

The access door to the wheelhouse opened and she tucked her feet under the bench to let the person pass, but he did not, and slid into the space that she had saved, sitting on her folded raincoat. She turned to apologise but instead floundered in a whirlpool of shock.

"Second class," said Pic, and poured wine from the bottle in his right hand into each of the two glasses in his left.

Age had not spared him, but neither had it overwhelmed him. His skin had thickened, but the classical framework beneath sustained its strength of form and balance of proportion. His features were fuller but not so weighty as to summon sympathy.

He was beyond the bounds of maturity and steeped in splendid vintage.

He concentrated on pouring without spilling and on matching precisely the levels in each glass. Only then did he switch his gaze to her, and there he let it linger, as he scrutinised the contemporary and searched for the previous.

"Hello you," he said.

"Hello you," she said.

She took one glass, he raised the other. "Skål!" he said.

"Skål," she said.

Bells rang and replied. The *Mariefred* accelerated.

"I'm sorry," he said.

"For what?"

"To hear about Vera."

Another islet slipped by. This one passed very close. A clutch of blossomed trees reached roots beyond the shoreline. "We had thirty years," she said. "Almost."

He looked at the islet too, and harboured a small smile. "I'm glad."

There would have been silence, but the water rhythmically splashed against the hull, the steam engine hissed and cranked, and the Italian man shouted enthusiastically to his wife sitting adjacent to him.

The poser didn't like the wine but sipped a little more. "You and I could have had thirty years."

"That was never on the cards."

"Nothing is all there ever is on the cards," she said. "The cards are decorated with invisible patterns that can only be seen in hindsight. When I knew what Heapy hoped for, I wanted to deprive you."

He looked at an islet in the distance. "You had every right to deprive me," he said. "I deprived you."

She sipped the wine, and suppressed a wince. "You gave me the only two times in my life when I was fully alive."

"I hoped you would be happy."

"Happiness isn't normal."

"Oh dear," he said.

"People confuse happiness with contentment. If one was happy all the time, one would never know contentment."

"Have you been contented?"

"No."

"Oh."

"Have you?"

"No." He drank some of his wine, she swirled hers. He said, "Do you think we would have been happy together?"

She perused the tiny red whirlpool in her grasp. "I doubt it."

"Contented?"

"I suspect not," she said. "Especially if I'd have had to live in the Soviet Union."

"I never left Sweden."

She leaned forwards onto the handrail, holding her glass above the bouncing water. "Then I might have been contented. Stockholm?"

"Zeus, no! One can't disappear in Stockholm."

"Where then?"

"The far north. Sami country."

"Cold?"

"In winter."

She poured a sliver of her wine onto the wind and into the waves. "Alone?"

"Even when I had company."

She sipped a little more and swallowed the bitterness. "Well I'm here now. Why did you ask me to come?"

"I cannot risk travelling to the UK. I've been officially deceased for three decades and I rather like that. I was informed of Vera's passing."

She tipped the rest of her wine into the Baltic water. "You've had me watched, all this time? Thirty years?"

"No. And it's twenty-seven."

"Then how did you know?"

"I've had reports. Infrequently. More so in recent months. The international climate is less cold."

"Who sent you the 'reports'?"

"Emira."

"So she still knows where you can be found."

"There are ways of communicating."

"Good old dead letter boxes."

"Of a kind." He drained his glass, refilled it, offered to do the same for her. She shook her head. He looked her in the eyes. "Not to your taste?"

She looked at his lips then back to his eyes, and shook her

head again. "And how did Emira know that Vera had died?"

"Emira's had a very profitable career."

"I bet she has."

"She travels a lot."

"Does she print her own tickets?"

He laughed a little.

"So why now?" she said.

"I cannot really rationalise a reason," he said. "Except that I wanted to see you again. To thank you. To reassure you."

"And yourself."

"Yes. And myself."

She stared south towards the thickly forested coastline of Sweden. "Let's go back," she said.

"Back to where?"

"To the beginning. The twenty-seventh of September 1956. Ten minutes past ten in the morning. The offices of Conrad Coward and Company. Why there? Why then?"

"We knew the hunt for you was underway. I desperately wanted to get to you before anyone else did. We thought you were still alive, but our initial inquiries had drawn blanks. So it was worth trying the PO Box."

"But why send me two hundred miles? Couldn't you have suggested somewhere closer?"

"Mr French couldn't get to London. He rarely took time off, and it wouldn't have been fair to ask him to do that."

"Mr French?"

"He had an associate standing by. That person followed you all the way back to your flat."

"Mr French."

"He heard most of what you told Coward. So we were absolutely sure it was you."

"And so you knew exactly where I lived from that day?"

"Yes – well two or three days later."

"Why didn't you come and get me?"

"It takes time to arrange things. To get the Anson. To make arrangements here in Sweden. French and his friends had established your links with Alice and Tinky and the driving instructor. We were nervous about what you might be saying to certain people."

"Hence your decisions to cripple Mr Coward, and Vera."

"We had no idea that Alice was Vera. Neither Heapy nor I

made the connection when we saw her onstage in London."

"You could have killed her."

"The business with the stage light was nothing to do with us. We were able to exploit it to get into her flat to look for the sketchbook, but we already had plans to do that without endangering her."

"So you are saying it was a genuine accident?"

"Who knows? It was only when Heapy lodged with Emira and saw the photograph she'd lifted from the passport we'd got from Stonorowich that we made the connection between the two of them. Her name didn't feature on the information French sent us about what Mrs Coward had unearthed."

"Mr French," she said again.

"Heapy knew him before the war. Same prep school. Mercilessly bullied when he failed to grow, but not by Heapy. He was eventually educated at home and ended up in the family trade of stocks and shares. We knew he could be trusted absolutely."

"What about French's 'friends'?"

"There are networks. French knew how to employ them discretely."

"But you sent me to Coward in the first place. How could I not confide in him?"

"We didn't anticipate you writing *War and Peace* for him, but French had told us about his proclivity for amateur sleuthing. French thought, quite rightly, that he could string you along and keep you in touch with us indirectly. What neither we, nor French, knew was that you and Mrs Coward had history. We had no idea that she'd served at Bletchley."

"Did you intend to terminate Coward?"

The *Mariefred* changed heading and more of the breeze caught their faces.

"Once French realised Coward was taking your testament home he grew wary. At the same time, Heapy learned that certain questions were being asked in sensitive places. We needed to stop the Cowards digging too deeply and give French a chance to get his hands on your chronicle."

"You didn't need to kill him."

Pic took a generous mouthful of his wine. "The accident was supposed to scare him. Nature always plays a part."

"Nature?"

"The weather. The road conditions; how fast he chose to drive; traffic. Some, or all, of those came into contention. Deflecting someone is not an exact science."

"Perhaps it was more exact for Heapy than it was for you?"

Waves splashed. The engine throbbed. "Perhaps."

"I would rather you would have killed me."

"No you wouldn't."

"Was there no alternative?"

"There are always alternatives. It was a calculated risk on several levels. We thought an accident might have done the trick, especially if French could then have brought some good sense to bear."

"I'm not sure you are being totally forthright with me."

"Well, you must think whatever you wish. As it turned out it was too late all round. His wife's enquiries had sounded alarm bells in sensitive places. Heapy discovered he was being scrutinised because people remembered he'd made enquiries about Stonorowich's surgical record. We had to take extra care. He lay very low for a couple of weeks while he got the plane sorted. Meanwhile we were trying to keep tabs on you."

The *Mariefred* turned more. A tiny jet of sea spray sprinkled onto her face. She said, "After all these years I still cannot understand why the hell Stonorowich did what he did in the first place. I can comprehend the espionage, but why the surgical hiding?"

"There's a fine line between genius and psychosis. According to Heapy, the code was brilliant yet simple, but Stonorowich was brilliant and complex. I've often thought it was simply some hare-brained scheme to ensure part of his cipher remained in the UK. Coventry - the anaesthetist -thought he might have stitched it in all his appendectomy patients, or at least the first six. The idea to commission paintings was probably just some whim that occurred part way through the process."

"But he didn't commission one of me."

"It looked like he didn't want us to know about you, because you had a special purpose. We did eventually furnish him with a canvas of you, just to let him know we knew."

"But it still doesn't explain why he stitched the code inside people."

"Well, for a start it was unlikely that it would be found by accident. I suppose the point was there would be three, or five or six, or sixteen or however many, copies of his cipher walking around in the UK and whenever Stonorowich desired he could let it be known where one of them might be discovered just by supplying a name – perhaps backed up by a photo of a painting. If that carrier couldn't be located, there were additional copies inside other patients. After that, coded messages could be read, but not in their entirety because the cipher had an appendix. Because of his special treatment of you we deduced the appendix was inside you. That was why it became so crucial to get to you first."

"But it wasn't, was it?"

"Yes."

"What?"

"The one you had was entirely different to those stitched in the other women."

"How do you know?"

He drained his glass. "Because we removed the nylon appendages from the two others that I had painted."

"You did what?"

"Heapy traced them."

The Italian couple stopped talking. The *Mariefred* turned more and the breeze gained speed and lost warmth. She said, "Edwin Heap killed them and cut them open?"

Pic held silence for what seemed an age. He waited until the Italian couple resumed conversation. "Heapy was in a very precarious situation. He was a servant of two executioners. It was a very delicate time. Britain's V Bombers were entering service. Heapy had high quality information. The Soviet bear was insatiable. It always wanted more."

She thought. Another wisp of spray sprinkled an out-of-focus pattern on her spectacles. "Stonorowich," she said.

"What about him?"

"He was feeding the bear. He was Heapy's contact."

Pic carefully lodged his empty glass in the slot of the seat, securing it there with the side of his leg. "Yes."

"And if Edwin refused to improve the contraband, Stonorowich would use the code to expose him."

"Not just Heapy; scores more. People in very high places."

"But Flight Lieutenant Heap was a double agent. He clearly didn't care about his country."

"He cared about people on the list. Coventry, French, two

or three others; and me."

The Italian man got up and went below. She didn't feel confident speaking even though she thought the Italian woman was probably not fluent in English. She spoke carefully and clearly but facing into the wind. "I was informed that the other women had not been internally damaged."

"Heapy knew what he was looking for. Coventry gave specific details. The nylon tubes were easily taken without disrupting things. The internal appendectomy sutures were undisturbed."

"With me it was different. It was stitched under my skin."

"Just as Coventry had said."

"And as you had sketched in your book using your own notation. Well, courtesy of Cole Porter."

The Italian woman started rooting through her handbag.

"We didn't understand it's significance at the time, but Coventry had told us that's what he saw, so I thought I should note it for future reference."

"But then you let me take the code back to England."

"My dear muse, you never had it."

She passed him her empty glass. "It was stitched in my hair."

"That was one Heapy had recovered from one of your predecessors."

She felt sick but was determined not to show it. She breathed the salt breeze deeply. "I did wonder if it had ever been inside me."

"Well it hadn't."

She sat back. "I never handed it over. Except to Tinky. Then I stitched it into an underskirt. Then I hid it behind a framed photograph that Tinky gave me when Vera and I moved into our house."

"And where is it now?"

"I slipped it inside Vera's sleeve the night before her funeral."

"Where is she buried?"

"She was cremated."

She saw his eyes swing up to the section of sky where thoughts often cloud. He lay his hand on hers and she sat back from the rail. He put his arm around her and she snuggled into his embrace. The *Mariefred* veered again, but this time to port, sheltering them from the breeze.

The Italian man came back with two cups of coffee. His wife ceased her searching and they resumed conversing.

Pic gathered the two glasses they had used and returned them and the bottle to the wheelhouse. When he sat down beside her again she said, "So did my appendix stay in Denmark?"

"Most certainly not," said Pic. "The surgeon was Swedish if you remember. Sweden got a copy, which helped secure my safety all these years."

"And where is the original?"

He reached into the inside pocket of his jacket and produced a packet of Swedish cigarettes that she recognised as being of thirty-year vintage.

"I gave up," she said. "Twelve years ago."

"So did I," he said. "Twenty years ago. But this selection I had already put on one side." He flipped the lid. The packet was full but contained only nineteen cigarettes. The final space was taken by a roll of nylon. She thought about removing it, but declined.

"No thanks," she said.

He eased the nylon roll so that it was just protruding. "I swear to you that this was once your appendix."

"Your oaths never proved valid."

"That is an eternal fallacy," he said.

"What is?"

"To confuse an oath with a promise."

"What's the difference?"

It was his turn to lean on the rail. "An oath is the truth; but all truths are temporary. Time sees to that. Time changes everything. It changes you, it changes me, it changes everything that there is. It's foolish to say I will always be *this*, because being *this* is not in one's control. *This* belongs to time. When time changes *this* changes also. My oaths were always true. At the time when they were made."

"You loved me?"

"Yes I did."

"And you loved Edwin Heap."

"And you loved Vera," he said.

She stared at the undulating surface of the sea. "My conception of her."

"And your conception of me."

"Yes," she said. "I loved my conception of you; my creation of you. I still love my creation of you. It doesn't have a name."

"That's very important," he said. "Never give it a name."

She leaned forwards next to him. The sea spray baptised them. "Just as you never named your conception of me."

"I never did," he said.

"What about your conception of yourself? Does that have a name?"

"In the mouths and minds of others."

"In your mind."

"I'm a painter," he said. "I have little use for words."

"Your love has many colours."

"One colour. Several hues."

She thought of Vera. "Do you think," she said, "there were other copies of the appendix to the appendix?"

He paused, peered out over the sea, then said, "We've always had our suspicions there was one more, but we thought it to be in safe hands."

She grasped his hand, and he gripped back. Without letting go, he stood up. "Come on," he said.

"Where are we going?"

But he was already pulling her passed the Italians. She stumbled against the calves of the man and he spilled a little coffee on his coat. "I'm so sorry," she said.

"That's all right," said the Italian man. His English sounded assured. She grimaced and gasped a little but the Italian man just grinned, as did his wife.

Pic did not let go as he took her to the lower deck and then coiled around to where a steep set of steps led down to the engine room. Without hesitation he descended, pulling her after him. By the time she found her balance in the bowels of the hull, Pic was already in animated cheerful conversation with the engineer. There was very little space down there and it was very hot and incessantly noisy as the steam engine chugged. Pic seemed to be feigning great interest in the vintage mechanics and sharing jokes with the engineer and the coal-dust stained stoker, who, much to her consternation, she presumed to be male, but felt deeply inclined to believe was a woman.

Pic rambled on and pointed at bearings and pipes. More

jests were exchanged and the engineer grinned and chuckled. The stoker opened the firebox door. She recoiled from the fierce glow but Pick put his hand on her arm and drew her close. He then produced the old packet of cigarettes, and once again flipped back the lid so that she could glimpse the contents. The macabre tube was still tucked tightly in among the untipped rolls of tobacco. He put the packet in her hand and encouraged her with his expression.

She understood. She held the packet for a moment focussing on its grotesque component. Then she cast it into the furnace.

For less than four seconds, it was flame.

They went to see the house in Mariefred. It was well-cared for. The bicycles leaning against the wall suggested it was a family home. The urge to walk up the path and see if the French window was still at the rear was almost irresistible but she hooked her arm firmly in Pic's and anchored herself. He seemed to understand her instinct and her correction of it, and softly signalled his empathy with a giggle.

"Is it like looking at your tomb?" she asked.

"Happily, yes."

"You and Flight Lieutenant Heap were not cut out to be spies were you?"

"No, I don't suppose we were."

He tugged slightly on her arm and they began to make their way back towards the quayside.

"How about an art dealer?"

"Not that either, I'm afraid."

"The gallery seemed to be doing well, way back in nineteen-fifty-seven."

"That was with the help of subsidies."

"From the Soviets?"

"Via Stonorowich. He also supplied the Colin Proctor cover name. It was a gift to him from Vera, as was her abandoned maiden name, which I believe he also put to good use in Berlin."

She didn't fracture the rhythm of her walk. "Yes, Mrs Coward thought she had traced Stonorowich and Vera Dalkandle to East Berlin."

"He was there from time to time. He *was* cut out for spying and became a very good one with fingers in several political pies. He was also a highly intelligent man. He devised that code, with all its various appendices, and he extracted very sensitive information through skilful blackmail."

"From Heapy?"

"I'm afraid so. Defence stuff. Nuclear. Technical details. V Bombers and the like." They turned a corner and walked downhill. The smoke from the steamer ascended over the rooftops that hid the quayside from them. They passed a bar where live jazz was being played. "Stonorowich had many covers in many countries."

"What happened to the picture of me on a train in Sweden – did you paint that during the war?"

"Just after it ended. It was a fantasy. The train wasn't in Sweden. It was in Poland. I've still got it. It has pride of place in the guest bedroom."

"And so how long were you Colin Proctor?"

"Three or four years. The last time I used that name was when I checked us in to the Drottning Kristina."

"Deliberately leaving me this address to find."

"Sooner or later Torn would have furnished you with it. Or Emira. Or Selma."

"Who was Selma?"

"The receptionist."

"Were they all in the know?"

"Of course not. They just knew what had to be done. Emira ran that side of things."

"Emira, who was never actually Mrs Proctor."

"Correct."

"Or your wife?"

"To do that I'd have to tell her my name. And I never reveal my name."

"You're Polish aren't you?"

"My mother was."

"And your father was a Greek god."

"I have no idea who my father was."

She cautiously extended the conversation. "Was your mother married?"

"Not to my father. So I have never been burdened with his name, nor carried hers."

"Unless she named you after him – your Christian name."

"She was Jewish."

"Was?"

"Was."

"But my forename is not particularly popular in Jewish communities. It is more Teutonic."

"German?"

"Or Prussian, even Russian."

They rounded another corner and the berthed *Mariefred* came into view.

"My name," she said, "is very Christian. But I think you've always known that."

"It is possible to un-know something."

"How?"

"To obliterate it in the mind. Paint over it. Replace it with something of one's choosing."

She squeezed his arm again. "You're good at that."

"It's the only way to know who one is. People talk about discovering who they are. That is something that cannot be discovered, only created. My mother, Stonorowich, Heapy, were all persecuted because of their inheritance. They were persecuted by others and plagued themselves. All because of their nature. I was tormented by mine. If the past is your present how can you face the future? Obliterate it? You cannot do that without also annihilating yourself. Painting over is different. That is not obliterating, it is reconstructing."

"You reconstructed me."

"You reconstructed yourself."

Smoke was rising more urgently from the funnel of the *Mariefred*. The sailor on the prow of the steamer positioned the gangplank and unhooked the safety cable. Passengers began to file on board.

He slightly tightened the arm that was linked around hers. "I'm glad you were so persuasive when you found your way back to the chalet at Vättern. I could have lost two very precious people."

She looked at him askance. "Instead, you just lost one."

"No," he said. "I kept both."

She understood.

As they got closer to the gangplank Pic's pace slowed. She said, "Did you purchase a return ticket?"

He said, "I know the captain. I didn't buy a ticket of any kind."

"Not even second class?"

"I was never that. And neither were you."

They stopped and admired the steamer. The exhaust smoke emitting from her stack was accelerating.

"You're staying here?" she asked.

"No," he said. "But I'm not returning to Stockholm."

"Then what are you doing?"

"I'm going back to the wild hinterland. It's first class."

"It's where you belong."

"Do you really believe that?"

"Yes," she said. "I really do."

"How about you?"

"I'm very much third," she said.

"Never," he said.

"Oh I think so." She squeezed his arm then slipped free of it and took half a step towards the ship.

"You were a first class steward," he said. "The service you offered was second to none. You were dispatched with an unsolicited cargo and kept it safe while refusing to deliver it."

"Well, it turns out you took it from me."

"That wasn't the cargo," he said. "The real payload was what you knew. By choosing not to offload that, you became a custodian of the sacred."

"Custodian of the sacred," she said. She walked a little further until she was alongside the vessel. He joined her. They stood before the name painted on the prow. The name of a ship and the name of a place. Two names in one.

"By not breaking the code, you re-wrote it," he said. He stepped closer to her. "Your devotion to me has been impeccable. You have given me thirty years of love, yet taken not one second for yourself."

"Oh I have taken many hours," she said. "Too many to be counted."

"How someone could be so selfless, I cannot comprehend."

"I've no wish to be comprehended," she said. "I find great stillness in being a poser."

"Thank you," he said. "For so intimately not knowing who I am."

"My pleasure," she said, and slipping one hand behind his head, she drew him towards her and kissed him.

The sailor who offered his hand as she boarded reminded her of a Swedish waiter she had met many years ago. She went straight up to the top deck and sat in the same seat that she had occupied that morning and from which she could not see the quay. The boat eventually pulled out, reversing and turning to head back towards Stockholm. The quayside came back into view.

He didn't wave. A few yards behind him, a vintage sports car, very reminiscent of the one she'd seen in a wartime photograph, was waiting, and the driver raised a hand. She unfurled her grip from the rail and raised her hand in reply.

The *Mariefred* picked up speed. Soon, the succession of tiny islands began their static procession. The seascape was idyllic, enchanting, and magnificent.

It didn't need a name.

ABOUT THE AUTHOR

Pete Hartley is based in northern England where he taught
drama for thirty years.

He has written extensively for the stage. Some fifty of his plays
have been performed by professionals, amateurs and student
companies. Six have won prizes, and one, *Mitigating
Circumstances*, was broadcast by BBC Radio.

He has also had short stories published and broadcast and now
markets his output under the moniker *uneasybooks* and blogs
as *uneasywords*.

Printed in Great Britain
by Amazon